HIGH PRAISE FOR
ZEPPELIN

"STEP ABOARD!"

—*Associated Press*

"THERE IS ACTION AND ADVENTURE APLENTY...THE WELL-DEVELOPED CHARACTERS ARE APPEALING, AND THE PLOT IS EXCITING. DETAILS OF ZEPPELIN FLIGHT ARE PARTICULARLY WELL DONE."

—*Library Journal*

"A SOLID, EXCITING NOVEL OF INTERNATIONAL INTRIGUE...THE PLOT IS WELL ORCHESTRATED, WITH TIGHT BINDINGS, RESULTING IN A SMOOTH FLOW...THE AIRSHIP IN EFFECT BECOMES AN ACTUAL CHARACTER IN ITS OWN RIGHT—AND A FASCINATING ONE."

—*Booklist*

"THIS NEW NOVEL BY A SPECIALIST IN EUROPEAN HISTORY IS ONE OF THE MOST INNOVATIVE STORIES WE'VE READ IN A LONG TIME."

—*Nashville Banner*

"USING THE TURMOIL AND TENSION OF THE MID-POINT OF THE DEPRESSION DECADE, AUTHOR RONALD FLORENCE HAS DEVELOPED AN INTERESTING ADVENTURE-SPY-HISTORICAL-ROMANTIC NOVEL... GOOD ESCAPIST READING."

—*The Cleveland Press*

Also by Ronald Florence

FRITZ
MARX'S DAUGHTERS

Zeppelin

Ronald Florence

BANTAM BOOKS
TORONTO · NEW YORK · LONDON · SYDNEY

This low-priced Bantam Book
has been completely reset in a type face
designed for easy reading, and was printed
from new plates. It contains the complete
text of the original hard-cover edition.
NOT ONE WORD HAS BEEN OMITTED.

ZEPPELIN

A Bantam Book / published by arrangement with
Arbor House Publishing Company

PRINTING HISTORY
Arbor House edition published March 1982
Bantam edition / April 1983

ISBN 0-553-23110-3

Published simultaneously in the United States and Canada

Bantam Books are published by Bantam Books, Inc. Its trade-
mark, consisting of the words "Bantam Books" and the por-
trayal of a rooster is Registered in U.S. Patent and Trademark
Office and in other countries. Marca Registrada. Bantam
Books, Inc., 666 Fifth Avenue, New York, New York 10103.

For Heather

It was not, as generally described, "a silver bird soaring in majestic flight," but rather a fabulous silvery fish, floating quietly in the ocean of air and captivating the eye just like a fantastic, exotic fish seen in an aquarium. And this fairylike apparition, which seemed to melt into the silvery-blue background of sky, when it appeared far away, lighted by the sun, seemed to be coming from another world and to be returning there like a dream—an emissary from the "island of the blest" in which so many humans still believe in the inmost recesses of their souls.

HUGO ECKENER
Chairman of the Zeppelin Company

Part I

Rio

One

Twelve hundred feet below, the city of Rio de Janeiro spread out like a toyland diorama. Miniature automobiles vied with tin soldier pedestrians for the streets. Model speedboats and harbor ferries skipped playfully across the waters of Guanabara Bay. Along Copacabana Beach, the string of modern apartment buildings and hotels glittered in the morning sun like diamonds in a tiara, their brilliance accentuated by the enormous black shadow pacing steadily across the beach and the silvery phosphorescent reflection on the water.

Although he had seen the view through the port of the radio cabin dozens of times, Anton Lehrmann never tired of it. The low altitude and unhurried perspective of the Graf Zeppelin transformed even drab cities into wonderlands; Rio turned to sheer magic. Looking up, Lehrmann saw the towering statue of Christ the Redeemer on the top of Corcovado at friendly eye level, like the great rounded dome of Sugar Loaf at the entrance to the harbor. For a few minutes, all he could do was stare, transfixed by the spectacle.

It wasn't until he heard the soft swish of rubber-soled shoes in the passageway outside that Lehrmann turned from the window. The door to the radio cabin was ajar, and through the crack Lehrmann caught a glimpse of the captain, walking aft to the passenger lounge. He wore a double-breasted blue suit and tie, but no hat. Lehrmann smiled to himself. It was a tradition on the Zeppelins for the captain to greet the passengers when the ship reached cruising altitude, and Lehrmann was glad that the new captain had at least chosen to follow the tradition, even if he did go hatless.

Still smiling, he began setting up his equipment, lowering the long wire antenna with its lead weight from the hatch below his feet, engaging the propeller-driven generator outside the window, and switching on the main 140-watt transmitter and receiver. He draped the earphones loosely over his neck while he waited for the units to warm up.

The length of its antenna and its altitude over the sea made the Zeppelin a formidable radio station. Lehrmann's earphones were soon clattering with Morse code signals as he tuned across the long-range low-frequency band, picking his way through transmissions from ships, airplanes, and ground stations, some as close as Montevideo and Rio, others as far away as Capetown and Hamburg. Later, he would sort through the signals, in case there were any transmissions of concern to the Graf Zeppelin. But for now, he ignored the babble, zeroing in on their assigned frequency to transmit a report of their precise on-time departure and their anticipated on-time arrival in Recife, where the ship would refuel for the long flight over the Atlantic to Frankfurt. For Lehrmann, the boredom of those routine messages—the Graf Zeppelin was almost always exactly on schedule in its regular service from Germany to Rio—almost balanced the exotic pleasure of being the chief radio operator on the most famous aircraft in the world.

What was routine for Lehrmann was still a miracle to much of the world in 1936. For over two years, the Graf Zeppelin had been the only aircraft in the world offering scheduled transatlantic service, and even those who had never seen the enormous streamlined shape floating in the skies could read endless newspaper stories about the engineering wonders of the Zeppelin. It was larger than all but a few ocean liners, the largest aircraft in the world until the construction of its cousin the Hindenberg. It had flown farther nonstop, lifted heavier loads, and carried more passengers more miles than any other aircraft, a record that was nearing one million kilometers and sixteen thousand hours in the air. And for the twenty passengers fortunate enough to book passage on each flight, there were luxuries of service and accommodations never equaled in air travel before or since. For diplomats, adventurers, businessmen, soldiers, and lovers, the flights could be crucial: the difference between the twenty-eight days for the crossing by ship and the four days for the flight on the Graf Zeppelin could mean the difference between failure and success.

Lehrmann knew that it was precisely because the Graf Zeppelin was a symbol of modern technological achievement, a rival to the Eiffel Tower or the new Empire State Building in New York, that the controversy over Captain Paul Whitman had arisen. And it went back long before their departure from Rio, when Whitman had first taken command.

Tall, with unruly blond hair and mischievous pale blue eyes that made people guess his age as much as ten years younger than his thirty-three, Whitman did not look like a commander. His easy walk and casual manner, his reluctance to wear a necktie off duty or a hat with his uniform, contrasted with the stiff bearing and haughty dignity of the regular Zeppelin officers. Most of them were ex-military men, veterans of the World War. Whitman, you could tell at a glance, was not.

But it wasn't Whitman's appearance that prompted the rumors and arguments in the crew quarters at the landing field in Santa Cruz, outside Rio, or in the hammocks deep inside the airship where the off-duty crew rested and slept. Nor was there any question of his ability—he had almost two decades of flying experience, including ten years in airships, a solid background in engineering from the famed Massachusetts Institute of Technology, and hundreds of hours logged at the controls of every kind of airship, much of it as a test pilot in the most trying circumstances. He was also liked by the crew, most of whom found his easygoing manner and relaxed warmth a welcome contrast to the haughty distance of the regular officers. But nothing could change the fact that Whitman was half-American. Although he was born in Wilhelmshafen, and had visited Germany periodically on his father's frequent business trips, and although he spoke German at home with his father as a young boy, Whitman had grown up on the East Side of Manhattan, been educated in American schools, carried an American passport, and had done almost all of his flying on American airships, most of it under the aegis of the United States Navy. It was only a quirk of circumstance and a tribute to his skills, which had greatly impressed Hugo Eckener, the head of the Zeppelin Company, that after six months with the German Zeppelin Company as a special observer, and only a single transatlantic flight on the Graf Zeppelin, he had been given temporary command of the most striking symbol of prestige of the German Reich. It was enough to set tongues wagging from Rio to Frankfurt.

The passengers in the lounge were so intent on the view below that they did not notice when Whitman opened the door from the control room and stooped to clear the six-foot-high lintel. He padded noiselessly across the carpeted floor to a window on the port side of the lounge and leaned over the back of a vacant chair, enjoying the view himself before he took on the task of greeting the passengers.

An elderly German man with a bushy white moustache, wire-rimmed glasses and an old-fashioned heavy wool suit was the first to notice the captain.

"Captain Whitman?" The man stood up, extending his hand and pushing the glasses up the bridge of his nose with the other hand. "Good morning. I am Otto Hutten. This is Frau Hutten."

The pleasant-looking woman, white braided hair stacked carefully on her head, smiled when she caught Whitman's eye. "So young to be a captain," she said. "And so handsome."

Whitman returned her infectious smile. He instinctively liked the Huttens. They seemed familiar. The word that came to mind was *homespun,* but even though he had been thinking and living in German for months, no decent German translation suggested itself. It made him realize that he hadn't met people like the Huttens in the entire time he had spent with the Zeppelin crews in Frankfurt and Friedrichshafen.

"Don't let me disturb your sightseeing," he said. "This view is too special to miss."

"*Jawohl,*" said Hutten. "The view is *wunderbar.* And the ship—so smooth and quiet. We cannot even hear the engines. We were not aware that the ship had departed until we saw the airfield so far below us." He leaned close to his wife, taking her hand in his. "We are simple people," he said. "For us, this voyage is a luxury. Already I think it is worth the expense, if only for this last view of Brazil."

"Going home?" asked Whitman.

"Home?" answered Hutten. He looked thoughtfully out the window at the harbor below before turning back to the captain. "To be truthful, I am no longer sure where home is. We have been in Brazil for over twenty-five years, since before the Great War. This is the first time we are returning to Germany. And after all we read and hear of the new laws and policies . . . who knows anymore what is home?"

He glanced fleetingly at the table in the rear of the dining room where three uniformed men sat. "This new politics in Germany," he added. "It is more than a simple man can understand."

"Otto," said Frau Hutten, squeezing his hand. "We said that we would go with open minds."

She turned to Whitman. "Yes," she said, "we are going home. We are old now and we have no children. Our only family is in Bremen. We are at the age when people need family. So we go back to Germany. We have decided to sell our land in Rio Grande do Sul.''

"Coffee?" said Whitman.

"Wine grapes," answered Hutten, his face brightening as he spoke. "Brazil is a splendid land for wine. People do not realize that some Italian and even French wines are made from our grapes. Brazilians in the fancy restaurants in Rio de Janeiro and São Paulo order expensive French wines without knowing that they are paying only to ship the grapes to France and back. Such snobbery . . .''

His sentence was interrupted by the approach of a crew member whose obsequious nod drew the captain to the corner of the room. "Sorry to disturb you, Captain," said Lehrmann. "But I've just picked up an emergency signal.''

"For us?"

"No. A distress call. I think it's from a ship.''

"Where?"

"It's difficult to pinpoint. They don't respond to queries. Only the same message over and over, an old-fashioned SOS. It is not a practiced hand on the key.''

"Can you get a directional bearing?"

"For now, only a rough line of position. They seem to be almost due east, somewhere south of Ascension Island.''

Whitman reflected for a moment, picturing the pilot chart of the South Atlantic. Their normal route to Recife would take the Graf straight up the coast of Brazil.

"We can hold our present course for at least two hours," he said. "That should give you the range for a second bearing and an approximate position for the ship. In the meantime, try to raise any ships that may be nearby and also the British wireless station on St. Helena. Tell them that we're willing to relay messages or render assistance as required.''

"Yes, sir," said Lehrmann.

"We have problems?" asked a voice from the table at the back of the lounge. It was one of the two junior officers accompanying Admiral Wilhelm von Teppler.

"No," said Whitman as he walked over to their table. "Our radio operator has picked up a distress broadcast, apparently from a ship at sea.''

As Whitman approached the table, von Teppler stood, bowing slightly at the waist. His erect bearing showed off the trim fit of his heavily decorated uniform, and Whitman noted the admiral's long, fine nose, silver hair brushed straight back, and the wine-colored saber scar running from his ear to the corner of his mouth, the kind the Germans call a "beauty."

The two junior officers belatedly jumped to their feet. They were still wearing their empty holsters. At the airfield in Santa Cruz, while the passengers were being searched for lighters and matches, Whitman had asked the officers to surrender their pistols. One of them had resisted, and tempers flared when Whitman finally insisted that they could not board the Graf until the pistols were locked up. Only a timely intervention by the German ambassador, there to see the admiral off, managed to smooth over the situation. Unlike the admiral, Whitman noted, the two junior officers wore black, red, and white swastika armbands on the sleeves of their uniforms.

"Of what concern to us is this distress message?" asked one officer.

"An emergency at sea can't be ignored," answered Whitman. "It's an unwritten law of the sea. If we were in need of assistance, you would certainly want a ship to come to our aid."

"I was under the impression that the Graf Zeppelin is never in need of assistance," said the officer, a short man with a bristly moustache and stubby haircut who slurred his words through partially clenched teeth. "Are you expecting problems, Captain?"

The admiral glanced briefly at the two younger officers before fixing his gaze on the captain. His eyes seemed to apologize for the comments of his companions.

Whitman knew the admiral by reputation—it was difficult to spend much time in Germany and not hear of Admiral Wilhelm von Teppler, the U-boat commander who had led all others in the number of "kills" on enemy ships in the World War. He had been almost as celebrated as the air ace Baron Manfred von Richtofen. Whitman could remember games of "dogfight" and "submarine" with his schoolmates, when they pretended they were sinking von Teppler's unseen U-boat with barrages of pebbles thrown into the pond in Central Park. Even then, something about the U-boats fascinated Whitman. Life under the sea would be claustrophobic, he knew, but he was intrigued by the ability of a submarine to float motionless, controlling itself with natural buoyancy instead of fighting its way up and down with sheer power like an airplane, working with the forces of nature instead of against them. By contrast, an airplane's assault on gravity seemed violent and unnatural.

After the war, the fascination with airplanes and submarines stuck. Engineering at MIT was a compromise between his father's strong-willed insistence on a profession and Whitman's own hopes of joining the Army Air Corps, and while still in college he learned to fly from an itinerant barnstormer in Newton, Massachusetts, trading jury-rigged repair work on the aging Curtiss Jenny for lessons. Airplanes were the future, everyone said, and while he liked the flying more than the courses in aerodynamics and structural engineering, secretly he still dreamed of the delicious quiet and peace of an aircraft that would float instead of fighting its way aloft.

Then one day he spotted a notice on a bulletin board, calling for volunteers to train for airship duty in England. Although he had never seen an airship, he read all he could find about them, and wrote a careful application to the program, arguing that his engineering and flying background should be as useful as the required military service. The application was summarily rejected on the ground that he wasn't in the Navy.

The next day he hitchhiked to Washington from Cambridge, bullied and charmed his way into the Navy office in charge of the program, and poured out so much enthusiasm and knowledge about airships that the officer pulled his application out of the reject file and restamped it on the spot. Two months later he was on a foggy airfield in England, staring at the R-34, a crude English copy of a German Zeppelin, but still the first airship to fly the Atlantic. He didn't take his eyes off the ship for hours, watching as it rode serenely and silently at its mooring, floating in the air. That, Whitman told himself, was how men should fly.

Whitman had never thought about von Teppler in the years since the war, and he was jolted when he saw the admiral's name on the passenger manifest in Rio. He learned that von Teppler had been posted for several years as a military attaché in the German Embassy in Buenos Aires. Even with the Germans deprived of the right to have submarines by the Versailles Treaty, it seemed an inappropriate assignment for an officer of the admiral's experience and fame.

"This is my first voyage by Zeppelin," said the admiral. "After so many years of maneuvers in which we had to evade airships, I finally begin to understand what we were up against. It is a formidable machine."

Whitman gestured toward a chair, waiting for a nod before he sat down. "From someone of your reputation," he said, "that is high praise. It's a splendid aircraft, built by magnificent craftsmen. It's an honor to fly it." His own words sounded stuffy to him and

Whitman was almost relieved when he saw the eyes of the officers focus over his shoulder. He turned around to see Hans Stifel, the senior watch officer, stride across the lounge to their table.

Almost as tall as Whitman, Stifel was a heavier man, with a full jowled face and a gait and voice that managed to convey an aura of perpetual impatience.

"I must speak with you," he said brusquely to Whitman.

"Of course."

"In private," Stifel insisted.

Excusing himself, Whitman followed his watch officer into the corridor outside the radio compartment. They stood inches from one another in the narrow passageway.

"Will you please explain why we are tracking this ship?" demanded Stifel.

"Because the ship is transmitting a distress signal," said Whitman.

"It is no responsibility of ours. We have a schedule to keep and an important passenger on board. Von Teppler must be returned to the Reich as soon as possible."

"We cannot ignore a distress call," Whitman said. "We will track it, attempt to direct assistance toward the ship, and offer any help we can provide. Those are my orders."

"You're very sure of yourself, Whitman . . . for an American. Perhaps you should consult with those of us who know better the procedures of the German Zeppelin Company."

"Do those procedures include ignoring ships in distress?" asked Whitman.

"They include, first and foremost, concern for the needs of the Reich. This is a *German* airship, or haven't you noticed the insignia on the tailfins?"

Whitman pictured the insignia, remembering vividly the first time he had seen it. He was training American airship crews in Akron, Ohio, when the Graf Zeppelin had landed on its way to Chicago in 1933. The enormous red, white, and black swastikas on the tailfins were a complete surprise to an American public expecting a quiet visit of a commercial airship, and they caused an intense stir in the newspapers and prompted outbreaks of fighting between German-American Bund supporters and anti-Nazi demonstrators. Whitman had been caught in the middle of some ugly name-calling involving the crew of the Graf Zeppelin. The German crewmen were candid enough to explain that the swastikas had been forced on a reluctant Zeppelin Company by the personal intervention of Josef Goebbels, the Nazi Propaganda Minister, who recognized the advertising value of the famed airship.

The insignia was only a symbol, Whitman knew, but absurd though it sometimes seemed, symbols were important. He could remember when one of his schoolmates discovered that Whitman spoke German at home with his father. "Which side are you going to fight on?" the other boy had shouted at Whitman. Their game of "dogfight" was dropped for a fistfight, and Whitman came home with a black eye that prompted intense questioning from his father at the dinner table. He finally admitted what had happened, and from that day until the death of his father ten years later, not a single word of German was spoken in the Whitman home.

"We carry fuel and lifting gas only for the journey to Recife," said Stifel. "A detour will imperil our safety and jeopardize our schedule. It is not done on the Zeppelins."

"We have fuel and hydrogen reserves for exactly this kind of emergency," answered Whitman. "As long as I'm in command we are not going to ignore distress signals from ships at sea."

"We'll see about that," said Stifel. He spun sharply on his heels and went forward to the control room.

As Whitman watched the other man walk stiffly down the corridor he realized once again that though the Zeppelin facilities in Frankfurt and Friedrichshafen were far away from the politics of Berlin, it was becoming impossible to shut out men like Stifel and the Germany they represented.

Two

Two hours later the Zeppelin was still flying within sight of the coast, close enough for passengers in the lounge to follow the gradual transition from the coffee lands of the south to the cocoa plantations and tropical forests of the bulge of Brazil. On the magic Zeppelin, the first hours of a journey of thousands of miles still felt like a sightseeing tour.

Whitman watched the view himself while he waited for Lehrmann to plot the two bearings. Then he leaned down over the chart on the crowded worktable in the radio room to trace the faint pencil lines with his fingertips.

"How reliable are the bearings?" he asked.

"Each could be off by as much as ten degrees," said Lehrmann. "Two hours at seventy knots gives us a base of only one hundred fifty miles, and the legs of the triangle are over a thousand miles. At best, it's a marginal fix. But the signals are definitely from that vicinity." He placed his finger on the intersection of the two lines, almost in the middle of the South Atlantic. "Approximately eleven hundred miles due east of here."

"No other ships within range of them?"

"None that I can reach. The British wireless station on St. Helena said they can do nothing. The only vessel they have would take over thirty-six hours to reach the ship, and they're not willing to dispatch a boat on the basis of our reports alone. There's also a P & O liner that has just rounded Capetown. They're at least three days away."

"Is the SOS still holding strong?"

Lehrmann cocked his head in concentration, holding one earphone tightly against his head before he handed it to Whitman. Whitman could hear the staccato tapping even before he put the earphone to his head: *dit-dit-dit, dah-dah-dah, dit-dit-dit.*

"They send the same signal about every twenty minutes," said Lehrmann.

"Any acknowledgement of our transmissions?"

"It's difficult to say. I suspect that it's not a regular radio operator; the transmissions are too slow and labored. But he did try to send the name of the ship." Lehrmann held out his log, with a printed notation: S-O-U-T-H-E-R-N S-T-A-R. "The copy was so rough that I had to fill in some of the letters. There was also one confused message which I copied as 'Storm damage. No control.' I've been transmitting back at very slow speed with many repetitions. I guessed that they might not be familiar with standard emergency procedures, so I've sent plain language messages in English. Southern Star must be English, I think, although the ship is not in Lloyd's Register. Perhaps an unregistered coaster, or even a yacht."

"Good," said Whitman. "Do you think anyone else can receive them?"

"I doubt it. It's probably a very weak signal, sir. We have the advantage of altitude and antenna length. It's not unusual for us to pick up signals that even ships with very powerful stations miss."

Whitman glanced again at the small pilot chart before they walked together to the main chart room, a spacious compartment that stretched the full width of the gondola. Whitman leaned over the chart table with a protractor and dividers, plotting the bearings onto the large-scale pilot chart of the South Atlantic.

"Fourteen hours away," said Whitman. "What's the latest weather bulletin?"

Lehrmann went back to his compartment for his log. "The German reports show nothing," he said, "but St. Helena reports a stationary front here—" He traced a shapeless blob in the empty ocean between Brazil and the tiny British islands of St. Helena and Ascension.

"Is it steady?" asked Whitman.

"Probably for a day or so."

Whitman traced his fingers over the chart, thinking out loud. "If we skirt the front, we could pick up the cyclonic flow. That would bring our ground speed up to ninety knots going out. And if the front holds, we could shoot back over the top and pick up a tailwind on the return."

He turned to the chief engineer, within earshot of the chart table. Like everyone else in the control room, he had been listening to Whitman and Lehrmann. "How's our fuel and gas?" asked Whitman.

"Normal, sir."

"Adequate for a detour of twenty hours?"

"Detour?" The tone pretended surprise. "*If* that front holds, the reserves should be sufficient."

Whitman studied the plot a last time, then turned back to Lehrmann. "Keep me informed of the status of the signals," he said. "I'm ordering a change of course to search for the ship. And please advise Recife that we will be delayed in our arrival, perhaps by as much as twenty-four hours."

Stepping forward into the control room, with its panoramic windows on three sides, Whitman nodded to the men working there. The hushed whispers that began a moment before suddenly stopped.

"Rudderman," he said, "come to oh-eight-nine. We are changing course to search for a ship in distress."

"Oh-eight-nine, sir," repeated the rudderman as he disconnected the autopilot and swung the rudder wheel, a small ship's wheel that was geared and linked to the huge rudders at the tail of the airship. The rudderman kept his eyes glued to the gyrocompass as he turned. The Graf Zeppelin was the first airship large enough to carry the weight of a gyrocompass, which meant that they could hold a course within one half of a degree instead of the two or three degrees possible on a magnetic compass.

"Signal engines to cruising speed," said Whitman.

The chief engineer clanged the five engine telegraphs all the way forward, lighting the signal indicators in the engine nacelles. Then he brought them back to cruising speed. An instant later, the airspeed indicator began moving slowly past seventy knots.

"Stein, how is it today?" said Whitman to the man laboring at the elevator wheel across the control room from the engine telegraphs. It was by far the most challenging task on the airship, and Stein, at thirty-seven years, was old to be an elevator man. He looked tired, his eyes were rheumy, and when he wasn't gripping the wheel, his hands shook with a noticeable palsy. But after watching him on the trip to Rio, Whitman could understand his reputation as the finest elevator man in the Zeppelin Company. Stein had a natural feel that simply couldn't be taught. He would be hard to replace when he retired with a pension after two more flights.

"He's smooth today," said Stein. "Won't be no spilled teacups. You tell the steward he can fill them right to the top if he wants."

From his experience in the American airships, which, like naval ships, were always spoken of as feminine, Whitman had a hard time getting used to the masculine gender of the German Zeppelins. The Graf Zeppelin, like its cousin the Hindenburg, was a *he*.

For a moment Whitman watched the artistry of the elevator man. Stein's tired eyes ranged over the instruments in front of him: the inclinometer that showed their angle of ascent or descent, the variometer that recorded their rate of climb, the altimeter, the gas and air temperature and pressure gauges. Above him were the toggles that would vent hydrogen to make the ship descend or release ballast to make it ascend, and directly in front of him was the elevator wheel itself, linked to the huge control fins almost seven hundred feet behind them at the rear of the ship. The control of the elevator was too delicate to entrust to an autopilot. Instead, the elevator man stood at right angles to the axis of the ship, using the feel in his legs to sense subtle changes in the attitude of the ship. A good elevator man was quicker and more sensitive than even the most accurate gauges, and the immediacy of his responses accounted for the smoothness of the flight. The work was so demanding that in bad weather an elevator man might be relieved after only thirty minutes at the wheel.

"You're right to go to that ship, Captain," said Stein when he noticed Whitman watching him. "No matter what the others say. We've been lucky"—he wrapped his knuckles against the wood frame of the wheel—"never had an accident. But I wouldn't want the Graf to have a bad name. Never know when we could be needing an assist." As he spoke, he worked the wheel in front of him. The sweat from his labor stained the back and shoulders of his shirt.

"What have the others been saying?" asked Whitman.

"Nothing, sir. It's all just idle talk. You shouldn't pay any attention. The men have nothing to do but talk."

For Hans Stifel, the senior watch officer, it was an automatic response to feel the slightest movements of the Zeppelin, even from his windowless cabin inside the hull. He was sitting at the tiny folding desk in the watch officer's stateroom, above the control room in the gondola, and he looked up when the airship began its turn. Unlike the captain's private quarters forward of his stateroom, Stifel did not have a gyro repeater compass, a *daughter* as it was called in Zeppelin jargon. But a glance at his small, handheld magnetic compass confirmed his suspicions. They had swung east. And he knew why.

From the shelf above his desk, he took down a blank notebook, the pages checkered with a fine grid of lines. He glanced at his pocket watch and noted the time of the turn and the crewmen on duty in the control room. The information would all be recorded in the ship's log, but Stifel wanted his own record. He also noted that he was not present in the control room when the order was given.

As he listed the names of the rudderman, the chief engineer, and the elevator man, he underlined the last name. Stein was one of the old veterans, a man Stifel's own age who had flown in the navy Zeppelins during the war. Stein knew too much for his own good.

He continued down the list, through the radio operator, the riggers, the enginemen. The most reliable men on board, thought Stifel, were the enginemen. They were new men, trained as

mechanics and enginemen in the Wehrmacht, the slowly rebuilding
war machine of Germany. They were men who knew the future
of Germany.

The future of Germany. It was the consuming thought for Hans
Stifel. Things were changing at long last, changing everywhere.
Men who had been nothing were suddenly something. Like Stifel
himself. Three years before, he had been unemployed, one of the
thousands of German war veterans who had staggered through
the rueful years of the Weimar Republic, dreaming of a better
time when they would be thanked for their sacrifices in the war,
instead of being punished with unemployment and poverty and
shame. In the days before he joined the Party, Hans Stifel had
waited in breadlines and slept in parks and doorways. He had
been driven to petty robberies to get enough money to afford the
flophouses of Stuttgart and Munich. He had applied for hundreds
of jobs, but his sole experience had been in the wartime Zeppelins, and when he refused to show his discharge papers to
potential employers, they refused to give him even a menial job.
Finally, he discovered that the National Socialist German Workers' Party, the Nazis, were not concerned with discharge papers
from the Imperial Navy. More than one top party official had left
military service under circumstances that were at least as questionable as Stifel's own past.

For Stifel, the Party had changed everything. As a latecomer
who joined after Hitler's election as Chancellor, Stifel had the
lowly status of a hanger-on, one of the hundreds of disenchanted
flyers and would-be flyers who gravitated to Hermann Goering as
the wings of the future. In that crowd, Stifel's experience in
airships was a liability. Goering thought only of airplanes for the
future of Germany.

But as things turned out, Stifel's half-hearted early member-
ship ultimately counted in his favor. When Hitler came to power,
the Brownshirts of the SA had seemed the most powerful group
in Germany, apparently unstoppable as they clamored for a
second revolution to follow the seizure of power. Then, almost
without warning, came the terrible Night of the Long Knives,
June 29, 1934. The leaders of the SA were taken out in the
middle of the night and shot, and the organization was effectively
dismantled. The next day the Brownshirts were nothing. Stifel
and the others who had waited on the sidelines were untainted.

Stifel's posting as a watch officer on the Graf Zeppelin had
been a fortuitous accident. It was only three months after the
Night of the Long Knives, in the wake of the death of President

Hindenberg. The German Zeppelin Company, until that time enjoying the special protection of the president, finally had to begin to come to terms with the Fuehrer and especially with Hermann Goering. Goering had never thought much of the Zeppelins until Josef Goebbels pointed out the propaganda value of the huge ships, which Germany alone could fly. Goering became an instant convert, decided that he wanted his own men in the Zeppelin Company, and Stifel was ready, experienced, and very willing. With a personal intervention by the future Reichsmarshal, the potentially troublesome naval record was expunged, and Hans Stifel found himself a full watch officer aboard the Graf Zeppelin.

Other party men were posted to the administration of the company and to the Hindenberg, but Stifel knew that the Graf Zeppelin was the big chance. He knew it as soon as he saw the gray pallor of Rolf Pruss's skin and the emaciated limbs that would no longer fill a uniform. The commander of the Graf was a dying man, his insides rotted with cancer. And that meant that Hans Stifel, the senior watch officer, was next in line for a command. Next in line to be one of the six fully qualified captains of the only airships in the world.

The plan had been perfect except for one detail: *Whitman*. The naming of the American to acting command of the Graf in Rio had come as a total surprise to Stifel. It was easy to concede that the American was more experienced, with his thousands of hours of flying experience and his years of education. But he was not even a German, let alone a member of the Party.

It had all happened, Stifel told himself, because of Hugo Eckener, the head of the Zeppelin Company. Old Eckener had been impressed by the American as far back as the 1920s, when Whitman had come over to Germany to serve as American liaison on the building of the *Los Angeles* for the American Navy, the first big Zeppelin built in Germany after the war. And as everyone knew, Eckener was a Nazi-hater from way back.

Eckener was a force Stifel hadn't reckoned with. His previous refusals to cooperate with the Nazis had earned him the status of an *unperson* in Germany; by order of Goebbels himself, Eckener's name could not be mentioned in newspapers or magazines. But it was impossible for even the Nazi propaganda machine to destroy overnight the reputation of a man who was one of the best known Germans in the world, a man who had once almost been nominated for the presidency of the German republic. The Nazis could put their men into the Zeppelin Company in 1936, but they couldn't run the company. Not yet. Whitman's appointment proved that.

It's not over yet, thought Stifel, and he smiled, knowing that just one mistake by Whitman could change everything. He turned back to his journal and made another notation before he started back through the crew quarters to the passageway that led through the hull of the airship to the rear of the passenger cabins.

Whitman waited in the control room until the Graf had leveled off on the new course, before he went aft to the passenger lounge to greet the other passengers. He planned to wait until everyone was relaxed and accustomed to the flight before explaining their change of course.

He went directly to the third table in the dining room, which was buzzing with a babble of Portuguese and Spanish. From the passenger manifest, Whitman knew that Señor Teodoro Lopez-Otero and his young bride were on their honeymoon voyage to Europe from Montevideo. Their hoped-for solitude had been violated by the only other South American passenger aboard, Senhor Mauricio Bernardino de Nascimento, of São Paulo, now encamped at their table.

The honeymooners had the polished, refined look of the wealthy young as they sat in their proper traveling clothes, undoubtedly the height of fashion, but excessively staid and conservative for a couple barely twenty years old. They had arrived at the airfield in Santa Cruz with nine pieces of matched luggage and two steamer trunks, and Nadia Lopez-Otero was incredulous when the Zeppelin Company personnel informed her that she and her husband could take only twenty kilograms of luggage each into the cabin area. Her distress, it turned out, was caused not so much by the weight limit as by the fact that she would have to sort the clothes herself, since she was traveling without servants. With the jaws of the ground crew around him falling slack at his words, Señor Lopez-Otero calmly requested that the rest of their baggage accompany them on the Graf Zeppelin, not batting so much as an eyelash when he was informed that the freight charge would be twice the cost of their tickets.

Whitman had often heard of the wealth of the South American rich, but until he had seen it himself, he did not realize how flamboyant that wealth could be amid such overwhelming poverty. In Buenos Aires and Montevideo, he saw huge Daimlers and Packards cruising the streets, blinds drawn on their rear windows so that the occupants would be spared the sight of crippled beggars on the street corners. Enormous mansions sealed their shutters against both the sun and the misery of the streets. And everywhere, he heard the rich talk incessantly of Europe, as if they were somehow only temporarily placed in the New World while their souls resided six thousand miles away in Rome or Paris.

Whitman found the Lopez-Oteros polite and unassuming, but their obliviousness still jarred. Wealth itself was no crime—if it were, there would be no passengers for the Graf Zeppelin at all. But the blindness to poverty, the ability to wear blinders and shut curtains and shutters, gnawed at him.

Yet they were certainly to be preferred to the man who shared their table. De Nascimento was a compact, nervous man with pomaded hair and a thin shiny moustache that he fondled constantly. He periodically brushed imaginary ashes off his immaculate white suit while he rattled off a monologue in Portuguese sprinkled with German and English phrases. Whitman gathered from a few minutes of the one-sided conversation that de Nascimento was on his way to Europe for unspecified business and booked on the return flight of the Graf.

Just as Whitman took advantage of a brief pause in de Nascimento's barrage of words to introduce himself, the steward arrived with a tea tray for "elevens." Señora Lopez-Otero took the china cup in two fingers, holding her pinky aloft in the best finishing school manner.

"One lump or two?" she asked her husband, looking directly into his eyes as if his answer would at least double her knowledge of him.

"Two," her husband answered, embarrassed by her gaze.

"And you, Señor de Nascimento?" She made no effort at Portuguese.

"Tea?" said de Nascimento, his words aimed at the steward. "I am a Brazilian. I will have coffee."

"Of course, sir." The steward returned with a tall silver coffee pot and a fresh cup.

De Nascimento sighted across the cup of coffee with his nose high and his eyes squinting. "It is brown," he said. "Have you no *cafezinho*?"

"I'm sorry, sir," said the steward. "We use only Abyssinian coffee, the finest available in Europe."

"Ah-ha," said de Nascimento. "You see, Señora, these Europeans do not know everything. You may believe me. I have traveled often on the Continent, to the finest hotels and restaurants. You must be careful and choosy. They think that because we are from the New World, we are barbarians like the North Americans.''

''Do you think all North Americans are barbarians?'' asked Señora Lopez-Otero.

Reluctant to hear the answer, Whitman excused himself to rejoin his interrrupted discussion with the admiral. He couldn't put his finger on the clues that disturbed him, but he sensed that de Nascimento was something of an impostor, the kind of man who made you want to check your billfold and wristwatch as you left his table.

''Good morning again, Captain,'' said von Teppler when he saw Whitman approach his table. ''Will you join me for tea?''

Whitman nodded to the officer sitting with the admiral. The other junior officer, the man with the cropped hair, was not there.

''It was wise of you to alter course,'' said the admiral. ''The sea is a lonely place. Few would venture forth at all if they did not know that others would come to their aid in a moment of distress.''

The face of the officer at the side of the admiral registered surprise.

''How did you know we had changed course?'' asked Whitman. ''Most passengers cannot perceive the turns of the airship. I suspect it is like a submarine in that regard.''

''Perhaps,'' said the admiral. ''But after so many years at sea my eyes function like a sextant. The reduction tables are in my memory. Your speed over the water is difficult to estimate, but I would venture that your present course is close to due east. That is not the direction of Recife.''

''Very impressive,'' said Whitman.

''Why have we altered course?'' said the junior officer. ''This was not part of the flight plan.''

''No,'' said Whitman. ''It wasn't. We have changed our course to come to the aid of a ship in distress. We appear to be the nearest vessel.''

''Vessel?'' persisted the officer. ''We are an airship.''

In the confines of the lounge, only twenty feet square, it was difficult to keep their conversation private. Already, heads were turned toward their table to listen.

''Excuse me,'' said Whitman, walking to the vacant table. He waited until the buzz of conversation ceased, then gave a short explanation in perfect German, describing the signals they had received, the fact that no other ship was in a position to render assistance, and the possibility of a delay of up to twenty-four hours in their arrival in Recife. He repeated the announcement in Spanish before he asked for questions.

The passengers sat quietly for a moment. Then suddenly the lounge burst into discussion, first at the individual tables, then between tables. Only the admiral remained silent. While the others questioned and complained, he sat expressionless, seemingly bemused by the dismay, confusion and excitement of the other passengers.

After answering as many questions and complaints as he could, Whitman came forward to check on the status of the airship. He was particularly concerned about superheating, the potentially dangerous overexpansion of the hydrogen in the gas bags, since they would now be spending almost an entire day under the equatorial sun. The overexpanded gas would automatically vent off, which would both shorten the range of the Zeppelin and build up an explosive concentration of oxyhydrogen in the exhaust shafts.

As he walked forward along the narrow corridor to the control room, his way was blocked by the open door of the radio room. Inside, Hans Stifel was talking with one of the officers in the admiral's party.

Whitman was surprised. It was strictly against Zeppelin Company policy for passengers to be in the control quarters, except at the express invitation of the captain, and it was absolutely forbidden for passengers to enter the hull of the ship, which was the only route the two men could have followed from the passenger quarters without being seen by Whitman.

"Stifel!" said Whitman. "This is highly irregular."

Stifel turned slowly to face Whitman. "We were just discussing that," he said. "You perhaps have not been properly introduced to Oberleutnant Beck of the navy."

The close-cropped lieutenant snapped his heels in an exaggerated acknowledgement of the introduction.

"Stifel!" said Whitman. "It's against company policy for passengers to be in this area. And surely you're aware of the danger of a passenger transiting the hull of the ship."

"There are no handrails along the gangway," he explained to Beck. "It's easy for an inexperienced person to fall off onto the outer skin of the airship. The weight of a man would tear it instantly."

"Oberleutnant Beck is not inexperienced," said Stifel. He moved toward the door. "You will please join us, Captain. These are matters which I believe we should discuss in private."

There was barely standing room for the three of them in the compartment. The room was purposely small, to save the weight of the metal shielding that kept the electrical interference from the engines to a minimum.

"This change of course is totally unauthorized," said Stifel. "I have reported it to Oberleutnant Beck, and he agrees with me that the so-called distress signals may be nothing more than a plot to free the admiral."

"Plot? What are you talking about?"

"There is no limit to the deviousness of our enemies," said Beck. "It is imperative that we contact the military attaché at the embassy in Rio de Janeiro, and that we send a priority message to the *Seekriegsleitung*. I am confident that the Naval War Staff will order that you return to the normal course of this flight immediately."

Whitman wanted to laugh at Beck's pompous seriousness, except that he knew the Naval War Staff was the one branch of the navy that was already controlled by the Nazis, while the high seas fleet commanders still held out their independence. Beck *was* serious.

"Oberleutnant Beck," he said, speaking slowly and with an effort to control his anger. "This is a commercial aircraft, operating under the authority of the German Zeppelin Company. Our operations, including the change of course to assist a ship in distress, will be reported by radio to company headquarters. If our return to Frankfurt is unduly delayed, all interested parties will be notified. But this airship is not subject to orders of the Naval War Staff or the military attachés of German embassies or any other military authorities. As long as I'm in command, that will remain the case."

"Do you and the German Zeppelin Company wish to be cited as conspirators in treason?" said Beck.

"Do you know who von Teppler is?" said Stifel.

"All that matters to me," said Whitman, "is that he's an admiral of the German navy, returning to Germany as a private passenger by his own choice."

". . . his own choice?" repeated Stifel. "He is returning to face a charge of treason."

Beck nodded, his mouth tight-lipped in concentration.

"According to the passenger manifest," said Whitman, "the admiral is a regular passenger, flying with two aides."

"Regulations," said Stifel. "The Zeppelin Company refuses to accept military prisoners as passengers. That will change."

"Perhaps," said Whitman. "But while I'm in command, the Graf Zeppelin is a commercial airship, and the admiral is to be accorded the rights of any other passenger."

"You leave me few options, Whitman," Stifel said. "I am making full note of your actions. It is my intention to file a report on your conduct."

"That is your privilege," said Whitman. "In the meantime, your duty is to assist me and the other officers and crew in operating this ship. And that means returning Lieutenant Beck to the passenger quarters. Now."

"Under the circumstances," said Beck, "I insist that you return my sidearm to me."

"Out of the question," said Whitman. "Firearms would jeopardize the crew and passengers of this ship, which is something I will not allow. Your pistol will remain locked in the bosun's safe until we have landed at Frankfurt and all passengers have left the ship."

"So!" said Beck. He backed out of the cramped room, glaring at Whitman, then stopped and clicked his heels as he raised his arm in a salute. "*Heil* Hitler!"

Stifel watched Whitman out of the corner of his eye, waiting for a response before he raised his own arm to return the salute.

Three

One thousand miles east of the Graf Zeppelin, and some two hundred miles south of Ascension Island, it was almost dusk. The sun was a fierce fireball in the west, igniting the sky to a flaming orange and gray, until it dipped toward the horizon and the reflections on the water dimmed enough to reveal patches of bluish white against the dark water, rolling quickly across the surface before they disappeared beneath the confused seas.

The woman saw the patches when she climbed out of the open hatchway, taking her first break from the pump and the radio. They were almost like whitecaps, but without any pattern in the waves. And unlike the dolphins she had seen under the bows of steamers, they didn't jump clear of the water or frolic in the breaking seas. These flashes seemed more like torpedoes, charging directly at the boat before they veered away at the last possible moment.

Then she saw one roll close to the boat, so close that she could make out the rows of gill slits behind the flat head, the beady eyes, the sucker fish attached along one side.

Sharks!

There were dozens of them, beginning their after-dark search for food. The boat, rolling lazily with the seas, was an intruder in their territory, and they had drawn close to assess.

Her first thought wasn't of herself, but of her cameras. For months she had lived only with her cameras. Everyone and everything else had been far away. But it took her only a moment to realize that it was too dark for anything but flash, and the sharks were too far away for the bulbs she had. She knew she didn't dare leave the radio for as long as it would take to set up a camera. Someone was still responding to her signals, and she had been straining to copy everything they sent. So far, she had only deciphered fragments, copying as best she could the individual dots and dashes, then looking up the letters on the back of the booklet that had been packed with the radio. She had missed so many of the dots and dashes that it was like a puzzle, and she could only guess at what they were saying. But they seemed to hear her, and as long as she kept sending, as long as the batteries of the radio lasted, they might be able to rescue her.

For a while, she had tried to send messages other than SOS, but the messages took too long to prepare. She had to look up the letters in advance and write out the dots and dashes. And there was really nothing else to send, except *Help!* She had no idea where she was. Nine days from Libreville, how many days from anywhere? And alone.

She remembered how everyone had warned her that the coastal schooners were unreliable, little more than privateers and smugglers. But the quaint wooden hull and raw cotton sails, and the bare-chested black crewmen at the dock in Libreville, were too romantic to pass up. Even the name of the old schooner was alluring: *Southern Star.* A shot of the transom would be the perfect ending to her photo essay.

At first, the captain kept saying the northeasterly winds couldn't last. "Nebba," he would say in his strange pidgin English. "Nebba fom de land. In one day, mebbe two, de wind he go fair."

But the strange northeasterly wind persisted, day after day, and they held stubbornly on the starboard tack.

"Aren't we being driven west?" she asked one afternoon. "We seem to be going out to sea. Shouldn't you take a sight to make sure we're still on course?"

The captain looked at her with a blank expression. He had no sextant, no tables, not even charts. His chart was in his head, a memory of stars and smells from the land.

That was the night that the crewmen first came to her cabin, laughing and singing as they pounded on the door. It was the first time she regretted taking the schooner. It wasn't fear yet, only a sense that the joy and excitement of the journey were gone, a realization that she was a woman alone with five men who had gone too long without women. And the wind had changed everyone. It blew relentlessly, always from the same direction, always hard enough to drive the boat rail down so the man at the helm had to fight the rudder with all his strength. And the longer it blew, the more the crew drank, first from bottles, then from the caskets of rum that had been loaded on the schooner at Libreville. She had heard of seamen taking a daily tot, so it didn't bother her, although she sensed an edge of fear in their incessant singing.

It was two days later when the wind stopped. It didn't slow or veer; it just stopped, completely dead. The seas were still running, and the boat slatted noisily with each wave, the sails alternately filling and collapsing, the slack rigging jerking with each roll of the boat. She remembered the radio then, the portable unit that the American consul had insisted she take along if she was going to risk a trip alone on one of the coastal schooners. But when she suggested to the captain and the crewmen that they send a message, they laughed. From their tone, she could tell that they were afraid of the radio.

"We be doin' a'right," the captain said. "One day, mebbe two, der be plenty wind an' we be doin' a'right." He poured more of the rum to salute his prediction, offering some to her. The others joined him in laughing and drinking.

He was right. That night the storm came. When they took

down the sails, except for the main, she went below, taking out a
book and forcing light from the reluctant kerosene lamp. She
resolved to make herself read until she was sleepy enough to
ignore the wind and the rain, the crash of the waves and the
rolling and pitching of the boat.

She slept soundly, or at least it seemed that she did, until she
awoke to a great crack, like a clap of thunder. The rain was
ferocious, pounding against the varnished glass porthole of her
cramped cabin in the stern of the schooner. When she could see
nothing through the port, she tried to fall asleep again, but there
was another crack, this one louder and with enough force to send
a shudder through the boat. Then suddenly the motion of the hull
changed, rolling quicker. She fell off to sleep again, content with
the sixth sense that told her that after the storm there would be
gentle, fair winds. The shouting from the deck and the scurry of
feet were reassuring. The sounds of men working.

She awoke, hours later, to an eerie silence. No voices, no
creaks from the helm, no slatting of sails, no sounds of bare feet
against the wooden decks. The boat seemed heavy in the water,
but until she stepped out of the berth and onto the sole of her
cabin, immediately tumbling across the floorboards into a bulkhead, she didn't realize how much they were listing. After
scrambling into clothes, she climbed up the ladder to the deck.
The seas were still running, and a steady dry breeze was blowing
out of the leaden sky. The first thing she saw was the stump of
the huge mainmast, broken off with a jagged wound. Holding
onto the taffrail, she inched forward, lifting up the main hatchcover
to peer into the hold where the water sloshed back and forth. The
water was coming through the seams, suddenly gaping open
without the tremendous tensions of the mast and the shrouds to
hold them against one another.

Aft, on the deck above her cabin, she could see the chocks
where the dory had been stowed. Empty. She knew what had
happened then, saw it all in an instant, but she was still calm
enough to finish her inventory. The hull seemed sound, even
with the water sloshing below. There was a gash in one side,
where the floating mast had probably smashed into the boat, but
it was at the waterline, and if she kept at the pump, she would
probably stay afloat. Both masts were gone, the forward mast
carried by the rigging when the great mainmast went. It had been
a clean break, as if a giant hand had swept over the decks,
clearing everything in sight. Possibly lightning, she thought, but
there were no blackened areas anywhere, and she remembered

that she had not seen a lightning flash when she awoke during the night. More likely an all standing flying jibe, the boom swinging over too quickly and catching the boat on the wrong part of a wave so that the wind against the seas had enough force to carry the mast and the rigging. The second clap, she decided, was probably the floating mast holing the hull.

And she was alone, somewhere in the South Atlantic.

The sharks were fascinating in their play. Long, lean creatures, built for one purpose, like the panthers she had photographed in the wild, weeks before. She tried to remember the little she had read about sharks, and wondered what would attract them to the wooden hull. Then she heard a thud and saw a flash of white close to the hull, near the gaping wound in the topsides made by the mast.

The cargo. A hold full of uncured hides, poachers' trophies on their way to Monrovia for shipment to the fur markets of Europe. The skins wreaked in the hold, and the odor of the rotting flesh that clung to them probably carried through the water, enough to attract the sensitive nostrils of the sharks. Did sharks have a taste for zebra and leopard? she wondered.

She didn't panic. The first task, she knew, was the pump, and once she found it she discovered that an easy rhythm would keep pace with the water in the hold. The cadence of the pump was almost reassuring—up, down, up, down, up, down—like soldiers marching. The rhythm was mesmerizing, and for a while she counted so intently that her eyes closed and she didn't realize that no water was going through the pump because a sliver of wood floating in the bilge had lodged in the leather flapper valve.

After an hour, she had won the battle of the waters, at least the first skirmish. She went back on deck to try to decide what else she could do. She spent a long time trying to figure out how to raise a sail, until she realized that there were no sails to raise, and no place to raise them. She sat down on the deck, pounding her fist against the hatchcover, cursing herself.

Then she remembered the radio and tore back to her cabin, still listing at a crazy angle so that she tumbled down the ladder into the cabin, banging herself black and blue in the process. The radio was in a wooden case, the instructions in French in a crudely mimeographed pamphlet. It was a military unit, used in Africa by the bush fliers who flew far into the jungle.

She tore open the wooden packing case as if it concealed a Christmas gift, so anxious to turn on the radio that she could hardly concentrate on the opaque, technical French of the directions. She saw from the packing slip that the unit was three years old, and she wondered whether it would work at all.

But there were tiny sparks from the wires when she tightened the knurled nuts on the brass key, and she knew the batteries were all right. She strung the antenna around the deck, crisscrossing until it looked like a spider's web.

Then came the exhausting tap-tap on the stiff key, impossibly difficult because she had no idea whether she was heard or not, or what a dot or a dash was supposed to sound like.

It was hours before she gave even a thought to the crew, and when she did, it wasn't anger. If anything, she felt a deep sadness, a realization that her naive trust and faith had been unfounded. She wondered how she would react when she developed the pictures she had taken the first days out, wonderful portraits that portrayed the crewmen as the last truly free men, the buccaneers of the African coast. She remembered how closely she had studied them, how she began to perceive infinite variations in the black faces that she had never noticed before. The photo essay would be important, she knew, and she was sad that it would have to end with their flight. She never doubted that they were safe in the dory. Sharks wouldn't follow them without the hides.

Looking up from the sharks, she glanced toward the setting sun, now sitting on the horizon, barely half a disc. She watched it slide down, wondering if she had ever perceived a sunset so intensely. With no other human voice, no landscape, nothing except herself and the sun, she watched the setting disc until she couldn't think of time, only that as long as the sun was above the horizon it was still one day.

How long? she wondered. *When would her hope fade? When would the darkness make rescue impossible?*

As the sun finally dropped below the horizon, in the instant before the day gave way to twilight, she thought she saw a brief flash just above the horizon—a glint of silver against the deep gray of the bands of sky that separated the heavens from the sea.

The flash of green that follows the sunset? She had heard of it, heard of photographers who had spent night after night trying to photograph it and failing. But what she saw wasn't green. It was silver, like a great bird, or a ship.

She strained, trying to make it out again against the darkening sky, but couldn't. In a few minutes it would be too dark for a ship to see her. They would have no way of finding her except by radio. She had been transmitting, on and off, for almost fourteen hours. The instructions said that the batteries had a useful life of four to six hours. She tried to remember how much of the time she had been transmitting, but it was useless. She knew only that it had been one long day, a day of pumping until her muscles ached, tapping on the key and listening until her head ached. And waiting. One long day in which she had kept busy enough not to think about how hopeless her situation was.

Four

Hans Stifel spent the long afternoon in his cabin, avoiding the control room where Whitman doggedly stood watch since they had turned east. He knew that Whitman had been up since midnight of the night before, personally supervising the loading and fueling of the Graf Zeppelin and eating breakfast with the ground crew at Rio, and he remembered that Whitman, like so many of the longtime Zeppelin officers, was a catnapper, one of those men who in an hour or two of deep sleep could recharge batteries that had been drained by long hours of service.

It was after six o'clock ship's time when Stifel heard footsteps in the axial passageway outside his cabin, followed by the opening and closing of the doorway to the captain's cabin next door. He could picture the interior of that cabin in exacting detail: the neat console of instruments, the reading lamp over the berth, the wardrobe with its shelves and hooks, the writing desk framed in lightweight aluminum and paneled in dark wood. The paneling in the lounge had been changed to lighter woods at the beginning of the season, to give an airy feeling for flights to the tropics. Stifel decided that it would be a good idea to change the paneling in the captain's cabin as well.

He pictured Whitman taking off his shoes and coat. And his tie. The man was never comfortable in a tie or a hat, it seemed. Didn't even enjoy the title of captain. More a mechanic than an officer, really. A test pilot. Stifel knew that Whitman would fall asleep quickly, and when he heard the light click off, he waited only twenty minutes before walking out of his cabin and down the ladder to the control room below.

As he came through the companionway, he heard a commotion in the control room. Fritz Zekner, the junior watch officer, was on duty, and the room was crowded because the captain had ordered an extra man to stand watch as a lookout. The large window panels of the control room took in a 270-degree panorama, around the entire front of the gondola, and from fifteen hundred Ɪeet altitude, with the sun behind them, they were in an excellent position to see anything on the water.

"*There!* Over there!" said the lookout. "At three o'clock."

From the bottom step of the ladder, Stifel saw the junior watch officer swing his own binoculars to the south.

"I see nothing," said Zekner. "The water is almost black. Perhaps it was a last reflection of the sun."

"Sir!" said the lookout, with a bold tone he would never have used with an officer older or more experienced than Zekner. "I've been watching the water long enough to be used to the reflections. This was something else."

"Rudderman!" said Zekner. "Did you see anything?"

"No, sir," the stout man answered. "But I was mostly watching the compass binnacle. And I didn't have no binoculars."

"Are you certain, lookout?" asked Zekner.

"Yes, sir. As certain as a man can be in this light."

"Rudderman!" said Zekner. "Prepare to turn right to . . ."

"Zekner!" said Stifel, striding into the control room.

"Sir!" answered the younger man.

"Are we still holding course oh-eight-nine?"

"Those were the captain's orders, sir."

"And what was the last bearing to the so-called distress signals?"

"Oh-eight-nine, sir. But that was two hours ago."

"Two hours?"

"Yes. We've lost radio contact. The radio operator said it could be a skip problem. It's apparently not unusual with weak signals in the late afternoon."

Stifel seemed not to hear the explanation as he studied the charts spread out on the navigation table. He worked through the ground speed calculations on the worksheet appended to the chart.

"Our ground speed is ninety knots," he said. "In two hours that puts us another one hundred eighty miles off course." He glanced up at the engine telegraphs, still registering on cruising speed. In still air, he knew, the airship would be making approximately seventy knots. They had a favorable twenty-knot tailwind helping them along.

"If this wind holds," he continued, "we won't make more than fifty knots going back. That'll add another three and one half hours of time lost." He pinned the junior watch officer in his gaze as he continued. "Do you realize who the man in the passenger lounge is? Do you know why he is returning to the Reich?" He didn't wait for a response before answering his own catechism. "Von Teppler has used his fame, notoriety may be the better word, to make repeated statements demeaning the Reich before the German communities in Argentina and Uruguay. It's only a matter of time before his statements attract the attention of enemies of Germany, before someone succeeds in publishing his filthy lies—just when the attentions of the entire world are turned toward the Olympic games and the glorious achievements of the Reich. He *must* be returned to Recife and then Frankfurt without delay."

"But the lookout has spotted a ship," mumbled Zekner.

"Where?"

"Lookout!" said Zekner. "Point out the ship. Do you still see it?"

The lookout pointed his hand to an approximate bearing, now slightly aft of the windows on the starboard side of the control room. "I haven't seen it again," he said. "It may be out of view behind us."

"Give me those," said Stifel, taking the heavy Zeiss 10x70 binoculars. He quickly scanned the horizon outside the window. "I see nothing," he said. "Nothing at all." He glanced at his wristwatch, then at the chart spread out on the main chart table.

"Rudderman!" he barked, "come around to a course of two-nine-five. It is time to abandon this unauthorized search."

"Shouldn't we check with the radio operator?" said Zekner. "And the captain? The captain's orders were to awaken him before any change of course."

"Whitman is sleeping and should not be disturbed," said Stifel. "He is obviously not accustomed to the hours of duty aboard a German Zeppelin."

Stifel leaned his head into the radio room.

"Exactly as I suspected," he said. "No signals of any kind for more than two hours."

"Rudderman!" he repeated. "Come to two-nine-five. A slow, even turn."

The stout rudderman looked around to Zekner, still nominally in command in the control room. He was waiting for a nod before he would follow the order.

Zekner looked back and forth, from Stifel to the lookout, unsure of what to do. He glanced down at the chart, then looked at the rudderman, making a tiny, almost imperceptible nod of his chin, a gesture that exactly reflected his half-hearted acquiescence.

As the rudderman swung the wheel, Stifel turned to the engineer on duty.

"Stand by for flank speed," he said. "We are resuming course to Recife."

Five

It was too dark to see the swells before they lifted the boat, but she could feel the wind picking up on the water. The boat listed further now, and it took longer to pump the water down to the level that she had decided was safe. It was an arbitrary standard, the depth of her ankle in the section of the bilge just beyond the frame where the old piston-action pump was bolted. Everything she did now was arbitrary, but rigid. She told herself that a rigid schedule was the only way to survive.

As she came up from the hold she tripped on the hatch opening. Her shin hurt, but it didn't seem to be bleeding, and she quickly channeled her cursing of the hatch and the darkness into an anger at her own stupidity. She had pumped in darkness for an hour. *How would they ever see her with no lights?*

She tried to remember the running lights on the schooner. At the dock and the first day out, she had photographed every part of the boat. There were wooden light screens on the main shrouds, with ornate, green-corroded bronze fixtures, but she couldn't remember any lamps. They would be carried away now anyway, she knew.

There was also a binnacle light on the compass, and she tried to remember if it had been used. All she could picture was the helmsmen checking the compass when they lit their pipes. They never even used a flashlight.

Flashlight? There was none in her cabin, only the tarnished brass kerosene lamp that hung over her bed, with the engraved soot shield above it. *Of course.* Why didn't she think of it before? She tore down the companionway, lost her footing on the steep stairs, and toppled into the cabin, banging her head and her arms until she was sore all over.

It was pitch dark in the cabin, and she finally found the kerosene lamp by feel, grappling along the wall and recoiling when she felt the splinters in the worn paneling. When her fingers found the lamp, she tried to wrench it from the wall, but it wouldn't budge. It was securely fastened by screws that she could feel with her fingertips.

A screwdriver. She had no idea where she would find tools, except in her camera box, and she wasn't sure she had one large enough. Again she fumbled in the dark, banging the already sore shin against a loose chair and the edge of a trunk before she found the box and snapped the three latches open. She grappled for the tool pouch, with the tiny syringe of oil and the set of miniature screwdrivers, trying by feel to identify the largest one. Her fingers were stiff from hours in the water of the bilges, and she slowly realized that she was too exhausted even to think.

Leaving the tools in a pile, she stumbled back to the lamp, fumbled in the drawer for a wooden match, and tried to light the charred wick. She tried three times before she realized that it was completely carbonized, and then she had to wait for it to cool before she could break off the charred fibers with her fingertips and roll it up again by feel. Another match, and it was burning.

For a moment she sat staring at the lamp, transfixed by the orange and gold glow of the flame. Then she went back to work, locating a screwdriver from the toolbox and digging at the embedded and corroded screws of the mounting sconce. Her largest screwdriver was much too small, and after she had tried each of the screws in turn, the small point finally snapped off in the slot of one of the screws.

She hammered at the fixture with the handle of the screwdriver, scraping her knuckles on the corrosion of the sconce before she caught herself. "Don't panic," she said out loud. "Think!"

Up on deck she found a timber and brought it down to pound on the soft paneling, beating a hole until she could see the mountings underneath. They were hopelessly rigid, oak stringers with long, well-bedded screws. Once upon a time it had been a well-built schooner.

Feeling the sweat dripping down her face and her temper rising to irrational rage, she sat down on the edge of the berth, staring at the lamp.

Think! she told herself. A light on deck, something that can be seen a long distance. *What?*

A fire? It was the surest light, but she knew she could never control it. And once it got out of control, she was finished. More boats were lost to fire than to sinking, she had read.

A torch? Soak the end of a timber in kerosene and hold it aloft. She pictured the Statue of Liberty. Then a photo caption for a news story. *Woman photographer waiting for rescue holds torch aloft while hungry sharks circle ship.* It was absurd, but what else was there?

She lifted the timber that she had used to pound the paneling and realized that she would never be able to hold a flare more than a few minutes. And if she fell asleep, the boat would burn. She didn't dare try to lash one to the hull.

She went topsides again to look for smaller timbers and suddenly remembered how absolutely black the tropical sky could be. There were millions, maybe billions of stars, tiny pinpricks in a velvet canopy. A flare would show up for miles. All she needed was enough kerosene, enough matches, enough timbers, and the strength to hold them.

As she staggered back down the steep companionway stairs, she fell again, stumbling across the cabin and lurching into her camera case. She shoved it roughly out of the way, heard the clink of broken glass and stopped short.

Flashbulbs!

She opened the reinforced box again and found the guns intact, along with more than a dozen of the large number sixty-four screw-based bulbs. She checked the batteries on the tester and they were good. She even had enough extension cords to rig the two flashers together.

Working by feel in the dark, it still took her only a few minutes to clamp the extension flash on the highest standing beam of the cabin structure. She unscrewed the reflector so that the bulb would shine equally in every direction, and decided she would flash one every half hour, starting immediately.

She positioned herself on the edge of the companionway and hooked both sets of batteries to the one extension, using the remote tripping button that she had used only weeks before for photographs of panthers feeding at night.

The first try was a dud, but she reacted without panic. Flash was something she knew. She quickly traced the wires, found them okay, then unscrewed the bulb and rubbed the base against the rough fabric of her slacks, cleaning off the minute corrosion. She put everything back together, made a last check of the wiring, and pushed the button.

Flash!

It was blinding, bright enough so that for a long time she saw only the stars from her own flash instead of the stars in the sky. To preserve her vision, she decided that she would flash the rest of the bulbs from below deck. Then she would have enough night vision to look for ships.

By the second flash, the routine was settled. After each flash, she would pump until the water was down to ankle level. Then she would come back to the little portable radio set to listen. There had been no sparks from the key for hours, so she didn't try to send SOS anymore. But she listened, reassured by the static she heard that the receiver was still working, even though she heard no signals.

Like the motion of the handle of the pump, the rhythm of her routine was reassuring. As long as she could flash the bulbs, pump the bilge, and monitor the radio, she was doing everything possible to assure her own rescue. It was only a matter of hours until a ship spotted her, she told herself. In fact, she decided, it was better at night. The flash would be visible much farther than the hull of a mastless ship in the fifteen-foot seas.

There was another thud as the hull listed enough for the sharks to make a swing at the hides floating close to the hole in the starboard topsides of the schooner. She realized that she would have to spend more time pumping to keep the ship afloat. She crawled down into the dark hold and braced herself over the pump, pulling back and forth, first with one arm, then with the other. Up, down, up, down, up, down. She counted the beat out loud, but her arms ached and her head felt heavy. She found herself thinking as much of sleep as of rescue. If only she could lie down, just a few minutes of sleep, enough to keep her arms from aching and her hands from cramping.

No, she told herself. *Back to the rhythm.* But no matter how hard she tried to concentrate, the rhythm gradually slowed—up,

down . . . up, down . . . up, down . . . up—until it was like a lulla-
by, and she fell asleep.

Six

After a long day of smooth flying, the passengers in the lounge
were oblivious to the drama of the search. At first, it had seemed
terribly exciting—the possibility of coming upon a ship crippled
somewhere in the South Atlantic in the role of rescuing angel.
But after hours of uneventful flying over the featureless ocean,
hours that were punctuated only by the elaborate rituals that
accompanied the service of meals, the passengers had all but
forgotten the detour. In the darkness of the moonless sky, they
were unaware of the most recent change of course, and in the
quiet of the lounge they had no sense that the engines were
racing to carry the airship back against the strong headwinds.
With nothing to do but wait, the passengers busied themselves
with books and talk.

With profound and overelaborate apologies to Nadia Lopez-
Otero, Senhor de Nascimento had "borrowed" her husband,
bringing him to the empty table in the corner of the dining room
for a one-sided discussion of finance. The young bridegroom
protested repeatedly that he had to get back to his wife, but de
Nascimento was firm, unwilling to give up what he correctly
perceived was the only audience for his monologue.

The bride listened with an ear half-cocked, hearing phrases
which de Nascimento thought were Spanish but which were
actually rapid-fire Portuguese with an occasional Spanish word.
"A responsible investment," she heard de Nascimento say over
and over. "An investment for the future. With the world in
tumult, we owe it to ourselves to invest in liquid assets. One
never knows when the difficulties of Europe may cross over to
our continent. One should be prepared."

She didn't like the Brazilian. His hair was oily, he talked too
much, and he seemed far too interested in her and her husband.
In a word, he was coarse. But there was no one else to talk to, or

even to listen to. She had imagined that as soon as the Graf Zeppelin departed Rio de Janeiro she would be enveloped in a world of European culture, surrounded by civilized men and women who talked of books and music and art. She expected to hear French, the language of culture, and instead she heard only a greasy Brazilian talking about investments.

The old Germans kept to themselves, and in any case, she decided after one glance, they were hardly people of culture. That left only the admiral and his companions. She thought nothing of the companions, but the admiral had an intriguing face. The wine-colored saber scar, his courtly manners, even the long drawn features of his face said that he was an aristocrat, a man of breeding. Not at all like most of the Germans in South America. And after the third or fourth furtive glimpse in his direction, she was sure that the book he was reading was French.

After half an hour of feigning interest in an out-of-date fashion magazine, she finally screwed up her courage to speak to him.

"Excusez-moi," she said in her schoolbook French, "but isn't the book you're reading French?"

"Madame!" He stood, bowing deeply at the waist. "You will join me at my table?"

Only one of the officers was there, and he frowned, then leaned toward the admiral. "Do not speak Spanish," he said. "You should speak only German."

The admiral looked down at him. "For your information," he said, "we were speaking French." The contempt in his voice was so obvious that Nadia Lopez-Otero could understand him without knowing a word of German.

He turned back to her and explained in French, holding out the book. "It is *l'Histoire de la guerre de sept ans*, by Friedrich the Great. A magnificent work of military history."

"How interesting," she said, with a prim, hollow grin. "Why do you read it in French?"

"Because he wrote it in French. Friedrich was a great admirer of French culture, a patron of Voltaire, and himself a man of the Enlightenment. What some of my countrymen do not realize in their new-found xenophobia is that in her hours of greatness Germany has been a nation of international culture. I have the companion volume, his autobiography, if you would care to read it."

"How very kind of you," she answered. She sensed the distress on the face of the officer with the admiral, who obviously could not understand a word of their conversation, and she anticipated the reaction of her husband, who could not help overhearing them in the infrequent pauses in de Nascimento's pitch. In any case, she couldn't think of anything to say about Friedrich, the Enlightenment, or Voltaire.

"Perhaps tomorrow," said the admiral. "I would be pleased to bring it for you." He stood up again, bowing stiffly as she returned to her table.

"It is not right to read foreign books," said the officer at his side. "You are a German, on a German airship, flying to Germany. You should read German books."

Von Teppler glared at him in silence.

In the opposite corner of the lounge, Otto Hutten was concentrating on one of the two books he had with him, reading slowly with his finger on the page, while his wife watched out the windows. She had a basket of embroidery work with her, but the view of the sea below had kept her from making even perfunctory progress on the embroidery.

After a while she looked up from the window.

"Excuse me please, Otto."

He looked up from the book slowly, adjusting the reading glasses on his nose.

"I'm sorry to interrupt you again," she said, "but is there such a thing as a firefish?"

"A *firefish*?" he repeated with a resigned sigh. "What is a firefish?"

"Like a firefly. A fish that makes a flash."

"This I have never heard of," he said, patting her reassuringly on the arm. He glanced back at the open book, adjusting the reading glasses once more.

"Are you sure, Otto?"

He looked up again. "Why do you ask such a question? What makes you think of a ... what was it? ... *firefish*?"

"Because I saw such a flash." She pointed out the window with her finger, toward the rear of the airship. He followed her finger with his eyes, to the invisible horizon, identifiable only because the stars stopped where the seas began. "There," she said. "It was on the surface. A while ago. I've been waiting for another one."

"I don't think there is any such thing as a firefish," he said.

"Perhaps we should ask the captain."

"Anna, he is busy with the business of the airship. We cannot disturb him for this." He patted her again on the arm, then put his hand over hers. "You've been watching the sea for a long time, Anna. Perhaps we should go to bed now. You are anxious and tired."

The mechanic on the number four engine was on the same side of the Graf Zeppelin as Frau Hutten, but several hundred feet to the rear, isolated in his tiny engine nacelle with the huge twelve-cylinder Maybach engine. While the passengers and the rest of the crew enjoyed the quiet of the main gondola, the enginemen spent their shifts cramped up with the engines that they babied like newborns, wiping them, oiling them, supplying them a steady diet of fuel and oil on demand. What others might consider the infernal rumbling of the engines at cruising speed was to the mechanics only the contented cooing of a well-fed baby.

Toward the end of his shift, the engineman had grown irritable with a throbbing headache. It had begun after the airship turned, when the engine telegraphs had ordered extra speed. Flank speed set up a vibration in the big Maybachs, a trembling that attacked a man's head from within, rattling his brains like a misbalanced flywheel, worse than a headache in the morning after a night of drinking too much beer.

After twenty-five minutes of the throbbing, he could hardly concentrate on the lubrication chart or the fuel flow meter, and when the relief man signaled from across the narrow gangway that led from the body of the ship to the engine nacelle, the engineman scurried across, handing over the oil chart and the fuel records without a word. He made straight for the crew quarters, padding quietly on rubber-soled shoes. No dinner tonight, he thought. He would go straight to his hammock.

As he crawled in, positioning himself at an angle so that his body wouldn't slump to the center, he shut his eyes tightly, hoping the pounding in his head would disappear. But as the clattering of the valve lifters and rocker arms of the Maybachs faded, instead of silence he heard the chatter of the off-duty crew.

"This Whitman," boomed the grating voice of one of the riggers. "He's got no idea what he's doing. First he has us going halfway across the South Atlantic. Then he spins on his tail and heads back. He's probably lost. Maybe in America they don't teach them how to read compasses. That's why the American airships all crashed."

"He didn't order us back," answered another voice, the high

chirp of one of the ruddermen. "Stifel did. Stifel's worried about the admiral getting back to Germany on time."

"What's so important about the admiral?"

"He made some speeches about the rearming efforts. In Uruguay and Argentina. That's all I know."

"Why can't they make up their minds about whether they want to go home or just fly around the ocean? It was different in the old days, when Eckener was in command. A hard man, that one, but he knew what he was doing."

Unable to sleep, and with the headache growing worse instead of better, the engineman leaned out of his hammock and shouted to the two men. "They turned back because of lightning. There's a tropical storm."

The rudderman shouted back to him. "Stick to your engines, greaseman. There was no lightning. I was in the control room. We're moving around a stationary front."

"I tell you there was lightning," snapped back the engineman. "I *saw* it."

"You're tired, greaseman. You spend too long by yourself, talking to those engines. You've started seeing things."

The engineman swung down out of the hammock and padded over in his stocking feet. "I wasn't seeing anything that wasn't there. I saw lightning, low on the water. It's the most dangerous kind. The captain was smart enough to turn back and keep us out of the storm."

The rudderman stood up, flexing his muscles and showing the bulk of his belly. "I tell you there couldn't be any lightning."

"I'm too tired to argue with a fool," said the engineman. "And I'm too tired to listen to your stupid talk. Be quiet so a man can sleep. And be thankful that we don't have to fly through a lightning storm."

"Enginemen!" said the rigger, speaking quietly now. "They'd see the devil himself after a shift with those monsters. And I'll tell you, the Hindenberg is worse. Diesels. Rumble like an earthquake. Makes your brain rot, all that noise and vibration."

"What kind of man is he?" asked the rudderman. "That engineman. You know him?"

"He's actually not as bad as some of the others. Permanent grease under his nails, but at least he doesn't talk in that mush-mouthed rumble like some of them. But still—lightning! Did you see that sky? Crystal clear."

"He couldn't see the sky," said the rudderman. "From the

engine nacelles they can only see down, behind the ship." He thought for a moment, then spied Lehrmann, the chief radio operator, sipping a cup of tea. He knew that the radio operators always picked up strong static on their sets whenever a bolt of lightning discharged.

Lehrmann listened patiently before he answered. "Lightning? Nonsense. The man must have fallen asleep. It's exhausting work out there. Noise, vibration, fumes from the fuel and the oil—it's enough to make a man see his own mother on the water after a full shift."

"But he was sure," said the rudderman. "And he's the only one on the ship who could see behind us. He said that it was because of the lightning that we changed course."

"You heard them," said Lehrmann. "It was Stifel. He ordered us to abandon the search because there were no further radio signals and no sightings. He wants to show Whitman up as a fool. It's no secret that he wants the command and that he hates the American."

Lehrmann thought for a moment. He didn't like being caught in a dispute between officers, but he had a duty to the ship. He loved that ship.

"Where's the engineman?" he asked.

Lehrmann tapped tentatively on the door, reluctant to disturb an officer. "Captain Whitman, sir?"

"Yes. Come in."

It surprised him that the captain woke so easily. He had looked dead tired when he went off duty, which was not surprising after the hours he had spent going over the Graf with the ground crews.

"Sorry to disturb you, sir." Lehrmann stood in the doorway of the cabin. "But there are some strange goings-on . . ." He reported the engineman's story, then realized that the captain had not had time to glance at the compass, and so had no way of knowing they had changed course.

Whitman glanced at the instrument console while he pulled on his shoes and jacket, leaving his tie dangling on the hook of the wardrobe. "How long have we been on the new course?" he asked.

They walked down to the control room together, talking as they squeezed through the narrow corridor and followed one another down the steep ladder between decks.

"What could the flash have been?" asked Whitman.

"Some kind of flare. A Very pistol, perhaps. Or it could have been nothing. But the engineman was certain he saw a flash."

"Are they still monitoring in the radio room?"

Lehrmann shrugged. "I went off duty before they changed course. There had been no signals for almost an hour when I left, but it could have been a reception problem. At twilight the reception on that band is often poor, especially with signals from a low-powered set."

At the bottom of the ladder, Zekner was still on the starboard side of the control room, in the traditional watch officer's position. Stifel was leaning over the chart chest in the adjoining chart room.

With no more than a quick glance at the two men, Whitman went straight to the radio room. One of the junior radio officers was on duty, sitting with his feet up on the equipment counter, headphones draped around his neck, and a Karl May novel open in his hands.

"Captain!" The radioman jumped to his feet.

"Have there been any further signals from the ship?" asked Whitman.

"I.... we have abandoned the search," stammered the radioman. "The senior watch officer ordered all equipment returned to routine monitoring." He held up his log in defense, pointing to the notation of Stifel's order.

"Go back to the frequency where the signals were heard before," ordered Whitman. "And broadcast a slow message in English indicating that we are still searching. Even if their transmitter is down, they may be able to receive us."

"I don't know English, sir."

"Copy the message Lehrmann sent this morning. If you send letter by letter it will be slow enough for an inexperienced operator to read."

Walking back through the chart room, Whitman ignored Stifel, who was huddled with Zekner. He glanced at the chart, where the reverse course had been sketched in, then laid out the parallel rules to calculate a new course.

"Rudderman!" he ordered. "Come to oh-nine-six."

"Oh-nine-six," repeated the rudderman mechanically. The squabbles of officers were none of his business, but like everyone else in the control room he was waiting for the fireworks.

As Whitman looked up from the chart he saw Stifel compose himself before he burst out. "Whitman!"

The captain looked at him without answering.

"You are endangering the passengers and crew of this airship. This whole search is absurd. Nothing has been sighted. There are no more radio signals. And we are losing valuable time. It is imperative that we reach Recife as soon as possible, and then make our way to Frankfurt. If you do not desist from this dangerous course of action, I will have no choice except to . . . ''

"Except to . . . ?" repeated Whitman. He watched Stifel search for support from the crewmen in the control room. The men were so astonished at the novelty of officers arguing in their presence that they either turned away from his gaze or returned expressionless stares.

"This is neither the time nor the place to discuss our differences," said Stifel.

"I have no secrets from my crew," said Whitman.

After a long silence, Zekner meekly asked, "Shall I have the lookout resume his station, sir?"

"Yes," said Whitman. "And advise the enginemen on duty and any riggers working on the envelope to stay alert. And station another lookout in the auxiliary steering compartment at the base of the tailfin."

"Yes, sir." Zekner moved briskly, eager to be out of the crossfire.

"Send up the chief electrician," said Whitman as the watch officer started to move up into the hull. "And have Stein take over on the elevators. I want to drop down to three hundred feet. With the water cooling it could be rough down there."

Whitman turned back to the charts and the dead reckoning position that had been plotted on the pilot chart. They had lost time, but with the considerable headwinds against them, they had not moved far from their earlier position on the chart.

The electrician, a gangly man with the goatee and pointed moustache of a World War I Zeppelin man, showed up in his coveralls and felt-soled shoes.

"How much light can we show?" Whitman asked him. "I want to light this ship up like Broadway."

"*Broadway?*" questioned the electrician.

Whitman caught himself. "Like the Friedrichstrasse in Berlin."

"Never been asked that before, sir," said the electrician. "Used to be that we showed as little light as we could. Especially at low altitudes. Guess you Americans have different ways of doing things."

Whitman grinned, humoring the man.

"The batteries for the galley are low," explained the electrician. "They were roasting those big Westphalian hams for dinner, and that really drains those batteries. But if we can do without the big radio and just run the seventy-watt standby unit, *and* if we shut down the galley completely, *and* if the passengers can do without their reading lights, I think we can rig some floodlights below us and power them off the generators in the galley and the radio room. That way we save whatever charge is left in the batteries as a reserve."

"Excellent," said Whitman. "Order all lights out in the crew quarters and distribute spark-proof flashlights. And have the steward explain to the passengers. If necessary, a man can stand by in the corridor outside the passenger cabins with a flashlight for the washroom and toilet."

Less than ten minutes later, the lights went out all over the ship. In the control room, there was only the glow of the compass binnacle light, powered from its emergency battery. A flashlight was snapped on at the chart table.

"Stein," said Whitman. "You need light for the altimeters? I want to take her down to three hundred feet."

"Every now and then would be helpful, sir. Unless you don't mind getting your feet wet."

Whitman laughed and the others joined him, relaxing the tension in the room.

"He's steady tonight," said Stein. "But when we get down to the water, it could be a little rough. Good thing they won't be havin' no more wine in the dining room."

Suddenly the water beneath the Zeppelin was illuminated by floodlights. From the control room, it was easy to make out the whitecaps and the pattern of the seas, rolling steadily across the course of the Zeppelin.

Whitman watched for a while without saying a word. He was trying to imagine what the Graf Zeppelin, lit up like Broadway, would look like from the water.

Seven

She woke up shivering, with water lapping against her knees. She glanced at her watch and realized that it had been over an hour since she fired a flashbulb.

Ignoring the water, she climbed up on deck, ready to set up her equipment for another flash. She had just screwed the new bulb in place when she looked up at the sky, expecting to see only the canopy of stars against the infinite velvet black.

She saw it as soon as she looked, pale and low in the sky, like a new star. She shook her head, then splashed water from the clogged deck scuppers on her face. When she looked again, it was still there. It was too high to be a ship, and as she concentrated, it seemed too pale to be a new star.

New star? she thought. Like the Christmas star? Even as a child she had a hard time believing in the Christmas star. Things like that just didn't happen. She wondered whether she was delirious from fatigue and hunger.

The only other explanation was even more bizarre. H. G. Wells. *War of the Worlds. No,* she told herself. There are no flying perambulatory tripods bringing men from the stars.

What else could it be?

Whatever it is, she told herself, *signal!*

Too tired and confused to think anymore, she went back to her cabin and gathered the remaining flash bulbs, taking them up to the top of the cabin structure so she could set them all off, one after another. She used a piece of rag to shield her hand from the hot bulbs, and fired them off so closely after one another that she didn't have time to lose the lingering stars on the retinas of her eyes. Finally, after eleven flashes, she quit, slumping down on the cabin top, her own strength as depleted as the supply of bulbs.

She closed her eyes, waiting for her vision to return. When she opened them, she couldn't see the object in the sky, but she could see that the boat had listed even farther so that the topside gash was under water in the troughs of the waves. And the sharks, fascinated now by the flashes as much as by the smell of the hides, rolled violently at the surface, heaving their bodies over and over, showing their white sides against the pitch black water.

Eight

"The Fourth of July," said Whitman. He spoke under his breath, knowing there was no time for a lecture in American history.

Everyone in the control room had seen the flashes, even Stein, who leaned back from the elevator wheel to look out the window beside him. They had been like a string of firecrackers. With no standard of comparison, it was difficult to estimate the distance, but in a hurried discussion everyone guessed that it was within ten or fifteen minutes flying time.

Word traveled quickly through the crew quarters, even to the men sleeping in the hammocks. Without waiting for orders, a rigging crew went forward to the mooring compartment to rig a heavy line on the big winch and prepare a bosun's chair to lower. When Whitman gave orders for the engine telegraphs to go to flank speed, even the enginemen in their remote nacelles knew that something exciting was happening.

Spirits everywhere were high. After a long season of routine flights, a perfect monotony of fortnightly round trips from Frankfurt to Rio and back, it felt good to be involved in an adventure. It was like the glorious days of the Graf Zeppelin's past, the flights around the world and over the Arctic, the first exciting Atlantic crossings.

Months of tension disappeared in an instant. Despite the routine of the scheduled flights, the year had been a tough one for Zeppelin men. The old independent Zeppelin Company had been replaced by the Deutsche Zeppelin Reederei, G.m.b.h., half-owned by Lufthansa and partially under the thumb of Air Marshal Goering. Early in the flying season, in March, both the Graf Zeppelin and the Hindenberg, then in its early tests, had been commandeered for propaganda flights over Berlin and other cities in support of the plebiscite on Hitler's reoccupation of the Rhineland. And there would be more propaganda flights for the Olympic Games in Berlin. It seemed that whenever Goering or Goebbels snapped their fingers, the great Zeppelin would have to dance. And among the crew, there was constant fear that political criteria would be applied to the coveted jobs, or that the ships would be taken off the commercial service and used to further the prestige of the Reich. But now, once again, they were flying as only the Graf Zeppelin could fly, on a mission that no other aircraft or ship in the world could accomplish. To the men of his crew, Paul Whitman was on his way to becoming a hero.

When the lights were switched off, the passengers had no choice but to sleep or rest in their cabins. With profuse apologies, the stewards had made up the cabins early, swinging up the backs of the settees to convert them to upper berths and laying out the linen, all monogrammed with the insignia of the Graf Zeppelin. Most of the passengers had responded without a grumble, except for Senhor de Nascimento, who had been looking forward to an evening of hard sell on Teodoro Lopez-Otero. To allay the concerns of passengers and prevent a panic that might interfere with the operations of the crew, the blackout was explained as a standard procedure for a rescue effort.

From his lower berth, Admiral von Teppler sensed that something was astir. There was nothing in particular, nothing he could hear, no turn that he could sense. But the airship felt less steady, buffeted up and down on the air currents like a submarine bobbing on the surface before its ballast tanks were equalized

He turned over on his stomach and inched toward the window, moving quietly so he would not wake Eisler, the lieutenant snoring in the berth above him. Von Teppler remembered when they had boarded the Zeppelin and he had argued that protocol called for him to have a private cabin. Beck had rudely flashed the orders from the Naval War Office, pointing to the specific order that von Teppler was to be escorted at all times.

Escorted, thought von Teppler. It was a cruel joke. Guarded was the real word. Guarded as if he were a common criminal. He had served the Fatherland for twenty-nine years, his father and grandfather before him had served for over seventy years between them. A century of uninterrupted devotion to Kaiser and Reich, and he was now guarded like a criminal by these upstart Nazis.

He was surprised to see how close they were to the surface, the waves below them clear in the bright illumination of the ship's floodlights. The seas were running a good fifteen or twenty feet, and from the whipping spray at the top of the crests, von Teppler could see that any kind of rescue operation would be difficult. The spray was blowing off the crests of the waves at a sharp angle to the direction of the seas. It meant that a new wind was confusing a leftover sea. It would be very bad in a submarine, he thought. The kind of seas he would be tempted to avoid by submerging.

As he lay there, he heard footsteps outside, walking partway down the corridor, pausing, then walking another few steps. As if someone were looking at the individual cabin doors. Then there was a light tapping at the door of the cabin next to his, Beck's cabin. Von Teppler listened carefully, but the voices were muffled and indistinct, until they finally disappeared and he heard only the sound of more footsteps, this time of two men.

In the control room, the rudderman and elevatorman fought to keep the airship on a steady course as it was buffeted by the low level thermals. Stein vented gas from the bow and stern of the ship to reduce buoyancy, and maneuvered the elevator wheel constantly to level off the changes in attitude as the nose rose and dipped with each up or down draft.

What made the job challenging, and made a man like Stein a master, was the difference between his instant sense of balance and the slow reactions of the Zeppelin. It took long minutes for the huge ship to respond to a swing of the elevator wheel. The secret was to anticipate the need for action, so that the ship was already correcting its attitude before the full effect of the thermal could be felt. Even in the cool evening air, Stein worked up a sweat in minutes, the palsy in his hand disappearing completely as he concentrated his energies on the task.

The rudderman was the first to see the schooner. He called out calmly, as if the sight were expected. "Dead ahead, sir. Boat on the water."

The others crowded the windows of the control room, leaving only a narrow corridor for Whitman, who brought the big Zeiss binoculars. He braced his elbows against the duralumin girders to steady the glasses, and carefully focused on the schooner lying dead in the water ahead of them.

The wooden hull was heeling precariously, exposing the heavily fouled and barnacled bottom. The superstructure was hidden from his view, but it was clear that the masts were gone. He scanned for a sign of life.

With the glasses fixed on the schooner, he gave orders to bring the Graf over the boat and into the wind. There was no time to drop a marker flare, which would give an accurate reading of the surface winds by its smoke. Instead, Whitman guessed that the ship would lie to the wind, and that if they came parallel to the hull, they could gradually reduce their speed until the engines would just hold a steady position against the wind.

"How low can you bring her, Stein?" he asked.

"I can set him right on the water, Captain. Have him walking across the surface like the good Lord himself. But if we have to lift in a hurry, someone could get a quick shower when I drop ballast. Hope they have raincoats down there."

The other crewmen were astonished by Stein's easy way with the officers. Previous captains had barely tolerated him because of his skills at the elevator wheel, and more than once he had been reprimanded for lack of respect.

Whitman, in fact, seemed to enjoy the man. He usually laughed heartily whenever Stein rattled off one of his long-winded homilies. This time, he was too intent for laughter

As they began their turn to come up into the wind, Whitman ordered the altimeter recalibrated with a bottle drop, a maneuver in which a bottle—a soda water bottle because of the variation in wine bottles—was dropped and its descent to the surface timed. At low levels, the technique was actually more accurate than the timing of the echo from a rifle shot or a compressed air blast. Once the distance was calculated, the barometric altimeters could be reset, and they would function with acceptable accuracy until there was a marked change in atmospheric pressure.

While the bottle was being dropped from the navigator's hatch below the control room, the rigging crew began lowering the bosun's chair from the mooring compartment close to the bow of the ship. It dangled in front of the control room windows like a fishing bait as the ship completed its turn into the wind and came up behind the hull of the schooner.

Whitman ordered the engine telegraphs to dead slow, and the Zeppelin's airspeed dropped quickly until it was barely holding its position against the wind. There was still no sign of life on the ship, but from behind, Whitman could make out the lettering of the cracked nameplate on the transom, even with some of the gilded letters missing: SO T RN S AR.

As he watched the bosun's chair descend, Whitman knew they

were in trouble. At first the chair dropped vertically, trailing aft because of the forward motion of the Zeppelin and the head-winds. Then it began to oscillate and shift to the side, caught in the sheered wind below. And as the speed of the Zeppelin dropped until it was almost standing still above the schooner, Whitman watched the schooner drift rapidly sideways, swept by the seas.

Whitman tried to calculate the drift, wondering if they could cut their own speed and somehow drift with the ship. It was impossible. The Zeppelin was subject only to the winds and the power of its engines; without forward movement, its control surfaces were useless. And the ship was lying broadside to the seas, at a sharp angle to the wind. Each was a creature of its own environment.

He was calculating, trying to figure how to make a 775-foot airship maneuver like a hummingbird, when the woman appeared on the deckhouse of the schooner. She looked up and waved frantically, then dropped to her knees, holding onto the rail of the pitching hull. She struggled up again, using her arms to pull herself, but when she raised her hands to signal, she lost her footing and collapsed on the deck.

"How steady can we hold her?" asked Whitman. He caught his error of gender but didn't bother to correct it as he waited for the assessments of the rudderman and the elevatorman.

"Without more speed from the engines, I can't hold him into the wind," said the rudderman. "Got full left rudder now, and the bow's still being driven off."

Stein fought the wheel before he answered. "He's fighting me," he said. "No control on the elevator. I can hold altitude with gas and ballast, but it'll be a roller coaster." He grunted as he whirled the wheel again. "He's not good tonight," he said finally, as if the great airship were a naughty little boy having a temper tantrum.

By now everyone in the control room could see the woman, and the excitement and frustration were building. The bosun's chair dangled uselessly, and no efforts on the helm and elevators would bring it close to the ship.

"She'll be too weak to take the chair by herself," said Whitman. "Someone will have to go down and get her. There may be others aboard as well."

"Sir . . . !" said the rudderman.

"I'll go, sir . . ." The radio operator.

"Sir . . ." The chief engineer.

Every man in the control room volunteered, even old Stein.

"No," said Whitman, his voice bringing instant silence. "Send one of the riggers. They're used to dangling on those ropes. But only a volunteer."

The order was relayed down to the mooring compartment, and as the bosun's chair started to come up toward the ship, the woman on the deck of the schooner began waving her arms frantically, sliding across the deck as soon as she let go of the taffrail.

"Is there some way we can tell her that we're sending a man?" said Zekner. He waited for an answer, then saw that Whitman was frozen at the window, staring at the water on the other side of the schooner, where the topsides dipped low in the seas.

"Watch the water on the far side of the boat," said Whitman. "Those white flashes, rolling on the surface." He took the glasses away from his eyes and squinted hard before he put them back.

"Makos," he said.

"What's a mako?" asked Zekner.

"A shark."

As the bosun's chair was lowered a second time, the control room buzzed with guesses about the man sitting with his back to them. He was watching above as the rope was unreeled, and when he was finally clear of the mooring hatch, he swung around on the rope.

"Jürgen," said the rudderman.

"The kid?" said Stein. "Isn't he too young to volunteer? I thought a man had to be eighteen to go without his mother's permission. The kid doesn't even drink beer yet."

Jürgen Steinbrenner was an apprentice rigger, a wiry young man who could scramble on the envelope and the internal rigging like a monkey. It was only his second flight on the Graf, but he was already a mascot to the crew, a cherubic young man who didn't know how to make enemies and whose milk-drinking, early morning exercise and limitless energy were a source of constant amusement and jokes

"How did they choose the kid?" asked the rudderman.

"By lots," came the reply. "Everyone volunteered, so they drew lots. He won."

"Won?" said Stein.

The bosun's chair dropped quickly toward the sea, bouncing as it came to the end of each spasm of eased line. It had been directly over the hull of the boat when it started down, but despite the frantic efforts ˙of the rudderman and Stein on the elevators, the Zeppelin crew watched helplessly as the boat drifted across their course.

"Can't bring her around," said the rudderman. "If the wind catches the bow at this speed, we'll be driven off."

"Come around for another pass," said Whitman. "We can come up below the ship, then let the two drift together until Steinbrenner can jump on the deck."

The engines speeded up and the airship began swinging in an enormous circle, a maneuver that would take almost twenty-five minutes.

As they pulled away from the schooner, he glanced at the clock on the wall of the chart room.

They were exactly one-half hour from their scheduled arrival in Recife.

Nine

Johannes Schaub, the assistant manager of the Zeppelin landing field at Giquia, outside Recife, glanced at his watch when he heard the sound of a car on the dirt road outside. It was 7:30 A.M., one-half hour before the scheduled arrival of the Graf Zeppelin.

Schaub was barely awake, dozing on the cot in the back room of the office. He had been dreaming of the incredibly beautiful black women he had seen the day before at the market in Recife, women with skin like *Milchschokolade*, smooth, rich, sweet skin that he could almost taste. The women at the market wore nothing under their loose blouses, and Schaub would sit for hours, watching the gentle bounce of their breasts as they swayed with heavy loads on their heads. There was nothing like them in Germany, where the women either bound their breasts tightly in the fashion of the twenties, or wore underwear so rigid that it was impossible to enjoy the curves of their bodies.

He liked duty in Brazil. It was difficult to deal with the Brazilian authorities, who were infuriatingly slow, resentful of what they considered German high-handedness. But Schaub liked the relaxed pace of life in Recife. When he wasn't against a deadline to make sure there was adequate Pyrofax fuel, or to repair the hydrogen generating equipment and the storage tanks for the weekly arrivals of the Graf Zeppelin, he had plenty of time for the market and watching the women. Although he would have been reluctant to admit it, he had learned from the Brazilians to appreciate the time he could spend just sitting and watching.

It was only because it was the night before a scheduled landing and refueling of the Graf Zeppelin that Schaub was at the field at all.

As he walked outside into the gray dawn, with the sun coming up over the ocean in the distance and the heavy shadows making weird shapes out of the palm trees, he saw the rooster tail of dust behind a speeding car on the dirt road. Like almost every first time arrival at the landing field, the car had ignored the signs and gone to the end of the road, until it was stopped by the tall wire fence around the hydrogen storage tanks. Now it was winding its way back to the office.

Schaub turned toward the red and white mooring mast, sticking up incongruously against the background of palm trees. Beyond the mast were shacks, the remnants of native huts that had been abandoned. Schaub remembered the day when he had first come to the field to inspect the huts. Two, three, even four families lived in each, as many as fifteen people, sleeping in hammocks hung so close a person could not stand on the dirt floor. The families lined up when the German officials came through, standing proudly beside their homes in clothes that were no more than miserable rags. He saw their dinners, pots of rice and beans. The dogs in Germany ate better. And he watched them miser the fuel for cooking, scraps of wood that they collected and burned in open fires.

It was one of those fires that had almost destroyed the Graf Zeppelin. The ship was landing at the field when a freak gust of wind and a sudden torrential rain drove it down onto a palm tree between two of the huts, tearing the outer fabric. A man in one of the native huts had been brewing coffee and to his astonishment a crewman from the Zeppelin jumped from the gondola of the ship, seized the coffee and poured it on the open flames before the fire could ignite free hydrogen from the airship. After that incident, the Zeppelin Company quietly bought up the native shacks. They were never leveled because the whole operation at Recife was considered a temporary expedient, there only for the Graf Zeppelin until more long-range ships like the Hindenberg were built, ships that could fly from Frankfurt to Rio without a refueling stop.

As Schaub stared at the shacks, he thought for an instant that he had seen a reflection of the sun on a mirror or a scrap of metal. He squinted, turning his head to shield out the glare of the sunrise, but he couldn't see it again.

"Where is the Zeppelin?" It was an officious voice, from behind Schaub. "You are holding a ticket to Frankfurt. Name, Enkmann."

Schaub looked up. A man had got out of the car wearing a lightweight suit and a hat, and carrying a large portfolio, like the envelopes artists use to carry their drawings.

"Good morning," said Schaub.

"My ticket!" said the man. "The name is Enkmann. And where is the Zeppelin?"

Schaub led the man into the office, watching him glance with disapproval at the modest sign and the decrepit furniture. He undid the string clasp of a manila envelope and took out the passenger manifest and one of the ten-inch-high booklets that were used as tickets on the Zeppelin.

"But where is the Zeppelin?" asked Enkmann as he took the ticket.

Schaub pointed to the blackboard behind him, with its neatly printed message in German and Portuguese: *The Graf Zeppelin will be delayed approximately twenty-four hours in its arrival and departure at Recife.*

"Impossible," said Enkmann. "I was told that the Zeppelin is always on time. It is imperative that I reach Dusseldorf . . ."

"It is usually exactly on schedule," said Schaub. "This is an emergency delay."

Enkmann started to snap back, then suddenly controlled himself, as if a warning buzzer had gone off. "What is now the scheduled arrival time in Frankfurt?" he asked in an almost polite voice.

"The flight from Recife to Frankfurt is normally four days," said Schaub. "They will probably try to make the crossing faster if weather permits. There is a new commander now, an American. I'm certain he will be anxious to adhere to the schedule as closely as possible."

"An American?" said Enkmann. "Is that the reason for the delay? Can you do nothing? This is a matter of . . ."

"I'm sorry," said Schaub. "A hotel room is available for your convenience in Recife. You can leave your baggage here. We will call for you at the hotel in time for the flight. You needn't worry. You are the only passenger boarding here."

As Enkmann's car sped off, Schaub noted that it was a large Mercedes, and new. Although the man had not flashed official identification or a diplomatic passport, he was obviously important. He remembered to jot a VIP notation next to the name on the manifest.

When the cloud of dust from the car settled to the field, Schaub looked out toward the huts and the mooring mast, remembering the glint he had seen before. The sun was higher now, and the long shadows were crisp on the dry earth.

This time he saw a man running from the doorway of one hut to another. He crouched low as he ran, and he was carrying something in his hand, like a tool. That, thought Schaub, was probably what flashed.

He watched for a minute, long enough to see the man run to the next hut, and Schaub now realized that what the man was carrying was a rifle or a shotgun.

Schaub ducked back into the office and rang the Interior Police. They maintained a large barracks in Giquia, near the field, mostly to provide security to the Zeppelin when it landed.

Then he went back outside, setting a chair up in front of the office so he could relax while he watched the chase.

Ten

Even when she realized what it was, when it was close enough for her to read the huge numbers on the side—LZ-127—the airship was like an apparition, as strange as a ship from outer space. She had never seen a Zeppelin before, only the photographs in the newspapers, and even with the trained eye of a photographer, accustomed to interpreting the tricks of perspec-

tive that lenses can play on an image, she was not prepared for
the immenseness of the Graf Zeppelin, or the way it floated with
such effortless majesty. As it closed toward her, she could make
out the gondola, itself twice as long as the *Southern Star*. And
the airship was fully eight times as long as the gondola tucked
under its belly, as big as a skyscraper or an ocean liner—but in
the air! There were rows of windows on the control room and the
whole underside of the gondola, but with the bright floodlights
shining into her eyes, she couldn't see the faces watching her
from the windows.

As the Zeppelin came overhead a second time, she watched
the bosun's chair descend, dropping in quick spurts until it was
close enough for her to make out the face of the man. *Man?* It
was a boy, his face angelic, the straight blond hair a halo in the
backlight of the bright floodlights. He waved to her and to the
airship above, and from the way he swung so comfortably,
without using his arms to steady himself, she could tell he was
agile and relaxed. He was almost close enough for her to reach
his legs, but when she stretched up with her arms, she found that
her strength and her balance were so weak that she could not
stand on the listing deck unless she held onto the taffrail with
both hands. As their eyes met, he smiled, and she could see the
fine teeth in his grin.

His feet finally touched the deck with a springy bounce, and
he reached out toward her.

"*Komm*," he said, bracing his feet as the ship pitched up on a
wave.

She started across to him, but the ship lurched downward
again. She lost her grip and careened down the deck, crashing
into the rail on the leeward side as water broke over her. Her
fingers just touched his legs when the ship lifted again in the
trough of the wave, flinging the bosun's chair overboard where it
swung hard against the topsides of the schooner.

She heard the boy shout, and she pulled herself up to look
over the rail. The rope from the bosun's chair had caught under
one of the heavy iron chainplates of the schooner. As the
schooner lurched under the hovering Zeppelin, the rope stretched
taut, growing smaller like an elastic band and starting to hum.
Then, with a crack like a gunshot, it snapped, flinging the
bosun's chair and the boy into the sea.

He went under, then bobbed to the surface, swimming in a
strong, deliberate crawl. Lifejackets rained down from above,
but the Zeppelin was drifting away so fast that the nearest one

landed on the far side of the wave behind the boy. He came up with the swells, until a wave crested over him and he disappeared again for a second. Then she saw him again, swimming with the same steady stroke, close enough for her to see his face when he lifted his head for a breath.

Then she saw a flash of white in the water.

It was over in an instant, before she could shout, before he could get a cry from his mouth. His body flew up out of the water, red and ragged where the legs had been. Then it fell back into the waves and disappeared among the rolling flashes of white. She stared at the spot, a scream welling up inside her, but it caught in her throat because the horror was too terrible for a scream, too terrible for anything but silence.

She felt the tears start down her cheeks. For the first time, she was truly terrified.

Eleven

The control room reacted in a single gasp, followed by a hush quiet enough for the men to hear the hum of the electric motor in the gyrocompass. Everyone was glued to the windows, watching the huge forms of the sharks circle and slash as they looked for more than they had found.

It was Stifel who spoke first, stepping out of the security of his niche in the chart room. "You're to blame, Whitman. You alone." Stifel's eyes searched the room as he shouted his accusation. "This entire operation was foolish. The Zeppelin wasn't built for sea rescues. We're so low now that a sudden downdraft could drive the ship into the sea. We've vented so much hydrogen in these insane maneuvers that we will be in danger on our return to Recife. And now you've killed one of our crewmen, a mere boy. And all because of your exaggerated American hero mania."

Eyes throughout the control room swung to Whitman, not yet accusing, but questioning, wondering about his judgment. Judgment was the one quality expected of a captain, and Whitman was still unproved. German crewmen did not normally question the decisions of officers, but the facts were clear. Jürgen Steinbrenner was gone, his death more horrible than anyone could ever have imagined.

Whitman answered their gazes with his eyes, sure of what he had to do, but unsure how to do it. He was, always had been, a man more comfortable with action than words, impatient when talk was substituted for decision. But a rescue needed more than him alone. It needed a crew. And from the looks in the eyes around him, he knew he had to persuade before he could act.

He walked steadily between the staring eyes toward the passenger lounge, where he knew most of the off-duty crew would be. It was the one place where they could watch the rescue effort. He heard them as soon as he opened the door.

" . . . hasty. Always we have been cautious. It is the mark of the Zeppelin Company."

"Of course. It's necessary to be cautious in a ship carrying three million cubic feet of hydrogen and one million cubic feet of inflammable fuel. Does this Whitman think this is a small airplane that can whirl about?"

" . . . a boy. He was only a boy. I remember yesterday, he was . . ."

"He thinks he's like the cowboys in those American films, who rescue the girl at the last moment. It's impossible in this wind and sea . . ."

As the eyes in the room spotted Whitman the voices quieted. He looked carefully through the room, fixing individuals one at a time in his gaze before he spoke. Except for an impromptu speech to the crew when he was first appointed to the command, a speech that had ended in laughter when he admitted he would have to practice calling the Graf Zeppelin a "he," it was the first time that he had spoken to the whole crew together. But then no other Zeppelin commander had ever done so, except for Eckener himself. By tradition, German officers gave orders; they didn't discuss them with their men.

"There's a woman down there," Whitman said. "She's barely holding onto the remains of that boat. The hull is holed and probably sinking. She is weak, from her actions she appears close to exhaustion. There may be other passengers alive as well. We have a duty to her, to anyone else down there, to all voyagers who take to the sea. I can't abandon that duty."

"What about your own passengers?" snapped de Nascimento. "We purchased tickets for travel to Europe, not for a tour to demonstrate the bravado of a captain who wants to be a hero. Would you sacrifice us the way you sacrificed that boy? They say the Zeppelin could crash when it's this low.''

Whitman zeroed in on him. ''You are not in danger, Senhor de Nascimento. No one on this ship is in danger. But if we don't do something, and do it quickly, that woman will die.''

''What about Steinbrenner?'' shouted a voice. ''You don't seem to care if he died. And he's one of us.''

A rumble of agreement went through the room.

''What would you have me do?'' asked Whitman. ''Abandon the woman and whoever else might be on the boat?''

There was no answer.

After a long while, an anonymous voice shouted out. ''Drop a life preserver and some food. A ship can come and rescue her.''

Murmurs of approval seconded the suggestion.

''She wouldn't last a day,'' said Whitman. He searched the passengers and crew one at a time, looking for the convictions behind their eyes. In the back of his mind he remembered stories he had heard of an early triangle flight of the Graf Zeppelin, from Europe to South America to North America and back to Europe. The passengers had paid $6,500 each for the flight, and when Hugo Eckener refused to land in Havana because of threatening weather warnings, the Spanish and South American passengers were so outraged that the passenger revolt could only be put down when the crew brandished revolvers.

As the comparison flashed through his mind, Whitman realized how different his own situation was. Then it was crew versus unruly passengers. Now it was a commander alone, an American commander on a German Zeppelin.

In the midst of the eyes that glared at him, Whitman saw Admiral von Teppler, his uniform jacket unbuttoned at the collar, but his demeanor and manner otherwise totally composed. His eyes were steady and unblinking when he returned Whitman's gaze, and even without a smile of acknowledgement, without the slightest change of expression, the message in the admiral's eyes was clear.

Whitman walked straight to the admiral, controlling his reaction to the glares of the crew members. Most of the crew, he knew, were confused, not so much afraid as unsure, waiting for someone to set a course of action that made sense.

''Captain!'' said von Teppler, fixing Whitman in his gaze. ''It *can* be done. It will not be easy, but it *can* be done. And *you* must do it.''

Next to von Teppler, Beck stood with his hands clasped behind him, glowering at Whitman. Everyone in the room seemed to be listening to them.

"How?" asked Whitman, playing his own devil's advocate. "The airship can only hold its position into the wind. The boat is drifting almost at right angles to the wind. There is no way to stay steady over it, not in this wind."

"It can be done," said von Teppler. "If the airship cannot be controlled, you must control the boat. Bring it into the wind, or at least head to the seas. If you can control its drift, you can maneuver to hoist the passengers from the deck."

"Enough," Beck said. "This talk is futile."

"The boat?" said Whitman, ignoring Beck. "We couldn't even get a man safely onto the deck. That was a fine young man who fell, as sure-footed as any man aboard."

"He did not know what to expect from the sea," said von Teppler. "He did not anticipate the motion of the boat."

The admiral looked hard at Whitman. "It can be done, Captain. We often faced the same problem in the U-boats. After a kill with a torpedo or a deck shot, we would sometimes want to pull alongside a crippled or sinking ship to take on survivors or to inspect and certify cargo. It was the same situation, exactly. Because of its shape, a surfaced submarine is only comfortable heading into the wind, but the ships would often lie as this one lies, hull abeam to the seas. With their rudders destroyed and no power in their engines, they could not control their course."

"What did you do?"

"Nothing a good seaman would not know. Warps, sea anchors. With the schooner, a steadying sail set on a jury-rigged mast would suffice."

"Could you show a man how to do it?"

Von Teppler thought for a moment, seemingly oblivious to the eyes and ears in the room that waited on his answer.

"No," he said finally. "I cannot show a man what has taken a lifetime at sea to learn."

Whitman waited, knowing the man would say more.

"I am willing to go myself," said von Teppler.

"Impossible," shouted Beck. He edged himself in front of the admiral. "Your orders are to return to the Reich. This cannot be permitted."

"You're not a young man, Admiral," said Whitman.

Von Teppler hinted a smile. "I have less to lose than a young man."

"I absolutely will not permit this," said Beck. "The admiral has been entrusted to my custody. He must be returned to the Reich."

"Your *custody,* Oberleutnant?" said von Teppler. "I am commissioned an admiral of the German navy. In my experience, admirals are not in the *custody* of junior officers."

Stung, Beck spun on Whitman. "You will not get away with this, American." He said the last word as if it were a curse.

"We can find you rubber-soled shoes," said Whitman. "What other equipment will you need?"

His face red, and lips clenched in anger, Beck moved to block the path of Whitman and von Teppler. Whitman took a single step, felt a hard object in his belly, and looked down to see a service 9-millimeter Luger P08 automatic in Beck's hand.

"Where did you get that?"

Beck's eyes scanned the room, settling on the tall figure of Stifel.

"Do you have any idea what a gunshot would do inside the Zeppelin?" said Whitman. "The muzzle flash would instantly ignite any free oxyhydrogen. If there was even a tiny leak in one of the gas bags, the entire airship would burn in minutes."

"Then do not force me to use it," said Beck. "I have a responsibility to the Reich, and I will carry it out. The admiral must be returned to Germany."

Men standing around them backed away as the captain faced Beck, his stomach still against the gun. Beck's thumb flicked the safety off.

"And I have a responsibility to my crew and passengers," said Whitman. "Give me that gun."

"Including Jürgen Steinbrenner?" said a voice that Whitman recognized as Stifel.

Whitman took another step, reaching up with his hands.

"I am warning you, Captain. If you force me, I will not hesitate to use the weapon." Beck's lips hardly separated as he spoke.

"Have you no sense of humanity?" shouted von Teppler. The voice seemed to come from a spirit other than the gentle admiral. "You call yourself a German. You speak of duty to the Reich. You have no idea what it means to be a German. Men such as you bring only shame and dishonor to the Fatherland."

Beck spun to glare at the admiral, the gun swinging to follow his gaze. "You...traitor, how dare you...?"

The rage distracted him only for an instant, but it was long enough for Whitman to grab his wrist and twist the arm down against his side. The gun slipped in Beck's grip, and with both hands, Whitman wrenched it free. He snapped the clip out of the pistol and stuffed it in his pocket before pushing the gun into his belt.

"Get out of our way," said Whitman.

"That is assault against an officer of the German navy," Stifel said: "Who do you think you are?"

"You," answered Whitman, "are relieved of any further duty on this airship. I will stand your watches. And if you continue to interfere with the operation of the Zeppelin, I'll have you confined to a cabin. Is that clear?"

There was no answer. As Whitman and von Teppler walked forward through the doorway of the dining room, there wasn't a sound in the room.

Twelve

The police truck stopped only long enough for Schaub to point to the huts by the mooring mast. There were six burly men in the back of the truck, wearing light green fatigues, their trousers stuffed into heavy boots and machine pistols slung over their shoulders. The Sigma sign of the Integralistas was on their armbands, but these undisciplined thugs were a ludicrous parody of the Nazis they imitated. If anything, thought Schaub, the Integralistas were a liability to Brazil and to the Germans. He couldn't understand why the German government would continue to supply them with weapons and advisors.

Schaub watched the truck speed across the landing field, stopping a few hundred yards from the shacks. The men formed a loose semicircle as they walked toward the huts, their machine pistols slung at their hips while they closed in for the kill . . . a pack of dogs after a rat.

Their first shots were tentative bursts, the Schmeissers spraying the houses at random in an effort to flush the man out. Answering shots came from one of the huts, and the police dove for cover behind the truck and the other huts. When the police tried to regroup, Schaub saw the man dash from the back of one hut and run for another. The police opened a murderous barrage on the first hut, raking it with a burst of automatic fire, before two of them walked slowly toward the doorway, their machine pistols at the ready. From the jaunty cockiness of their strides, it was obvious that they expected to find only a bullet-ridden body inside.

Schaub found himself quietly cheering for the lone man, so foolish against such incredible odds. So far he was outwitting the police.

The police moved down the row of houses systematically, attacking each one with the same technique: encirclement, a heavy barrage from the machine pistols, a slow search. Each time, the man managed to dash out before they got him.

After the fourth hut, one of the police spotted the man running. He fired wildly from the hip, but the man dove to the ground and scrambled into the shelter of the palm trees. Schaub caught glimpses of him running through the dense groves.

Three of the police jumped into the truck to give chase, gunning the engine until the wheels spun up clouds of thick dust from the dry airfield.

The man sprinted deeper into the thickets of the palm trees, but the police soon had the headlights of the truck pointed into the deep shadows, and they opened another of their murderous barrages, raking back and forth with clip after clip of shells. It was impossible for the man to be alive, thought Schaub.

Then, just when he expected the police to go in for the body, he saw the man walk out, his rifle held over his head with one hand, his other held up in a defiant fist. He was wearing the loose cotton pants and drawstring blouse of a peasant. His feet were bare.

Minutes later, the truck stopped again in front of the office to show off their prize to Schaub. Two of the police stood up in the back and kicked at the prisoner, catching him off balance so that he fell onto the ground before he could stand. His hands were tied behind him, and blood streaked his beard and his thick, shaggy hair.

"You know him?" asked the police sergeant. He grabbed the man by the hair and twisted his head viciously so Schaub could see the face. The eyes, dark and deep set, glared with hatred.

Schaub glanced for only an instant and turned his head away, repulsed by the brutality of the beating the man had received.

"No," he said.

"Another stupid peasant from the Sertão," said the sergeant. "They come to the city to look for work. Especially now, with the fevers in the backlands. They're dying like flies back there. It's a good thing, too. There are too many of them for the land."

He turned to look at the prisoner. "Look at him. Stupid, uneducated . . . peasant trash. Of course they can't find work in the city. They're not suited. So they rob. This one is so stupid that he tries to rob empty shacks."

Schaub noticed one of the police staring at the prisoner. The prisoner turned his face away, shielding his eyes in his chest, but the policeman walked around to the other side and squatted, pulling a crumpled poster out of his pocket and comparing the picture with the man in front of him.

"It's him," said the policeman. *"Conselheiro."*

The others suddenly looked at the beaten man, grabbing the poster to make their own comparisons.

The sergeant came over and pulled back the prisoner's hair, painfully wrenching the man's neck. He looked closely, glanced at the poster, and said, "It's him, all right." He smashed his fist into the man's face.

The man's head spun away. Then he looked back at the sergeant with the same glare of patient hatred.

"This scum calls himself a *revolutionary*." The sergeant said it with the inflection he would have used for *child molester*.

"Why does he call himself the Counselor?" asked Schaub.

"They call him that. The ignorant peasants. It's the name of a revolutionary leader in a famous Brazilian book. You remember in November, when the peasants rioted here on the field? He was their leader. Your great airship stayed up for four days waiting to land until we broke them. This one was captured and sent to Fernando de Noronha. Only last week we heard that he had escaped."

"What do you think he was doing here?" asked Schaub.

The sergeant laughed. "Maybe he was returning to the scene of his glory."

The other police joined his laughter.

"Glory? They were shot down like rats." Schaub started to laugh himself, then stopped abruptly. "Unless . . . unless he was here with some crazy idea of revenge. That would explain why he was here this morning, when the Zeppelin was scheduled to land."

The sergeant looked over at the prisoner. "That scum? What would he know of an airship?"

"Yes," said Schaub. "That must be it. He probably thought that his rifle would bring down the Graf Zeppelin. He didn't realize that the bullets would do nothing more than make tiny leaks in the gas cells. The riggers can easily repair them even in flight. It takes more than bullets from a rifle to destroy a German Zeppelin."

The talk of armament intrigued the sergeant. "What would it take to bring down the Zeppelin?" he asked.

"The Zeppelin? Even a machine gun wouldn't bring it down. It would take an incendiary bomb, or a cannon. Perhaps a mortar with an explosive shell."

"Well, no need to worry about this filth," said the sergeant. "He won't attack anything now."

"Why would he try?" asked Schaub. "If he just escaped from that prison, a fugitive, why would he try to attack the Zeppelin?"

The sergeant shook his head, glancing in the direction of Conselheiro. "These revolutionaries," he said, twirling his index finger in a small circle at his temple, " . . . all crazy."

Thirteen

As the bosun's chair began its third descent, Whitman took the helm himself, something no other officer had ever done. Von Teppler's long frame was draped over the dangling chair, a heavy coil of rope hanging from one shoulder and his hands full with wire, life preservers, an axe, and a rigger's knife. Despite the paraphernalia, he managed to make clear signals with his hands to the winchmen in the mooring compartments above him, and to Whitman at the helm

He dropped quickly to within a few feet of the level of the deck of the ship, then motioned Whitman forward. The schooner had settled lower in the water, and its motion had steadied, although the decks were now occasionally awash in the seas. The boat was still drifting rapidly beneath the hovering Zeppelin.

By reversing and accelerating the engines of the Graf, Whitman brought the airship briefly over the deck of the schooner. He watched for von Teppler's signal to the riggers. There was only an instant when they would be directly overhead, and Whitman knew there would be a delay before the riggers reacted to a hand signal. If von Teppler was to come down on the sloping deck, the signal would have to come before the boat was underneath his feet.

Suddenly, in a motion so swift that it was impossible to follow with the eyes, von Teppler reached up with the rigging knife and sliced through the rope, letting himself fall straight to the deck. He came down on all fours, and grappled for a handgrip as he slid down toward the leeward rail, now partially submerged. The woman stared at him in disbelief, her arms and legs locked around the taffrail.

On deck, von Teppler was a whirlwind of activity. As soon as he had his footing, he scrambled up to the woman, strapping her into a lifejacket. Then he disappeared belowdecks and slowly came back up to try the helm of the schooner. From the stern, he worked his way forward, lugging the heavy coil of rope and tying one end to the samson post at the bow of the schooner. With the axe, he tore loose one of the hatch covers and part of the rail on one side of the deck, then lashed it all together in a formidable if unconventional sea anchor, which he pushed over the bow. He paid out the line, and when it finally took, he went back to the helm, fighting the wheel until the boat slowly rounded up into the seas.

The motion on the boat slowly became more irregular, pitching with the seas instead of lurching in soft rolls as it had done with the seas abeam. But the boat held its position, drifting in a slow, controlled course that Whitman could follow in the Graf Zeppelin. Once the boat came around, Whitman discovered that by feathering three of the engines and cruising at quarter speed on the other two, he could keep the Graf steady over the schooner.

With a corkscrew signal, von Teppler called for the rope to be lowered again, and it came down weighted by a monkey's fist of knotted line. He had already strapped the woman in the bosun's chair. His agile motions on the deck of the schooner, even when waves crashed over the bow, pitching the hull violently, made it seem like child's play. When the monkey's fist dropped, he grabbed it on the first try and tied the end to the bosun's chair, moving so quickly that it was hard to be sure that the line was even there when he signaled with the up motion of his fist.

"Steward," said Whitman as he watched the chair come up

from the deck, "have her taken to an empty passenger cabin. She may want some bouillon or hot tea. I think you can ask the other women passengers to lend her some clothing. And take the medical kit, in case she's hurt." Whitman spoke without taking his eyes off the rising chair.

He kept his eyes fixed on the chair until he saw the hands of crewmen reach down from the hatchway of the mooring compartment to pull the limp form aboard. Then he looked down to the deck of the schooner, expecting to see the admiral. The sharks were either gone or invisible in the graying light of the early dawn. And there was no sign of the admiral.

"He went below," said Zekner, reading the question on Whitman's face.

There was a long silence while they waited for the admiral to reappear on the deck.

"You don't think . . ." said Zekner, filling the awkward silence. "They couldn't be right, could they? It couldn't be a . . . ?" He didn't finish the sentence, but there was no doubt what he was thinking. And even if it made no sense when they looked down at the sinking hulk below them, it was hard to drive the question away.

"He must be taking a leak," said Stein. "A gentleman like the admiral wouldn't just go off the deck with everyone watching, especially with women passengers on board."

No one laughed. Everyone just stared, waiting for the admiral to reappear.

"You're sure he's belowdecks?" said Whitman.

"The woman is all right," interrupted the steward. "She's exhausted, and she has a nasty bruise on one leg, but she was well enough to give us a nice smile. Señora Lopez-Otero offered to lend her some clothes. After a good sleep, I'd guess she'll be just fine."

A soft hum, almost a muffled cheer, went through the control room at the news.

"Captain Whitman," said the steward, waiting for Whitman to turn around.

"Yes?" Whitman seemed reluctant to take his eyes off the boat for even an instant.

"She's American, sir. Her name is Margaret Bourne."

American? Whitman caught his reaction short, turning back to stare at the deck of their schooner, still empty, still pointing into the seas, still awash with spray and water as the seas broke over the bow. While he tried to focus his thoughts on the possibilities, including the death of the admiral by drowning or accident or the now invisible sharks, a figure calmly stepped out of the cabin hatch onto the listing deck carrying a small suitcase in one hand with a crude rope sling wrapped around himself.

The rope went down, Whitman maneuvered into position, and less than fifteen minutes later the admiral was at the hatch of the mooring compartment.

Whitman had gone forward, and he extended his own hand to pull the admiral aboard. Instead, the admiral, still dangling in the slipstream with a rope sling around his chest, held up the small fiberboard suitcase.

"What is it?" asked Whitman.

"I have no idea," said von Teppler as he pulled himself through the hatch. "But she wouldn't leave that hulk until I promised to get it for her. She is very strong-willed." He heaved himself up onto the catwalk over the hatch.

"She is also a very beautiful woman," he added.

"And you," said Whitman, taking the admiral's hand in both of his own, "are a damn brave man. That was a fine piece of work down there."

"Not really," answered von Teppler. "I am only an old man with little to lose. It is you who risked your command. But believe me, Captain"—he winked, then grinned broadly—"the lady was worth it."

Fourteen

"Yes?"

Wide awake and refreshed after a few hours of sleep and a chance to wash and change uniforms, Whitman felt that he could take on even the questions and complaints of passengers, which was what he expected from the steward.

"It's Miss Bourne, sir. She's up now, and she asked if you would join her for lunch. I explained to her that the captain never dines with passengers, but she is persistent."

"I will," said Whitman.

"But . . ." stammered the steward, "there is no precedent."

"There's no precedent for what happened last night, either,"
said Whitman. "I'll tell her myself."

She was sitting at the fourth table in the dining room, with her
back to the door, looking out the window at the calm seas below.
After only a day of flying, the other three tables had become
Stammtische, standing tables to which recorked bottles of wine
and mineral water were brought each day from the meals of the
previous day.

She turned around at the sound of the door opening, and
Whitman realized immediately what the admiral had been
talking about. She was wearing the same brown suit that
Nadia Lopez-Otero had worn the day before, and at first
glance they appeared to be the same size. But a suit that had
been staid and conservative on the señora was filled out to
stunning proportions by Margaret Bourne. Her long legs made
the skirt seem short, and her wide shoulders and full breasts
lifted the jacket with each breath. The throat of the blouse was
unbuttoned, showing the dark tanned skin of her neck, a
splendid contrast with her green eyes and the bright sparkle of
her teeth as she smiled. With one hand, she brushed back her
hair, brown with auburn highlights. It hung straight down to
her shoulders, without the prim waves on top that were the
fashion of the day.

"Captain Whitman?"

He nodded as he walked over to the table.

She stood, a little awkward on the leg that had been bandaged
around the shin. He saw that she wore no stockings, and that the
long legs had the same bronze suntan.

"I'm Margaret Bourne." She extended her hand. "Everyone
calls me Maggie."

"You slept well, I trust?"

"Never better in my life." She caught herself, suddenly
realizing that the captain was not the stiff German she expected.
"You're English?" she quizzed, grinning now.

"My mother was American. I grew up in New York."

Her palm came up to her forehead in a gesture of mock
dismay. "Incredible! Shipwrecked in the middle of the South
Atlantic and I'm rescued by a German Zeppelin with a captain
from Gotham."

He pulled out a chair for her, then sat next to her at the
table.

"I'm from San Francisco," she said. "At least I was. I've

been traveling so long that I can hardly remember home anymore.''

The steward interrupted with the menus, neatly printed in ornate covers.

"If you would prefer, Miss Bourne," he said, "I can have the cook prepare a light soup for you."

"Thanks," she said. "Right now I think I could eat a horse."

The steward looked surprised, his meager English challenged by the American slang. "I'm terribly sorry," he said, with a tone of genuine regret. "We do not serve horse flesh. Today's lunch is Rhine salmon and roast gosling."

She laughed, and Whitman joined her.

"Sold," she said. "Please."

"Could we also have a bottle of the Moselle?" added Whitman.

"Another precedent shattered," mumbled the steward as he jotted a note. "Soon I will not be able to keep track of them."

"What did he mean?" she asked as the steward went to the next table.

"I'm afraid American humor catches some of my colleagues at a loss," Whitman explained. "The precedents are my dining with a passenger and drinking wine during a flight. Apparently my predecessors never did either."

"And you?"

"My first time. Actually, this is my first flight in command."

"I'm honored," she said. "Seriously, Captain Whitman, I don't know what to say. After what happened to that poor boy last night, and after all you've done, it sounds plain silly to say thanks."

"It's the admiral who deserves your thanks," he said. "The crew and I just did our jobs."

"The admiral speaks enough French to have explained why the Zeppelin went on the search in the first place. I didn't completely understand him, but I take it your decisions weren't exactly popular."

"Only because there were some on board who didn't realize what a delightful castaway we were rescuing."

She laughed with a smile that wrinkled the corners of her eyes and flashed her teeth. "That sounded an awful lot like 'What's a nice girl like you doing on the deck of a sinking rotten old schooner in the middle of the ocean?' ''

He smiled back, a response that was part of speaking English, something he wouldn't have done in German. "Something like that," he said. "It's not the way we usually pick up passengers. It would be useful if we had something for the log and an explanation for the officials in Recife of why we're arriving with an extra passenger. As the steward would say, it's another precedent shattered."

She twisted in her seat, gazing over the calm conviviality of the dining room. "I really can't believe I'm here," she said. "It's not a dream, is it? I've never traveled in this kind of luxury. At least I can't remember it. When I woke up this morning, I found my legs braced against the bulkhead, as if I were still on that pitching deck. It wouldn't have surprised me if my arms had been pumping up and down. I can still feel the aches in my shoulders. And then, suddenly . . ." Her eyes swung around the room again.

"It's not a dream," said Whitman. Something wistful in his voice made his words seem more than a reassurance.

"Your baby?" she asked.

He nodded, not sure whether he was amazed at her perceptiveness or his own obviousness. "I'm not sure for how long."

"Sounds like a good story," she said.

They talked while they ate, with the steward nervously returning to their table to offer extra portions as she hungrily devoured the plates of food he put before her. Everything about her seemed so American to Whitman, the easy smiles, the relaxed table manners, the open conversation. It made him realize how long he had been in Germany, speaking and thinking German, never seeing a smile like hers or laughing openly at easy, relaxed talk.

"I'm a photographer," she explained. "Free-lance, now. I used to do assignments for the *Chronicle* in San Francisco before I . . ." She caught herself, stopped short, restarted. "I just finished five months in West Africa, working up a photo essay on the coast. It's the kind of story you might see in *National Geographic,* except that they don't hire women photographers, and I was hoping for a little more depth than they can usually handle. I have a book in mind, and my publisher will back me if I can come up with the plates. That's why I care so much about that case that the admiral brought up from that wreck. When I get back to civilization . . . " She stopped short again, laughing this time. ". . . back to civilization? It's hard to imagine anything more civilized than this."

"What put you on that schooner? It didn't look safe for a sail across San Francisco Bay."

"I just missed the liner and I didn't feel like waiting another six weeks in Libreville. And when I first saw those coastal schooners, I thought they were marvelous, the most romantic boats I'd ever seen." She went on to describe the storm, and waking up to find herself alone on the boat.

"They just left you?"

"That's sure what it looked like. I woke up, and it was just me and that mastless mess. For a while I really felt like calling the Marines."

"Do you have photos of them? If they ever made it back, they could be caught."

"What would that accomplish? They've already lost their boat. That means that they'll end up laborers, if they even survive in that dory. Believe me, being a laborer in Libreville is enough punishment for anyone. I suppose it's partly my fault anyway. I think they would have been all right if I hadn't frightened them. When I started talking about the radio, and asking about taking sun sights, I think I became an evil spirit in their eyes. It was as if I'd brought the storm."

"I trust you won't do the same for us," said Whitman. "We have a full day of flying before we get to Recife."

She grinned at him as she sipped the white wine in the tall-stemmed green glasses. "Believe it or not," she said, flicking her tongue over her lip, "I actually forgot how delicious wine could be. You forget everything except survival down there." She glanced around the room again. "And then to suddenly be in an elegant dining room, eating smoked salmon and roast goose with a dashing captain . . . it's as big a shock as my first days in Africa."

Whitman didn't quite control his blush. He was still getting used to hearing himself addressed as "captain," and the "dashing" in English, along with her smile, made him feel he was living out his childhood fantasy, a captain in the Lafayette Espadrille with a flowing white silk scarf. He almost laughed at the memory. "Have you met the other passengers?" he asked.

Her eyes roved around the room and Whitman watched her smile at Otto Hutten. Hutten returned the smile with a shy grin, then came over to the table.

"Captain Whitman, Miss Bourne." His heavily accented English was almost comical. "Frau Hutten and I would wish to tell Miss Bourne that if there is anything we can do . . . we have some Brazilian money with us, and if perhaps we could help in travel arrangements from Recife to wherever . . ."

"That's really kind of you," she answered. "I haven't even thought about it. Recife is about a million miles from anywhere, isn't it?"

"You will please remember our offer," said Hutten. "Also," he said to Whitman, "Frau Hutten and I would extend our condolences to you and the crew and the parents of that brave boy. We were asleep last night, but we heard this morning of the tragedy. It was very brave of you to carry on, Captain."

"Thank you," said Whitman. "It's really Admiral von Teppler who is the hero."

"Yes," said Hutten. "We have also heard what he did. Do you think it would be proper for me to address him? I would like to commend what he did."

Whitman glanced over at the admiral's table, then turned back. "I think the admiral would enjoy talking to someone other than his present companions."

He watched as Hutten made his way to the admiral's table and stood waiting for the admiral to look up.

"Excuse me, please, Herr Admiral," said Hutten. "I do not wish to disturb your luncheon, and I apologize if I do not know the correct forms of address. Things have changed so much since I was myself a soldier that I no longer know how to speak to an officer. My wife and I wanted only to say that what you did last night makes us proud to be Germans. There is much that we read and hear about the New Germany, and it is sometimes confusing. You have reminded us that there are still men who understand the true values of our Fatherland. For this, we thank you."

Von Teppler stood stiffly and bowed. Before he could speak, Beck got to his feet. "The admiral does not speak with other passengers."

Whitman and Maggie Bourne watched it all. Whitman was already standing behind his chair, getting ready to go forward to the control room. For a moment he said nothing, and when he finally spoke, the lighthearted tone was gone from his voice.

"The Germany I know," Whitman said softly, "is changing."

Fifteen

Conselheiro woke up on a cold cement floor, aches in every inch of his body testifying to the efficiency of the police truncheons. As he opened his eyes, he felt caked blood on his face, and when he looked down, his blouse was torn and streaked with blood. One foot was throbbing with pain, and swollen to the size of a football.

He recognized the cell. It wasn't really a cell, but a bullpen, three windowless walls, a fourth wall of bars, a barred hole in the ceiling for light and air, open to the rain.

When he was last there it was with twenty other men, crowded so close that they had to make rules among themselves about who could sleep and for how long. The lucky ones got a section of floor for an hour; the others stood like cattle in a slaughterhouse pen, ankle deep in their own excrement and urine.

He had been there for one week then, until the ridiculous court ceremony they called a trial. The charges against him were never read out, he had no lawyer, no chance to speak before the judge announced his sentence: life imprisonment on Fernando de Noronha. It was the only sentence worse than execution.

The next day he was taken to the island, thrown in with murderers and maniacs, the dregs of Brazil. He quickly swallowed his pride and learned from the murderers and maniacs how to build a wooden platform so he wouldn't have to sleep on the ground and be bitten by rats and stung by scorpions. He learned to scramble for bananas before they were picked and eaten by other prisoners, and his body learned to survive the chronic diarrhea that came from eating green bananas. The alternative was slow starvation on the two meager servings of gruel slopped out each day by the guards. The sun was so hot that the guards would not venture out of the shade to enforce the labor in the rock quarries, and like the other prisoners, he spent his waking hours dreaming of freedom, planning suicidal escape schemes that offered only the promise of quick death by drowning instead of the slow tortures of the prison.

For Conselheiro, the worst punishment of all was the overhead flights of the Zeppelin. Every week, the Zeppelin flew over the island on its way to and from Germany, its schedule so regular that Conselheiro knew from the tally of days exactly when the airship would next appear. He would wait and watch until the great silver form appeared overhead, so close that he could make out the monstrous red, black, and white insignia on the tail.

Every time he saw it, he remembered the terrible day in November 1935 when the fighting on the landing field was finally over, and the Integralistas and the police stood triumphant over the bodies of the peasants who had come to demand food, jobs, and medicine. Survival was all they wanted, and the answer to their demands was bullets from the machine guns. The Integralistas denied that they were supplied and supported by the Nazis, but the landing of the Zeppelin, which had been circling aloft for over one hundred hours, waiting for the fighting to stop, was almost an admission of guilt.

Conselheiro knew that as long as he lived, he would never forget that sight. Bodies on the field were thrown into the back of trucks. The survivors were led away with long ropes tied around their necks, like a chain gang. He turned around as they were marched off and behind him the silver ship was slowly descending to the field, floating serenely like a leaf in the river, oblivious to the blood that stained the dry earth. Every time the Zeppelin flew over Fernando de Noronha, Conselheiro thought of that day, of the men and women and children who had fallen on the field, of the dreams that had died in the fusillade of bullets from the Fascist machine guns.

Now he was alone in the cell, alone with his bruises and cuts and a thirst that made him think of Fernando de Noronha.

"Jailer!" he shouted. "Jailer! Bring water."

There was no answer.

He shouted again. "Jailer! For the love of Christ, bring water." He banged the bars with his fists.

From the other room he heard a chair slide on the dirt floor, then the water pump. Finally the jailer shuffled in, wearing a shabby khaki uniform with a wide belt and a ring of keys. He had sandals on his feet, and a bucket and a cup in his hands. He placed both on the floor, then pushed them close to the bars so Conselheiro could scoop up the water.

He spilled as much water as he brought to his mouth, but after thirstily gulping three times, he splashed more water on his face and wiped at the caked blood. When he looked up, the jailer was staring at him.

"You are truly the man who is called Conselheiro?" asked the jailer. He spoke with the accent of the Sertão. "The stories are true? You are responsible for the deaths of fifty soldiers, twenty with your own hands?"

Conselheiro looked at the man, crouched on his haunches back from the bars. "I fought," he said. "I fought for the people of my village and the other villages of the Sertão. If I killed, it was because the soldiers killed our people. They cut them down with machine guns before we ever fired a shot. The bodies were taken away in trucks and dumped into the rivers. I saw it with my own eyes."

The jailer stared as if Conselheiro were the president of the Republic of Brazil granting an audience.

"And you truly escaped from Fernando de Noronha? From the island?"

"There were logs. A raft. We drifted on the currents to Bahia."

"Why did you not go into the Sertão? There you would have been safe. They would never have found you among the people of the villages."

"I have a reason," said Conselheiro.

"But now you will die. I have heard them talking."

"Then I will die. It's easy to die. We of the Sertão have practice. If it's not hunger or the guns of the police, it's the fever."

The jailer stared longer at him, then went into the other room and came back with more water, a bar of rough soap, and a clean shirt. He handed them to Conselheiro without a word, then watched while the prisoner slowly washed himself, moving his arms and legs tentatively to see if any bones were broken. Only the swollen foot seemed badly hurt.

"They are careful," said the jailer. "They know how to make pain without breaking bones or killing a man. It's a science for them."

"This is not the science that the people need," said Conselheiro.

When he finished washing he put on the clean shirt and put the soap into his pocket.

"In one hour, I will bring food," said the jailer.

They stared at one another for a few minutes, until finally the jailer, uncomfortable in the silence, spoke.

"Tell me, what were you going to do on the landing field? They say that you were going to try to shoot down the airship."

Conselheiro watched the face of the jailer, letting the man's words play through his own ears. The jailer was not educated, and from his accent he was a newcomer to the city. That much was obvious. From his sandals, it appeared that he was as poor as the thousands of others who had found jobs working for the corrupt government, menial jobs that paid only enough to keep a man from starving, enough to exact some kind of loyalty from people who would otherwise revolt.

"I was not going to shoot the airship," said Conselheiro.

"Then why were you on the field? You can tell me. I am not with them." He gestured toward the barracks and armory that both knew were next to the jail. "I am only a jailer. It is only a job."

"Is this why you left the backlands?" asked Conselheiro. "To be a jailer?"

"Sometimes a man cannot choose. I have a wife. Four children. Two children have already died. I cannot let the others starve."

"They eat well now?"

"Better than the bandits on Fernando de Noronha."

Another silence while the two men assessed one another, each wondering how much the other could be trusted.

"You still did not say why you were on the field," said the jailer. "They say that you would not talk, even during the beatings. You are a strong man." He paused, waiting to see the other man react. "But I think a fool."

"I am not so foolish as to work for them and still see my children hungry."

The jailer reacted angrily. "What else can a man do?"

It was what Conselheiro wanted. He had gotten to the man. The jailer was curious, desperate, and ashamed.

"There are many things a man can do," said Conselheiro. "Many things."

Sixteen

The jangadas were the first hint of land. Swooping triangular sails were scattered across the blue-green waters like leaves in a pond as the heavily laden wooden rafts raced home from the fishing grounds with their catches. With steady southerly breezes behind them, the same breeze that had helped the Graf Zeppelin make a quick crossing from the middle of the South Atlantic, the jangadas ran swiftly toward the invisible beaches in the distance. At fifteen hundred feet, the Zeppelin was low enough for passengers to make out the helmsmen on the rafts, sitting on low wooden benches, the catch of fish at their feet as they swung the long tiller-oars while their apprentices worked the crude centerboards and splashed water on the sails to keep them taut. The fishermen plied every trick to squeeze speed out of their rafts, hovering on the edge of capsize, so intent on the water ahead of them that they didn't notice the Graf Zeppelin overhead until the great black shadow or the silvery reflection on the water appeared in their vision. Then they would gaze up in wonder, watching the stately progress of the huge airship for only a moment before returning to the serious business of their race for the shore. The first jangada back would have an advantage in marketing its catch, and in a culture where all life was marginal, where every penny mattered, the race to the beach was a matter of daily life or death.

The journey that would take them until long after dark, and that some of them would never finish, was a matter of minutes for the Graf Zeppelin. Soon after the jangadas disappeared behind the airship, the long sandy beaches of the coast came into view, stretching as far as the horizon to the north and south. When the Graf crossed the beach, the land seemed to swallow the reflection on the water, leaving only the great black shadow, stretched by the afternoon sun into an immense cigar that paced their progress into Recife as if it were a pointer on the map below.

The Zeppelin crossed the heart of the city with its graceful colonial buildings, flying over the upper reaches of the three rivers to where another city grew up, a city of mangroves and shanties built on stilts. In that city people could live an entire lifetime without stepping foot on dry land. Life in the mangroves was ruled by the rivers and the mud, and the tiny crabs that were hunted day and night to fight off starvation. It was a city where infant mortality rates exceeded fifty percent, where typhoid fever could kill off whole villages in weeks, where entire religions were structured to salute death as the welcome release from a life of unbearable hardship.

But from the Zeppelin, the countryside was a fairyland, a lace filigree of bright sparkling buildings and dark water, glistening foliage and sunlit earth, interwoven into a delicate chiaroscuro—an ornament to dazzle the passengers of the Graf Zeppelin on their journey from the glamor of Rio to the culture of Europe.

The first landing of the Zeppelin in Recife, in 1930, required the services of three hundred Brazilian soldiers, supervised by a Zeppelin man who had arrived in advance by steamer. Two 10-ton hydrogen generators, forty tons of crude materials, and seven hundred thousand cubic feet of Pyrofax gas in cylinders had been brought to the field in advance, and American technicians were brought in to operate the equipment. A special U.S. Navy kite balloon was even borrowed to regulate the flow of hydrogen from the portable generators to the ship. The airship dropped dozens of mooring lines as it hovered over the field, and the soldiers manhandled it to a temporary mooring mast that had been hastily erected in quicksand with a foundation of one hundred tons of concrete.

By 1936, in the third year of regular transatlantic service, the landing procedures had become routine. A permanent mooring mast had been erected, with piping for the hydrogen, fuel, and water to replenish the depleted stores of the airship. And with the development of modern mooring techniques, many of them pioneered by the Americans, the complex maneuvering to bring the 775-foot airship to the mooring mast was entrusted not to ground crews but to the skills of the commander.

These landings were the supreme test of a commander. His skill in anticipating thermal updrafts, windshifts, and the ponderous reactions of the airship, and his timing in ordering movements of the rudders and elevators, the venting of gas and the dropping of ballast, and the speed of the engines, made the difference between a smooth and safe landing or potential disaster. A minuscule miscalculation could result in crushing sections of the frame. The slightest spark from metal striking metal could ignite free hydrogen vented during the landing maneuvers, setting off an inferno that would destroy the ship. The responsibility was so awesome that if the weather were less than perfect, the commanders would often order delays for hours or even days. And even in the most perfect weather, the crew would watch the captain with total concentration, especially a new commander who had not proved himself in the service.

As soon as he came into the control room, when they were still over the city of Recife, the contrast between Whitman's style of command and the traditional approach of the German commanders was evident. The Germans were cautious, nudging the great ship in incremental movements, working closer and closer to the mooring mast in steps, then pausing until the ship was almost motionless before moving again. It was a safe and sure technique, and caution after all was the operating motto of the German Zeppelin Company.

By contrast, Whitman was bold, even in his first landing as the commander of the Graf Zeppelin.

"Elevatorman, vent to an altitude of one hundred meters," he said when the landing field came into view.

"In a single burst, sir? We usually vent down in stages. There could be ground thermals."

"A single burst," said Whitman. "It's smoother and it conserves gas."

As the man pulled at the toggles suspended in front of him, the craft hung in the air, then began to ease down, the needle of the altimeter swinging quickly as the hydrogen vented from the maneuvering valves at the top of the gas bags. After a second, smaller pull on the toggles, the altimeter settled at one hundred meters, low enough to read the letters and numbers displayed on top of the field shed to indicate the windspeed and direction on the ground. At the larger airship fields, like Frankfurt and Lakehurst, New Jersey, the windspeed and direction were displayed on electric billboards. Recife had only interchangeable numbers that were placed in position by ground technicians. They were fine if there were no last minute shifts or gusts.

"Wind—one hundred seventy-five degrees, eighteen knots," called out the watch officer. He was standing at the window with his binoculars trained on the ground.

"Steer three-oh-five," said Whitman.

"Three-oh-five," repeated the rudderman.

"All engines to quarter speed."

"Quarter speed," repeated the engineer.

"Shouldn't we wait until the wind drops?" The watch officer posed the question carefully, a suggestion rather than a challenge. "It can be tricky here with the onshore breeze and the afternoon thermals. If we wait an hour or two, it will be cool enough for the wind to drop."

"We've lost enough time," said Whitman. He saw the men in the control room exchange knowing looks.

"If you're certain, Captain," said the watch officer, the slow cadence of his voice certifying that he wanted to be on record as an I-told-you-so.

As they crossed the far edge of the landing field, Whitman ordered a turn to 175 degrees, bringing them into the wind and slowing the craft.

"Prepare to stop all engines for weigh-off." He watched the magnetic compass as the ship swung around. When they were almost, but not quite, to the new course, he ordered, "All engines idle."

"We're not around yet, sir," said the rudderman.

"All engines idle," repeated Whitman, his voice firmer.

The rudderman and the engineer shrugged at one another and the engine telegraphs clanked up and back to *idle*. With the props feathered, the Zeppelin coasted around to complete its turn, the airspeed indicator dropping steadily until they were making almost no progress against the wind. It was an elegant, economical maneuver.

"Elevator neutral," said Whitman. "Commence weigh-off."

Weighing-off was an essential maneuver when an airship either landed or took off. During flight, gas and ballast were released from different parts of the airship to control the altitude and attitude of the craft, and consumables from different sections of the ship would be exhausted. As a result, the ship could become slightly out of balance, with more lift forward or aft. The slight misbalance was of little concern during powered flight, because the dynamic lift of the moving ship and the constant corrections of the elevatorman sufficed to keep the ship level. But during landing and lift-off, the ship rose or descended without its engines, and it was essential that the craft be precisely balanced by idling the engines and releasing gas or ballast from the bow or stern of the craft until the inclinometers read exactly zero. When the lift of the hydrogen exactly matched the weight of the ship and its ballast, the Zeppelin was said to be weighed-off, and it was ready for a smooth, level ascent or descent using lift alone.

Whitman moved to the elevatorman's station, and with the ship still moving forward, he checked the inclinometer, a looped glass tube filled with colored fluid that rose or fell depending on the attitude of the ship.

"Vent bag nine ten seconds," he said.

The elevatorman glanced sideways at Whitman, as if the order were sheer madness. "We're still moving forward, sir."

"Bag nine, five seconds," said Whitman again, firmly. There was a hint of impatience in his tone.

He watched the man pull the toggle, then saw on the inclinometer that the stern had settled by a few degrees.

"Release two hundred kilos of water from station three."

Again the elevatorman glanced sideways. This time he followed the order without question.

The inclinometer dived, then rose, finally leveling off exactly on center, just as the airspeed indicator dropped to the pin at the bottom.

The elevatorman looked in amazement at Whitman. *How did you do that?* his eyes asked.

"Vent one hundred kilos at station four," said Whitman.

"But we're exactly on keel, sir," protested the confused elevatorman. The watch officer and the radio operator were now watching the indicators over his shoulder, and their heads wagged in disbelief.

"We're still moving forward," said Whitman. "We still have dynamic lift. When we come to a dead halt, we'll be bow-heavy."

The elevatorman pulled the toggle, and all eyes watched the inclinometer rise, hover, then slowly drop as the ship lost speed. It finally halted exactly on balance.

"All engines ahead quarter speed," said Whitman, moving forward to the rudderman's station. Behind him the telegraphs clanged and the ship gradually accelerated toward the mooring mast in the distance.

"Down elevators five degrees. Steer one-seven-zero."

The ship responded slowly, swinging into line with the mooring tower.

"We're closing too fast," said the watch officer. He spoke under his breath to no one in particular, but his words were acknowledged by nods from everyone except Whitman.

"It's blowing more than eighteen knots," said Whitman. "The ground station is wrong."

"Wrong?" repeated the watch officer.

"Look at the trees. Palm trees don't bend over in eighteen knots of wind. Not like that."

"Perhaps we should delay our landing, sir. A wind over eighteen knots could be dangerous here."

"Elevatorman, vent all bags ten seconds," said Whitman.

"*Ten* seconds?"

"Correct. Order the mooring crew to prepare to drop starboard and port cables."

The ship dropped fifty meters, smoothly but rapidly, until the mooring cone was directly ahead of them on the field.

"Engines two and four idle," said Whitman. When he did not hear an immediate clang, he repeated the order and added "Now!" His voice was sharp enough to prompt immediate action by the engineer.

The entire control room crew, used to the slower maneuvering of the German commanders, were suddenly alert at their stations. Whitman's orders came one after another, without pause or hesitation; the effect was like Adrenalin shots. He seemed to anticipate every motion of the ship, calling for corrections even before the ship had time to complete a previous maneuver. The men in the control room no longer had time to question or think.

"Course one-seven-five."

"Engine five idle."

"Elevator neutral."

"Come up to one-seven-seven."

"Vent all bags three seconds."

"Release port mooring line."

"Rudder to one-seven-four."

"Release starboard mooring line."

"Engines one and three idle. Stop engines two, four, and five."

"Stand by to accept mooring cone. Signal ground crews to leave the lines slack. Let the ship do the work."

"Rudder one-seven-six."

"Engines two and four astern one-eighth."

"Steady."

"Elevator down three degrees."

"All engines stop. Elevator neutral. Rudder neutral."

A collective breath was held as the mooring mast loomed directly ahead of the ship, the palm trees on the ground almost doubled over by the wind outside. The airspeed indicator was barely lifted off the zero, and the inclinometer registered absolutely level as the ship inched under momentum toward the solid, triangular mast.

"Release forward emergency ballast."

"Sir?" questioned the elevatorman.

"Forward emergency ballast! *Now!*"

Heads spun toward him, eyes wide and questioning. The maneuver would have the effect of making the bow of the ship leap up, above the cone of the mooring mast, which was now directly in line with the nose of the Zeppelin.

From the control room windows, everyone could see the water ballast splash out of the bow compartment, drenching the hapless ground crew holding onto the mooring lines. The bow of the Zeppelin started to drop slightly, then as the water fell, it rose to level again, eased forward, and with a gentle nudge, hooked onto the mooring cone at the top of the mast.

Every eye in the room turned back to Whitman as breaths held in anticipation of disaster exhaled.

"How did you know . . . sir?" asked the elevatorman, voicing the question in every mind. "How did you know he would dip his nose at the mast?"

Whitman pointed below the ship, to where the long shadow of the mooring mast merged with the shadow of the Graf. "The shadow cools the earth," he explained, "and where the earth is cooler, there is less thermal lift. As soon as the bow came over that spot, it dropped. Except that you were ready and beat her . . ."

He caught himself and corrected the gender before finishing the sentence, " . . . *him* to it."

"You know him well," said the elevatorman.

Every eye in the control room followed Whitman as he walked back toward the passenger lounge. Congratulations were not in order. A captain is supposed to know his ship. But no one could resist a subtle, almost inconspicuous nod as Whitman walked by, if only to acknowledge that American or not, Paul Whitman was now a Zeppelin commander.

And for his part, Whitman acknowledged the nods with something like a grin. He figured he could allow himself that.

Seventeen

Hans Stifel was the first one down the ladder. He had waited in the corridor outside the galley, on the starboard side of the gondola, and as soon as the stern of the airship was secured, he opened the hatch and scrambled down the ladder, walking straight across the field to the Zeppelin Company offices.

The passengers followed as soon as the stewards secured the ladder, led by Nadia Lopez-Otero, who opened a parasol when she got to the bottom of the ladder. There was no time for the passengers to travel into Recife. The entire refueling operation would take only a few hours, and passengers were asked to leave the airship mainly for their own comfort and safety. The ventilation system was inefficient when the Zeppelin was standing still, and there was nothing more dangerous than the loading of thousands of cubic feet of hydrogen and flammable fuel into the gas bags inside the envelope of the airship.

The passengers gravitated to the tables under the covered porch of the field office, duplicating the seating pattern they had followed on the airship. The Lopez-Oteros sat at the front table on the right, what would have been the starboard side if the porch could fly. Senhor de Nascimento, with no more than a cursory query with his eyebrows, joined them, oblivious to the fact that they had not signaled his welcome.

"What a perfectly horrid place!" said Nadia Lopez-Otero. "It is so . . . so desiccated." She fanned herself as she spoke but did not bother to unbutton the tailored jacket of her navy suit. "It feels like the desert."

"No, dear," corrected her husband. "In the desert the heat is dry. It is not nearly so oppressive." He wriggled his neck, trying to free the flesh that was pinched by the tight, starched collar of his shirt. "This is a humid air; the vapors of water make the heat unbearable."

She looked up at him, smiling at his infinite wisdom.

"The northeast," said de Nascimento, gesturing with one hand toward the ramshackle shacks in the distance. He brushed the sweat off his glossy moustache with the fingers of his other hand. "The shame of Brazil, the racial backwater. If you have an opportunity to see the natives, you will notice that they are predominantly of the darker races, although mongrelization has whitened the skin of some. That's the real horror of it: with the races, as with coffee and milk, a mixture dilutes the qualities of both."

The Lopez-Oteros listened with faint distasteful looks, expressing not so much disagreement as discomfort that the topic would even be raised

De Nascimento went on, paying no attention to the reactions of his audience: "Brazil, you see, is the perfect laboratory to demonstrate the validity of modern racial theories. In the south, which is predominantly white, there is prosperity, progress, industry, the achievements of culture. In Rio or my own city of São Paulo, you will see the most modern buildings, the most advanced factories, the most elegant theaters—proofs of the genius and industry of the white race. Here in the northeast" —again he waved toward the shacks—"where the lesser races predominate, there is only poverty, ignorance, blight. A shameful decay of good land. And in the interior, where the Indians live, it is a veritable jungle, a habitat fit only for animals. In terms of the theory of evolution, of course, the Indians are only a step removed from being animals. The correspondence of race with progress is quite exact."

Nadia Lopez-Otero looked away in boredom, trying to ignore the loud Brazilian. Her husband, sitting directly across from de Nascimento, could not avoid the challenge.

"Excuse me," he said, "but I have read that the climate is a major factor. Along with the productivity of the soil. Could it not be true that the droughts and the exhausted soils have contributed to the poverty? This was once the wealthiest and most important part of Brazil, was it not?" He tried to seem profound as he spoke, gesturing with his shoulders back and his head twisted slightly to one side as if the table were a podium. The stuffy vested suit, the obviously uncomfortable shirt and collar, and his boyish features made him look like a little boy masquerading as a professor

"Precisely," answered de Nascimento. "Under slavery this was a prosperous region. Whites ran the plantations, provided the genius of leadership. The blacks did what nature has always meant them to do—manual labor. With each race following its natural function, the economy prospered. Until certain fools brought so-called *enlightened* ideas to Brazil. Slavery was abolished in a ridiculous imitation of the laws of other lands, lands without the racial mixture of Brazil. The result is this bastardization of races and cultures. The consequences are apparent." He waved his arm in a grand semicircle, as if the barren landing field and the shabby shacks in the distance were the whole of northeast Brazil. "Anyone who will admit the truth of this poverty and decay cannot deny the validity of modern racial theory. It is one area in which I believe the Germans have come to understand Brazil."

At the table behind them, Admiral von Teppler looked up at the word "Germans," saw de Nascimento speaking, and looked away, an expression of contempt on his face. Eisler, sitting at the admiral's side, kept his eyes on the admiral, but leaned his head in the direction of de Nascimento, trying to make out the unfamiliar language.

Beck and Hans Stifel, sitting at another table behind them, were too engaged in their own conversation to notice.

Across the doorway to the office, the Huttens were sitting with their backs to the Brazilian, looking out at the landing field.

"Do you hear what the man is saying?" Hutten asked his wife. "This, I fear, is what we will hear all over Germany. It is the same hatred I have read in the book of that madman, *Mein Kampf*. First it will be the Jews. Then, who know? Madness."

"Shush!" said Frau Hutten. "They will hear you. You must not speak so when there are so many other people around."

"What have I to fear?"

Margaret Bourne had been stretching her legs since they landed, walking as far as the police on the field would allow. Her leg was still limp from the bruises, and she walked to loosen it, insisting to anyone who asked that she needed the exercise more than anything else, including a telephone call to the American consul or transportation to Recife. Even after a day of decompression in the smooth luxury of the Graf Zeppelin, it felt strange to be back on solid land.

When she came back under the shade of the porch, she noticed the Huttens looking out over the field, toward the swaying palm trees in the distance, beyond the looming form of the moored Zeppelin.

"Beautiful, isn't it?" she said. "I had no idea Brazil was like this. Someday I'd like to come back and do a photo essay. Not just the landscapes, but the people. Did you see those houses built on stilts in the rivers? A whole city on the water. Imagine!"

They both smiled at her.

"You will join us, Miss Bourne?" said Otto Hutten. He stood and pulled back a chair for her.

"Excuse please our poor English," he said. "We have both studied English, but we have little opportunity for practicing."

"You're doing fine," said Maggie.

"You have your travel plans completed now?" asked Anna Hutten. "We still have some Brazilian money if it . . ."

Maggie shook her head. "Not really. It feels so good to be on solid land, to see trees and grass and earth. I guess I'm in no hurry."

"Where will you go?" asked Otto Hutten. "To the United States?"

"I guess so," she answered half-heartedly. "They tell me I can drive into Recife and stay at a hotel until I book passage to the States. But to tell the truth, I really don't look forward to another voyage by sea, at least not yet. If I had my choice, I suppose I would . . ."

She glanced toward the sign on the Zeppelin offices, a look of surprise on her face as if her own idea had caught her unaware. "Would you excuse me?" she said as she hurried inside

Whitman was standing with his back to the door, going over the loading manifests for the Zeppelin, sheets that specified exactly how much Pyrofax fuel and water were to be loaded, along with the food and other provisions for the transatlantic crossing. The balance of weight was exacting, and although the only cargo to be boarded was a shipment of biological samples in ice that had to be stored in the galley of the Graf Zeppelin, it was close enough to the peak heat of the day to complicate the pressurization of the hydrogen bags. The gas in the cells was already expanded from the heat of the sun, which left little room for additional hydrogen to replace the amounts that had been vented off during flight. Fortunately, Whitman's landing had been economical, and the airship would not have to remain on the ground until evening to take on additional hydrogen.

"Captain Whitman?" She spoke from across the room.

He turned. "Miss Bourne. How's the leg?"

"Fine," she said. "It's Maggie, please. No one has called me Miss Bourne since I was almost expelled from Vassar."

He laughed. "As long as you're not a passenger anymore, Maggie it is. Your car should be here in a few minutes, and we have a schedule of steamer service from Recife, if you want to take a look."

"That's what I wanted to speak to you about."

"The steamer service?"

"No. My not being a passenger."

He looked puzzled.

"Can I book passage on the Graf Zeppelin to Europe?" she asked.

"On this flight? I thought you would have had enough travel for right now."

"Only enough of the sea. I was originally on my way to New York, but I think it would be just as fast to fly to Frankfurt and take a ship from Southampton or Le Havre. I suppose I could even try to book on the Hindenberg to New York. I'm getting to like travel by Zeppelin."

"That would be quite difficult, Miss," interjected Johannes Schaub. "The Hindenberg is fully booked for its transatlantic crossings."

"How about this flight of the Graf Zeppelin to Frankfurt?" she asked.

He glanced down at his desk. "There is a cabin available," he said. "The fare is twenty-one hundred Reichsmarks, of which one half must be paid in Register Marks. In dollars, that would be . . ."

"May I wire New York?" she asked. "I can have my publisher send the money."

"I'm afraid we wouldn't have time for that, Miss. The Graf Zeppelin will be departing in less than two hours, and company policy requires that all tickets be fully paid in advance."

"Surely we can make an exception in this case, Schaub," said Whitman. "Miss Bourne was rescued with little more than the clothes on her back. I would think that she could wire and have the fare paid at our office in New York."

"Captain Whitman," answered Schaub, "you and I can neither make nor break company policy. There is of course no charge for her passage to Recife. That is absorbed by the company as a humanitarian act. But for further passage, the fare must be prepaid in acceptable currencies." He lifted the thick notebook of regulations as if to prove his point.

"How much is the fare?" asked Whitman.

"For a private cabin, from Recife to Frankfurt, twenty-one hundred Reichsmarks, of which half..."

Whitman reached into his jacket pocket and withdrew a leather billfold, taking out a blank check on the Dresdener Bank.

"Captain Whitman, I..." She smiled as she protested.

"There is really nowhere else I can spend it," he answered. "You'll be doing me a favor if you repay me in dollars."

"This is most unusual, Captain," said Schaub. "You realize that according to the German Banking Law of 1935, currency exchanges by private citizens are forbidden?"

When Whitman did not look up from his checkbook, Schaub added, "There is also the matter of a passport. Company policy requires that all passengers embarking for Germany carry a valid passport and a visa for either transit or temporary stay in Germany. I doubt that there will be time for Miss Bourne..."

Whitman looked at him. "We can wire the American Consul in Frankfurt," said Whitman. "By the time the Graf Zeppelin lands, he will have a temporary passport prepared for Miss Bourne. If the immigration officials insist, it can be delivered to the Graf Zeppelin before she disembarks."

"As you wish," said Schaub. "But the company policy is quite clear..." His voice trailed off as he busied himself writing a ticket. Then he switched to German to add, "I hope you realize, Captain, that it is not customary for officers to involve themselves in the affairs of passengers, even passengers as..." He stopped again at Whitman's glare.

"There is also another passenger boarding here," he said, handing the manifest to Whitman. "Herr Enkmann. There was no VIP notation on the original manifest, but I think he must be at least semiofficial status. The ticket was prepaid in Dusseldorf, and he is in a great hurry."

"Everyone on the Graf Zeppelin seems to be in a great hurry," said Whitman. He shrugged to Maggie Bourne and added in English, "Modern times. I'm afraid we don't even have time for you to go into Recife to shop."

She looked down at the suit she was wearing. "If the other passengers don't mind, I'll be just fine. This suit is more luxury than I've seen in months."

Whitman was considering a compliment and imagining Schaub's reaction when he heard the Kleinschmitt teletype machine in the back of the office clatter. The red light on the top of the machine blinked on to indicate that a message was being received.

Schaub walked over to the machine, catching the tape as it came out of the printer. He handed it to Whitman without cutting it and pasting it on a blank.

> DEUTSCHE ZEPPELIN REEDEREI, RHEIN-MAIN FLUGHAFEN, FRANKFURT. 20.05 GMT.
>
> ATTN: CAPT PAUL WHITMAN, ACTING COMMANDER, GRAF ZEPPELIN, LZ-127. ZEPPELIN REEDEREI, RECIFE DE PERNAM-BUCO, BRAZIL
>
> RADIOED REQUEST RE CREW ASSIGNMENT DENIED. REPEAT DENIED. OFFICER HANS STIFEL TO REMAIN ON BOARD GRAF ZEPPELIN WITH DUTIES SENIOR WATCH OFFICER. HIS PRESENCE REQUIRED AT HEARING RE DEATH OF RIGGER JÜRGEN STEIN-BRENNER DURING UNAUTHORIZED COURSE DEVIATION GRAF ZEPPELIN IN FLIGHT RIO DE JANEIRO/RECIFE DE PERNAMBUCO. ALSO, INFORM ELEVATORMAN WERNER STEIN HE IS REQUIRED TO SUBMIT FLIGHT WORTHINESS EXAMINATION UPON ARRIVAL FRANKFURT.
>
> S/ HEMPE, D.O., DEUTSCHE ZEPPELIN REEDEREI.

"Who the hell is Hempe?" said Whitman.

"Director of Operations, sir."

"Director of Operations? I've never heard of him. He's not a Zeppelin man."

"He's a new man, sir. Appointed just last week, after you were awarded the command of the Graf Zeppelin." He leaned close to Whitman, whispering so no one could hear. "Goering's man. Transferred from his personal staff straight into the Zeppelin Company."

Goering's man. Everyone close to the Zeppelins knew it was only a matter of time before Goering's private empire expanded to encompass the Zeppelins. The only photograph on the wall of the Zeppelin office in Recife was of Hitler, but Whitman remembered the ubiquitous photographs of Goering in Germany, the pudgy face, the cunning eyes, the enigmatic grin. It was all he knew of the shadowy man, except hearsay and rumors. But then what did anyone really know about politics in Germany in 1936? If you believed the propaganda in the newspapers, Hitler was the salvation of Germany, the only hope after the financial

and social ruin of the Weimar Republic. And if you believed
what some people were saying outside of Germany, or even
whispering inside, Hitler was nothing but a buffoon, and wouldn't
last in office for another year once the Germans came to their
senses. No one knew for sure. Whitman had stopped reading the
newspapers, trying to avoid the question. It wasn't politics that
had drawn him to Germany after all, but technology, a conviction
that the Germans could do things with the airships that no one
else was willing to try.

It was impossible to make much of the cable. What purpose
would a hearing serve? The Nazis had a reputation for being
sticklers on laws and legality, at least their own brand of legality,
but an inquiry? There were no secrets that weren't in the log of
the Graf Zeppelin.

"Does Eckener know about this?" asked Whitman.

"Probably not, sir. The operational authority is now in Hempe's
hands."

"And what is this nonsense about Stein taking a flight worthiness exam? He's the best elevatorman in the world. He needs
only one more flight after this to qualify for a pension. After all
the years he's put in for the company, he deserves it."

"It is company policy, sir. A flight worthiness examination
may be required for any crewman over the age of thirty-five on
the request of a senior officer."

"I did not request any exam," said Whitman.

Schaub's eyes dropped. "Stifel did," he said. "As soon as the
Graf landed, he came in and sent a priority cable to Frankfurt.
This"—he pointed to the long strip of tape on the counter in
front of them—"is a reply to his message. He sent it directly to
Hempe."

Whitman picked up the tape, holding it out in his fingers.
"Hans Stifel is not leaving here on the Graf Zeppelin," he said.

"Sir," said Schaub. "With all respect, sir. I think that would
be a mistake. Hempe is not a man to welcome challenges to his
orders."

Whitman looked down at the tape, then tore it in pieces,
dropping them neatly in a wastebasket. "While I'm in command," he said, "Hans Stifel is not flying on the Graf Zeppelin."

He turned angrily toward the door.

"One other thing, Captain," Schaub called after him.

Whitman stopped.

"A man was picked up here, early this morning. He was over

in those shacks beyond the mooring mast. With a rifle. The police said he's a revolutionary.''

"Why was he there?"

Schaub shrugged. "Who knows? Perhaps he thought he would shoot down the Graf Zeppelin. Some of the Brazilians, especially the poor peasants from the backlands, still think the Zeppelin is supernatural. The evil eye, that sort of thing. No need for concern, though. The man's in jail now, and the police sergeant said he will probably be shot.''

"For being on the Zeppelin field? They would shoot a man for that?''

"They say he's dangerous.''

Part II

Spain

Eighteen

It had been a stifling day in Madrid. The occasional cooling breeze from the Sierra de Guadarrama never materialized, and even at seven o'clock in the evening, the temperature was close to one hundred degrees. In the wealthy districts, the shutters of the few rich who had not yet fled the city were opening to catch whatever zephyrs of breeze could be found, and in the cafes, workers were loosening their shirt collars and setting aside their militia rifles for long, cool drinks. It was so hot that for a change there would be talk of something other than the civil war.

Neither the heat nor the climate of war seemed to affect the clerk as he left the side entrance of the Bank of Spain, at the southwest corner of the Cibeles. He paid no attention to the sandbags piled in front of the Palaccio de Communicaciones on the southeast corner and the steady stream of cars arriving and departing from the Ministry of the Army building across the way. Dressed in a black cutaway jacket, striped trousers, a white shirt, and a black four-in-hand cravat on a stiff celluloid collar, and carrying a rolled umbrella, the clerk might have looked very much in place in the city of London. But in the Madrid of the second month of the civil war, where a necktie ranked second only to a clerical collar as a symbol of Nationalist (pro-Franco) sympathies, the clerk's attire appeared outrageously anti-Republican.

In fact, the clerk was oblivious to politics. For fourteen years he had dressed every day, summer and winter, the way he thought a banker should dress, as callous to the stares of workers on the street as he was inured to the heat. Stoically, he refused to loosen the stiff collar that chafed where the heat had produced a prickly rash on his neck.

From the doorway of the bank, he walked a full block north on Castellana before crossing over one street to look at the elegant windows of the shops on the Calle Serano. Although sporadic artillery fire and bombs had already been heard in the outskirts of

97

the city, some of the shops were still open and filled with goods, even as the walls next to their windows were covered with painted slogans and exhortations. The red letters of ¡ *No Passaran!*, the most stirring La Passionaira's slogans, was overpainted with the blaring white *¡Arriba Espana!* of the Nationalists. And the Nationalist slogan in turn had been overpainted with a Republican exhortation calling for the arming of the people and the redistribution of land holdings.

The clerk hardly noticed the graffiti, and when he did, he averted his eyes. He was a clerk of the Bank of Spain, he told himself. Above politics. Or more precisely, beneath politics. From where he worked, deep inside the vast vaults of the bank, he was insulated from the tumult of the war. He sat all day in a tiny wrought-iron cage, working over an enormous hand ledger where he kept track of the supreme treasure of Spain, the gold reserves. Counting both the coin reserves and the bar stock, and including those portions of the reserves that were in Bilbao and on deposit in Paris, the reserves that day totaled over 2,258,569,908 pesetas. His last task before leaving the bank was the conversion of the totals to sterling at the current exchange rate, a calculation made each day to record the wealth of Spain in the currency of international finance. It came to more than ninety million pounds sterling, over five hundred million dollars.

To most people the numbers meant nothing. But to the clerk, they were the glory of Spain. Spain might be backward in her cities and her industry. She had not achieved the spoils of victory in recent wars. She suffered continued humiliation in losing colonies and international prestige. But still, he told himself, she had the glory of her gold, the gold of the New World that had first made Spain great four hundred years before. Never would she suffer the disgrace of Germany, where inflation had once made a currency so worthless that a day's salary had to be carried in a wheelbarrow. Spain had a real currency, backed by the fourth largest gold reserve in the world. And as chief clerk in the reserve section of the Bank of Spain, it fell to him each day to total that glory of Spain.

He crossed the Calle Serano in front of a lingerie shop, where he lingered to stare at the camisoles, corsets, and stockings arranged so tastefully in the windows. Then he moved on, crossing the street to his tram stop.

The tram was crowded with workers, carrying rifles and shouting slogans to those in the streets. They interrogated the clerk with their eyes, as if they expected him too to carry a rifle

and defend Madrid against the threat of Franco and the Nationalists. The clerk averted his eyes until he reached his stop, in an
area of middle-class apartment buildings. Then he jumped down
and walked quickly up the street, stopping first at a butcher to
pick up the lamb kidneys that he always bought on Thursdays,
then across the street to the bakery, where he bought two rolls,
one for his dinner and one to eat with his coffee in the morning.

Outside a tobacco shop he paused, wondering if he could
afford a cigar. He saw from a poster on a kiosk that the bullfights
had again been canceled for Sunday. Although he was not a fan
of the *corrida*, the cancellation of the bullfights, more than the
armed men in the streets or the slogans on the walls or the
occasional gunfire he heard at night, told the clerk that the
revolution and the civil war had changed Spain. As he had heard
someone say in a cafe, there would be enough bloodshed now for
Spain to be her own *corrida*.

From the tobacco shop he went straight to the yellow apartment building and walked slowly up the dark stairs to his own
door. He fumbled with his key, juggling the newspaper-wrapped
packages and the umbrella before he finally swung the door open
and walked into the spotless room. He left the light off to enjoy
the apparent coolness and walked across the room to open the
heavy shutters.

After two steps, he heard the door click shut behind him.
When he turned around, two men were standing there, one
brawny like a mason, looking awkward in an ill-fitting suit. The
other was tall and gaunt, with a broad-brimmed hat pulled down
over his eyes. The gaunt man was holding a revolver.

"I have nothing," said the clerk. "What do you want of me?"

The brawny man answered by pushing him down into a
straight-backed wooden chair.

"What do you want?" the clerk said again. "I am not a
wealthy man."

"Shut up," said the gaunt man. "Speak when I tell you to
speak."

The clerk remembered stories he had heard, what had happened
to the rich when the news of Franco's rising first reached
Madrid. Wealthy families had been accosted on the street,
dragged from automobiles and even railroad carriages. Their
offense? *Wealth.* Wealth alone was enough to brand a man a
Nationalist, a follower of Franco, an enemy of the people.

The gaunt man switched on the electric light, a single bare
bulb that hung from a wire over the table. He signaled to the

other man to move the chair under the light, and the brawny man easily picked up the chair and the clerk, moving them as if they were weightless.

"What are the plans for the gold?" asked the gaunt man. His wretched Spanish grated in ears that were accustomed to the gentle lisping sounds of Castilian, but the clerk could not quite identify the foreign accent.

"I know nothing," said the clerk, purposely exaggerating his own haughty diction.

The gaunt man raised the revolver and slammed it across the clerk's face, smashing his upper lip against his teeth. The clerk winced, then stared down at his shirt front, where a trickle of blood from the corner of his mouth dribbled onto the shirt. "I am only a clerk," he said, dabbing at his mouth with a handkerchief.

He watched as the pistol came up again.

"I do not make the policies of the bank," he blurted. "I am only a clerk."

Again the gun smashed into his face, the side of the barrel coming down flat against his nose and lip. The brawny man put his fingers over the clerk's mouth, holding him still until he stopped writhing. The blood flowed freely from a nostril, and the pain was excruciating as his flesh seemed to pulse with the trembling of his heart. He could feel his knees knocking together and his hands shaking. He saw the gun go up again.

"No, please . . ." He held up both hands. "Please. I will tell you anything you wish to hear. *Please.*" His eyes shut tightly as he waited for the gun to come down.

"What are the plans for the gold?" asked the foreign-accented voice again. The clerk thought the accent sounded German.

"I am not sure. I think the trucks will take it," he said.

"Where?"

"To the south, I think."

"The south?" said the brawny man behind the chair. He too had an accent, which the clerk immediately identified as Catalan, perhaps from the Balearics. He tried to concentrate on anything that would identify the two men.

"Where in the south?" said the gaunt man. His face was close to the clerk, but with the broad brim of the hat pulled down, the clerk could not see the features of the thin face in the harsh light of the single overhead bulb. The brawny man was invisible behind him, but the clerk could tell from the powerful, rough hands that the man was a worker.

"I do not know where," said the clerk. He saw the revolver move, and quickly added, "Valencia, I think. I also heard talk of Cartagena."

"Cartagena?"

"The naval base."

"Why Cartagena?" asked the brawny man. He spoke more to the gaunt man than to the clerk. There was no answer to his question.

"How much of the gold?"

"I do not know."

Again the revolver came up, the barrel turning sideways toward the temple and ear of the clerk. "Answer me quickly," said the gaunt man, "or I break the bones of your face until it is unrecognizable." His accent seemed even stronger when he spoke a full sentence. The clerk was certain that it was German.

He looked at the gun, fascinated for a second by the blue-black iridescence of the barrel as it moved in the glare of the electric light.

"How much of the gold?" asked the gaunt man again.

When the clerk hesitated for another instant, the gun slammed into his temple, snapping the head sideways against the powerful hands of the brawny man.

The clerk writhed, gagged a scream, then spat blood.

"One thousand five hundred million pesetas," he said. Then his head collapsed on his chest.

The gaunt man calculated quietly for a moment. He looked up and realized that the sum was beyond the comprehension of his companion.

"When?" he said.

The brawny man shook the clerk, who finally repeated, "When?"

"*When* are they moving it?"

"I do not know." He watched the gun, a streak of blood, *his blood*, gleaming on the barrel.

"Truly," the clerk begged. "I do not know. I am only a clerk. They tell me nothing."

"You lie," said the gaunt man. "These clothes, they are not the clothes of a clerk. You are the officer in charge of the reserves. When are they moving the gold?"

"No. Please. I am only a clerk. I know nothing except..."

The blow was harder than the others, and the cracking sound of the bones under the metal of the revolver said that it was perhaps too hard. As the powerful hands of the brawny man held the clerk, the body began to twitch in spasms. Then the eyes rolled upward. The brawny man shook the body until the other man said, "It's useless."

The hands let go and the body toppled to the floor.

"Why would they send it south?" asked the brawny man.

The other man emptied the pockets of the clerk. There was a cheap leather change purse with a few coins, and a billfold with identification papers. He opened the miserable newspaper-wrapped packages of the clerk, lying on the floor by the umbrella, and found only the lamb kidneys and the two rolls.

"He wasn't lying," said the gaunt man. "He is only a clerk."

"Then must we find another man? Someone who knows more."

"No," said the gaunt man. "There's been enough killing for now."

They left as they had come, through the front door of the yellow apartment building, making sure they were seen and that the gaunt man was heard asking directions in his German-accented Spanish.

Nineteen

David Sinclair sat bored at the table in the back room of the cafe on the Gran Via, listening to stories he had heard a thousand times. How the Russian general insisted on a fresh Spanish virgin every night in his room at Gaylords Hotel. How the Franco troops included Moors who had been blessed under the sign of the cross so they could fight against the atheistic Spanish republic. How Mussolini had warned the troops he was sending to aid Franco that they would be shot if they did not return victorious. The stories were true. Sinclair knew because he had uncovered most of them himself. But he was bored to hear them again when there was a real war raging outside.

He was the best known of the journalists who gathered every evening in the cafe. Some of them had not written a word for months, but they called themselves journalists because in those early days of the civil war everyone had to have a label. Foreigners were no longer tourists, but *volunteers*, which meant that they knew which faction they would fight with, or at least which factions they would fight against. Those who didn't know, or who pretended a neutral objectivity, were journalists. In the late summer of 1936, the Spanish civil war had almost as many journalists as soldiers

But Sinclair was not like the rest. Although few people in Spain had ever read his articles in American magazines like *The Nation* or the *New Republic*, or the earlier reporting he had done for a San Francisco newspaper, he was *known* in Madrid, if only for a single quote, a line from an article he had written after a two-month stay in the Soviet Union. "I have seen the future and it does not work," he wrote, and that one line, a parody of Lincoln Steffens, made Sinclair an overnight hero of the anti-Stalinist Left. After that, he no longer had to seek stories; they came to him, a steady stream of informers and spies, men with tales to tell and axes to grind. Those who asked in the front of the cafe would be directed to the table behind the bead curtain, to the man with the blond beard and dark shirts that made him look more like an English poet seeking his manhood in the trenches than a reporter in search of a story.

Yet for all his fame, a fame that drew a circle of reporters around him every night, from Italy, France, Canada, England, Austria—reporters satisfied to pick like jackals at the scraps of information drawn by his reputation—Sinclair was not satisfied. With the sound of Nationalist artillery echoing in the background, and armed militia combing the streets, carrying their rifles like badges, with daily parades of the Fifth Brigade to remind the population of the city that the siege of Madrid was coming, Sinclair was growing impatient with words, troubled by the impotence of what came so easily. He knew he had written well, reporting on the lies behind the promises of Soviet propaganda, the massacres by the Italians in Ethiopia, the scorched earth policies of the Japanese in China. For years, his articles had been widely read and praised. But deep down, he knew that Margaret had been right: everything he had ever written had been from the sidelines, the comments of a safe observer.

Two bottles of wine had already been emptied and the old stories had gone through a whole round when the bead curtain jiggled. Sinclair looked up to see Kruger, the gaunt Austrian, his hat pulled down over his eyes. The brawny Minorcan was with him.

"Kruger!" said someone at the table. "Did you find out?"

"It was the wrong man," said the Minorcan. No one paid any attention to what he said.

Kruger sat down without taking off his hat, poured wine from the bottle and downed a glass quickly. "You were right," he said to Sinclair. "The gold is to be moved. By truck. They are taking it to Valencia or Cartagena."

"Valencia?" said someone. "Then the government is leaving Madrid. They are abandoning the city to go into exile in Valencia." The speculation set off a buzz around the table.

"How much of the gold?" said Sinclair.

"One thousand, five hundred million pesetas."

Sinclair calculated for a moment in silence. "That is three-fourths of the entire reserves."

"Three-fourths?" said Kruger. "What happens to the rest? They leave it for the Fascists?"

Sinclair sipped at his own wine. The mystery was too easy to solve. "The rest will go to Paris," he said.

"Paris? Why?"

"Insurance," said Sinclair. "In case they lose the war. The politicians of the Spanish republic may call themselves Loyalists, but their first loyalty is to themselves."

The buzz of a moment before escalated into a rumble as the journalists scribbled their notes. They were all composing the same sensational story, of how the Spanish republic was preparing to abandon Madrid to the Fascists, fleeing into a safe exile in Valencia. In a day or two, the story would be printed in every language represented at the table, often in obscure journals that reached a minuscule audience, but still in print. The world would know of the perfidy of the Spanish government. They buzzed with the excitement of the scoop. Except Sinclair.

"Did you say Cartagena?" he asked Kruger.

"Yes. That's what the man said. Valencia, perhaps Cartagena. But he was only a clerk."

"The naval base," said Sinclair. He sipped more of the wine and looked away from the table, to a torn poster on the wall—a peasant with a rifle held aloft in his hand and a slogan exhorting the people to arm.

"The gold is not going to Valencia," he said finally.

Kruger, basking in the success of his mission, looked up from his wine. "What do you mean? If the government isn't fleeing into exile, what's happening? I didn't kill a man to make riddles."

The jackals around the table pounced. "Kruger was the wrong

man to send," said someone. "I told you. Killing is all he knows..." "We could be traced," said another anxious voice.

Sinclair waved them silent. "You killed him?" he asked. A swallow of wine caught in his throat.

"He was only a clerk."

Only a clerk... Human life had already become cheap in Spain. Sinclair looked back at the poster. It's war, he reminded himself. War means killing.

"He found the information, didn't he?" he said. "And if anyone saw or heard him, they'll suspect the Germans."

Kruger grinned. "What do you think is happening to the gold?" he asked.

"The man said Cartagena?"

" 'Valencia, perhaps Cartagena,' is what he said."

"He wouldn't have mentioned Cartagena unless he heard it somewhere," said Sinclair. "It makes sense. The naval base is a closed port. That's what they would insist on, total secrecy."

"They? You make no sense, Sinclair."

Sinclair flared. "You see the Russian airplanes and troops coming to Spain," he said. "How do you think it is paid for?"

"Paid? It's fraternal aid. The Communists are hoping that Spain will follow in the steps of the Bolshevik revolution. They missed their chance in Germany and Austria. Now Spain is their hope."

"Bullshit! Fraternal aid? You believe that? You think that's the way they operate? They're not as stupid as the propaganda they put out. If they're sending guns and planes, it's because they expect to be paid. With Spanish gold."

The table fell silent. If what Sinclair said was true, this was a story to shock every reader who had ever turned an eye toward the war in Spain. Spanish gold shipped to the Soviet Union. The sellout of the Republic to the Russians. The end of an independent Spain. Questions and arguments flew fast and furious as scribbling pencils embellished Sinclair's pronouncement into a tale of the ultimate perfidy—the Republic selling out the people, the Russians selling out the Republic. The great idealism that had made the Spanish civil war the focus of Leftists everywhere, the Mecca for fighters for freedom and the International Brigades, was now so much propaganda.

"Spain is finished," said someone.

"Freedom and democracy are finished," pined another. "It's the beginning of the age of barbarism."

The pronouncements went on and on, lubricated with more

bottles of red wine as the journalists trumped their righteous indignation into declarations of their own importance. After they wrote their stories, they assured one another, the game would be up. How could any government dare such perfidy once they exposed it?

"Words!" Sinclair said finally.

"What?"

"Words! It's all *words*. Nothing else."

"Words are power," came the answer. "Have we not exposed the so-called peasant generals who all speak Russian? The volunteers who are all experienced Communist agitators?"

"Words."

"What else have we?" asked a plaintive voice across the table.

Sinclair stared at the man without answering.

Even after months of war, the American-owned and operated telephone network in Madrid still worked. You could call New York night or day, and with luck a call would go through in a matter of hours.

Sinclair was not surprised to hear that his call went through, and even less surprised when Morrison, his agent in New York, told him there was no possibility of another advance. Sinclair had written nothing in weeks, he was behind on articles that had been commissioned and paid for, and even the infinitely patient Morrison was beginning to suggest that it was time to snap out of the funk.

But what Morrison said next was a surprise. Sinclair could remember every word.

"I thought you might like to know, David. I just heard from Maggie. The intrepid lady left Africa, managed to get herself into and out of some outrageous shipwreck, and she's on her way to Frankfurt."

"Margaret?" Sinclair was almost speechless. "Frankfurt? Wasn't she supposed to be coming back to New York?"

"It's hard to keep track of Maggie these days. Since you two split up, she's been the freest of the free spirits."

"When will she be in Frankfurt?"

"Believe it or not, in three days! She's on the Graf Zeppelin. First class only for that lady. Don't ask me how she did it. All I got was a cryptic wire asking for money."

"You have her telephone number in Frankfurt, someplace where I can reach her?"

"David, I don't think that's wise."

"She's my wife, damn it. Where will she be?"

"All I know is that she's en route from Brazil to the Rhein-Main Airport in Frankfurt. Really, David, weren't you two going to lay off one another for a while? I've been enough of a friend to you and to her to know . . ."

Sinclair could think of nothing else. As he walked back to the cafe, images flashed through his mind. Margaret that last night in San Francisco, telling him what he realized should not have been a surprise. "I'm leaving," she said, and it came out so flat and simple that he took a while to register the words. There was no argument, no chance for persuasion. She was just leaving, wearing the tweed jacket that she always took on assignments, carrying the big camera case and a small suitcase. "An assignment?" he asked, and she said, in the same flat voice, "No, David. I'm leaving."

He had come close to begging, to promising that it would be different, reminding her of what it had once been, what she had said about his life and his writing, how much it had once mattered to her. She had always been his biggest fan, seeing detail and life in his stories that no one else recognized. For a long time he had written mostly for her, hoping that somehow the uneasiness and awkward moments when they seemed miles apart would disappear in her admiration for his writing. But there had come a moment—he hadn't really noticed it all at once—when her reaction changed, and his writing stopped mattering. He could still hear her.

"You're *watching* life, David. On the sidelines, an observer. You see it all, and it comes out eloquently in your words. But you don't believe in anything. You don't care about anything. Nothing really matters. And I just can't live life that way."

For a while he had tried to change, tried to convince her that it wasn't so. He wrote stories with more feeling, with poignant scenes that could move a reader to tears. She actually cried at his pieces on Ethiopia. But it wasn't enough, and on that last night she said it all again. "You never *really* care. Nothing really moves you, David. Not me, not even the people you write about. You don't write for the Ethiopians or the Chinese. You write for David Sinclair, to hear the praise. And what makes it all so very sad is that you're good. The best, really. If you could only feel and care . . ."

When he got back to the table at the cafe, the journalists had already left for their typewriters. Only the Minorcan was still there. He was always there, because he had nowhere else to go. He was an accidental exile of the war, and he sat at their table in the cafe, doing errands in return for occasional meals and wine, while he dreamed of returning to his island of Minorca. In the weeks that he had been there, he had said no more than a few sentences.

The Minorcan was a simple man, and he didn't pretend to understand the complexities of the politics of the war. Sometimes someone would try to explain the factions to him, the POUM and the PSUC and the CNT and the UGT and the FAI and the splinters which didn't yet have initials for their names. But he could not understand the minute differences any more than he could understand why the war in Spain was an international crisis. A Fascist general in Africa had staged an uprising and come to Spain, expanding his power and his territory until he was a threat to the Republic. The Republic meant freedom, especially for his own island of Minorca. The Fascists would mean something else—rule by the army and the Church and the great landowners and the wealthy. This much the Minorcan could understand. But he could not understand what any of this had to do with Russia or Italy or Germany or the United States or England, or why educated men from those countries would come to Spain to write stories of the war, or why volunteers would come from many lands to make the war of the Spanish people their own. He knew how to kill Fascists, and he knew that the Fascists and the bosses and the men who lived well when others were starving were all enemies. It was all he could understand, and for him it was enough.

After a few minutes of the unfamiliar silence at the table, the Minorcan leaned close to Sinclair, whose eyes turned inward in glum introspection.

"With your permission, Señor Sinclair—" The Minorcan spoke awkward schoolbook Spanish, as if he were addressing a schoolmaster. "I am not an educated man, only a fisherman, I do not understand all the things of which you and your friends speak. But this gold you speak of—it is the gold of the people, is it not?" The Minorcan pictured bracelets and brooches and rings, such as the wealthy women of Madrid wore. It seemed to have little to do with the war.

Sinclair nodded, hardly looking up from his wine.

"Could you tell me, Señor Sinclair—if this gold belongs to

the people, how can it leave Spain? What is this gold to the Russians?''

Sinclair started to wave the Minorcan away. He was still thinking of Margaret, feeling sorry for himself. He didn't need naive questions. But as he looked up at the sincere eyes of the Minorcan, the simple honesty of the question struck him. Unlike the journalists, the Minorcan was totally without guile, asking a straightforward question that wanted only a straightforward answer.

So Sinclair answered, and without a sophisticated audience to demand eloquence and wordsmithing, he spoke in simple terms, without artifice or posturing, explaining that once the Russians took the gold, the Republic would lose the last guarantee of its independence. Even if they received arms and planes in return, these would be Russian arms and planes, manned and flown by Russians, serving first and foremost Russian interests. Spain would then be in a vise, with Franco and the Nationalists and their German and Italian allies on one side, and the Republic and the Loyalist forces with their Russian allies on the other. Between those jaws, Spain would be crushed, nothing but a practice battlefield where the Fascists and the Communists could prepare for the greater battles to come, when they fought for the whole world.

"How could it be different, Señor Sinclair? Always the mighty will use the land of the poor as a battlefield?"

"It could be different," said Sinclair. "If the Republic used its gold to buy its own arms, its own planes, weapons that were not controlled by the Russians or anyone else. *Spanish* weapons, to fight for a free and independent Spain." He paused, hearing his own words for the first time. What was happening in Spain *was* a prologue for the rest of Europe, and finally, for the world. The end of the Republic *would* mean the end of independence, the collapse of the world into the two abysmal pits of fascism and communism, the death of freedom and democracy. They were the same grand, abstract words he had used many times, but they seemed different now: he meant them.

"Such arms can be bought?" asked the Minorcan. "You speak as if there were a store where a man could put down his money and come away with airplanes and guns. We cannot buy shells for hunting the rabbits now."

Sinclair laughed. The innocence of the Minorcan had a way of stripping questions down to raw essentials. "Switzerland," he said. "It's almost a store. There is a man from the Northrup Corporation who would sell airplanes to donkeys if they could pay in cash. There are planes just waiting on the ground in Texas, *looking* for a customer. They tried selling them to the Republic, until my country's Neutrality Act put the squeeze on." He stopped when the puzzled expression on the Minorcan's face told him that he had lost his audience.

But even as he spoke, ideas began to gel in Sinclair's mind. Inchoate at first, like the loose facts that could only slowly be pieced together into a good story. For the first time in months he wasn't bored or depressed. He was excited.

He turned back to the poster, looked at the expression on the face of the peasant-soldier—pure exhilaration, passion, determination. Margaret was right: the real war was fought with bullets, not words. But a man of ideas could aim those bullets.

"You're a fisherman?" he asked the Minorcan.

"Like my father and his father before him. On Minorca there is only the fish and the cheese and the shoe factories."

"You have a boat, then?"

"Of course..." Sinclair waved the Minorcan quiet as the waiter showed up with another bottle of wine.

"How fast is your boat?"

"Fast? It's for fishing. It isn't necessary to go fast to place the nets. Before we got the diesel engines, we used only the sails or the oars. You can tell a Minorcan fisherman by the muscles of his back."

Sinclair looked at the brawn of the Minorcan. He looked like a man who could move a mountain.

"Does anyone in Minorca have a fast boat?"

The Minorcan thought for a moment, concentrating hard.

"I have a cousin..." said the Minorcan. He looked around, afraid to finish the sentence.

"This cousin of yours...?" Sinclair knew enough about islands like Minorca to realize that *cousin* was a term of acquaintance as much as relationship. "This cousin of yours, he is...?"

The Minorcan leaned close. "*Contrabandista*," he said in a conspiratorial whisper. "He smuggled tobacco from North Africa. It is very..." He finished by rubbing his fingers together in the universal sign of money.

"Now sometimes he brings arms and ammunition from the mainland. From France too. So we will be ready on Minorca when the Fascists come. His boat is swifter than the patrol boats of the revenue police in the Guardia Civil."

"What kind of arms does he bring in?" asked Sinclair.

"Rifles, pistols. Once there was a machine gun, but it would not work and we couldn't get the ammunition for it anyway."

"How big is the boat? Big enough to go to Cartagena?"

"Cartagena?" Again the Minorcan had to stop to think With his eyes he paced off the back room of the cafe and the distance through the bead curtain to the street beyond. "The boat is perhaps fifteen meters long," he said. "With very powerful engines. It would be nothing to go to Cartagena if there were enough fuel. But why would he . . . ?"

Sinclair waved him silent again. He tried to picture the island of Minorca, poised at the end of the Balearics, as close to France as it was to Spain. He had never been there. What he knew was from books and hearsay, but even a vague memory of the map told him that the island could be perfect—isolated, astride the sealanes, close enough to both Cartagena and the quiet ports of southern France. And from there it would be a quick ride up to Switzerland. The idea was beginning to gel.

"Your cousin, he's a good man? You'd trust him?"

"He is not an easy man," said the Minorcan. "For too many years he has fought with the Revenue Police. He trusts no one, especially with the Fascists on Majorca now."

"Can *he* be trusted?"

"If he says he will do something, he will do it. All of my cousins are such men. But I do not understand these questions, Señor Sinclair."

"*All* of your cousins? How many men are there who can be trusted?"

"Eight, perhaps ten. In our village."

"They can all fight? Handle a gun?"

"Of course. As boys, we learn to shoot by hunting rabbits in the hills. And every man can use a knife. If we had no bullets, we could still kill Fascists. But I . . ."

Sinclair didn't look up. He was lost in scribbling on a pad, sketching a crude map, then some numbers. He wrote notes next to the sketch, crossed them out and wrote new notes, finally adding an exclamation point in the margin.

The Minorcan watched every move of Sinclair's pencil. He had never known a man like Sinclair, a man with so many ideas he had to write them down. He wondered what it was like to have such a mind, what ideas went through that mind.

"Would you like to go back to Minorca?" Sinclair asked suddenly.

"I dream of it every night," said the Minorcan. "I am not at home in this Spain. They do not even speak my language. But I have no money for a ticket, and it is impossible to get on the trains without having bribe money for the ticket sellers and the conductors. Also, from Barcelona there are almost no ferries to Minorca now. They say it is too dangerous, because of the Italian airplanes from Majorca. They fly everywhere and bomb the ships that come to Minorca. My cousin has said . . ." He caught himself and leaned close to Sinclair. "My cousin has said that if he had a machine gun for his boat, he would shoot the Italian airplanes into the sea."

With a one hundred peseta bribe and a flash of his international correspondent identification, Sinclair bought two tickets on the 0710 Express to Barcelona. It was a troop train—it seemed that every train in Spain was now a troop train—but the ticket seller admitted that he did not know where the troops would come from or why they would be sent to Barcelona.

"It makes no sense," he explained. "Without arms, the troops can do nothing. And we have no arms. All the weapons are in the hands of the troops with the Russian advisors."

"Maybe it will change," said Sinclair.

Twenty

Early evening was a delightful hour on the Zeppelin. The airstream through the open windows was cool and dry, and once they left the turbulent thermals that wafted up from the parched land, the ship seemed to glide effortlessly, the rudder easy, the elevator steady. To compensate for the decreased lift of the cooling hydrogen, the airship flew with a slight upward pitch of three degrees, using the dynamic lift of the great hull to maintain its altitude without jettisoning ballast. The lifting attitude meant a slight increase in fuel consumption, but it also meant a ride as smooth as a sailboat beam reaching in a steady breeze on a flat sea.

To the passengers lounging in the dining room, enjoying

aperitifs and hors d'oeuvres, the serene ride was all the more carefree because it was so simple and obvious. Any child with a balloon at a circus can explain the principles governing the flight of a Zeppelin. Hydrogen is lighter than air. Fill a balloon with hydrogen and it rises. Build a lightweight, rigid structure to hold the hydrogen balloons; cover it with a streamlined, protective skin; equip it with engines and propellers powerful enough to move it through the air; and you have an airship. And unlike an airplane, the engines need only enough power to drive the airship laterally through the air, not the incredible power to overcome gravity.

How different the experience was for a passenger in an airplane, constantly aware of the struggle between the airplane and its environment, symbolized in the roar and vibration of the engines that must not only push the airplane through the air, but generate the lift to get it off the ground. And even after it has been explained over and over, the flight of an airplane can seem impossible. The concept of the lift generated by a moving aerofoil is difficult for most passengers to comprehend. So they fly on faith, on the trust that the airplane has somehow gotten off the ground before and that it probably will again. Amid the roar and trembling of the great engines, they tighten their seatbelts and pray, trusting to a technology they do not completely understand, hoping against fear that they will not hear a missed beat or a sputter that will mean the engines upon which they are so dependent may suddenly fail and let them crash to earth.

Such worries were impossible in the Graf Zeppelin. The constant pampering of the huge Maybach engines, monsters that poured out 2,650 horsepower at flank speed, was no concern of the passengers. If an engine ever stopped, the airship would still float, drifting until the engine was repaired, or continuing on its way with the power of the remaining four engines. Passengers had no reason to worry about the vibration of the engine mounts or the lubrication charts or the fear that an ignition wire might break loose in a shower of dangerous high-voltage sparks. From the comfort of the lounge, most of them forgot the airship even had engines.

The passengers could also remain blissfully oblivious to the concerns that kept a large crew of mechanics and riggers and electricians busy on round-the-clock shifts: the necessity of constantly shifting water between the internal ballast tanks, the fresh and used water tanks, and the recirculating toilet systems, to keep the ship in equilibrium even as the stores were exhausted; the constant inspections for loose wiring, broken connections, or the smallest sign of metal fatigue, a crack in a frame ring or one of the cruciform or cantilever girders that strengthened the framework, or a fatigue vibration that could break an axial support wire, leaving the ends red hot or allowing two pieces of wire to slap against one another and create sparks; the incessant monitoring of the hydrogen cells for *ripeness*, the contamination of a cell by air that would turn the pure hydrogen into explosive oxyhydrogen, the checks for blockage in any of the complex venting systems that might trap free hydrogen inside the outer envelope of the ship; or most important of all, the search for leaks in the doped goldbeater skin gas bags that held the highly explosive Blaugas fuel.

The use of Blaugas was an innovation of the Graf Zeppelin, and the key to the range and load-carrying ability of the ship. Unlike heavy diesel fuel or gasoline, the Blaugas—a propanelike fuel with a specific gravity almost identical to air—did not lighten the ship as it burned off. There was no need to vent hydrogen to compensate for reduced weight, or to build the heavy and complex condenser systems the Americans used to recapture water from the exhaust vapors in order to offset the weight of the burned fuel. But Blaugas had its disadvantages. It was perhaps the most explosive fuel that could have been chosen. And because its specific gravity was the same as air, it neither fell harmlessly below the ship nor rose through the vent ducts when there was a leak. Instead, the leaking Blaugas would tend to stay where it was, waiting inside the ship for the slightest spark to convert the Zeppelin into a raging inferno.

But an accident was a million-to-one chance, the brochures assured the passengers, making short shrift of the fact that the passenger gondola was slung beneath three million cubic feet of highly flammable hydrogen and one million cubic feet of explosive Blaugas, in one of the most complex and sophisticated structures ever built, with girders and frames of experimental alloys, fastened with experimental techniques, and fabricated with an emphasis on lightness that bordered on the fanatical. From the dining room of the Zeppelin, the passengers remained oblivious of the technical details and the maybes. To them the Zeppelin was a carefree traveling lounge, an elegant observation post far above the mundane life below, a place where one didn't have to worry about the possible.

As the ship cruised toward the coast after departing Recife, it flew over a parched plain where emaciated cattle scraped at the scraggly brush. The shadow of the Zeppelin, stretched thin by the setting sun, crossed the fields, and the cattle looked up to bellow their displeasure. A mangy shepherd dog howled at the heavens, chasing frantically after the Zeppelin until it had successfully driven the great ship out to sea. Passengers watching from the windows laughed as the proud dog strutted back to its resting place, content with the knowledge that it had once again driven off an intruder.

It was a carefree moment on the Graf Zeppelin, one of a thousand such moments that made up a crossing. Thoughts of the flammability of the fuel or the dangers of sparks or even the threats of politics were unthinkable at such moments. They were a thousand feet above the sea, gliding serenely in the safest and smoothest form of transportation known to man. As the Zeppelin Company proudly noted in its brochures, there had never been a single passenger fatality in all the millions of miles of commercial Zeppelin travel. Statistically, it was an incomparable record.

"Captain Whitman?"

Whitman looked up at the steward from his wicker chair in the starboard corner of the control room. Both the chair and the corner were traditions of the Zeppelins, made famous by Hugo Eckener himself when he commanded the Graf Zeppelin on its pioneering flights. Every commander since had used it. It was a splendid place to think, and Whitman had a lot of thinking to do.

"It's the second night out," said the steward.

Whitman knew exactly what he meant. It happened on every flight as the novelty of travel by Zeppelin wore off.

When passengers first boarded, they were amazed by the luxury of the Zeppelin. They were shown their spacious twin-bedded cabins, with broad downward-sloping windows that could be opened for fresh air. Even before departure, they would find seats in the dining room and lounge, and it wouldn't be long before they heard the only regular sound in flight, the clink of fine crystal and china from a food service that rivaled the finest passenger liners. The flight was generally so smooth that passengers were rarely inconvenienced by a spilled wineglass or teacup, let alone motion sickness. One regular passenger used to lure first-timers by balancing his pen on its cap before the lift-off and offering to wager that it would remain standing throughout the flight. He rarely lost.

Despite the luxury, or perhaps because of it, by the second night out the passengers would begin showing the first signs of restlessness. The prohibition against smoking would take its toll, and the lounge and cabins that had seemed so spacious when they boarded would gradually seem confining. The Germans would miss a promenade deck for constitutionals. The South Americans would begin disappearing for long siestas, forsaking the confines of the lounge for the only privacy the airship offered. As passengers realized that the journey would have little of the excitement they had anticipated from air travel, occasional boredom threatened to escalate into constant irritability. It did little good for the stewards to point to the proud boast in the Zeppelin Company brochure: "You *fly* on an airplane, but you *travel* on the Graf."

From experience, the stewards would begin scheduling progressively more elaborate meals, knowing that the anticipation, consumption, and discussion of food could be a weapon in the war against boredom and irritability. Each meal would be prefaced with a presentation of the menu and a brief discussion of the dishes, and even the most modest tea service would be accorded the full ritual and paraphernalia of German cuisine. Every item of silver and glassware would be carefully wiped with a clean white *serviette* before being placed on the table. Every dish, no matter how simple, would be presented on a silver bowl or salver, covered by a glass or silver dome, held in a white-gloved hand. After each course, the table would be cleared down to service plates. A breakfast of cold ham slices, boiled eggs, rolls, toast, butter, marmalade, and fruit could consume over an hour with this service. Lunches and dinners, with their accompanying wine service, could consume as much as two and one-half hours.

But between the meals, the only diversions were still reading, conversation, and the familiar panorama of sea and sky outside the windows. Some passengers brought no books and found nothing they liked in the modest library on the Zeppelin. Others had no interest in the view. After a single day, language barriers and the complex organization of the *Stammtische* had already established stringent rules of discourse. Easy initial topics had been exhausted, and passengers were sometimes putting as much energy into avoiding conversations as pursuing them.

It was the second night out.

"I didn't want to bother you, sir," said the steward, "but the man who boarded in Recife has been a bit troublesome. Seems to have a chip on his shoulder."

It took Whitman a second to translate the German into the American idiom.

"I heard it in an American film," explained the steward. "The man's name is Enkmann. He gave us quite a time of it at the baggage inspection. We found some cigars in his traveling bag, and you know what they say, sir—'where there's smoke, there's fire.' Well, he didn't want that portfolio of his opened, and he was quite sticky about it. The usual stuff about his reputation and all that. Of course, we found four boxes of matches inside. He claims that someone must have planted them.

"Then before we were off the ground he began complaining about there being no smoking compartment, even after we explained that he maybe had the Graf Zeppelin confused with the Hindenberg. Nothing seemed to satisfy him. He ordered a beer, insisted on a *Dortmunder Pils*. It turned out we didn't have any on ice, because of those tissue samples. I tried to explain the situation, but the man became quite livid, carrying on about our priorities and you being an American and all. I promised him that we would somehow find room for his beer in the refrigerators, but I suspect he'll be a troublemaker. I thought you should know, sir."

"Thanks. I'll try to talk to him." It was the part of Zeppelin flying that Whitman liked the least, the need for diplomacy with passengers and their demands. And it was always a complaint about priorities.

It was ironic, he thought, but he had the same complaint to make himself. He had been thinking about it since they left Recife. The priorities of the Zeppelins were changing, away from the dreams he once had, toward something unknown and frightening.

The tissue samples that had been loaded onto the airship in Recife were a good example. The tin case, packed with ice, held cultures of the microbes that were suspected as the cause of the epidemic that had been devastating the peasants in the Brazilian backlands. If all went well, the Graf Zeppelin was to deliver the cultures to the Hoechst Laboratories in Europe, where a vaccine would be made and brought back on the return flight of the Zeppelin. By ship, the same voyage would take over two months, and the English doctor from the clinic had said that even with refrigeration the microbes could not live that long. Flying those samples was an opportunity for the Graf Zeppelin to save thousands of lives.

But to the Zeppelin Company, it was a low priority mission. The slight delay on the ground while the samples were loaded onto the ship resulted in complaints from some of the passengers, and the Zeppelin Company ground personnel answered the complaints with haughty shrugs and sarcastic comments about the English doctor from the missionary hospital and the incompetence of the Brazilians. To the company, the vaccine mission was an inconvenience, required by a certain *noblesse oblige,* but like the rescue of Maggie Bourne, an unfortunate detour from the straight and narrow schedule of the Graf Zeppelin.

And yet, thought Whitman, it was exactly what the Zeppelins could and should do. With a greater range than any other aircraft in the world, able to carry loads that were unthinkable in an airplane, and with a reliability that was impossible for an airplane, the Zeppelins were capable of missions of mercy that could be the difference between life and death for whole populations. But that vision, he knew, could never be shared by the Nazis. For them, the Zeppelins were just one more propaganda machine, another chance to display the swastika, to show off the uniqueness and might of German technology.

He glanced over at the open filigree girders of the control room, a masterpiece of design and construction, a framework as lightweight and rigid as only the structural engineering and metallurgical techniques of the Zeppelin Company could have produced. The Nazis were at least right about something, he thought. It *was* a unique technology, a design and construction that no one else in the world could equal. The British had tried with the mighty R-101 and failed miserably in a tragic crash. The Americans too had tried, developing flying techniques that added to the potential of airships, techniques that Whitman would have liked to share with the Germans. But the Americans too had failed, and it was finally only Hugo Eckener and the Zeppelin Company that had given the miracle of reliable commercial travel to the world. And now, with Eckener an *unperson,* shunted aside from the Zeppelins he had created, the Nazis seemed determined to throw it all away. Whitman felt like he was flying back to a Germany he hardly knew, and little wanted.

He thought of the cable in Recife, with its terse promise of an inquiry. It seemed like more Nazi blindness. What was there to investigate? The death of Jürgen Steinbrenner? It was a terrible tragedy, but still an accident, no different from a rigger falling off the envelope during mid-flight repairs, or the horrible American incident when ground handlers were suddenly lifted two hundred feet into the air by an accidental ascent of the Akron, and then fell to their deaths when they could no longer hold onto the lines. Whitman remembered the investigation then: the goal was not to find fault, but to develop procedures that would make sure there was never another incident like that one. The same could be done for Steinbrenner's death in the rescue. Zeppelin flying procedures and training could be expanded to incorporate the kinds of maneuvers necessary for rescue missions. But from the tone of that cable, it was hardly what the new Director of Operations of the Zeppelin Company had in mind

What would this man Hempe do? Whitman knew nothing about him except that he was Goering's man. And he knew nothing about Goering beyond the rumors and hearsay that everyone in Germany read and heard, and the occasional scuttle-butt of crew members. Like the other Nazi leaders, his face was familiar; everything else about him was strangely obscure.

He tried to put himself in the place of the Nazis, to view the whole incident from their perspective. It was the admiral who had angered Stifel and Beck. Why? What had he done? Why was it so important that he be returned to the Reich, under what was obviously an armed guard? Whitman suspected that it was a secret that he would never be told, a grievance too terrible or too petty for the ears of a non-Nazi. But then what would be the premise of an inquiry? That he had delayed the Zeppelin from its all-important schedule? Or could they twist things far enough to suggest that the whole rescue had been part of some American conspiracy?

It seemed preposterous, and yet conspiracies were perhaps the only possible explanation to paranoid minds who saw the whole world ready to pounce on an innocent and victimized Germany. One more example of the classification and labeling mentality that was so essential to the Nazis, the same mode of thought that could pigeonhole all Jews and Gypsies as automatic enemies of Germany. Americans were still neutral in that typology, at least they were the last time Whitman had forced himself to read through a copy of *Der Angriff* or the *Völkische Beobachter*. The Nazis, it seemed, still held hope that Charles Lindbergh or Henry Ford would persuade the rest of the United States to support their America First cause. But Whitman and Maggie Bourne were no Lindberghs, and the simple fact that she was American and rescued by an American——*half*-American, he corrected himself—

captain, was perhaps enough to raise the specter of conspiracy. Incredible, he thought, but possible.

He cut his thoughts short with a grin he couldn't control, and a vivid image of Maggie Bourne. In a way they were right, he thought. At that moment there was nothing he would have enjoyed more than spending more time with her, listening to those expressions he had almost forgotten, the loose idiom of American conversation. *I could eat a horse. Call out the Marines.* And her smiles, open and easy, with no purpose except friendliness. Being with her had made him feel very American, and it was a damned good feeling.

His smile embarrassed him. An ocean to cross, an inquiry to face, a future of questions he could hardly pose, let alone answer, and he was feeling homesick and enjoying the delicious feeling of being with a splendid woman—after an hour in the lounge of the Graf Zeppelin, he reminded himself, with a woman who herself seemed to have spent lately as little time in the States as he had. Still, he found that he couldn't shake from his mind either her smile or the admiral's prophetic words. "Believe me, Captain, she is worth it . . ."

As much as he would have liked to talk more with her, professional restraint kept Whitman from going back into the passenger dining area. The exquisitely smooth flying did not require his attention in the control room, but it was one thing to have lunch with a recently rescued castaway, another thing altogether to spend too much time with one passenger on the Graf Zeppelin. That would be exactly the kind of unprofessional attitude that would feed the talk of conspiracy, and that Whitman himself, as a professional flyer, would frown on.

Enkmann, the man who boarded in Recife, had taken over the fourth table in the lounge, directly opposite the Lopez-Oteros and Senhor de Nascimento. At the earliest opportunity, de Nascimento, recognizing a kindred spirit and a potential mark in the German, came over to the table to introduce himself. His German improved strikingly when he sat down with the stranger.

"You are going back to Germany?" he said. "I trust that your business ventures in Brazil have been successful."

Enkmann nodded, then turned his head to avoid further talk with the Brazilian.

"And you have bought Brazilian gifts to take back with you?" asked de Nascimento.

Enkmann looked puzzled. "What could I have possibly bought that would be appropriate as a gift?"

"Ah, *mein Herr!*" said the Brazilian, pulling his chair closer to the table. "Brazil produces the finest gemstones in the world—topaz, amethyst, aquamarine, tourmalines They are famous throughout the world."

"I am hardly interested in trinkets," said Enkmann. He was already trying to play subtle eye-games with Nadia Lopez-Otero, catching her glance, then looking away, or staring back until she blinked in embarrassment.

"Trinkets?" De Nascimento pretended insult. "I am not speaking of trinkets, *mein Herr,* but of valuable gems. Investment quality gems. Perhaps you did not know that Brazil mines the finest diamonds in the world."

"I told you," said Enkmann, sipping at his beer with unconcealed disgust. "I am not interested in jewelry."

"Of course," said de Nascimento. "Of course. But surely you are interested in investments. A sound investment for the future."

"No. I have told you. I am not interested."

De Nascimento reached out for Enkmann's arm, leaning close to him until he was what he considered a comfortable talking distance. Finding the Latin closeness uncomfortable, the German recoiled, twisting his arm from the Brazilian's grip.

"There are people in Germany who will pay large sums for diamonds," said de Nascimento. "People who *must* buy diamonds. They are a prudent investment now."

"Then why don't you sell your diamonds to those people?"

"If I could, *mein Herr,* I would be a very wealthy man. But I am a Brazilian. I cannot engage in such transactions inside Germany. It is forbidden. But you . . . you could find such a transaction very lucrative. As I say, there are many people in Germany who are only too anxious to translate their fortunes" —he glanced around the room, then again leaned close to Enkmann—"ill-gotten fortunes, to be sure, into portable wealth."

"Who are these people you speak of?" Enkmann asked the question with a tone of genuine ignorance.

"*Mein Herr!* In the wisdom of its racial policies, Germany is cleansing itself of unnecessary peoples, peoples who only pollute the purity of the great German race. Need I say more?"

"They are buying diamonds? The Jews are buying diamonds? Why would they invest in jewelry when they are being forced to leave Germany? It makes no sense."

"Not jewelry, *mein Herr*. Investment stones. There is no more portable means of transporting wealth."

"But it is forbidden for the Jews to take monies with them. Your whole scheme is absurd."

"You will think about it, please, *mein Herr*. We will speak again before the ship lands in Frankfurt."

Margaret Bourne shared a table with the Huttens, delighting in their charming broken English. And in turn, Otto Hutten was pleased to have the beautiful young woman as an audience for his descriptions of his vineyards, and his twenty year effort to develop a *Spätlese* vintage in the occasional frosts that came late in the Brazilian growing season.

At one point, Anna Hutten tried to change the subject, sensing that even the polite young American woman would soon be bored with the details of their vinicultural experiments. But she realized quickly that her efforts to divert her husband from the consuming passion of his life were sure to fail. She turned instead to her window, watching the sea below as the ship moved steadily off the coast. The water seemed to change color in sharp lines, from the green of the beaches to a green-turquoise in the shallow coastal waters, and finally to a dark blue that bordered on violet-black offshore.

She looked up briefly when the steward handed her the menu for the evening meal—*Pâtés à la Reine, Filet de Boeuf roti, salades assorties, fromage et fruits, café*—then went back to her window, looking up only when she spotted the steward on another of his trips through the lounge.

"Excuse me," she said, gesturing toward the window. "Could you please tell me the name of that island?"

He leaned over the table to look out at the rocky island below, dominated by a strange needlelike pinnacle of stone.

"That is Fernando de Noronha," he said. "We use it as a navigation checkpoint, the last one on this side of the Atlantic. Our next landfall will be the Cape Verde Islands."

"Does anyone live there?" she asked. "It looks lovely. The palm trees are so green, and the rocks and the sea seem so peaceful."

The steward grinned. "You would not find it very hospitable, *gnädige Frau*. It's a prison colony. Like Devil's Island, but even more formidable. It is five hundred kilometers from the coast. Only the most dangerous Brazilian criminals are transported there—murderers and revolutionaries. Supposedly, it is a place from which there is no escape."

"How sad," said Anna Hutten. "It must be very painful for those prisoners to look up and see the Graf Zeppelin flying overhead."

Twenty-One

For over a day, no one had spoken to Conselheiro. After the initial interrogation and beatings, the Integralistas had given up on him. His kind they knew. He would never talk, even if they tortured him to death. Soon enough he would either be sent back to Fernando de Noronha, or they would get permission to shoot him. And if it turned out to be the former, they had plenty of time to break his legs to make sure he would never escape again.

The jailer saw him three times, bringing water and food and carrying away the slop bucket. After the first dinner, he too said nothing.

Then, on the second day, the jailer squatted on his haunches outside the pen while the prisoner ate his lunch. When Conselheiro looked up from the tin plate of gruel, the jailer caught his eyes.

"You said there are things a man can do," said the jailer. "What are those things?"

It was the question Conselheiro had waited for. He ate the gruel slowly, letting the jailer wait for an answer. When he saw the jailer twitch with anxiety, Conselheiro gestured in the direction of the barracks he knew were outside the cell. "Why do you think they fight?" he asked.

"The Integralistas? Who can know? Maybe they like to wear the green shirts and carry the guns. They were smiling after they beat you. I think they like it."

"They are like the men who perform in the *capoeira*," said Conselheiro, referring to the stylized ballet fights of the region. "We know it is not a true fight, but a ritual. We know that the fighters do it for the tourists because they're paid to do it, as our fathers were paid or forced to fight one another for the entertainment of the rich landowners. The Integralistas are the same. They fight because they're paid. They are mercenaries.''

"So? For money, perhaps I too would fight.''

"Where do you think the money to pay them comes from?''

"Where else?'' said the jailer. "The government.''

"Since when has the government ever spent a single *milreis* for the northeast?''

The jailer shifted position nervously, then got up and brought in a stool to sit more comfortably. He closed the door behind him so no one would hear him talking to the prisoner.

"If it is not from the government, where does the money come from?''

Conselheiro looked up to the barred opening in the ceiling of the cell. Sunlight streamed through, and a corner of blue sky was just visible.

"It is new money,'' he said. "Brought in from Germany. The Integralistas are paid by the Germans.''

"I don't understand,'' said the jailer.

"Do you understand the sum of two million *milreis*?''

"Two millions?''

"That's how much money they bring on the Zeppelin to pay the Integralistas.''

"Why would they bring it on the Zeppelin? And why to Recife?''

"Because a ship would take almost two months. With the inflation, it would be worthless after two months. And they do not bring it to Recife. They bring it to Rio. But the Zeppelin stops in Recife for fuel.''

The jailer looked confused and skeptical. "How do you know this?''

"I was not the only prisoner on Fernando de Noronha. Another man was a payroll robber. He knew about the Zeppelin.''

"Why did he tell you?''

"To escape.''

"And why do you tell me?'' asked the jailer.

Conselheiro grinned, a gap between his teeth revealing how effective the Integralistas had been with their beating. "The same reason,'' he said.

"Two millions, you're sure?''

"I'm sure. It is two million, on each flight, to pay the Integralistas. If they're not paid, they will not fight.''

The jailer calculated silently, trying to comprehend the sum.

His life was measured in pennies. Two millions was an impossible sum, enough to buy the world.

"And with your rifle you were going to hold up the great Zeppelin? Did you think you would be a highwayman like Lampiao? You don't even have a horse."

Conselheiro's grin widened into a broad smile. He knew he had the jailer.

"I was only checking my plan," he said.

"They say that the bullets of a rifle would not even hurt the Zeppelin."

"Of course," said Conselheiro.

"Then what were you going to do?"

Conselheiro laughed. "If I told you, you would leave me to die and do it yourself. I will tell you nothing until I am free from here."

"If they caught me, they would kill me," said the jailer. "They would torture my wife until she told where I was, then they would kill me."

"Your wife can go back into the Sertão. They will never find her. And in two weeks, when the Zeppelin returns, you will have one million *milreis*. You will be richer than the owners of the greatest *latifundia*. You could go to the south and live like a gentleman. Or do you prefer seeing your wife and your children slowly starve to death?"

"How do I know you have a plan? How do I know you are not simply lying to me?"

"Would I go to the Zeppelin Field and risk capture for nothing? Am I such a fool?"

"Perhaps. They say even a few days in the sun of Fernando de Noronha makes a man a fool."

"And I say that a man who turns down one million *milreis* is a fool."

The jailer walked back and forth outside the pen, looking over at Conselheiro, trying to see something behind the grin that stuck through the mangy hair and beard.

"How do they carry it?" he asked suddenly. "The money. How is it carried?"

"In wooden cases," said Conselheiro without hesitation. "It is packed in steel boxes that are then enclosed in wooden cases."

"And what form is it?"

"Form?"

"Is it coins? Actual *milreis*?"

"No. It is paper bills printed in Germany, each of one hundred *milreis*. They are wrapped in bundles and packed into the boxes.''

It seemed to satisfy the jailer. He had no way of checking, and the quickness and exactness of Conselheiro's responses answered his doubts.

"Wait," he said. "The Integralistas change shifts at five o'clock. At night there are only two on duty, and they usually play cards in the front. There is no one by the side door. I will be back with your dinner after five. We will talk then.''

Twenty-Two

The irregular rhythm of the diesel engine kept Sinclair awake in the hardwood pilot berth of the fishing boat. For a long time, he had tried to sleep, twisting and turning in the cramped berth, trying to find a position that did not transmit the vibrations of the pounding diesel directly into his bones. There was no escaping the rhythm. He tried to concentrate on it, as if he could break it down and defeat it. Old lessons in poetry came back, dactyls and iambs, forgotten metric patterns. Nothing quite fit the beat of the diesel.

A flash of pesetas in a Barcelona bar had led the way to the fishing boat, a colorful high-prowed trawler that looked no different from hundreds of others in the crowded docks of the fishing fleet at Barceloneta. After a long negotiation the captain agreed to take Sinclair and the Minorcan across to Minorca. Sinclair thought he had gotten a good deal until he realized that the misbalanced diesel was part of the bargain.

Twice during the night the pounding diesel suddenly slowed, then stopped.

"Is something wrong with the engine?" asked Sinclair the first time, after he had extricated himself from the pilot berth and climbed to the deck.

The captain waved him quiet. He scanned the horizon slowly, not looking up until his ears and eyes told him there were no airplanes or boats near them. Then he restarted the engine, grinning when it resumed the vibration that seemed sure to shake the boat to pieces.

When Sinclair gave up his efforts at sleep and came on deck at five in the morning, the sky was just tinged with dusty gray in the east. The Minorcan was sitting on a low hatch cover, his eyes fixed on the distant horizon. He saw Sinclair and pointed to a faint mirage in the southeast, a wisp of brown against the lead gray sky.

"Beautiful, isn't it?" he said. "The most beautiful island in the world."

Low clouds scudded across the smudge of an island, and the land alternately seemed to merge with the clouds and the sea, disappearing and reappearing as the boat chugged on through the dawn. Sinclair went below in the hope of finding hot coffee. When he came back on deck, the island suddenly loomed over them, as if they had covered dozens of miles in a matter of minutes. He had not made enough landfalls in small boats to be used to the phenomenon.

The boat turned around a tall stone bluff, and they were in the outer reaches of Puerto Mahón. As they came up the channel, Sinclair suddenly understood all that he had so hurriedly read about the island. It was the most magnificent natural port he had ever seen, a fully protected anchorage that made San Francisco or Naples look like gunkholes. Puerto Mahón had been selected by the fledgling United States of America as its first overseas naval base. American warships operating out of the harbor defeated the Barbary pirates in the young nation's first war, and from 1802 until Annapolis was opened in 1845, Mahón was the site of the United States Naval Academy. Farragut, according to the books, was still a hero on Minorca.

The narrow entrance widened into the bays and coves of the vast anchorage, with the buildings of the town built on a steep hill behind. The eyes of the Minorcan ignored the hills and the ships lying at anchor in the harbor. Instead he focused on a large factory standing on a hill across from the town. A colorful sign on the side proclaimed: *Mahón*.

"Mayonnaise?" asked Sinclair. He had read the stories of how the sauce was invented in the port during the Napoleonic wars.

"No, Señor Sinclair," answered the Minorcan. "Gin. From the British we have learned to make gin. That is the largest factory. It is our own drink, available nowhere else in Spain."

"Is that what made you homesick?" asked Sinclair.

"Everything about my island makes me homesick."

Sinclair studied the edges of the harbor as the boat made its approach to a low stone quay. The civil war had not really come to Mahón. Fishing boats spread nets on their stubby masts and on the quayside for last-minute repairs, and men and women trudged toward the docks and the market square with empty baskets, walking with that quiet somnambulist gait that says morning has not quite come.

When they stepped up on the dock, Sinclair asked, ''Where is your cousin's boat?''

''Not here, Señor. We must travel to Ciudadela, at the other end of the island. It would not be safe here.''

''Safe from what?'' asked Sinclair. It looked like the safest harbor in the world.

The Minorcan grinned. ''The Revenue Police have their office here, in Mahón. Come, we can take a taxi.''

The drive over the spine of the island took over four hours, and the driver and the Minorcan did not stop talking the entire time. From the little Sinclair could make out of the rapid-fire Minorquin, the main subjects were fish, cows, cheese, births, and deaths—in that order. Sinclair was more interested in what he could see of the villages they passed, the English-style horizontal window sashes in place of the vertical French windows of the rest of Spain, and the blue-eyed fair children that told of a more lasting influence of the English.

After dozens of stops and starts, the car coasted along a stretch of road paralleling the coast into Ciudadela, a picturebook city built around a spacious square of terra cotta, green and white. With the Minorcan shouting directions to the driver and greetings to pedestrians at the same time, the taxi skirted the square to a steep switchback road that led down to a stone quay alongside the narrow harbor. They screeched to an abrupt halt in the midst of a collection of cafe tables on the quay.

The Minorcan bolted from the car, shouting to men at the tables before he ran to the doorway of the cafe, where a slim, pretty girl with prominent cheekbones and long, coal black hair stood barefoot in a loose cotton shift.

''Pedrito?'' she said, putting down a tray of glasses and walking quickly toward him. He hugged her and led her to where Sinclair was standing.

''Señor Sinclair,'' he said. ''This is my sister, Montserrat. We call her Monsy.''

She half-curtsied and smiled, rows of perfect white teeth in a shy grin. She looked down when Sinclair returned her smile.

"She dreams of traveling in Europe and even America," said Pedrito. "On her own she studies French to talk with foreigners. I tell her that when she gets there she will see that there is nothing and she will come home to Minorca to find a man. But she is young." He shrugged.

He then introduced Sinclair to the men, going through the names so rapidly that Sinclair couldn't remember a single one. He referred to Sinclair as The American.

They sat down at one of the tables, and from inside the cafe Montserrat brought out a tray with ordinary glass tumblers, each filled halfway with neat gin. Sinclair listened and watched as the Minorcans sipped and talked. Then he followed with a sip of his own, choking at the bite of the warm perfumed liquor. A few more sips and he was no longer aware of the taste. As the others talked, he could recognize only a few words of their Minorquin— his name, gold, Fascist.

One man, at the opposite end of the table, kept his eyes on Sinclair as Pedrito talked. He was short and stocky, with the bull neck and powerful shoulders of a scrapper. The others periodically looked to him for approval of their talk, and Sinclair gradually realized that he was Manolo, the *cousin* with the fast boat, the leader of the group of men.

"This idea is yours?" one of the men asked Sinclair in Spanish.

"And his," said Sinclair, reaching out to touch Pedrito's shoulder.

"Pedrito?" said one of the others. They all laughed. "It will never work if it was Pedrito's idea," said someone through the laughter. He looked at Sinclair to explain. "Pedrito is a man of muscle, even between the ears."

Sinclair tried to join their laughter, but he was still an outsider, and they had a long headstart on the gin. Instead, he watched the men closely, knowing he had to learn the style and rhythms of these men if he were to use and depend on them as a team.

After a few rounds of gin, an old woman began bringing out platters of food—grilled *gambas*, huge tasty prawns cooked over an open fire, followed by whole red mullets, heaping plates of soft fried potatoes, a salad of green vegetables covered with fresh mayonnaise laced with garlic. They shoveled away like trenchermen, piling away plate after plate of the fish and potatoes, washing it all down with a greenish wine that reminded Sinclair of the new wines of Grinzing he had tasted in Vienna. Montserrat stood behind Sinclair as he ate, her long black hair grazing his shoulder as she leaned forward to refill his wine glass whenever he took a sip. When she cleared away the plates, leaving only the wine and a wooden board with cheeses, the men turned again to Sinclair. One asked him a question, this time in Minorquin, from which he could pick out only a single cognate— *Russian*. Montserrat, seeing his difficulty with the language, translated the question into Spanish for him.

"How do you know the gold will be on the Russian ships?"

Sinclair answered in Spanish. "The dockmaster in Barcelona. He has a tongue like a washerwoman."

The men laughed, all except Manolo. He had still said nothing, and he leaned forward now, looking right at Sinclair. "The dockmaster of the port told you about the shipment of gold?" he asked.

"No. Not in so many words. But he's a vain man, and the thought of his own photograph and name in a newspaper often loosens a man's tongue. He's proud that his office is now in charge of all ship movements from Spanish ports, and he was eager to impress a reporter with his importance. As an example of the difficulties of his job, he told me that he must route a convoy of four Russian freighters in a single day."

"How do you know that it is the gold that these ships will be carrying?"

"What else would they ship from Cartagena?"

"It does not require four ships to carry the gold." Manolo's tone was self-assured.

"No, it doesn't," said Sinclair. "But would you put one thousand five hundred millions of pesetas of gold on a single ship?"

The men around the table gasped, taking hasty gulps of wine before they could digest the sum. Only Manolo seemed unimpressed. He still stared into Sinclair's eyes, not lowering his gaze in the manner most Spanish consider respectful for close conversation.

"Cartagena," he said. "It is no fishing village. It's a fortress."

"Exactly," said Sinclair. "I've been there. The walls are a meter thick, of solid stone. And because of that, the guards are lax. The navy thinks that a fortress built to resist attack in the eighteenth century is still impregnable."

"For such a shipment they will bring in extra guards."

"I don't think so," said Sinclair. "Extra guards would mean extra attention. I think they will want to keep the shipment as quiet and secret as possible. That's why I believe this plan will work.''

He took out his notepad and looked around. ''Is it all right to talk here?''

Manolo nodded. ''Every man on this island hates the Fascists.''

Sinclair opened the pad to his sketches, then began to explain the details of his plan. Montserrat stood behind his chair, translating the odd Spanish words he used, some of them English terms that he had cannibalized into Spanish. When he pointed to details on the sketch, she would trace over his drawings with her fingers, looking him straight in the eyes, sometimes asking questions to be sure she understood him precisely before she turned back to the others to explain it all in Minorquin.

After a few minutes of her translations, Sinclair motioned toward a chair at another table, asking her why she did not get another glass for herself so she could share the wine. She hesitated and he leaned over to grab the chair, moving himself to the side so there would be room for her at the table. When he turned back, the glances of the men told him he had made a mistake. In Minorca, women waited on men; they did not join them in serious business. How different from Margaret and her demands for independence, he thought.

When Sinclair finished explaining the plan, there was a long moment of silence. He waited for Manolo to speak, but it was another man who asked a question.

''Let me understand, Señor Sinclair,'' he said in slow Spanish. ''You want us to steal the gold to buy airplanes for the Republic?''

Sinclair nodded.

''And you know of a man in Switzerland who will sell such airplanes for the Republic?''

Another nod.

''Why?''

Sinclair responded with a quizzical look.

''Why for Spain? Why would you do this? You are an American.''

Sinclair hesitated, self-conscious about the words he would use, language that suddenly seemed too grand and abstract. ''Spain is where the war against the Fascists must be fought,'' he said. ''The fight here is the beginning of the fight everywhere. And without its own arms, the Republic will lose that fight.''

His words brought smiles of approval around the table, except for Manolo. Without taking his eyes off Sinclair, he reached down to his ankle and drew a knife from a scabbard under his trouser leg. The blade had been ground thin, like a fisherman's knife, and he ran the ball of his thumb over the sides of the blade, twisting it in his hand in a mesmerizingly slow motion. Before long everyone was watching the blade, waiting for the moment when the thumb would caress the edge.

"It is foolish, this plan," he said.

Before Sinclair could answer, Manolo went on. "*You,* American, you do not understand the Spanish. When Napoleon came to Spain, he had been victorious everywhere, against the greatest armies of the world, armies equipped with the finest weapons. And still he was driven from Spain by our guerrillas. This is the kind of fighting we know. We wait for the invader, and from behind the trees and the rocks, we wage a thousand little wars, until even an army with the most modern guns is driven off. To drive out the Fascists will be no different. Their weapons and their airplanes are nothing, because the Spanish know how to die."

"What you say is true," said Sinclair. He had to force himself to take his eyes off the knife in Manolo's hand, and the thumb that slowly caressed the blade. "But what can a guerrilla do against an airplane? The Republic has the men for a great army, but the Fascists have airplanes and Germans to fly them. And against airplanes, your army is defenseless. It's like sending a man with a knife against a man with a gun."

Manolo flashed the blade under his chin. "Knives like this one have killed many men with guns."

Sinclair started to answer, but Manolo waved him silent with the knife. "Tell me," he said. "Have you seen Majorca since the Fascists have come? Have you seen what they do to the people?" He paused to hear the sympathetic sighs of the others at the table. "We do not like the Majorcans. They are rich and we are poor, and they govern us with no feeling for our island except contempt. But now we must forget our feelings for the Majorcans because what is happening on their island could also happen on our island."

Every eye at the table turned to Manolo, ignoring even the knife in his hand as his eyes mirrored the poetic tone of sadness that Spaniards seem to reserve for talk about death.

"It is no longer Spaniard against Spaniard," he went on. "Now on Majorca there is a Blackshirt from Italy, a terrible man with a beard like coal and a chest like a barrel who calls himself General Count Aldo Rossi. His real name is Arconovaldo Bonacorse, and he is no more a count than I am the king of

France, but under his orders, and with the Blackshirts giving courage to the Fascist cowards on the island, they have begun the massacres. Anyone who is denounced is shot. I have seen it. Every evening, on the Ramblas in Palma, the trucks come, big gray trucks. They go out into the countryside when the men are still coming in from the fields, with their shirts still clinging to their backs from the sweat of the day, meet them at the gates of their houses, while their dinners are still waiting on the stoves inside. Then, in the fields outside Palma they line the men up in even rows, to make the work of the gravediggers easier. They shoot them with no ceremony, not even words. Tell me, Señor Sinclair, what will your great plan do for these men? How will your plan help the peasants to defend themselves against these Fascists? No, I say that to use precious petrol for anything except more runs to Majorca with guns would be a crime against the people."

"It's true," said Sinclair. "And this killing will happen all over Spain. I too have seen such killing. Have you seen what happens when airplanes are turned against the peasants? In Majorca, the airplanes of the Italians have perhaps bombed the ships, or the installations in the harbor. But in Ethiopia . . ."

He saw the puzzled look on Pedrito's face and explained, giving his voice the same flat emotion he'd heard in Manolo's words. ". . . in Ethiopia, in Africa, the Italians sent their airplanes against the villagers. The planes would come in low, with their machine guns spewing out bullets. Sometimes the Ethiopian soldiers would mount their horses, and with their pitiful swords and spears, they would charge the airplanes. To an airplane, a man with a rifle is no different from a man on a horse with a sword. The planes fly so low that you can see the faces of the pilots with their leather helmets. They seem to smile as they come over the village and let loose their bombs, like seeds thrown into a furrow on the ground. Everything in their path is blown into tiny pieces. The bombs do not distinguish between soldiers and civilians, or between women and men. Babies are torn from the arms of their mothers by the force of the blasts. Legs and arms and heads fly up into the air. And all the while, the machine guns on the airplanes search out those who try to flee the bombs. Sometimes they wait before firing, letting those who would escape run until they almost drop from exhaustion. And then, with a single burst from the machine guns, they cut them down. The dust does not even clear from the first attack when the next wave of airplanes comes in. And when they finally leave, there are only craters where there was once a village. The dogs and vultures are all that is left.

"Against these airplanes there is only one defense, and that is more airplanes. The Nationalists will have airplanes from the Italians and the Germans to attack the villages, just as the Italians attacked the villages in Ethiopia. And if the Republic does not have airplanes of its own, the fate of the Spanish villages will be the same as the fate of the Ethiopians."

"What about the Russians?" said Manolo. "The Russians have airplanes."

"*Russian* airplanes," answered Sinclair. "With *Russian* pilots. The Russians are no different from the Germans and the Italians. All of them will use Spain as a battlefield, a place where they can practice the techniques of war. It's easy for them because Spanish will do the dying. As you said, the Spanish are good at dying. But to fight and win its own war, the Republic needs its *own* airplanes. That's what the politicians will not understand."

There was a long silence when Sinclair finished. Manolo picked at his fingernails with the blade of the knife, his fingers moving delicately for a man built so powerfully. The men around the table stared at him, waiting. He was their leader.

Sinclair turned his gaze away from Manolo, worried about the answer that would come like a verdict. For an excrutiatingly long moment he found himself staring at Montserrat. The animation in her eyes when she had been translating his thoughts had given way to a serene calm, a gaze so open that he found returning her look almost painful. He'd often fantasized a girl like Montserrat, the undiscovered woman, a beauty that had not been corrupted by fashion and makeup, a mind uncontaminated by modern ideas, a girl ready to give anything to a man. It had never really occurred to him that there *were* such women, that he would ever meet one. As he stared at the glistening black hair and the wide, dark eyes that suddenly looked down when she realized that he had caught her gaze, he pictured himself as she would see him—a foreigner, a soldier of fortune, a freedom fighter. He enjoyed the image enough to forget for a moment that he was waiting for the answer of the man at the other end of the table.

Twenty-Three

It was the first day in fourteen years that he had not shown up for work, but no one missed the chief clerk of the reserve section of the Bank of Spain. He had always kept to himself, working alone in his cloistered wrought-iron cage, going off by himself during the siesta break. No one ever saw the results of his labors except during the monthly audit reviews, or on the rare occasions when Señor Ortega Lupe de Cortelos, the managing director of the reserve section, gave up his usual pursuits of horses and women to make an appearance at the bank.

Had it not been for the meeting, the absence of the clerk would not have been noticed even on the second day. At noon, Señor Ortega was meeting with senior officials of the bank and representatives of the government of the Republic to discuss the forthcoming shipment of gold. A senior naval officer asked Señor Ortega exactly what proportion of the reserves was in coins, and finding that he did not have the answer ready at hand, Señor Ortega ordered a porter to bring the chief clerk to him.

"I'm sorry," said the porter when he returned. "He is not in the bank."

"What do you mean?" Señor Ortega turned red with rage. "He has never missed a day of work in over a dozen years. He is the most reliable man in the entire staff of the bank. Go back at once and bring him to me."

"Sir," said the porter, tugging at his short gray jacket, "the clerk is not here today. No one remembers seeing him yesterday either. Perhaps he is ill."

Señor Ortega felt the eyes of the others in the room, and he stiffened with embarrassment. How could a managing director not even know that his chief clerk was absent?

"Report this matter immediately," he said to the porter. "And have a man sent to investigate at the home of the clerk." He reached down and scrawled out a note. "I want a report made to me directly."

"Is this a problem?" The voice was Gregory Orlov, ostensibly the representative of the Moscow State Bank, but actually, as the Spanish officials knew well, an agent of the NKVD, representing the People's Commissariat for International Affairs. Orlov had been silent during their earlier meetings, and the sudden question was unsettling to the Spanish officials.

"He is nothing," assured Señor Ortega. "Only a clerk."

"Does he know anything of the plans?" asked Orlov.

"Of course not. He is only a clerk, in charge of the ledgers in the reserve section. He knows nothing at all." Señor Ortega nervously wiped the sweat beads off his forehead with a handkerchief from his breast pocket, then glanced down at the sheets of paper in front of him to conceal the distress that colored his cheeks bright red against his bushy sideburns.

"If we can go on," said the naval officer, "I think we should review the logistics for the transfer."

Every eye in the room was on Gregory Orlov as the officer continued his peroration. "There are one hundred fifty trucks that have been commandeered for our use, divided into three convoys of fifty trucks each. The first convoy has already departed, following the main road to . . ."

He walked over to an easel-mounted map, using a long wooden pointer to trace the route, lingering dramatically at the road junctions before it went down to Valencia on the coast.

"Valencia?" said an official from the Ministry for Foreign Affairs. "But our shipment is to be from Cartagena."

Heads around the table anxiously nodded in agreement.

"Precisely," said the naval officer. "The trucks in the first convoy are empty. A decoy."

"Excellent . . . very clever . . ." mumbled voices across the table. Orlov did not look up from his papers.

"Then at midnight," the naval officer went on, "the main convoy will depart for Cartagena in two groups of fifty trucks each. Every truck will carry four heavily armed men in addition to the driver and a relief driver. After every fifth truck, there will be an armored car with a machine gun."

The naval officer turned to Orlov, waiting for his comment.

Orlov glanced at the map, then turned again to Señor Ortega, who was still digging in his documents.

"This clerk who is missing," said Orlov, "he is not privy to the details of the shipment?"

"Comrade Orlov!" said the naval officer. "The only person outside this room who is aware of these plans is Señor Indalecio

Prieto, the minister of the navy. Even the officers who will be in charge of the escort convoy to Cartagena, and the companies of seamen who will be loading the cargo, know nothing of these plans. Our security in this matter is inviolable.''

"*Inviolable?*" repeated Orlov. "An interesting choice of words. How very Spanish of you to speak of your plan as if it were a woman."

No one in the room seemed sure whether to laugh or not.

Twenty-Four

Pedrito's tiny, double-ended fishing boat looked like the sort of craft Arab fishermen and traders might have used to visit Minorca a thousand years before. High bow and stern posts gave an exaggerated sheer line to the white lapstrake topsides, and a colorful talisman was painted on the bow to ward off any evil eye that might threaten catches of fish. There were no seats, only a cambered deck with removable hatches that could be lifted for access to the storage space below. When Pedrito saw Sinclair looking at the hatch covers, he grinned. "For fish," he said, "or sometimes guns."

The steep sides of the harbor at Ciudadela gave the feeling of a fiord, except that the passage was serpentine, turning and twisting back and forth in switchbacks. Tacking out in a sailboat would have been a nightmare, but it was an ideal defensive position. A few men with rifles on the banks could have held off almost any boat that tried to come up the channel. Like the great harbor at Mahón, it did much to explain the insularity of the Minorcans.

When they reached the open water of the bay, Pedrito hoisted the simple lateen-rigged sail, brown and patched with age, the Egyptian cotton resewn so many times that the seams were perforated like used telegraph tape. Broad-reaching, with the sail swung out to one side, they looked even more like a miniature Arab trader.

"Watch for an elephant," said Pedrito when he saw Sinclair staring at the moonlit rocky shore.

Sure he had misunderstood, Sinclair didn't ask Pedrito to explain. An elephant was no more likely on that barren landscape than a polar bear. Yet there was an incredible beauty in the cool colors—the antiseptic glare of the moonlight, the blue-white reflections on the sea, the shadows of the pine trees nestled in sheltered pockets among the cliffs. It was the beauty of a virgin coast, of an island never subjugated or tutored in ways other than its own, even as it was invaded by Arabs and Greeks, Italians and French, English and Americans; an island that could go on catching its fish, making its cheese, and drinking its gin, secure in the isolation that kept it poor enough to be left untouched even by the civil war. Sinclair thought of Montserrat. How like her the island was, how peaceful and . . . content?

"There!" said Pedrito, shattering Sinclair's reverie. He pointed high on the cliffs to a natural stone figure. In the eerie moonlight it did look like an elephant, a great bull proclaiming his lordship of all around him. "It is called Cala Morell," said Pedrito. "The most beautiful cove on our island, and therefore in the world."

He furled the sail and restarted the engine to drive through the breaking surf at the mouth of the cove. What had appeared from offshore a desolate stretch of rocky cliff opened up into a sheltered cove, protected on all sides from even the strong northerly breeze. The water inside was flat calm as they tied up between a cork mooring buoy and a line fastened to an iron pin in the rocks ashore.

They climbed the hillside to an isolated cottage with an unkept field behind and a rutted dirt road in front that seemed to lead in the direction of Ciudadela. Sinclair paused at the top of the hill to look at the breathtaking view over the cove, past the moonlight-streaked black water, to the elephant guarding the entrance. When he looked up, he saw Pedrito smiling at him. "You see, Señor Sinclair? It *is* the most beautiful place in all the world."

Yellow light glowed in the windows of the cottage, and inside they found Montserrat sitting at the round wooden table, reading by the light of a kerosene lamp. The walls were scrubbed, but in need of whitewashing, and the tile floors were chipped and cracked. The furniture was heavy, simple, ageless. It was a humble house.

As the two men came in, Montserrat quickly closed her books and cleared them off the table. Sinclair saw only a single title as she moved the stack to a shelf in the corner of the room, a worn guidebook to Paris, the pages falling out from too many readings. From the photograph on the cover, it looked at least twenty years old.

"You see?" said Pedrito. "It's as I told you. She dreams of nothing but France. They say that when a woman learns to read she will never be happy again. Do you believe that, Señor Sinclair?" He was oblivious to the crimson blush his words had prompted on his sister's face, and the embarrassed smile that hid her feelings.

"But she's a good woman," he added, "and beautiful, no? She could make a fine wife, but she's interested only in the books, instead of men."

She was beautiful. Her skin was rich and deep, almost sienna in the yellow glow of the kerosene lamp. Her eyes were dark green, the color of olives. She dressed in the black of an older woman, but Sinclair guessed that she was about twenty years old. Only a brooding depth in her eyes made him unsure whether to think of her as a girl or a woman.

Pedrito insisted that Sinclair take his own bed, as he had insisted that Sinclair sleep in his house. He would be comfortable on the pallet in the big room, insisted Pedrito, and after giving Sinclair another glass of gin, this time from a brown crock that was kept on a shelf near the dining table, he pointed the way to the bedroom, shut off by a heavy planked door with iron hardware.

A heavy woolen curtain hung across the bedroom on an iron rod, dividing the already small room into two alcoves. Sinclair's own alcove was barely large enough to turn around in but managed to include a sturdy wooden bed frame, a chair, and a tiny bureau. On top of the bureau there was a towel, a bar of soap, and a bowl and pitcher of water. Someone had carefully prepared the room for him.

A mirror hung on one wall, next to the window. Over the bureau was a crucifix and a framed photograph of an older couple, posed rigidly facing the camera. Sinclair glanced at the couple, then stared at himself in the mirror, confirming what his aching muscles had already hinted. He was tired to the bone. His normally trim beard was overgrown on his cheeks and throat, his hair was filthy, his eyes bloodshot and baggy, and after two days without washing, his clothes and body were rank and gamy. He undressed, poured water from the brightly colored pitcher into the bowl and lathered himself, feeling the grittiness of the soap

and rubbing roughly until he felt clean and raw. He toweled off
and lay back upon the bed, naked on the coarse blanket. After a
few minutes he snuffed out the lamp, and in the moonlight
through the high window, he could see the gleaming enamel of
the crucifix. The close, plain room had the feel of a monastic
cell.

It was so quiet that for a long time he concentrated on
listening to his own heartbeats, until he heard a rhythmic sound
from the other side of the curtain. He looked toward the curtain
and saw that it was actually two curtains pulled together with an
overlap. At the point where they joined there was a slit, slightly
open from where he sat. He saw a glint of movement through the
slit, then froze.

When his eyes adjusted to the dimness, he could just make out
the shining highlights of a woman's hair, gleaming against the
blackness as a brush moved languidly down, again and again,
like a little girl counting the strokes. He wondered: were the
dreams of a Minorcan girl who already wore the black shift of an
old woman any different from the dreams of rich little girls in
lacy white summer dresses of eyelet cotton, with sashes of satin?
Little girl? In any society except the overcivilized, Montserrat
was a woman, and had been for at least five years.

When she suddenly stopped he thought for an instant that she
had sensed or seen him. She stood slowly, her movements
graceful and feline as she turned to face the wall under the
windows, the wall where a mirror was hung in his side of the
alcove, and presumably, in hers. As she stood there, her shoulders back and her legs poised, she was no longer a little girl. Her
skin was soft and supple in the dim light, and the brushed hair
gleamed with sparkling highlights. Her eyes and mouth had the
maturity of a woman, and her pose was without a trace of
awkwardness or embarrassment.

Holding her body erect, she reached behind herself and unbuttoned the shift, then with the slightest wriggle of her shoulders
and hips, she let it fall to the floor at her feet, stepping out of it
with slow, deliberate movements. Her body was lean and young,
subtly rounded at the hips, the legs lithe, the breasts rising in soft
globes, promising a fullness that would soon follow. As she
stood, she arched her back, letting her hands glide slowly down
her sides to her waist, the fingers tracing tenderly along the
smooth skin. She lifted the edges of the worn and patched cotton
panties, then slipped them down her legs, raising her knees and
pointing her toes as she slipped them off. She wore nothing else.

Naked, she turned her body slightly, and he could just glimpse the expression on her face, a dreamy wistful gaze that hinted of Paris and silk gowns and perfume. Her fingers slid down her sides, lingering on the skin as she undulated against the hands. Her body responded to the touch of her fingers, swaying gently like a reed in a zephyr of breeze and he could almost feel the goosebumps on her skin, until he realized that it was the tumescence of his own flesh that he sensed so vividly.

He looked away, embarrassed by the unrequited intimacy. As his eyes focused on the heavy wooden door, he thought of Pedrito, asleep on the simple pallet in the other room. An image of Margaret flitted through his mind, running for the train in Union Station in San Francisco. She turned and waved, as if he were one more old friend seeing her off. Nothing else was left.

He turned back to the curtain and saw Montserrat sitting on the edge of the bed, lifting one leg, then the other as she stretched out on the rough wool blanket. When she lay back, he could no longer see her face, only the lean body, one knee lifted slightly, the young breasts flattened. He watched her fingers glide over the supple skin, slowly fondling her breasts as if she were discovering their sensations for the first time, tracing the aureoles of the nipples until they stood erect like ripe *fraises des bois*. The fingers of one hand slipped teasingly over her flat tummy, tracing lightly over the skin and leaving silky tracks in the fine sweat, until the fingertips just disappeared over her lifted thigh.

He watched the heel of her hand rise and fall, the rhythm gentle and slow and sensuous like the brushstrokes in her hair. The other hand caressed the nipples, first one then the other, until they stood erect and dark against the skin. Her breathing became coarse and audible, each breath distinct in a rhythm that seemed to mimic her hand. Then he realized that it was also his own breathing he was hearing, that he too was pacing the movements of her hand, slowing his breaths as her hand slowed, quickening as she quickened. He could feel his whole body begin to respond to her rhythms—steady, persistent, irresistible. Her hips lifted as she thrust herself against the hand, and her back arched, the muscles suddenly taut as the pace of her hands turned almost frantic. Suddenly her breathing became rapid and throaty. Her back arched higher and the gasping breaths gave way to a muted moan as her body shuddered once, then again, and again, before it finally came to rest.

Sinclair's own body couldn't find the same release. His

muscles were tense, his throat dry, his fingers aching. He looked down at himself and saw his skin covered with sweat. His hands gripped the wooden bedframe so tightly that his knuckles were white, as if he were forcibly holding himself back from bolting through the curtain.

He closed his eyes tightly and turned his head away, trying not to listen as her breathing became more regular and slower, until finally he could no longer hear the individual breaths but only the scarcely perceptible murmur of sleep. Images tumbled in his mind . . . fantasies of himself as a warrior taking a woman on the eve of battle. Yet he knew he couldn't take this woman. As much as he wanted her, a reserve inside him seemed to seize and crush the urge, shifting his mind to a catalogue of reasons, excuses. What if Pedrito discovered? What would become of the plan without Pedrito? His cousin? His men? In the rush of words and reasons, the impulse died. Sinclair was back to words.

He listened hard for Montserrat's breathing again, but there was only the peaceful murmur of sleep. He thought of her dreams of Paris and silk and perfume. As his eyes closed, he pictured her in a long white dress of eyelet cotton, with a flowing satin sash, her hair rustling in a spring breeze. He fell asleep with that image in his mind.

Twenty-Five

For over an hour Whitman watched the moonlight play on the sea swells. The Zeppelin was close to its landfall at Cape Verde, and he was enjoying the solitude of the control room after an unpleasant evening in the passenger lounge.

It had begun shortly after they left Recife, when Nadia Lopez-Otero demanded that the steward seat her at the captain's table for dinner. It was to be expected, her tone insisted; her manner made her notions of rank and privilege amply clear. Just from the way she pronounced the word *airship* the steward knew that the wealthy young woman had conjured up a fantasy of the voyage that had little to do with travel by Zeppelin. She pictured a combination of the breathtaking excitement of flight in an airplane with the luxury of travel at sea, complete with glittering ballrooms, elegant dinners at the captain's table, and captivating conversations with cosmopolitan diplomats and titled nobility. Now, after days of flying, instead of excitement and culture, she had found only the banal prattle and cloying attentions of the Brazilian hustler de Nascimento to listen to, and only the back of her husband's motorcar magazines to stare at. With no hope for relief from the daytime ennui, dinner at the captain's table had become her paramount expectation.

"But this is not a steamship," the steward patiently explained. "The captain cannot dine with the passengers."

"He ate lunch with *her*."

Predictably, the dinner was a disaster. The Señora arrived in a pale pink satin evening gown, daring in its cleavage, suited perhaps to a formal ball on the *Bremen*. Instead of the compliments and admiring stares she anticipated, she was greeted by the other passengers, including the admiral, with looks of dumbfounded astonishment. Whitman arrived after she did, actually because he had to consult with the navigator, but in the Señora's eyes it was a deliberate effort to upstage her. He greeted the other passengers as he came into the lounge, and he spoke to her and her husband not in the cultivated French she expected, but in Spanish, and with a broad American twang.

Everything Whitman did, it seemed, was wrong. She glanced with annoyance at his uniform, as if she expected at least a dinner jacket. She actually seemed put off by his rugged if handsome features, his tousled hair, his failure to wear a hat, and especially his refusal to acknowledge differences of rank among the passengers. He failed to compliment her appearance adequately, knew no one in Montevideo, and nothing about the upcoming seasons in Paris and Rome or the holiday plans of the European aristocracy. Before they were through the first course of jellied consommé, she had run out of conversational gambits and patience. By the time the plates were cleared for the fish course, a deadly silence had fallen over the table.

Her young husband attempted to fill the uncomfortable silence by discussing technical questions about the Graf Zeppelin, but that talk only compounded her disappointment and boredom into anger. She did look up briefly when Whitman, searching for a Spanish word to describe certain aerodynamic shortcomings of the shape of the Graf Zeppelin, said that the actual shape was perhaps too *falico*. Her eyes quickly swung away as she realized that the figure of speech was not the introduction to a risqué if at least tantalizing topic. For the rest of the dinner she paid her husband and Whitman no attention at all, preferring to flicker her eyes at the German who had boarded in Recife, himself no aristocrat, but at least a man who knew how to admire the cleavage of her gown.

It was late when Whitman got back to the welcome solitude of the control room. He stopped to look at the latest plot on the large-scale pilot chart, then went forward to watch for the landfall. They had flown over one thousand miles of open sea, navigating only by dead reckoning, and he couldn't conceal a certain anxiety about the navigator's prediction of the time of landfall.

Celestial navigation with sextant, chronometer, and reduction tables was almost unheard of on the Zeppelins. Whitman's own aircraft sextant, in its fitted wooden case, was a curiosity to the German navigators, who relied instead on a refined system of dead reckoning, keeping track of the position of the airship by plotting its speed and course, and making allowances for surface winds. Periodically, floating acetylene flares were dropped to the ocean surface from a hatch in the chart room, so the bright flame at night and the smoke column in the daytime could be used to calculate the true ground speed of the Zeppelin and the drift or set from its chosen course. Generations of navigators had refined the simple system until they could repeatedly make accurate landfalls after flying over thousands of miles of open water. It had gotten Hugo Eckener safely across the Pacific and the Atlantic, even across the vast frozen reaches of Siberia. No one in Zeppelin service ever questioned it.

But even after he had seen it work in difficult circumstances, Whitman couldn't help wondering what the navigators would do if visibility or wind conditions made it impossible to take bearings off the flares. "Never a problem," he was told. Still, Whitman never flew without his sextant and reduction tables, to the amusement of the navigators.

The tall lighthouse on Cape Verde appeared only three minutes after the time predicted by the navigator. Whitman went back to the chart room to congratulate the man, who acted surprised. It was his job, the smile suggested. Before Whitman left, the navigator was already busy with preparations for another flare drop.

It was past midnight on the ship's chronometer over the chart table as Whitman continued down the corridor toward the passenger lounge. Had someone at that instant asked him why he was going to the lounge, which at that late hour would be almost certainly deserted, he would have probably answered with a shrug and a shy grin. Somehow, with the moonlight bright on the violet-black sea, the evening seemed incomplete, and though weary from a long day, and with a bothersome feeling of social malaise after the awkward dinner with the Lopez-Oteros, he wasn't at all sleepy. If anything, he was flush with the sheer excitement of flying that magnificent aircraft. And while he might never have admitted it, he was also hoping that Maggie Bourne might on an off chance still be in the lounge, ready with one of those raw American expressions that made him feel so deliciously homesick.

He hesitated at the doorway, glanced over at his hat on the rack with the binoculars, then went into the lounge. It was almost deserted. Enkmann and de Nascimento sat at a corner table, deep in conversation. In the opposite corner, at the table that had been the admiral's by day, Maggie Bourne sat with her legs draped over a chair, alternately gazing out the window and down at an open book in her lap.

Enkmann and de Nascimento looked up at Whitman, then without a word returned to their huddle. He took a few more steps, then stopped, not wanting his footfalls to startle Maggie Bourne.

She looked up slowly.

"It's Cape Verde," he said. "We're across the Atlantic, almost back to Africa."

She smiled. "What a difference! I still can't get over it."

He stood over a chair, as if he were just passing through. "What keeps you up so late?"

She gestured at the book in her lap, an unlined notebook filled with neat printing. "I'm trying to write up a journal of my trip on the schooner. Otto Hutten gave me the notebook yesterday, but it's hard to get much written during the day. They're lovely people, the Huttens, salt of the earth—but I think he must be starved for company. His English is so charming that I can't bear discouraging the chatter."

"I suspect one reason for all the talk is apprehension," said Whitman. "They've been away from Germany for a long time."

"It shows." She closed the book and put it on the table, waving toward the chair until Whitman sat down. "Hutten's been reading a novel," she went on, "*The Forty Days of Musa Dagh*, by Franz Werfel. He reads very slowly, and every so often he looks up from the book and describes some horror scene of the Turks butchering the Armenians. Then under his breath he says that if you change the Turks to the Nazis and the Armenians to Jews, it's not a novel. I guess he's really not sure what he'll find in Germany."

She watched Whitman's expression, suddenly serious. His face was drawn, his eyes gray and ringed, the weary fatigue of a man exhausted with worry and work.

"How about a brandy?" she said. "You look like you've had a long day."

"No, thanks. That glass of wine at lunch was enough to set tongues wagging in the crew quarters. In fact, if our friends over there"—he shrugged toward Enkmann and de Nascimento—"hear one word about FDR or baseball or anything else American, I suspect they'll report both of us as dangerous conspirators."

She laughed, the warm spontaneous laugh he remembered from their lunch. Her smile and her warmth were an incredible contrast to Nadia Lopez-Otero and to everything European that Whitman had come to dislike. For the Europeans, smiles were guarded signs, turned on and off deliberately to signal feelings and intentions. Sometimes, the German smiles seemed almost Japanese, a cover for embarrassment. Even laughter, except among the closest of friends, was controlled, measured in doses as politeness required. The American notion of easy spontaneous laughter, or an open smile that said *I feel friendly*, was unknown to the Germans. Maggie Bourne made him feel more relaxed than he'd felt in almost a year.

"Baseball?" she said suddenly, with another flashing grin. "My God. I think I almost forgot about baseball. I haven't seen a score for months."

"You're a baseball fan?"

"Absolutely. *Yankees.*" She clapped her hands together. "You can't imagine what it's like to be back. It all comes to you in a rush, and you suddenly realize how long you've been away. And it's funny what you miss. Amos 'n' Andy. Will Rogers. Kate Smith on the radio with that 'Hello everybody.' FDR and the fireside chats. John L. Lewis with those big bushy eyebrows and that knockout voice. I feel like I've been away for years instead of a few months."

"You're not back yet," he said, his voice cautious, muted. "Believe me, Frankfurt is nothing like New York. They call FDR names you wouldn't believe. No Benny Goodman or Duke Ellington. Clark Gable is a nobody. They don't show W. C. Fields. Even Charlie Chaplin is persona non grata. Too many people were making jokes about a striking resemblance between the Little Tramp and . . . ?" With a quick toss of his eyes in the direction of Enkmann and de Nascimento, he didn't finish the sentence.

"Chaplin? He *does* look like those photographs of Hitler." Her voice saddened. "For some reason, Chaplin makes me think of what's wrong with the States, the things that really got to me before I left. Out on the Coast everyone was talking about the new film Chaplin is making, a silent about workers and assembly lines. *Modern Times,* I think it's called. Before it was even released, some of the critics, probably goaded on by old William Randolph himself, were saying that it was pink. What frightens me is that panic reaction. I did some photographs in the migrant camps in California, workers who were escaping from the dust bowl. Every time a few of them got together to demand enough pay to live on, the papers would call it communism."

Whitman leaned forward on his chairback, looking straight at her as he lowered his voice.

"You might be in for a shock when you see Germany," he said. "I've stopped following the politics. I can't stand reading the newspapers, and from Friedrichshafen, even from Frankfurt, it's not the same as being in Berlin. But the country has a feeling that's not like anything I've ever seen before."

"You sound almost like Otto Hutten, which is pretty strange when you're wearing that uniform, and serving as commander of this."

"I'm uneasy. Look, German comes as easily to me as English, and there are people in Germany who are very special to me, like the people who built this ship and the men who fly it. Or the Huttens. To me they're the real Germany. It's just that there's another Germany now, and it's changing faster than I can follow, or want to follow . . ."

"What will happen to you?" she asked. "I gather from that blowup in Recife that you're in hot water."

Whitman shrugged. "Who knows? In the Germany I left there would have been no questions about our detour. If anything, they would have given the crew medals, which is exactly what they deserve for the way they handled this machine. Not just Jürgen Steinbrenner, the rigger who fell . . . but all of them."

"I assumed that he and the admiral and you would be heroes."

"I'm afraid that right now, all bets are off," he said.

"Worried?"

"About myself, no. The worst they can do to me is send me home. But yes, I guess I am worried. About Germany. The New Germany could be the end of this"—his eyes roved around the ship—"and everything it means. There was a time, during the

World War, when the Zeppelins meant death and destruction.
The Germans were bombing English cities, and the English press
equated the bombing with the rape of Belgian nuns. Now, eight
years of peacetime flights have shown that the Zeppelins can
mean something else to the world. They've earned a reputation
for reliability and elegance and economy. They mean peace
instead of war. What worries me is that the New Germany
doesn't care much about that tradition."

Whitman talked easily. Maggie was a good listener, and he felt
relaxed without the automatic restraints that instinctively cen-
sored his thoughts and speech in German. Ever since he had
come to Germany, he realized, he'd been walking on eggshells,
treading lightly on questions of politics and authority and even
the future.

"What happens to a man like the admiral?" she asked. "If
anyone is the old Germany, he is. I've never met anyone like
him. Aristocratic, haughty, pompous actually. But underneath, I
have the feeling that he's special, a fine and generous man."

"He's one of the great heroes of Germany," said Whitman.
"That medal he wears around his neck is the Pour le Mérite,
roughly their Congressional Medal of Honor. It's not given
routinely."

"It doesn't surprise me. Dangling off that bosun's chair was
more than enough for a medal. He's hardly a kid. With men like
him around, one can at least hope that the good Germany will
come out on top."

"I wish you were right, but unfortunately, it's not men like the
admiral who . . ." Whitman caught himself in midsentence, suddenly aware that he had gone too far, at least for talk in the
lounge of the Graf Zeppelin. "I think maybe we're getting too
serious," he said.

She smiled mischievously.

"About politics," he added, and her smile broke into open
laughter.

"How long do you plan to stay in Germany?" he asked, after
his glance toward Enkmann and de Nascimento sobered both of
them.

"I haven't got a single plan beyond a hot bath. I'm not much
on planning these days, which may be why I end up on sinking
schooners in the middle of the South Atlantic. There should be
enough money waiting for me in Frankfurt to repay you and to
buy a ticket to New York. Beyond that, I have no schedule and
no obligations. And for me, that's a delicious situation to be in,

at least until the money runs out. For the first time in a long
while I feel really footloose and fancy free.''

There was a delightful combination of control and abandon in
the way she talked, a sense of a woman in command of herself
and her feelings. Without realizing quite how or when, Whitman
found himself thinking how special she was, a woman of striking
independence and self-confidence who could still laugh and
smile without a trace of guile.

"How about seeing some of Germany?" he asked, amazed
even as he said it that she had made him temporarily forget the
responsibility of his rank. He went on before his own reaction
took hold. "If you're really a baseball fan, I think I might be
able to wangle some tickets to the exhibition game they are
staging at the Olympics. Two amateur teams I've never heard of.
They're probably terrible, but I'd guess that watching German
fans at a baseball game might be worth the price of admission.''

"Olympics? I'd almost forgotten. There were no newspapers
in the jungle. I guess the Germans will put on a real spectacle,
won't they?''

"It's the one thing they're very good at. I'm just hoping that
the American team will put on its own spectacle. That could top
anything the Germans come up with. I've heard that watching
Jesse Owens run is a spectacle all by itself. He's supposedly so
light-footed that you can only see his feet coming off the track,
never setting down. And the rest of the squad looks pretty
strong.''

Maggie leaned forward. "The Olympics. If I could get hold of
a camera, that'd be spectacular.''

"You'll have competition.''

She queried with her eyebrows.

"Leni Riefenstahl, the woman who did that film of the
Nuremberg Party Rally, *Triumph of the Will*——she's going to
have carte blanche at the Games. She'll probably have thirty
cameras going at once. They're even arranging to have the
Hindenberg fly over when the light is right for her cameras.''

"I don't think she'll mind my taking a few snapshots. If they
let an American command their prize Zeppelin, I can't imagine
any trouble for a woman who just wants to snap a few photographs of beautiful bodies on an athletic field. Were you going to
the Olympics anyway?''

"Yes. At least part of them. My kid brother is on the
American team.''

"Really?" Her eyes shot up in amazement. "What event?''

"I was surprised too. He's on the sailing team, crewing on the Six Meters. He's a terrific sailor, the two of us used to do pretty well in the Star class, but I don't think he's sailed a Six Meter more than twice, at least not that I know about. But then he's a pretty enterprising kid. All his letter said was that he was coming to Germany to try out the beer and the Fräuleins."

"You're close to him?"

"Yes and no. We're ten years apart in age. A long time ago we decided that one of us was a mistake, and ever since we have kidded about which one it was. We always did a lot together, especially sailing, but my father died when Henry was only thirteen, so I have had to be something between a big brother and a father to Henry. I think you'd like him."

"I'm sure I would. Baseball, Jesse Owens, your own brother sailing . . . it sounds too good to resist. I'd love to go. Where do I buy a ticket?"

For an instant, the Zeppelin, the hearing, Goering, Germany—all seemed miles away. He was alone with a splendid woman. "The tickets, I'm afraid, will mean some poking in the black market, or using influence, if I still have any after fraternizing with the passengers on the Graf Zeppelin."

She grinned, winked. "Okay, Captain, I get the hint. You want us to be hush-hush. I'll do my best." She extended her hand, shaking his formally and adding in a loud voice, "Thank you for telling me about the islands, Captain. It was very interesting."

"My pleasure, Miss Bourne."

She winked again and added in a low whisper, "It really does feel good to be back. Thanks."

Twenty-Six

Orlov was in the midst of his breakfast when the police report was brought to his suite. At first glance it looked like an entry in a penmanship contest, written in precise flowery script on unlined parchment-like paper, ornate initial uppercase letters like an illuminated manuscript, not a single letter crossed out or corrected. The entire report comprised one long paragraph, which managed to include the name of the deceased clerk four times, writing out all of his Christian names so each entry consumed an entire line. The name of the *sereno*, the ubiquitous concierge who stood guard day and night at most Spanish apartment buildings, was repeated twice, as was the name of the police officer who had filed the report. Even the scribe who had penned the masterpiece had managed to get a full mention. When all the names and the florid boilerplate were taken out of the paragraph, there was nothing left. The bank clerk, concluded the report, was killed by unknown assailants in the course of a robbery.

Orlov read through the report quickly and threw it down on the table. He knew it wasn't true. He had already visited the apartment building, walked to the flat after leaving his car and driver two blocks away on the Calle Serano. Most of the private vehicles in Madrid had already been commandeered to help transport militia to the front a few miles away. Orlov and a few high government officials were almost the only ones with private cars, and he knew he would attract attention in a residential neighborhood

The building was shabby, a worn remnant in a once fashionable section of the city, the kind of apartment building where urban *hidalgos* trying to hold onto the dignity of their empty titles found cheap but respectable rooms. Harmless people, thought Orlov. And doomed. When the revolution came, they would disappear, as the poor Whites had disappeared in the USSR. And of one thing Orlov was certain: no one who lived in that building was likely to be the victim of a robber. What fool would attack one of these humble *poseurs* when it was so easy to prey upon the truly wealthy, the hapless rich who had not yet fled the city? The rich were easy marks now, careless about their possessions and their money as they frantically sought an escape from the Republic to the safety of Andalusia or Argentina. A robber would know exactly where to find those who had not yet fled, locked behind drawn shutters in the wealthy quarters, afraid to go out because the Republic was too busy with a civil war to protect personal wealth.

He glanced at the police report with disgust. It was like everything the Spanish did—all style and appearance, like the showy but concealing movements of a matador. It was the same with the plans they had made for the shipment of the gold—all secrecy and charade with no real concern for security. The decoy convoy, the talk of inviolable security—it was all only an effort to make sure that no one would find out that the gold of Spain was being shipped out of the country, as if the possession of those bars of yellow metal would somehow make this pitiful country great and powerful. The plan was the desperate move of politicians anxious to save their own necks, afraid that anything they did could someday backfire in their faces.

Theoretically, Spain was an exciting post for an NKVD agent. Although most of the nation was not yet industrialized enough to follow the orthodox Marxist pattern, the political and social situation was close to Russia before the great Bolshevik Revolution: a growing urban class, a semifeudal landholding structure in the countryside, strong regional rivalries that divided city and country from one another. The Nationalist uprising, like the civil war in Russia, was the opportunity for the triumph of a revolution. But until the Fascists were defeated, Orlov had to work with the Spanish bourgeois politicians and their endless petty pride, the kind of pride that would cover up even the strange circumstances of the death of a bank clerk.

He shuddered with a twinge of fear, a fleeting memory of names he had almost forgotten, names of those who had been purged because of failures. What if the clerk knew too much? Talked too much? It could make shambles of the idiotic *inviolable* security of the bungling Spanish. The ultimate responsibility for the shipment was Orlov's, and it was he who would pay if that gold did not reach the Soviet Union intact. He knew exactly what the payment would be: *oblivion*.

He caught hold of his fear and glanced again at the trite prose of the report. This time something caught his eye. The *sereno*, according to the report, had said that two men left the apartment building not long after the clerk came in that day, and that they were both foreigners. Orlov was not surprised. Foreigners were accused of everything in Madrid. Fear of revolution and civil war had made the city nervous, and with foreigners pouring into the city from all over Europe and America, they were the logical scapegoats. The *sereno* had gone on to say that one man was almost certainly German, and the other a Catalan, or perhaps from the Balearics.

. . . *or perhaps from the Balearics*. Why would the *sereno* add that? The language of the Balearic Islands, Orlov knew, was similar to Catalan, but with subtle differences of pronunciation and vocabulary. Enough differences to be obvious to someone who knew either. And the very fact that the *sereno* suggested the possibility of the Balearics made Orlov wonder. It was like identifying a speaker as a Ukrainian, *or perhaps from Odessa.* Why mention Odessa at all unless the characteristic speech patterns of the city were obvious in the speaker's Ukrainian?

But it made no sense for a German to be with someone from the Balearics. The Germans had their strong points in the north and west of Spain, not in the Balearics. The islands were in the Italian zone of influence, occupied by Italians, defended with Italian airplanes. In any case, Orlov guessed that the German wasn't a Nazi. There were dozens of German agents in Madrid— he had lists of most of them in his files—but it wasn't the German style to act so crudely.

He thought for a minute, then glanced at the map of Spain on the wall of the sitting room that had been converted to an office. The map was covered with pins and lines that traced the shifting front in the West. He had never paid any attention to the Balearics, but one of his political officers had duly drawn a heavy black line around the biggest of the islands, Majorca, to signify the Italian occupation. Ibiza, to the southwest of Majorca, was also outlined in black. To the northeast, so far away that it looked as much a part of France as of Spain, was another island, this one without a black line. *Minorca.* He knew little about it, except that the Republican navy had made no plans for the defense of the island because they assumed that the Nationalists would never risk an attack on a harbor like Mahón with less than a full battle fleet. And the island wasn't worth that kind of effort to the Nationalists.

But on the map the island suddenly took on a very different aspect. Securely astride the sealanes from Spain to France, safely in Republican hands, a rumored haven for smugglers. And quiet. Quiet enough to be a safe haven. Quiet enough to be unnoticed.

But how did a German fit in? It made no sense. The German agents in Madrid were incredibly ineffective, concentrating all their energies on military intelligence when in fact the Republic had no real military plans. Stupidly, with blind faith in Franco, the Germans ignored the political situation, the economy, the development of consciousness among the masses. And they knew nothing of the true situation of the Republic. They would never have suspected the gold shipment, and they would never have sent someone who could be recognized as a German.

But whom did that leave?

Orlov glanced at his files, accordion-pleated folders filled with dossiers, a matchless collection he had built up in his years as a political officer and brought to Spain as his private tool.

He skipped quickly through some of the files. The Anarchists might kill a clerk, but they would be more likely to blow up the bank building itself. The Trotskyites would attack Gaylords, or the offices of the Russian liaison mission. The only reason someone would single out that clerk would be a suspicion that something had been planned for the gold. And the only hints of that kind of suspicion had been scattered rumors in the obscure hectographed flysheets of the so-called anti-Stalinist Left.

He flicked through his files and pulled out the folder he was looking for, then thumbed through the dossiers inside. Martine, Torrado, Grimaldi, Sinclair, Kruger—all self-proclaimed anti-Stalinists, all traitors and parasites, would be hangers-on of the splinter parties. As journalists they had written streams of hateful articles questioning the motives of Soviet policy, articles that were worse even than the slanders that poured out of Josef Goebbels's propaganda machine. No one else had ever mentioned the gold reserves of Spain in print.

But not one of them would have the nerve for action. They were quibblers, typewriter revolutionaries, led by the coward of cowards, David Sinclair, a man who had abused the hospitality of the Soviet Union by writing the most calumnious lies after touring the country for only two months.

Orlov sighed as he put the police report back into its string-closed envelope. He was sure that he knew why the clerk was killed. Sensationalist journalists looking for a story, hoping to discredit the USSR. They had pumped the man to find out what he knew, and he probably knew very little, just enough to give them grist for their rumor mills. With a little effort, Agitprop could send their stories into oblivion. The Spanish would never admit the gold shipment, and without evidence the journalists would convince no one of their speculative stories.

He started to close the files, but something still nagged at him. Something that didn't fit. They didn't just ask questions of the clerk. They *killed* him, beat him to death. Why? These journalist parasites were not the kind of men who would kill, not even for a story that could embarrass the Soviet Union.

Orlov picked up the dossiers again and started to read them, one at a time, looking for any hint that might tell him who, and why.

Twenty-Seven

"It seems too easy, Sinclair," Manolo spoke without looking at the other man. "No Italian patrols the whole way across. The fuel waiting in St. Lucia. Getting inside the gates of the fortress. It is as if they were expecting us."

Sinclair glanced over, unsure how to answer. It *had* been easy. They had departed from the Cala at twilight, crossing hundreds of miles of open water at night, the powerful gasoline engines of Manolo's boat throbbing in a steady, droning rhythm as the boat rode up and over the six-foot seas.

The preparations had taken a whole day. Sinclair watched the men fuel the boat and clean the rifles and pistols. He wanted to help, but he had no idea how to handle the heavy barrels of petrol or how to strip and clean a weapon. He felt like an outsider.

Montserrat had brought them dinner from the cafe—a heavy crock of fish soup, bread, cheese—and they had eaten and drunk heartily before they went down to the boat for a long siesta. Sinclair wanted to join them, but as much as he wanted to be another warrior, to drink heavily before battle as they did, he was afraid that his stomach could not take the crossing after drinking. And he knew that excitement and apprehension would make sleep impossible. Instead, he climbed the hillside behind the cove, up to a flat shelf of rock, sheltered by an overhanging so that it looked like a canopied terrace. In the center was a prehistoric stone table monument like those he had seen on the road from Mahón to Ciudadela, and against the back wall someone had piled straw to make a pallet. The view was spectacular, taking in the whole cove, across to the narrow entrance where the surf crashed against the rocky cliffs. The elephant was silhouetted against the sunset, standing alone, guarding its private preserve. The water in the cove was so clear that Manolo's boat seemed suspended in air. The gray hull looked like another workboat, rust streaks around the cleats and

155

hawsepipes, with no hint of the powerful engines below. Yet knowing about the men and the cache of arms inside, Sinclair felt like an admiral about to order his fleet into battle. It was a feeling he had never known. For the first time, he was not watching or reporting, but *doing,* leading. He was in command, of men and himself. And Margaret was right: it felt good.

He heard a pebble roll down the slope behind him, turned, and saw Montserrat climbing down to where he stood. When she saw him, she lowered her gaze, glancing up again only when he extended his hand as she reached the shelf.

"Señor Sinclair." Her voice was delicate, unsure. "It's very beautiful here, isn't it?"

He nodded.

"They say these *taulas* were built thousands of years before the birth of Christ. I like to think that the men who built them also came here for the beauty."

"Yes," he said, looking directly at her. Her hair flowed behind her in the gentle breeze, and her skin was aglow with the honey colors of the reflected sunset.

"You will be leaving soon," she said.

"Yes." He glanced at his watch. "In an hour."

"Will you come back?"

He didn't answer, sensing the fragility of the moment.

"Last night," she said, her eyes returning his gaze for only a moment before they dropped away again. "Last night, I saw you."

He blushed full crimson, turning from her, embarrassed to acknowledge his voyeurism.

She went on. "When I lay down on my bed to sleep and closed my eyes, I saw you. In a dream. I know it's only foolishness, Señor Sinclair, but I dreamed that after you and Pedrito and Manolo did this, you came back to Minorca, and we talked of France and Switzerland and the places you will go. It's the south of France where you will go first, is it not? I have read that it is where all the finest people go for holidays. I know it was only a silly dream, but...."

He reached over and took her shoulders in his hands, turning her toward him before he gently lifted her chin with his fingertips.

"It's not silly at all. Nothing in France or Switzerland compares with the beauty of this. A man could be very happy here." Looking at the delicate, simple beauty of the girl, he thought how very true his words were. He could picture himself there, away from the whirl and the demands, the guiles and the sophistication. With a woman like Montserrat, a house like Pedrito's, a kerosene lamp, a stack of paper. In a place like that, he wouldn't even need a typewriter. Words would flow from a pen. And if they didn't flow, she would be there, always, to soothe and comfort.

"I will come back," he said.

Her lips were parted as he kissed her, but even as he felt the supple fullness of her mouth, he knew she had never really been kissed by another man. She was like the island—pure, unspoiled beauty. Her eyes came up to his, then stopped, fixed over his shoulder. When he turned, Pedrito and the others were already busy on the deck of the boat, making last-minute preparations for the departure.

They said nothing more, and as he walked down to the boat, he never looked back. But he walked self-consciously, aware of his bearing and the swagger of his steps because he knew her eyes were on him. And all the way to Cartagena, even as the boat pounded and pitched over the seas and the engines throbbed in his ears, he couldn't get her out of his mind.

Now, it was the eyes of the others that were on him. It was an awkward moment, when the command of the mission was floating between Manolo and Sinclair. In Minorca and on the water, Manolo had been indisputably in charge. His boat, his fuel, his navigation, his seamanship had gotten them safely across to the tiny fishing village of St. Lucia, just outside the entrance to the harbor at Cartagena. The men were accustomed to sailing with Manolo, to his style of terse, barked commands without explanation. But once they left the boat for Cartagena and the naval base, it was Sinclair's plan that gradually became the focus, and without a formal ceremony, the passing of the sword or the new captain reading his orders, the men were unsure where to look for leadership. Each time Manolo or Sinclair spoke, the eyes of the men flicked back and forth, as if they were at a tennis match. And, as much as anyone else, Manolo saw his leadership slipping away.

The harbor in front of them, the old port of Cartagena, was still. Ships bobbed lazily at their moorings, tenders and workboats were lined up at the supply docks. On the inner ring of moorings, closest to the docks, three small freighters of about four or five thousand tons were rafted next to one another. Dark gray ships, almost the color of Manolo's boat, their hailing ports obliterated so they looked like Spanish coasters. Warships of the Republican fleet stood guard on the outer moorings, two destroyers and an old battle cruiser, draped with flags and moored fore and aft so they could turn their maximum firepower toward the entrance of the harbor to protect it from seaborne attack. One more freighter, the same size and color as the three rafted ships, was tied at the loading dock of the armory, the concrete quay where ships would normally charge their magazines with armaments.

The armory was in the one area of the naval base that was heavily guarded, a secure island in the midst of the otherwise open base. Like many navy towns, Cartagena lived in a symbiosis with its base. Bread and milk and meat and casual labor had come into the base from the town for so long that the sentries no longer troubled themselves checking identification. The gates stood open from morning to night, except in the smaller fenced area that enclosed the armory and the massive stone naval headquarters building, a glass-roofed structure built in the eighteenth century to withstand bombardment by a French or British frigate. A high iron fence with gates flanked by sentry boxes surrounded the two buildings.

From outside the fence, Sinclair and the men could see rows of parked trucks around the armory, some lined up, others parked helter-skelter amid the pyramid stockpiles of projectiles and barrels of lubricating oil.

"They're loading one of the ships," said Sinclair. He pointed down at the dark gray freighter at the armory dock. The big cranes were still, but a small crew of sailors could be seen scurrying across the dock, carrying compact wooden cases with rope handles at either end.

Manolo looked down at the freighter, then let his eyes follow the fence that led from the water alongside the dock all the way around the armory and headquarters area. The sentry boxes stood out from the perimeter of the fence like pillboxes.

"How will we get inside?" he said. "We have six pistols. They have machine guns at the sentry boxes and squads of marines at the gate. You said there would be no guards."

Sinclair squirmed in the itchy uniform. They had bought the uniforms that morning, at a shop in Cartagena that asked no questions. Like most navy towns, Cartagena sold three commodities freely: women, drink, and uniforms. The uniforms were the only tickets they needed to get inside the base.

"Well, Sinclair," repeated Manolo. "We used up the petrol to get to St. Lucia. Now, how do we get inside past those guards? And how will we get a truck out?"

Pedrito glared at Manolo, annoyed at the challenge to Sinclair.

"He has a way," he assured Manolo. "In the notepad, he has a way."

He turned to Sinclair, waiting for the explanation.

In fact, it was the one flaw in Sinclair's plan. He had seen Cartagena before, early in the war, when he wrote about the ill-preparation of the Republican navy. He had seen then how the marine guards were more concerned with the pleats in their trousers than with the security of the base. And with the faith of an author in the capabilities of his hero, he had left a hiatus in the outline of his story, an ellipsis that would be filled in the course of the action by the clever ability of a man of action. He *knew* that on the spot he would see his way through.

Manolo stared at him, waiting for specifics. The rest of the men were standing behind them, lounging against a low stone wall, smoking cigarettes. They could hear every word of the discussion and feel the tension of the long silence.

And still, Sinclair's mind came up blank. He had made a mistake.

Then Sinclair heard the buzz. At first it was like a hive of hornets, and he thought it was inside his head, the beginning of the kind of headache that came when he was stumped over the typewriter. But this was different. He closed his eyes for a moment to seal off the world, and suddenly, vividly, he remembered where he had heard the sound before.

"Machettis," he said, looking up at the darkening sky.

"What?" said Pedrito and Manolo simultaneously.

Sinclair's effort at an answer was drowned out by the simultaneous shriek of sirens from the corners of the base, handcranked sirens that were out of synchronization with one another so that their combined output was a deafening maelstrom: *Ooooh-aaaah-ooooh-aaaah . . .* An instant later, the lights at the base went out, as if the main switch had been pulled, leaving only the dim starlight until the antiaircraft floodlights came on.

"I know that sound anywhere," said Sinclair. "They used the same planes in Ethiopia, along with the Bredas. The Bredas roar; the Machettis only buzz. They must need the range of the bigger planes."

The planes were still invisible, and their buzz was now completely muffled by the sirens. Sinclair searched the sky, watching as the guns on the ships out in the harbor started firing, each shot leaving a bright flash and a wisp of luminescent smoke. The gunners were firing blind, and the high *rat-a-tat* of the light machine guns and the deeper *poom-poom* of the cannons did little more than identify the ships as targets to the planes.

"The secret was not kept so well, eh?" said Manolo. "Even the Italians know."

"Do they?" said Sinclair. "Would they bomb if they knew what was here? They're after the ships."

The first load of bombs fell on the headquarters building, smashing in the glass roof. The armory was unscathed.

"Those planes could take out the ships easily," said Sinclair. "They must think they can capture them intact someday."

Horsedrawn fire trucks came out of the shed at the perimeter of the base to race across the parade ground toward the headquarters building. Three of the sirens had stopped, and over the wail of the fourth, megaphones called for all hands to report for human chains to carry buckets of sand and water to fight the fires in the wooden interior of the building. Inside the fence, the marine guards scattered in panic as the planes came back for a second run, strafing this time. A few of the marines ran for the inside of the building, melting into the lines with the buckets. Others just disappeared into the vastness of the base. They had been drilled and prepared for an attack from the sea, not for marauders from the air. Only the rigid guards in the sentry boxes remained at their posts, as oblivious to the chaos as tin soldiers.

"Now," said Sinclair, "let's go."

"This was your plan?" said Manolo.

Sinclair's answer was drowned out by the noise of the planes.

Once through the open gate, they followed the columns of men running toward the building, until they got to the rows of trucks in the stockpile area. Ducking behind the trucks, they worked their way toward the armory. In the chaos, no one noticed seven more men in uniform. Instead of the fear he anticipated, Sinclair felt exhilaration. For the first time he understood why leaders were so often brave. They were too busy to feel afraid. His thoughts raced on—planning and plotting as he moved across the ground.

"These are the six-ton trucks?" said Sinclair.

Manolo nodded.

"Can you start one?"

Manolo was under the hood before the question left Sinclair's lips. He pulled a length of wire from under his blouse, feeling with his fingers in the dark before he motioned to Pedrito to get into the truck.

"Just the starter pedal," he said. "And easy on the spark."

The truck turned over but wouldn't start. Sinclair turned angrily to Manolo. "You said that you . . ."

"More gas," said Manolo as he fiddled under the hood.

This time the truck started. Manolo quickly gave the signal to kill the engine, pulling his index finger across his throat.

The sentry boxes outside the armory were built more for appearance and the comfort of the guards than for effectiveness. Enclosed on three sides, with a sharply peaked roof that formed an overhang in front, they were impossible to defend except from the front. With sparks, debris, and water spraying off the fires in the adjacent building, and steam and smoke pouring out in dense clouds from the fire-fighting efforts, the sentries retreated into the comfort of the boxes, with only a glimmer of their white and red uniforms visible in the blackout lights.

Motioning to Sinclair to go straight up to the sentry box, and to the others to stay low, Manolo worked his way along the side of the building, watching as the sentry stepped out, holding his rifle with its white strap in front of him at a fancy port arms.

"Halt!" he shouted at Sinclair. "State your business."

Manolo's pistol caught the guard on the neck, just below the nape of his plumed guard regiment helmet. The man fell forward.

"Is he dead?" said Sinclair. He had seen death before, but only as a reporter.

Manolo shook his head no, grinning at Sinclair's naiveté.

Four of the men were already at the heavy door of the armory, trying to slide it along its track.

"Is it locked?" said Sinclair.

"That kind of door is closed with a winch from inside," said Manolo. "Or sometimes with a tractor from outside. I don't think we can open it without a tractor." He waited for Sinclair to look up at him. "What was your plan for the door, Sinclair?"

Sinclair felt the massive timbers and iron straps with his fingers. Manolo was right. They could never push it open.

Then Pedrito came up, feeling along the edge of the door for a purchase point. He put his back against the stones of the doorway and his legs up against the timbers, flexing his knees. Sweat began to pour off his face as the muscles of his jaw and forehead tightened into knots. He looked over at Sinclair and Manolo, his face twisted with pain, and he began to grunt, puffing like a locomotive starting from a standstill. The door creaked, but wouldn't budge.

"It's no use," said Manolo.

Then the door creaked again. The blood vessels and muscles

of Pedrito's face looked like they would burst through the skin as the grunting accelerated and the door finally slipped open, enough so the others could hook their hands into the opening and pull with him.

They came in with their revolvers out, crouched and facing in every direction, not sure what to expect inside.

The vast building was eerily silent. There were no windows, no light except the flickering flashes from the fires that could be seen through the open door. Even Sinclair, buoyed by the luck of the timely Italian attack, was taken aback by the emptiness of the building. No guards at all? he wondered. Would even the Spanish go that far?

Staying low, they worked around the edges of the vast space, until they could make out the tall stacks of crates along both sides of the center of the armory. The wooden crates were piled in even rows on pallets, stacked as high as a man could reach. Up close, they looked much like the crates that they had seen loaded onto the gray freighter at the dock, each about one hundred centimeters long and twenty centimeters wide

Sinclair quickly counted the crates in a stack. Fifteen across, five deep. Seventy-five per layer. Each stack was eight layers high. Six hundred boxes per stack. As his eyes gradually adjusted to the dim light, he could make out ten stacks lined up in two rows. Six thousand boxes.

"They look like rifle ammunition crates," said Manolo. "What else do you expect to find in an armory?"

Grabbing the rope handle at the end of one crate, Sinclair started to lift it off the top of a stack, then realized how heavy the case was. About fifty kilos, he guessed. A broad smile crossed his face. What else could weigh so much. Fifty kilos per case, six thousand cases—three hundred tons of gold!

Pedrito, seeing the smile, reached for the crate, lifting it off the top of the stack and lowering it to the floor. Sinclair leaned close to read the markings. The case looked new, made of rough sawn softwood. Number codes with interspersed letters were stenciled on the wood.

Manolo pulled his knife from the scabbard on his ankle, wedged the butt of the blade under one of the planks, and pried open the top.

Underneath there were four metal canisters, each sealed with wax. Sinclair frantically tore the rest of the wooden strips off the top of the crate and pulled out a canister, breaking through the wax with his fingernails and prying the two halves open.

Inside were neatly packed rounds of 7-millimeter rifle ammunition for the Italian Mannlicher rifles with which many of the Republic troops were armed.

Sinclair pulled out the shells, then dumped the rest of the canisters onto the floor.

"Those shells would be useful on Majorca," said Manolo. "But they weren't worth the petrol."

Sinclair ran to another stack of crates, pulling one down. It was identical to the crate they had opened, softwood with rope handles on the ends and number codes stenciled in black on the wood.

"If there is no gold," Manolo said. "If we have wasted the petrol that could have helped kill Fascists on Majorca . . ."

Sinclair looked toward the front of the building, where tracks led to the doors and beyond them to the dock in front. The entire center section of the building where the tracks led was empty except for stacks of wooden pallets. Desperation made his mind race.

"That ship at the dock," he said. "It's not the first of the freighters. It's the last. They must have finished loading them this afternoon. The gold is already on the ships."

Pedrito was at the door, using the cranked wire winch at the side to wind it open. Through the opening they could hear and see the chaos left by the raid of the planes—shrieks, jets of water from firehoses, thick billows of smoke.

"The ship has left the dock," said Pedrito. "It's hard to see through the haze and smoke, but I think it's mooring with the other three."

"How long would it take them to get out of here?" Sinclair asked Manolo.

"What makes you think they're leaving? Maybe they brought this ammunition from Russia."

"*Four* ships? One could carry this easily."

"And one could carry the gold easily," answered Manolo.

"But we knew there would be four," said Sinclair.

Manolo went to the doorway to look out at the ships. He studied the harbor for a moment, then looked back along the side of the building, where the fire-fighting teams had most of the small blazes under control.

"You still think we're a match for ships in a convoy?" he said. "It's one thing to take it from a truck. Six of us can take the guards on a truck, and we have surprise on our side. But a ship? We're not pirates."

"We can do it!" said Sinclair.

"Halt!" The voice rang out from the open doorway at the side of the building. "What are you doing in here?"

The lights went on, flooding the armory, showing the enormous cleared area in the center where the empty pallets were stacked.

Sinclair and the others scrambled through the doorway toward the loading dock. It was still dark on the docks, and they ran toward the water's edge, where the fence came down into the harbor water. A man could easily swim around the edge of the barbed wire that topped the chain fence.

As they ran, shots rang out, ricocheting off the concrete loading dock. Sinclair dove to the ground, then saw that Pedrito and Manolo had made it to the water. When the firing stopped, he started to get up and felt an arm drag down against his leg.

"Señor Sinclair. It's me, Luiz. I'm hit."

Sinclair looked back, his eyes focusing on the leg of the man, soaked in blood and twisted horribly, hanging only by skin and tendons. He saw Pedrito start to come out of the water toward them, but he waved him on while he dragged Luiz toward the fence and the comforting darkness. Until then, Luiz had never said a word. All Sinclair knew about him was that his wife had been killed in Majorca and that he had escaped with his children to Ciudadela.

"You must go without me," said Luiz. "I will only slow you down and they will catch all of you. You can trust me. I will tell them nothing of the plan. I will die before I tell them anything."

"No," said Sinclair. "We're in this together."

Sinclair watched the man grimace with pain, then look up toward the sky.

"No more planes," said Sinclair.

Luiz cringed again from the pain. Sinclair pictured what the marine guards would do with the man. It wouldn't take an expert to coax information from a man hurt that badly. A prod to the wounded leg would make even the strongest man talk.

"It will work, Señor Sinclair?" he asked. His eyes were fixed on the black sky, suddenly still without the cross streams of airplanes and tracer bullets. "The plan will work and you will be able to get powerful airplanes like these for the Republic?"

"Yes," said Sinclair, "it will work. We'll make it work. He quietly raised his revolver to the temple of the other man, backing himself away from the muzzle. The gun felt awkward, heavier than he anticipated, the grip too large for his hand. As he started to squeeze, he hesitated, closing his eyes, bracing for the recoil. For an instant, he thought of the cafe in Madrid, the poster on the wall, and Margaret, her voice cold as she called him only an observer of life.

He cringed at the recoil, turning away without looking at the face of the man he had shot. Then he stuffed the gun into his belt. It seemed to nestle easily where it had once dug into him.

Twenty-Eight

The Zeppelin had flown within sight of land for most of the day. The African coast came into view not long after they crossed the Canary Islands, and Maggie gave up her seat with the Huttens for the starboard windows behind the admiral's table. She was staring at the vast empty spaces when von Teppler pointed out a caravan stop, a collection of low white buildings and palm trees that seemed to pop up out of nowhere.

Maggie took the proffered chair at his table, fascinated as he explained that he was familiar with the area from his days of naval patrols off Morocco before the war. He seemed to know the whole coast below, from the tall buildings of Casablanca and the Great Mosque and Tower of Hassan in Rabat, to tiny medieval towns like Sale, with its roguish history as a pirate headquarters. From the altitude of 1500 feet, and with the admiral's detailed knowledge, the panorama was a spectacle no guidebook or tour on the ground could equal.

"We're not far from Europe," he said as they approached the curve of the coastline south of Tangiers. "I can feel it. Always I have strong feelings on approaching Gibraltar from the sea. You Americans seem to be at home everywhere, even in the most primitive areas of the dark continent. For my part, I readily admit that I am European to the core. Only in Europe do I feel truly at home."

Eisler looked up at the word *Europe*, the only term he had understood in von Teppler's French. Since they departed Recife, the task of sitting with the admiral had fallen principally to Eisler. Beck, the senior of the two officers accompanying the admiral, had spent most of his time in his cabin, whether because of embarrassment after his losing confrontation with Whitman, or because with Stifel no longer aboard there was no one to share his views and provide moral support.

Though bored at first, Eisler gradually assumed a style and attitude of his own, a manner far more relaxed than his colleague. He no longer objected to the admiral reading books in French, no longer demanded to see the long memoranda the admiral wrote to himself in French, and no longer commented on the admiral's occasional conversations, usually with the American woman, and again in French. Since he could understand nothing of what was being written or said, Eisler took to amusing himself with a continuous game of solitaire that consumed his attention from early morning until he gave up in defeat late each night.

"To my generation," the admiral went on, "the internationalism of a man like your Captain Whitman is quite incomprehensible. He is remarkable. He seems at home in all cultures, what in German we would call a *Weltbürger*. You would say . . . I am not sure how to translate this."

Maggie looked up and spotted Whitman at the opposite side of the lounge. Her smile invited him over.

"The admiral says you're a *Weltbürger*," she said. "Sounds like something to eat to me."

"Citizen of the world?" offered Whitman.

The admiral stood, bowing slightly. "Captain Whitman! You will join us? We were admiring the remarkable vista of the Moroccan coast, and the gracious Mademoiselle Bourne was humoring me with her attentions."

Maggie smiled. "I really should get back to my journal," she said, excusing herself before either of them had time to protest. Whitman's eyes followed her as she walked back to her usual seat with the Huttens. The admiral read his mind.

"She is strong-willed, Captain. I suspect that any effort to argue with her can only end in failure."

Grinning in agreement, Whitman took the chair she had vacated.

"That remark about *Weltbürgertum*," he said. "What did you mean?"

"It was a compliment, Captain. For a man of my generation, nationalism is an affliction, an incurable disease. To command the vessel of another nation would be inconceivable. Yet you, an American, seem totally relaxed in your command of a German airship. And this at a time when some people in Germany have made remarks that are highly critical of your nation. It is not so very long ago that our nations were on opposite sides of a terrible war, after all.''

It took Whitman a moment to realize that the admiral had smoothly slipped into French. He leaned back in his chair, unbuttoning his jacket and stretching his legs beneath the table.

"It's quite simple," he explained. "The United States doesn't have any active airships now. The Macon crashed in the Pacific almost a year and a half ago. We still have the Los Angeles—a German-built ship—but it's been decommissioned. So I came to Germany to study developments at the Zeppelin Company. And from there, circumstances just took over.''

"On the contrary, Captain.'' The admiral leaned forward in his chair, placing his elbows on the table and putting his fingers together like a child saying prayers. "Circumstances do not *take over*. Men make their circumstances. As I have made mine.''

Whitman questioned with his eyes, realizing that the admiral would go on without encouragement.

"There is no puzzle," said von Teppler. "I am a man out of my time. Politics, technology, the age of the masses—they have all passed me by. I remain a *Junker*, a man of the eighteenth century.''

"You don't mean the nineteenth?'' said Whitman.

"Explicitly, no. The nineteenth century belongs to the merchants and the industrialists, to steamships and railroads and great factories. Just as the twentieth belongs to airplanes and submarines and politics and the masses. For my part, I was never happier than when I was a naval cadet, training on a square-rigged barkentine. We sailed without an engine, like the navies of the eighteenth century, and before the wind and the sea, we learned to respect authority and rank and class. We learned humility in the face of the forces of nature. Since that time I have had the privilege of serving on and commanding some of the most modern naval vessels of our age, with the most advanced equipment. Yet I continue to miss those days, that feel of delicate balance between the ship and the wind, that sense that one is respecting nature and using her, instead of fighting her. Perhaps my feelings are only a form of nostalgia, which is what I like to think. Or perhaps my son was correct, and I am an anachronism, a man whose views have no place in the world today.''

Whitman smiled, remembering his own early dreams of flying an airship.

"You find my nostalgia amusing, Captain?"

"I'm smiling because I think you've put your finger on what I love about the Zeppelins. These great bags of cloth and cord and wire and alloy are the sailing ships of our century, machines of grace and elegance and style. And they're probably doomed for the same reason that sailing ships were doomed. In a world measured by speed, no one has time for this elegance and style. It's only a matter of time before airplanes will fly scheduled runs over the Atlantic, taking less than a day for a journey that requires four in the Zeppelin."

Von Teppler shook his head. "It is not speed that will decide the fate of the Zeppelins, Captain. It's war. So long as war remains the obsession of our age, there will be no place for these graceful ships. Airplanes are essential for war. Airships are not. If I'm not wrong, your own navy, like mine, has concluded that there is no real role for the airship in a modern war. The tradition of elegance, the grace of the wind filling a sail, the beauty of these wondrous machines—they mean nothing today. What do these men know of grace and elegance? It is pearls before swine."

Whitman had never heard a German of rank or position speak with such candor. Most of the Germans he knew were silent about their politics, knowing that it was unwise to be too open in discussions with a foreigner.

Even more than the candor, he was struck by an intimacy in the admiral's tone. Although they used the *vous* with one another, the admiral's words seemed to invite Whitman into his confidence.

"Are you sure you want to tell me this?" said Whitman.

"Whom else can I tell? Even my own son would not listen to me. We argued about this many times, even before he volunteered for the air service."

"Your son is a flyer?"

"Was. He was killed in 1933."

"I'm sorry." Whitman said it automatically.

"There is nothing to be sorry about. He died in the service of the Fatherland. At least that's what the official commendation said. He was killed in a mishap in the Soviet Union, where the Luftwaffe—it was in the guise of the so-called sport flying clubs then—was training in secret."

Whitman almost gasped. It was perhaps the best kept of

German secrets, the joint military training and weapons development program that the Germans and Russians had undertaken in the Soviet Union, long suspected by British and American intelligence, but never proved

"I tried to speak out to my fellow officers," von Teppler continued, "and my reward was exile to Buenos Aires. I spoke out there and now I find myself returning to Germany to face a navy inquiry. You're surprised? I have nothing to fear. I will face fellow officers, men of my own class who will honor my right to state my views. And at least I am permitted to return to Europe, to the Fatherland." He glanced down at the mountains of the Rif below, then let his eyes wander forward in the direction of Gibraltar.

"Believe me, Whitman, I do not oppose all wars. The military is and must be the backbone of the nation, especially in a nation as immature and insecure in its political development as mine. But it is one thing to fight wars as they were fought in the eighteenth century, when war was entrusted to a professional caste, led by men of enlightenment and restraint. When Friedrich the Great waged war"—he tapped the book of memoirs with his fingertips, then spun the book around for Whitman to see the title on the spine—"it was a game of political chess, with Europe for a board and professional armies as players. When one great mind outmaneuvered the others, as Friedrich so often did, the war was over. Now, the demand goes out for the *destruction* of the enemy. Whole populations are put under the guns, weapons are deployed which can annihilate mankind and civilization as we know it. And we entrust this awesome power not to the enlightened, not to men such as Friedrich, but to *madmen*."

Whitman started to raise his hand, hoping to restrain the looseness of the admiral's tongue. Even with the protection of speaking French, there was no guarantee that someone would not hear their conversation.

Von Teppler ignored the hand.

"When my son was killed," he went on, "I realized that Germany was preparing a revanchist war. His death was only an accident, like the death of that young boy who was killed in the bosun's chair. But the deaths that will follow if Germany is allowed to pursue this course of madness will be no accident. They will doom Europe to generations without leadership.

"Many years ago, I visited the French Cavalry Officers School at St. Cyr. There's a monument there, in front of the school, listing the names of those graduates of each class who have fallen in war. To go through the years of the nineteenth century is to read a history of wars: in the years of peace, only a few died; in the years of war, there are many. But then the list comes to a most terrible year: 1914. The inscription for that year is shorter than for any other. It reads, in its entirety, *La classe de 1914*. Do you understand, Whitman? A whole class of young leadership killed off. Gone. And it's the same in Germany. The finest of our sons were killed in the Great War. And who comes forward to take their place in the leadership of the nation and the military? Nazis—madmen! Men with no sense of honor or courage, barbarians, rude upstarts without tradition or education or appreciation for the meaning of culture and civilization. Alone, they are weaklings, cowards before the authority of true leadership. But with the strength of their numbers, with the power of their masses and their organization, they have the means to destroy Germany.''

Von Teppler looked straight into Whitman's eyes, his features as animated as when he had verbally lashed Beck on the night of the rescue.

"Do not underestimate them, Captain. A man like that watch officer does not forget easily. Precisely because he has no sense of honor, he cannot let a public reprimand pass lightly. He and his kind always find their revenge. Look at their leader! The little Bohemian was trampled, humiliated, in his service as a corporal in the Imperial Army in the Great War. And in time he will find his revenge on the General Staff. These madmen will stop at nothing. They believe that power can erase their crassness and their origins. And the military—already they have changed the name from *Reichswehr* to *Wehrmacht*—will be the source of their power.''

"Do you really think we're headed for war?'' asked Whitman, an inflection of astonishment in his voice. Except for a few hysterical commentators on the occupation of the Rhineland, Whitman had heard no one suggest the possibility of war in Europe. Some threats and bluffs perhaps, some pressure for the hard diplomacy that would be necessary to undo some of the more punitive clauses of the Versailles Treaty. But *war*? It was unthinkable. "Surely the Germans are in no position to wage a war, at least not against France or the Russians. It's only a year and a half since Hitler threw off the Versailles limits on the German armed forces. That little army and navy, and that primitive Luftwaffe—they're no threat.''

"Don't be blind, Whitman. It's a shell game. While you're

watching one shell—listening to Hitler's demands for defensive weapons or seeing the occupation of the Rhineland—he is busy under the other shells. No one, even inside Germany, wants to see what is happening. Three and one half months after Hitler announced the end of the Versailles limitations, a submarine was launched at Kiel. Other submarines followed at the rate of one every eight days! That could only be done if the parts were prefabricated, in secrecy. And we know that in Holland and Finland and Spain, the Krupp Works have set up dummy companies to develop the tooling and design for these parts. It's the same with the rest of the war machine. While the world is distracted by their antics, these madmen are preparing for war."

"But they have no training," said Whitman. "No tactical or strategic experience. The Germans have had no military involvement since 1918."

Von Teppler glanced out the window, at the coast of Spanish Morocco.

"There will be opportunities, Whitman. And they will be seized upon."

"But Hitler has said that he will remain strictly neutral in the Spanish conflict."

"Watch their actions, Whitman. Don't be mesmerized by their words."

Whitman let his eyes follow the admiral's to the window. He was torn. As much as he wanted the admiral to go on, he was afraid for the man, afraid of the repercussions of the man's candor. "We're over Tangiers," he said. "In a few minutes we reach the Straits. I should return to the control room."

Von Teppler caught Whitman's eyes as he turned away from the window. "Captain! My generation is too set in its ways, too old-fashioned. We have tried to lead the nation and failed. And we are now no match for them. I can speak out, but even now I cannot be sure that my words will be heard. Even my fellow officers may be deaf to what I say. My only consolation is that they will respect my right as an officer to speak."

"And if they ignore you?"

"Then I will have no choice. I shall retire from active service. When he was too old to serve the Kaiser, my grandfather built a house in the Frisian Islands. On Juist. He had it constructed by shipwrights, with oak beams joined as the ribs of a ship are joined, and heavy walls planked of pitch pine. From there, I can turn my eyes to the sea, and live with the wind and the waves. I will have served the Fatherland for twenty-nine years. Perhaps that's enough. As long as my fellow officers will hear me out, I shall have no regrets.

"But someone, someday, will have to stop them. If no one will listen to the men of my generation, then perhaps it is you—the Americans—who will inherit the responsibility."

Flattered, and at the same time frightened by the admiral's tone, Whitman tried to wave the thoughts away with his hand. "Admiral, I'm not even a military man. I was too young for the war, and too committed to airships for the peacetime navy. I'm just a civilian, like the captain of an ocean liner."

"There will be no civilians, Whitman. Believe me. That age and that choice are gone."

"I hope you're wrong," said Whitman.

"So do I, Captain. So do I."

In the control room, Whitman found the crewmen crowded at the forward windows, looking up under the curving nose of the Zeppelin to the sky above. No one paid any attention to the sweeping view of Gibraltar, towering fourteen hundred feet into the sky, its peak almost within reach of the portside windows. Or the smaller Spanish fortress at Ceuta, visible from the starboard windows. Straight below, between the Pillars of Hercules, the seas surged through the narrow straits connecting the Atlantic and the Mediterranean. How could anyone pass up such a sight? Whitman wondered. The gateway between two continents—Europe and Africa—spanned by the views from two sides of a narrow compartment.

As he moved forward, the crowd of men parted. Someone handed him a pair of field glasses.

"Junkers 52s," said someone as Whitman raised the glasses.

He saw the planes immediately. There were three inverted vees of the low-winged, 3-engined transports, ten planes in each vee, flying in tight formations. Along the edges, low-winged pursuit planes, new Messerschmitt 109s, guarded the formation as it winged from Spain toward Africa. There were no identification marks on the transports, but the wingtips of the Messerschmitts were painted black—the markings of the Condor Legion.

"Never seen so many of them together," said Lehrmann, the radio operator. "Except on the ground, and once in a flyover at Nuremberg. I wonder where they're going?"

"Find out," said Whitman. Even without markings, it was obvious that the transports were German. The Junkers 52 had

been in production for years as a civilian transport, but a fleet in
those numbers could only come from the Luftwaffe.

Whitman took an approximate bearing of the course the planes
were flying, then followed Lehrmann back to the radio room.

"We have crystals for the frequencies they usually use," said
Lehrmann. He switched on the voice radio that was used for
communication at airfields and between the Zeppelin and nearby
aircraft.

"You want to speak with them, Captain?"

"If you raise their squadron leader," said Whitman.

Lehrmann called twice, and got only static on his receiver. He
switched frequencies and called again, then went back to the
original frequency. There was no answer to any of his efforts.

"They must not be monitoring," he said.

"Or else they're observing radio silence," said Whitman.

"Why would they guard silence, sir? They're just transports."

To Whitman, the answer was obvious. Von Teppler's words
seemed a prophecy. The only reason a fleet of transports would
be flying south, with a heavy fighter escort, would be to assist in
transporting Franco's army of Africa from Spanish Morocco to
the Spanish mainland. Each plane could carry eighteen passengers. Each sortie of that fleet would bring over five hundred
men.

And the Nazis, who had proclaimed their neutrality in the
Spanish conflict, were even going to the extreme of radio silence
and unmarked planes.

But to Lehrmann he said, "Keep trying."

Whitman walked out of the radio room and scrambled up the
ladder to his own quarters. He dug into his kit bag, throwing
clothes onto the sole of his cabin until he found what he wanted,
the Leica Model IIIa in its hard leather case. He had bought the
camera as soon as he arrived in Germany, one of those treasures
of German engineering that could not be equaled in the States.
He had hardly used it, except for a roll of film that he shot as a
test, but he had spent hours admiring the design of the camera
and the finely machined controls that were engraved like a fine
watch or a masterpiece of the gunmaker's craft.

Back in the control room, he twisted and extended the collaps-
ible 50-millimeter lens, setting the focus on infinity and guessing
at the correct exposure for photographs against the bright daylight sky. Through the viewfinder, it was not an exciting photograph. The standard lens took in too much sky, the clouds were
too pale to stand out without a strong filter, and the planes

showed up as no more than tiny black dots. But he knew that the resolution of the Leica lens was high enough for the individual planes to stand out in an enlargement. And it wasn't often that you could see thirty transports, with escorts, flying in close formation.

He snapped six shots, one after another, bracketing his exposures because the Agfa film was unfamiliar and he wasn't sure how to set the aperture. Then he collapsed the lens and stuffed the compact camera into the side pocket of his jacket.

Only dimly, in the recesses of his mind, did he admit to himself his real reason for taking the photographs—that he was aware of being present at a historic moment. Those planes, even with no markings on the Junkers transports, marked the entry of Germany into an international war. The nightmare the admiral had described to him only minutes before was starting to come true.

He watched until the airplanes were out of view, above and beyond the Zeppelin on their way toward the airfields of Spanish Morocco. When he finally turned to go back to his quarters, to stow the camera in a secure place, Lehrmann was coming toward him from the radio room.

"Any response?" Whitman asked.

"Nothing," said Lehrmann. "They don't seem to be interested in talking to the Graf Zeppelin. I guess they're too busy."

Exactly, thought Whitman.

Twenty-Nine

Everyone on the dock was working. One man painted a sign, tracing out the letters in white paint. PRACTICO DE PUERTO. Sinclair had thought all along of the single English word, PILOT. It was the problem of thinking in one language and working in another. Up close, the sign was crude, whitewash on a weathered wooden board. But from a distance, even the end of the dock, it had the authenticity of the signboard on a pilot boat.

Manolo's boat sat alone at the end of the flimsy fishing dock at St. Lucia. It had looked out of place when they pulled in, too businesslike in its gray paint alongside the colorful fishing boats, and Sinclair was afraid of the reaction of the fishermen until Manolo brought out cartons of cigarettes and asked questions that left the clear impression that he was scouting locations for a smuggling run to North Africa. In those days when it was impossible to ship fish to the markets, and when cigarettes were more negotiable than money, the fishermen were eager to be included in his plans, eager enough to keep silent.

On deck, two men were erecting a short mast with a crosstree, leading the wire guys to deadeyes on top of the cabin house. In the cockpit, another man was busy with a needle and thread, sewing a square of white cloth to a larger square of red to make up code flag *H*. The red and white flag had the same significance in all waters: Pilot aboard. Inside the cabin, Sinclair saw men oiling weapons, checking and coiling lines, counting out ammunition. Manolo's broad back and shoulders were just visible in one of the engine hatches, where he was pampering his two big powerplants. Each man looked up when he saw Sinclair, then without a word or a smile went back to work.

The silence was a bad sign. The men had been excited when they left Minorca, their energy crackling like overcharged batteries. Sinclair couldn't help contrasting the enthusiasm of that last afternoon in Cala Moreli with the sullen moroseness of these men going about their tasks with glum, mechanical detachment. They were troubled, and he knew that men with troubles on their minds cannot function with the efficiency his plan demanded.

As Sinclair walked down the dock toward the ship, Pedrito jumped off the foredeck and walked toward him.

"What's wrong?" Sinclair asked.

"It's not the same, Señor Sinclair. The men do not feel the same."

"Nothing has changed," said Sinclair. "This was always the second plan. The trucks were just a chance. This was always the main plan. And it will work. We've thought of everything."

He saw men look up at the sound of his voice, then return to their tasks.

"It's not the plan that troubles the men," said Pedrito.

"Then what is it? Do they want overtime pay? Or are they just scared?"

"No, Señor Sinclair." Even as Sinclair's voice became caustic and sarcastic, Pedrito's remained calm and steady. "They are angry because of Luiz. They say it wasn't necessary for him to die. A death fighting the Fascists they can understand, but this was not necessary. This is what the men believe.''

"We were surprised," said Sinclair. "They opened fire without warning. There was nothing we could do. He was badly shot.''

Pedrito shook his head. "We saw what killed Luiz. It was not the bullets of the *marineros*. It was you. You shot him with your pistol because he was badly wounded. You were afraid he would slow us down so we could not get away.''

Sinclair's face reddened. The impact of what he had done had already hit him hours before. He couldn't think of the killing without feeling a hard cramp in his gut.

He answered nervously, the words coming too quickly. "Do you think I wanted to kill him? There was no choice. His leg hung only by the tendons. Can you imagine what they would have done to him? It's too easy to torture a wounded man, to make him say things he doesn't want to say.''

He searched for a hint of agreement in Pedrito's face. "You said all of these men were willing to die in the struggle against fascism. Well, this is the struggle. This may be the most important thing any of them will ever do in that struggle.''

"The men do not believe that anymore, Señor Sinclair.''

"Why do you think I am here?'' Sinclair asked the question loudly enough for the others to hear. "To get rich? Do you think I would risk my own life for nothing?''

There was no answer, and for the first time he was afraid. He had never seen so much distrust as in the eyes that surrounded him. What did they see when they looked at him? The same thing Margaret saw—a man of words, a journalist, an observer? What was he doing here with these men and this boat?

He cut off the errant thoughts. It was too late to rewrite the page or rethink the plot.

"There was no choice," he said. "There was nothing else I could do. What we're doing is too important to sacrifice." He gradually expanded his voice until it projected to all of the men, and he spoke slowly, making each word important. "Nothing has changed. We knew about the ships and we were right. We knew how many ships, and we were right. And we know what they carry on the ships. It's not just gold that goes on those ships. It's the future of Spain. And if it goes to the Soviet Union, then Spain will never be free. You will never live in freedom on Minorca, and your children will never be free. None of us will ever be free.''

On the boat and on the dock, the men slowly stopped working. First the man painting, then the men on the cabin top and in the cockpit, and finally even Manolo. And as Sinclair saw that he had his audience, he let the words flow. His Spanish was slow and precise, and he chose his words carefully, remembering when Montserrat had translated for him. He knew that some words, like *death* and *man* and *freedom* and *dignity* had a special ring for the Spanish. And he knew how to use alliteration and repetition and onomatopoeia to make the words shout out with profundity and significance.

It was more than hollow rhetoric. As he spoke he became convinced once again that his plan could work. It had to work. For the first time in his life, he believed, cared.

"If we don't do it," he said, "then the gold will be gone forever. And Luiz *will* have died in vain. *Por nada*. We will have wasted the precious petrol, and we will have wasted a precious life. And there will be thousands of other precious lives wasted. I say that lives in Spain are too valuable to waste. Not a single Spaniard should die unless it is for the freedom of Spain. This is what I believe. This is why I am here. This is why I say we must do this."

The men sat in silence when he finished. Then they began talking among themselves, making long, involved arguments in Minorquin, as if they were settling the verdict for a trial. Gradually, the arguments coalesced, until it was only Manolo talking and the others nodding. Sinclair felt like he was standing in front of the judge's bench, waiting for the announcement of his sentence.

It was Manolo who spoke finally, standing on the deck of the boat and looking down at Sinclair at the dock.

"No more killing, Sinclair," he said. "These men are not enemies of Spain. The men in Cartagena and the men on the ships are not our enemies. We must save the killing for the Fascists." He said it as if it were an ultimatum.

Sinclair nodded, but it wasn't enough for Manolo.

"No more killing?" he asked.

"No more killing," said Sinclair.

With no change of expression, Manolo wiped off his hands and got into the cockpit to start up the engines.

They drifted just ahead of the rocky shoreline, with the engines idling. Whenever they drifted too close, Manolo would ease the engines into gear for a moment, just long enough to get them clear of the rocks and into open water. The signboard was in the cockpit, the flag ready to hoist at an instant's notice. To an observer on the ships steaming out of the narrow mouth of the harbor, with the sun in their eyes, the low gray boat was invisible against the rocks.

"We must wait for the last ship," said Manolo. "When the first three have gone around the point, the fourth ship will be alone."

"But what if . . . ?" Sinclair stopped in the middle of the question, panicked with a thought that had never occurred to him before. There was no reason to believe that the gold would be divided among the four ships. Any one of them could easily carry the entire shipment, and it was probably a wiser plan to put the gold on one ship, leaving the other three in ballast as decoys. The choice was between all or nothing and divided risk, and it was hard to argue that either was the logical choice. And if it was all on one ship, there was only a twenty-five percent chance that the last one carried the gold. In truth, Sinclair silently calculated, the odds were that it wouldn't be the last of four ships. It would be the second or the third. They could be waiting for a ship that was traveling under ballast.

"What is it?" said Manolo.

Sinclair knew he couldn't voice his doubts. "You're sure it isn't carrying a pilot already?"

"There are no civil pilots in Cartagena," said Manolo. "The port is run by the navy. And the exit is so easy that the ships need no pilots."

They watched the last ship come steaming through the distant harbor opening and gradually turn to make course around the lighthouse on the point. The ships had come out at invervals of twenty-five minutes.

"You're sure there will be no escort?" said Manolo.

"Escorts would attract the Italian airplanes," said Sinclair.

Manolo looked from the ship to Sinclair and back again. "We'll soon see, won't we?"

As the third freighter disappeared behind the lighthouse on the point, Manolo took the wheel of his boat, engaged the engines, and pushed the throttles slowly forward. Two men busied themselves lashing the signboard to the cabinside, and another man hoisted the code flag to the crosstree of the stubby mast.

Sinclair had no duty. He tried to watch the ship ahead of them, but all he could picture was the expressions of the men when they searched the holds and found nothing.

Moving at thirty knots, and with the ship steaming toward them at eight knots, they covered the water quickly. Within minutes they were close enough to see men standing at the rail of the freighter, looking down at them.

"The channel has been changed," shouted Manolo, as he throttled his engines down to match the speed of the ship. "You will need a pilot."

One of the men at the rail, his jacket and cap identifying him as an officer, leaned over to wave them away. "We need no pilot," he shouted through a megaphone. "We are in convoy."

"In the bombing raid last night a plane was shot down in the channel," shouted Manolo. "Until it is cleared away, we must take you around the obstruction."

The officer scrutinized the pilot boat as if something were awry, then looked ahead to the lighthouse on the distant point before he shrugged his shoulders and began shouting orders to his crewmen.

The ladder was lowered from the rail of the steamer, and Manolo gave the wheel to Pedrito as he and Sinclair stood on the open aft deck of the boat. They were wearing gray trousers, shirts and caps, a plausible enough uniform for port pilots.

As soon as the ladder was down to the water, they jumped to the platform and scrambled up the steps. They were almost at the top when the officer on the freighter noticed something, perhaps the signboard with its crude lashings, or the obviously hand-sewn flag, or even the temporary structure of the mast and crosstree. Whatever it was, the officer turned open-mouthed to face the two men who stepped through the lifeline gate.

He was too late. Sinclair had seen his expression change, and pulled the gun from inside his shirt, leveling it at the officer. It felt easy in his hand. He was in command again. "Do as we tell you and no one will be hurt," he said.

"What do you want?" blurted the officer. "We carry no arms."

"Shut up!" said Sinclair. Up close he saw from the insignia that the officer was the master of the ship.

Manolo leaned over the rail and signaled. Four more men scrambled up the ladder, all carrying pistols. They moved quickly across the deck, herding the crewmen of the steamer toward the forepeak, surprising even themselves with the ease of the takeover. It was as if no one on the ship knew what the cargo was.

Sinclair and Manolo led the master forward to the pilot house,

where another officer and a helmsman were steering the ship.
When the other officer saw his captain at gunpoint, he started to
reach up behind the wheel, to where a rifle hung in brackets on
the bulkhead.

"No," said Manolo and wrestled him to the floor.

Sinclair moved toward the radio equipment in a niche behind
the steering station. It was on, but silent. When he picked up the
headphones, there was only the crackle of static.

Through the windows on the sides and front of the pilot house,
they could see the crew of the steamer being herded forward
along the decks, then down through the forward hatch to the
crew quarters in the forepeak. While Sinclair held the three men
in front of his pistol, waving it ominously when the master
started to talk to the other officer in Russian, Manolo went to the
helm and bent the speaking tube into a comfortable position.

"Pedrito!" he shouted into the tube. "Pedrito, do you hear
me?"

"Yes," came the muffled answer. "I hear you fine."

"How many men there?"

"Two. They think we're Spanish pirates."

Manolo turned to Sinclair. "You like that?" he asked. "Pirates."

Sinclair smiled, feeling relaxed.

"I will take these three forward," said Manolo. "You watch
our course."

"Leave this one," said Sinclair, gesturing toward the ship's
master. "In case there is anything on the radio."

Manolo stopped for an instant. "We don't need it. There will
be nothing."

"Leave him."

Manolo left with the others, unwilling to argue in the limited
time they had.

The captain looked at Sinclair as the others left. "What do
you want?" he asked in halting Spanish. "We carry no arms.
We are only . . ."

Sinclair waved him over to a chair, the officer's chair behind
the helm.

"Relax, *tovarich*," he said in a Russian more halting than the
captain's Spanish. "I'm going to let you watch."

"But we carry no arms. There is nothing. What do you
want?"

Sinclair breathed deeply. The smells of a steamer were strong
in the pilot house, not the fumes from the stack or the raw

sweetness of bunker fuel, but the scent of stale sweat and uncirculated air. Sinclair knew that on small steamers like that one, men went for days without washing. There's no one to wash for. And even when they scrub themselves before going off to the whores in a port, the ship never loses the smell of the men.

What surprised him was how few men it took to operate the ship. The normal crew of the freighter was nineteen, including the master, two mates, and a chief engineer. Routine maintenance and watches could keep that many men busy, even on a small ship. The engines should be constantly inspected and lubricated; the automatic pressure lubricators cannot be trusted on old steam engines. The battle against rust is constant, and the ordinary seamen are supposed to spend part of each day with a chipping chisel and paintbrush. There is always something that needs repair—chafing gear, mooring lines, lashings. But these are reserve tasks. As few as two or three men can actually run the ship. A single duty officer and a helmsman can handle the bridge. A mechanic's mate or engineer can handle the engines if nothing goes wrong. Holding course on a flat sea is child's play.

Manolo had locked the wheel, trusting that the ship would not swing too far off course in the flat sea. That left Sinclair with nothing to do at all.

Sinclair watched the men on the foredeck peel the tarpaulins off the center cargo hatch, then swing the ship's crane into position over the hatch.

"You're wasting your time," said the captain as he watched out the bridge windows. "There is nothing."

Sinclair was troubled by the calm of the man. How could anyone be so composed when he was sitting on one hundred fifty million dollars worth of gold? He remembered his speculation when they were watching the ships. Perhaps this one was nothing but a decoy. Perhaps all the gold was on one of the others and they were ransacking the ship for nothing.

Suddenly the ship lurched, then seemed to slow down. Sinclair leaned over the speaking tube.

"What's happening?" he shouted. "We're slowing down."

"It's no good," answered Manolo. "There isn't enough steam in the boilers to handle the engine and the crane. It's one or the other."

"Who cares about the engine?" said Sinclair.

There was no answer.

"What do you want with it?" said the captain, still in the

calm voice that troubled Sinclair. "What will you do with cases of machine parts? They are useless to you, whoever you are."

"Shut up!" said Sinclair.

He watched as the crane swung over the hatch, the men struggling with it as if they were unsure just what to do. The block at the end of the rig stayed in position, not dipping toward the open hatch.

He looked at his watch. They had been on the ship for over forty minutes.

"Manolo!" he shouted into the tube. "What's wrong? What's taking so long?"

Then he saw Manolo on the deck, directing men first one way then another. Looking closely, he saw that Manolo had the knife in his hand. Manolo's words—*if there is no gold, Sinclair*—were vivid in his mind. The plan was for Manolo to work in the engine room, directing steam to the ship's cranes. There was no reason for him to be on deck, and if he was, there was no way for the cranes to operate. Maybe they had discovered that the cargo wasn't there.

He heard the earphones crackle in the radio niche.

The captain looked over, then quickly turned his eyes away, as if he were afraid Sinclair would discover his secret

Sinclair picked up the earphones and held one up to his ear. He wasn't sure he could understand Russian without knowing the exact context or seeing the speaker's lips. It had been a long time, and he had never really learned the language, only enough to get by in the USSR. He had lied to the Minorcans when he told them he could speak Russian.

The words in the earphones were garbled, but he gradually realized it was Spanish. He smiled at the captain as he listened to the routine weather broadcast from Valencia.

Then he saw Manolo come up onto the deck. The crane was still in the same position, not moving. He wanted to ask what was happening, but he was afraid of the answer.

As he watched, Manolo rigged a heavy block and tackle to the crane, then swung it out over the hatch. The hook on the tackle dropped down the center of the hatch with a man dangling from the end. At the edge of the hatch, a man was relaying arm signals. Two other men had taken the end of the line to a windlass, putting their backs to it.

Slowly, a net appeared in the hatchway, wrapped around four wooden cases. From the distance, they looked identical to the cases that had been in the armory.

"Fools," muttered the captain. "Why do you want this?"

"Shut up!" said Sinclair, waving the gun menacingly. He had his own doubts. He didn't need more from the captain.

He watched as the net came down onto the cases. With the top loose, he dug inside, then turned to look up at Sinclair in the pilot house. The other men crowded around the case as Manolo waved with a thumbs-up gesture.

Sinclair heard himself sigh.

"What is so exciting?" asked the captain.

Sinclair looked at the Russian, sitting with a dull, blank expression on his face, as if they were stealing nothing more than sacks of potatoes from the mess stores. He suddenly realized that the captain knew nothing. Nothing at all.

"Why are you so excited about a box of machine screws and washers?" asked the captain.

"Because we are stupid Spaniards," answered Sinclair.

The net swung out over the edge of the ship and down toward the waiting boat. The operation looked complicated, but in the calm sea, and with Manolo's boat securely lashed with double spring lines so that the two boats moved together on the sea, it was simple to lower the pallet directly onto the deck of Manolo's boat.

It came up again, then went down into the hold. Sinclair tried to keep count of the number of boxes in each netload. He knew there were approximately fifty kilograms in each crate, which meant that they needed sixteen crates to be safe. There had been four in the first load. There were six on this one. One more of six.

He watched the net swing over and down to the waiting boat.

"You are fools," said the captain. "Fascist fools. What kind of a fool would steal screws?"

"Shut up!"

He saw the net go down for the third time and come up with six more boxes. It was all they needed. With each lift of the net, the operation had gone smoother and faster. They were almost done.

Then he saw the net dip once more into the hatch. He waited until it came up with six more crates.

He opened the sliding door of the pilot house.

"It's more than we need," he shouted. "We will go too slowly if we're weighted down."

The men ignored him as they swung the crates over the side and down to the launch.

Suddenly Sinclair had a new fear. Why did they need him?

Manolo was a smuggler. And this was the biggest haul he had ever made, enough for six men to live like kings on Minorca for the rest of their lives. He looked at the captain, seemingly oblivious.

"What will you do with me and my men?" asked the captain. "After you have taken your screws."

Sinclair glanced at his watch. They had been on the ship for two hours. He glanced down at the binnacle compass. The ship had swung over to 130 degrees, 14 degrees off its original course. He started to turn the wheel, then realized that he didn't know how to unlock it. Was he spare baggage now, unable to do anything? His contribution had been the plan. They didn't need him for anything else.

Finally, Pedrito came into the pilot house.

"Why did you take more boxes than we planned?"

Pedrito smiled. "It was too easy. The plan was so perfect that Manolo said we should take more. There was room on the boat, and if one thousand kilos can kill Fascists, then one thousand five hundred kilos can kill that many more Fascists. No?"

Sinclair watched the expression of the captain, a blank look of fear.

"He didn't know," said Sinclair. "They didn't know what they were carrying."

Pedrito laughed. "Truly, you are an extraordinary man. Even the captain of the ship did not know. But you did. Spain needs more men like you."

Sinclair watched the face of the captain, still oblivious.

"He should go in the forepeak with the others," said Pedrito. "We must go."

"The course," said Sinclair. "We're not on the proper course. It was one-four-four degrees when we boarded."

"It's no problem," said Pedrito. He reached down, released the wheel lock, then swung the wheel. "We were afraid when Manolo said there wasn't enough steam for the crane. But like you, he's a clever man. He found a way for us. You saw it."

He locked the wheel again, then turned back to Sinclair. "Come, we must hurry now. And this one should go forward with the others."

"You go," said Sinclair. "I'll bring him. I—I want to make sure there's nothing on the radio."

Sinclair stared at the captain after Pedrito left. Then he burst out laughing.

"Do you know what has happened, *tovarich*? Do you know what's in those crates?"

The captain stared at Sinclair, sweat rolling down his face, adding to the stains of his filthy shirt and jacket.

Sinclair wanted desperately to tell the man. He wanted to tell the stinking, flat-faced captain what they had done right in front of his eyes, in front of the eyes of the Spanish navy and the NKVD and the CPSU and the whole world. He wanted to tell the man how David Sinclair had outwitted all of them. His idea, his plan. He was no observer anymore. He was in the heart of the struggle. Someday the whole world would know. Margaret would know.

He cringed as he thought of her, on her way to Germany, so close. In the whirl of action, he had almost forgotten her. Now he knew he had to find her, make her come to Switzerland, make her listen.

"What have they done?" asked the captain. "What have your Fascist pig comrades done while you sit here watching me?"

"Shut up!" screamed Sinclair. He raised the pistol, pointing it at the face of the captain.

He hesitated for an instant, long enough to let his anger pass. Then he pushed the captain ahead of him, down the ladderway to the deck.

Below him, on the deck of the steamer and on Manolo's boat, every man stood with his head craned toward the sky, as if they had just seen a comet. Sinclair took his eyes from the captain to follow their heads, up to the immense form of the Graf Zeppelin, floating at an altitude of perhaps 1500 feet, blithely ignorant of the drama below.

Thirty

Gregory Orlov sat alone outside the door of the interrogation room, a bottle of vodka open on the table in front of him, a look of repugnance on his face. Through the partially open door, he could hear the two Guardia Civil officers working over the man.

The door opened once, and he caught a glimpse inside. The officers had their jackets and Sam Browne belts and shiny three-cornered hats off, and both were sweaty under the arms and across the backs. They were doing a thorough job. Typical of the Spanish, thought Orlov. The only job they did with thoroughness was heavy-handed cruelty.

His anger at the stupidity of the Spanish authorities and their "inviolable" security was tempered only by the fleeting satisfaction that his hunches had been right. He had gotten reports on the circle of journalists who hung out at the cafe on the Gran Via, the so-called anti-Stalinist leftists. He knew that Torrado and Martine were the authors of the spurious hectographed flysheets that had circulated in Madrid with rumors about the gold, and he noted with satisfaction that a few rumors in the air had caused no stir at all in the city. Only he, it seemed, had even bothered to read them.

He had spent long enough with the dossiers and reports to conclude that Kruger, the Austrian, had probably killed the clerk. Alone in the group, Kruger had a reputation for violence, including some unsolved "assassinations" during the 1934–35 uprising in Austria. He had said nothing to the Spanish police until he was sure he needed them. Their procedures were too thorough and crude to be wasted prematurely.

The rest of the group was also still in Madrid, except for Martine and Sinclair. Martine, the French labor reporter, was too fastidious to be up to anything. He was an annoying parasite, but if he had gone off to France, it was only to shake loose enough funds from the unions to support more of his petty muckraking in Madrid. David Sinclair was another matter. He had left Madrid, destination unannounced. Every question about him came up with blanks.

Orlov glanced at the vodka bottle. He had drunk more than half of it while he waited for the Guardia Civil officers to finish with Kruger. They thought they would get the man to talk, but Orlov knew the Austrian would say nothing to them. Kruger would taunt them, perhaps tell them lies, probably just insult them and their mothers. It wouldn't matter how much they beat him. A determined man like Kruger could absorb an incredible amount of pain. The very process of fighting off the pain, of refusing to yield, would help him keep body and soul together. But he was still vulnerable. Orlov had seen it work dozens of times. When the beating stopped and a calm voice followed, the man was vulnerable. The collapse of will would register in the glassy and lifeless eyes. Then, if the voice was right, color would start to come back to the sallow skin and the spasm-ridden muscles would begin to relax. And then the right questions, asked the right way, would get answers.

The whole process was crude and repellent. Reason and research were the proper and satisfying way to get information, the way of a gentleman. But with eleven days until the ships docked in Odessa, Orlov did not have time to be a gentleman. The price of failure was too great. He needed to know where David Sinclair was, and he had to find out from Kruger.

He downed another glass of vodka before rehearsing what he would say. He would speak German to Kruger, relaxing the man after the screaming Spanish interrogation of the Guardia Civil officers. And calmly, he would tell Kruger what happens to murderers in Spain. Not the firing squad, with its opportunity for a moment of glory, the final grand gesture of refusing the blindfold and shouting, "Long Live Freedom!" or some comparable tripe. No, he would explain, murderers get the garrote, a typically cruel Spanish device. He would tell Kruger how the cord is sometimes not pulled quickly enough, so that the man does not die instantly. He would describe how the throat muscles can tighten involuntarily against the cord, how the eyes bulge, how the man soils himself and the body begins to spasm in the ugly gurgling of the death rattle. And when his words began to play hypnotically, when Kruger's will to resist collapsed in the face of a vision of that squalid, brutal death, then Orlov would ask his questions. Innocent, seemingly unimportant questions. The kind of questions that weren't worth dying for. And Kruger would answer.

They always did.

Thirty-One

More than Gibraltar, or the Mediterranean, or even their landfall on the coast of France, it was the Rhine River, the frontier of Germany, that stirred the passengers on the Graf Zeppelin into the excitement of journey's end.

Otto Hutten was the first to spot the river. Glued to his

window in anticipation, he called out when he saw the towers of Colmar in the heart of Alsace. A few minutes later, the great gray river came into view, broad and stately between the red banks, like a highway connecting three nations. Hutten began to sing softly to himself in a gravelly, off-key voice:

> *Die Luft ist Kühl und es dunkelt,*
> *und ruhig fliesst der Rhein;*
> *der Gipfel des Berges funkelt*
> *im Abendsonnenschein.*

Tears welled in his eyes as he sang.

"You know it?" he asked Maggie.

She shook her head.

"Otto!" said Anna Hutten. "How would she know? It is not even the Lorelei here. This is still France."

"When we left, it was Germany," he said. "What does it matter which country? Does the river know politics?"

He turned back to Maggie. "The song is from a poem of Heinrich Heine, *Die Heimkehr*. The homecoming."

He sang the words again, softly, not embarrassed by his scratchy voice or the tears on his cheeks. "It tells of how the air is cool and how it darkens, and how peacefully the river flows, and how the peaks of the mountains sparkle in the setting sunlight. Tell me, have you ever seen such a sight?"

"It's beautiful," said Maggie. "Truly beautiful." She beamed at him, sharing his obvious joy. All his qualms about Germany seemed to disappear as he looked down at the river.

"There," he said, pointing up the valley of the river. "You can see the spire of the cathedral at Strassburg. And over there, across the river, is the Black Forest."

"I'm very happy for you," said Maggie. She watched him take Anna's hand in his own as the tears of joy started down her face too.

"You're almost home," said Maggie.

"Yes," said Hutten, choked with emotion. "Almost home."

The city of Mainz, at the junction of the Rhein and Main rivers, was in view below the airship when the steward came aft, working his way obsequiously to the admiral's table.

"Admiral von Teppler?"

Von Teppler and Eisler both looked up. Beck, who had

emerged from his self-imposed seclusion after they crossed the Rhein, did not respond.

"We have a message for you from Zeppelin headquarters in Frankfurt," said the steward. "They ask that you and your . . . escorts . . . remain aboard the Zeppelin until the other passengers have disembarked."

Catching the hint of puzzled anxiety in the admiral's usually cool expression, the steward added, "I suspect it's for a special reception of some sort, sir. We rarely have such a distinguished military officer aboard. When the Spanish Enfanta flew with us on the great triangle flight, there were receptions for him everywhere we landed. He always had to leave the ship last."

"Thank you," said von Teppler. Unlike the now ebullient Hutten, his tone seemed sober and sad at the sight of Germany. Alone of the passengers, he did not look out the windows at the river valley below.

Maggie flagged the steward as he left the admiral's table.

"Should I disembark with the other passengers?" she asked. "Paul . . . Captain Whitman said that there might be some problems with the immigration authorities if I were to disembark without a passport."

"There's been no word, Miss Bourne. I suppose the safest thing is to stay on board until we speak with the authorities on the ground in Frankfurt. I'm sure there will be no problem. They are very hospitable to passengers on the Graf Zeppelin."

The Rhein-Main Airport was immense, the center of German civil aviation, with a huge new section given over to a display of Luftwaffe airplanes. As they came in over the enormous new hangar that had been built for the transatlantic service of the Hindenberg, the ground crew readying the lines on the field looked like worker bees, scurrying to envelop and protect the arriving queen. The landing itself was anticlimactic, not at all like the sudden dramatic descent at Recife. There was no hesitation, no checking of wind direction, only the brief pause in the beat of the engines during the weigh-off, then a steady descent until the ground lines were secured by the practiced crew on the field.

They came down in the lee of the great hangar, where the surface winds were almost dead calm, and the whole operation was over before most of the passengers were even aware of the touchdown. Only when the doorway that led forward from the lounge was hooked open, and the steward and cabin boys began bringing luggage forward into the lounge, did most of the passengers give any sign that they realized the flight was over.

Enkmann was the first down the gangway, followed by de Nascimento, then the Lopez-Oteros with their enormous piles of luggage. Passengers, baggage and crewmen moved every which way in such confusion that there was no time for the good-byes that usually conclude a voyage of so many days. In the hubbub, no one noticed that the admiral and his two companions had disappeared from the lounge.

When they reappeared minutes later, the passengers and most of the crew had already disembarked down the gangway, crossing the tarmac toward the low building that served as the Zeppelin terminal.

After watching them, Whitman walked back into the lounge. Maggie was sitting at the Huttens' table, her only luggage the notebook that Otto Hutten had given her and the fiberboard case with her photographic plates. Whitman wondered how she managed to look so fresh and clean after three days in the same clothes.

On the other side of the lounge, von Teppler stood at attention, resplendent in the full dress uniform of a German admiral, the stripe down the leg of his trousers echoing the color in the swastika armbands of his escorts. A saber was slung across his hip, decorations spread across his chest, the Pour le Mérite hung prominently from his neck, which seemed even longer and more aristocratic than Whitman remembered under the stiff tunic collar of the uniform jacket. The admiral seemed taller too, his nose thinner and more prominent, the saber scar more obvious. He seemed exactly what he had called himself, a man of the eighteenth century, an officer in the court of Friedrich the Great.

"Captain Whitman," he said, "I thank you for a most comfortable crossing. It was a privilege to witness your skills as the commander of this airship."

The cool formality surprised Whitman. He suspected that somehow the dress uniform, or perhaps the fact of being on German soil, had retransformed the admiral into a proper Prussian officer.

Before Whitman could respond, Beck clicked his heels sharply. "I will have my sidearm now, Captain," he said, his first words to Whitman since their confrontation.

"Yes," said Whitman. "I had almost forgotten."

"I did not," said Beck.

When Whitman turned to go up to his quarters for the Luger,

he saw a long car cruising slowly across the tarmac toward the Zeppelin.

Von Teppler seemed to spot the car at the same time. He stared for a moment, then said, "May I borrow your field glasses, Captain?"

Whitman nodded, then went through the open doorway, down the narrow empty corridor through the control room, and up the steep ladderway to his cabin. He took the pistol from his safe, along with the clip of ammunition he had removed when he first took the pistol from Beck, dropping the clip in his pocket as he came back down the ladderway with the Luger in his hand. In the chart room, he retrieved his field glasses from the rack.

The admiral and the other men were already in the narrow passageway at the door. The admiral took the glasses with a nod, then raised them to his eyes as he sighted out over the tarmac.

Whitman saw the muscles on von Teppler's face tighten. The veins on his closely trimmed temples stood out against the bony scalp, and the saber scar turned bright red against the skin of his cheek and jaw.

"My pistol!" said Beck, extending his hand.

"Captain!" said the admiral, holding out the glasses. "Would you mind looking at that car for me? Tell me what insignia you see on the sides."

"My pistol!" repeated Beck.

Ignoring him, Whitman held the pistol in his left hand while he raised the heavy 10x70 field glasses with his right hand, scanning slowly until he zeroed in on the car.

"It's a black Mercedes," said Whitman. "Looks like government issue, but I see no insignia. And no flags on the fenders." He looked up at the admiral.

"Exactly, Captain. That is not a navy staff car. It is *Sicherheitsdienst*, Heinrich Himmler's personal thugs." The admiral turned to glare at Beck, who now had the pistol in his hand.

"I was to return to face a navy inquiry," said the admiral. "I expect to face my peers, not that Nazi scum."

Whitman watched the admiral's expression gradually change from outrage to a calm, cool mien, the anger giving way to arrogant silence.

Beck, his confidence restored by the pistol in his hand, glared at Whitman. "You!" he said, waving the pistol at Whitman and at Maggie Bourne. "Get out of the Zeppelin!"

"Are you giving me orders?" said Whitman. He glanced at

Maggie. She was listening to a conversation in German that she could not understand, but the tone of what was said, and the expressions on the faces, along with Beck's gun, were enough to transform her face. There were tiny lines around her eyes and mouth that Whitman had not seen before, and her eyes, wide open, flickered from Whitman to the admiral and back again.

"You are not giving me or anyone else orders on this ship," said Whitman. He stood directly in front of Beck, blocking the lieutenant's view of the admiral.

Beck tried to sidestep, but Whitman followed him. Beck's face reddened with anger. "Get out," he said again, "unless you also wish to be charged with treason to the Reich."

"Treason?" Whitman watched the admiral's expression, expecting outrage or surprise. But there was no change in his proud bearing. He felt like he didn't know the man at all, that their talk of the day before had never happened.

"Admiral von Teppler," said Whitman, "is it your wish to leave the Zeppelin with these men?"

"My wish? I am afraid, Captain, that my wishes do not matter now."

"I am still in command of this ship," said Whitman. "And while I am in command . . ."

Beck waved the gun menacingly. "Your command, American, is a matter of . . ."

"Captain Whitman," said the admiral, still without a trace of emotion in his voice or on his face. "I am an admiral of the German navy. I have never disobeyed an order and I will not do so now. It is my duty to follow orders. *C'est une question d'honneur.* May I suggest that your efforts on my behalf can only cause difficulties for yourself?" He waited, catching Whitman's eyes before adding, "Remember, Captain, circumstances do not take over. Men make their own circumstances." There was the slightest hint of a smile in his expression as he said it.

Beck waved the gun at Whitman, snarling, "Get out of the Zeppelin, you and the American woman. Now!"

Whitman kept his eyes on the admiral, waiting for a change of expression, a hint of defiance. When he could wait no longer, he abruptly led Maggie by the arm down the stairway.

At the bottom, the long black car pulled up, and two men got out, wearing baggy gray suits and calculated menacing expressions. "Where is von Teppler?" one of them asked.

Whitman didn't answer. He led Maggie a few steps further, then turned to look back at the Zeppelin.

Von Teppler was standing in the doorway, staring straight ahead, one hand on the hilt of his saber, his gloves folded in the other hand, his chin jutting defiance. Above him, behind the Zeppelin, black and gray cumulus clouds towered up thousands of feet, broken by slanting beams of afternoon sunlight that had burned holes in the cloud cover. Backlit against the clouds the Zeppelin seemed oblivious to the drama in its shadow. The only markings visible on its skin were the huge red and white swastikas.

"What will happen to him?" said Maggie. "Who are those men?"

"*Sicherheitsdienst*," said Whitman. "Security Police."

"What will they do? And what did he mean when he said it was a question of honor?"

Whitman looked from the silhouette of the Zeppelin to the car, speeding away across the tarmac with Admiral von Teppler and the men in the baggy gray suits. "Honor," he repeated. "The code of a Prussian officer. The old Germany."

Thirty-Two

The seas and the wind were out of the east, and the gray boat labored, pitching up over the swells when Manolo caught them in time, driving through others in a shower of spray as solid water pounded over the deck, running down into the cockpit before it drained through the scuppers. Manolo had been at the helm for seven hours, refusing all offers of relief. Lines of gray fatigue were clear on his face even in the faint red glow of the compass binnacle, the only illumination on the boat.

"Why will you let no one relieve you?" asked Pedrito.

Manolo answered with a shrug.

Pedro looked down at the compass. They were steering east-northeast, well off the course that would take them up to the coast of France.

"You're too tired to steer," said Pedrito. "This course will take us back to Minorca."

"That's right."

"But Señor Sinclair's plan was to . . ."

Sinclair, awake but groggy, was halfway out of the narrow companionway hatch that led from the cockpit into the cramped forepeak. He had tried to sleep, but excitement, even more than the violent motion of the boat, had kept him awake. He heard his name and climbed through the hatch. Off the port bow, the sky was streaked with gray and brown.

"Where are we headed?" he asked.

"We need fuel and rest," said Manolo, his eyes on the spray-soaked windshield of the cabin house. "The engines cannot run forever without changing the oil. They're like men, they must rest."

"Rest? When we have this?" Sinclair gestured at the wooden crates lashed down on the sole of the cockpit. "It's no good to anyone until we deliver it in Switzerland."

"There's time for that," said Manolo. "First we rest."

"Time?" Sinclair's face twisted with anger, not so much at the thwarting of his plan, but the usurpation of his authority. He was clearly no longer in command.

Pedrito stepped between the two men. "We *are* tired, Señor Sinclair. All of us. Perhaps it would be wise to rest. A day, two days. You have seen how beautiful Minorca is. You can rest your body and your mind. If we're rested, we will not make mistakes."

"Time is what we don't have," said Sinclair. "This is war. How long do you think things will last once those German and Russian airplanes begin arriving?"

He had directed the questions to Manolo, but the short man didn't look up and didn't respond. He watched only the water ahead of the boat and the compass.

"There is always time," said Pedrito. "The island and the sea, they're good for a man's soul. Even for a man like you." He turned toward the transom of the boat, putting his bulk between Sinclair and Manolo, cutting them off from one another. "You know, Señor Sinclair," he said, "I have never seen Montserrat look at another man as she looks at you. She is very beautiful, is she not?"

"She's a pretty girl."

"And you care for her, no?"

Sinclair pictured the beach at Cala Morell and the secret spot he had found on the hillside over the cove. He remembered the suppleness and hunger of her innocent kiss, the look in her mysterious olive eyes. How tempting it was, the girl and the place. It was a place to forget everything, to find a house like the little whitewashed cottage, a place to do some serious writing, the book he had always promised himself. And this was the perfect war to write about, a war with good and bad, innocent and evil, the timeless passions of ideology and religion fought with the weapons of modernity. The dream was vivid. It had lived a long time in the recesses of his mind. And now he had *the* story of the war to write—not another scoop to report, but his own story, how he had led a band of fishermen and smugglers, men who could neither read nor write, on a mission so bold and so important that it could decide the course of the war. Descriptions of the men and the boat flitted through his mind, taking shape in prose.

Manolo said something to Pedrito in Minorquin, and they swapped places, Pedrito taking the wheel and Manolo standing next to Sinclair at the transom, looking out at the phosphorescent wake behind the boat.

"What is it?" Manolo asked. "What is it that drives a man like you?"

Sinclair gestured toward the wooden crates. "This," he said. "And the fight we must all fight."

"I don't think so," said Manolo. "You're not even Spanish, yet this plan of yours matters more to you than to any of us. We've all lost friends and relatives to the Fascists. If they win, or if the Communists take over the Republic, we know what will happen to us. That's why we fight. But to you, it will be nothing. You can go home. Or to another war. It's not the end for you."

He paused, waiting for Sinclair to look at him.

"I think there's something else," he added. "A hatred, a fear, a woman perhaps. Nothing else can possess a man as you are possessed."

"What are you getting at?" Sinclair asked angrily. "Do you think I would do this for a woman? What—to buy her a trinket?"

"No, Sinclair, I don't think you are a man to buy trinkets. But every man tries to prove himself to a woman. Some do it by fighting, or by beating the woman. Others try to be powerful, or rich, or to act the hero. It's the way we are."

Sinclair looked away, afraid Manolo would read more in his face. He suddenly felt vulnerable.

They left the boat concealed in a grotto near the cove, and chugged into the harbor in Ciudadela in Pedrito's little double-ended fishing boat, six of them crowded in as if they were just back from a long fishing trip. No one on the quay seemed to notice that there were too many men in the boat, or that they had no catch to unload. At the siesta hour, no one in Ciudadela noticed much.

Before the others were ashore, stretching their legs as they wobbled unfamiliarly on the steady land, Manolo was negotiating at the gasoline dock for more fuel to take back to the cove.

The men scattered, back to the quiet, shuttered houses where they could fade into the life of the town as if nothing had happened. For them, it had been one more expedition, not very different from a run for arms to southern France or a run in the old days for tobacco in Morocco. And with no price tag ever put on the crates in the cockpit of the gray boat, it was less real to them than tobacco or arms would have been. Tobacco had an instant value, like a load of fish. It could be sold anywhere, bartered at any shop, in any man's home. And with arms, they could see what the shipment would do, see the grateful looks of the men on the beaches in Majorca when they unloaded the cases. The crates on the sole of the cockpit were too abstract to have any meaning. After all, as Manolo had said, they were *contrabandista*, not pirates.

Sinclair and Pedrito crossed the bridge to the quay that led down to the cafe. The old woman at the cafe saw them and ran inside, appearing a moment later with Montserrat, barefoot and wearing the familiar black shift. Even in the distance, Sinclair could make out the enigmatic smile on her lips. He could feel her eyes studying his walk.

When he and Pedrito were close to the cafe, Montserrat began running toward them. Sinclair was embarrassed as he watched her lean, tawny legs and the cloth of the shift stretching tight over her breasts, the erect nipples pressing their shape into the threadworn fabric.

She threw her arms around the neck of her brother, kissed him on both cheeks, and chattered at him in Minorquin. She flashed a broad smile at Sinclair.

"My sister thinks we're heroes," said Pedrito to Sinclair. "To her, you are El Cid." He watched the blush come to Montserrat's face, then added, "I think maybe I will help Manolo with the barrels. I cannot let him know he is as strong as he thinks he is."

When he left, the two of them were alone on the quay. There

was no one else at the tables of the cafe, or on the nearby fishing boats. Even the old woman had disappeared inside.

"Will you have some wine?" asked Montserrat.

When he looked at her, she lowered her eyes.

"I'm very happy that you've come back," she said.

"I'm happy to be back," he said, trying to keep his tone casual. Her shy gaze and direct words made him acutely uncomfortable.

"Pedrito and Manolo will go to the Cala tonight," she said. "With the fuel. Manolo always does it immediately. He doesn't like to be unprepared."

She seemed aware of his discomfort. "Do you want to rest?" she asked. "Perhaps a bath? There's no one in the room upstairs."

Sinclair looked down at himself. His body ached with fatigue, stank with the sweat of close quarters and nervous anxiety. A hot bath, a rest, a bottle of wine ... he remembered the table at the little cottage, the kerosene lamps. He could picture himself sitting with a jug of wine, beginning an outline on a pad of coarse paper. He smiled at Montserrat, and she responded with big olive eyes open wide, looking straight at him.

"Come," she said, "we can walk up through the square."

Her hips swayed gently as her bare feet gripped the worn cobblestones. He walked alongside her, glancing across the harbor to where Manolo and Pedrito were loading fuel barrels onto the fishing boat.

"I knew you would come back," she said. "I just knew it." She watched her feet as she spoke, not taking his arm or his hand, but walking close to him, brushing against him often enough for him to anticipate the accidental contacts. "I've never known anyone so famous."

"What makes you say that?"

"This morning a man was in Ciudadela asking about you. He said he had read some of the things you had written and that he had heard you were here."

Sinclair stopped in his tracks. "A man? Here? Who was he?"

"He never gave his name. He came in a taxi, in the morning. For a long time he wandered around the harbor, looking at the boats. He tried to talk to the fishermen, but most of them speak little Spanish, so they sent him to the cafe and he talked to me."

"What did you tell him?"

"I told him nothing. I said that I didn't know anything about you. But inside I was proud that you are such a famous man."

"What did he look like?"

"A big man, but not so big as Pedrito. He had a flat face and he was perhaps fifty years old. He was dressed like a man from the city. He spoke Spanish well, but with an accent, perhaps a German accent."

Sinclair thought of the others at the cafe on the Gran Via, the only ones who knew he was in Minorca. No one fit the description. A German looking for him in Minorca? It seemed impossible.

"What else do you remember about him?" Sinclair took her slender arms in his fingers.

"The taxi driver said that the man came to Minorca on an airplane. By himself. The plane brought only him."

"By airplane? Alone? Are you sure?"

"That's what the taxi driver said."

He looked past her, to the open square of the town, with the post office and the town hall, all frozen in the quiet of siesta. There was only one man important enough to have flown there alone—Orlov, the NKVD man. His Russian accent could be mistaken for German. Sinclair was surprised that they had discovered so soon, more surprised that they had tracked him to Minorca. And strangely, he was pleased. He knew what Orlov thought of him and of his writings. Well, now he had gotten to Orlov, shown him what David Sinclair could really do. And it was too late for Orlov to stop them.

"What happened to him?"

Montserrat squirmed in his grip. "Señor Sinclair—you're hurting me." He looked down and relaxed his grip on her arms. There were red streaks on her skin where his fingers had been. "I'm sorry," he said.

She rubbed her arms. "You're very strong."

He smiled. No woman had ever said that to him before.

"The man went back to Mahón," she said. "No one told him anything about you, so he went back. Do you know who he was?"

"I think so. He won't be a problem."

Montserrat led him up a dim stairway at the back of the cafe. The room at the top was stark—a brass bed, a bathtub behind a screen, two chairs, a plain table. There was a view out over the square to the post office and the terra-cotta buildings, but the room felt like the seedy rooms that are hired by the hour in port towns.

Montserrat brought hot water for a bath from the kitchen downstairs, and when Sinclair came out of the tub with a towel wrapped around him, she was sitting on the bed, staring off at the quiet square outside. She got up shyly, looking up at him, reading his thoughts. She glanced down at herself in the worn, black shift, then turned around. "Please do not watch me," she said as she began to unbutton the shift.

Sinclair remembered the movement of her hands unbuttoning the shift, and he thought of the grace of her body behind the curtain in the darkened alcove, the rhythmic undulations of her legs and tummy, the uplifted nipples of her breasts, the glitter of the moonlight on her black hair. But as she walked toward him, the grace was gone, hidden in the shyness of her steps. He reached out and she quickly brought herself close to him, hiding in his arms like a frightened child. Then she looked up, her lips full and moist, her eyes wondering. As he kissed her, she pressed her thighs and breasts against him with a surprising desperation.

He tried to pace himself, but with her eager body close to him, he felt his own body responding too quickly. He fought for control, tried to think of anything but her supple skin and lithe body. It was too late. Before he could pull himself back, they were on the squeaky bed, his hands locked on her slender shoulders, his face buried in her neck, his body exploding inside her. And then he was spent.

He rolled away, avoiding her eyes. From the dry stillness of her body, he knew she hadn't been aroused. The memories that had been so vivid, her tawny skin covered with fine sweat, trembling like a reed, swaying in a rhythm that consumed him—all seemed distant. He wanted to say something but couldn't find the words.

She turned, nestling her back against him, hiding her face from his. She was still like that for a long time, his hand resting on her arm, her hair against his face.

"David?" It was the first time she had used his given name, and he was afraid she would ask about their unsatisfying lovemaking. He kept her back to him until she said, "Will you tell me about France and Switzerland? Someday I will go there. I will dress up in fine clothes from the fancy shops and have my hair cut in the newest style and wear tall shoes and speak only French."

"I like your hair like this," he said, teasing it with his lips, thankful that she hadn't asked a question he would have been too embarrassed to answer.

"It must be wonderful to go so many places and see so many things. Pedrito said that you even saw the Zeppelin flying overhead. Have you ever . . . ?"

Zeppelin! He bolted upright. His idle thoughts—the whitewashed cottage, the adoring black-haired girl—faded quickly as he tried to count the days. On the pounding boat, days and nights had merged. He had almost lost count. Three days—Margaret was almost in Frankfurt, perhaps there already.

"The post office? Is it open? Can I make a call now?"

"Yes, of course. It is open through the afternoon."

He dressed quickly, still carrying his jacket as he ran out the door.

"David . . . Señor Sinclair . . ." She sat up, hugging the bed-clothes around herself. "Will you be back?"

He left without answering.

Thirty-Three

Whitman and Maggie were hardly away from the crowd of security guards, ground handlers and policemen on the tarmac when they were accosted by another phalanx of officials inside the terminal—Zeppelin Company administrators in double-breasted blue suits, customs and immigration officers in a panoply of uniforms, and Gestapo in their baggy gray suits.

"Whitman!" someone shouted.

"Herr Kapitän! This way please."

Everyone seemed to want him at once.

Only one man sought Maggie, and he stood out from the others in a trim, well-fitted suit of fine worsted. His hair was long at the temples and collar. Obviously an American.

"Mrs. Bourne?" he said. When she turned toward him, he extended his hand. "Frank Cooper. American Consulate. I have a temporary passport for you."

Ignoring his own name and the persistent shoving of the officials who had crowded around him, Whitman listened for Maggie to correct the "Mrs." He was ready to say it himself when she turned to him, a shadow in her eyes.

"I meant to explain. There was so little time. It's . . ."

Before she could finish, they were separated by the sea of prodding officials. Whitman looked around and recognized none of the faces. The old-time Zeppelin commanders and engineers who had taken administrative positions with the company were not there.

Two men started to lead him by the arms, and he instinctively shook free, twisting loose from their grips and scanning through the faces until he spotted Zekner, the junior watch officer of the Graf Zeppelin.

"Did those samples get unloaded?" Whitman asked him.

"The samples?" Zekner seemed surprised. "With all the excitement, I . . . I forgot."

"Make sure, would you? They have to get to the Höchst Laboratory right away if the vaccines are going to be ready for our return flight."

Whitman flinched at the word *our*. With the threat of that hearing, and the new questions that would certainly be asked about his removal of Stifel from the crew roster against the explicit orders of the new operations manager, "*our* return flight" was at the very least presumptuous.

"I'll take care of it," said the younger man. "And good luck with . . ." He nodded his head toward the Zeppelin Company offices in the back of the terminal building.

"Thanks."

Whitman went directly to the crew counter. The unsmiling immigration officer barked *"Pass und Papiere, bitte."*

It was a formality, even with Whitman's American passport. With extended residential status, Whitman was all but a German for immigration purposes. Even so, there was the ritual of the stamps to undergo, and he knew the Germans loved those stamps. The ability to dispense or withhold the stamp made even the lowliest bureaucrat into a powerful official.

While the sour-faced immigration officer tilted Whitman's passport in different directions, reading off the other visas in a mumble so indistinct that only the contemptuous tone was discernible, Whitman looked for Maggie. She was nowhere in view.

Through the glass partition that separated him from the immigration line for German citizens, Whitman saw Otto Hutten, hunched over in exasperation as he unsuccessfully argued with an official seated below the partition.

"This cannot be correct," said Hutten. His face was red, and his fists tightly clenched as he tried to control his anger. "We are German citizens. We have always paid our taxes, here and in Brazil."

"Citizens," spat out the official. "Because you were born here? What rights do you think you have after twenty-five years? The right to come back and be a burden on the State? In the New Germany it takes more than birth to be a citizen. Some of the Jews were born here. Does that make them Germans? A citizen has responsibilities toward the State."

"Responsibilities?" Hutten pounded his fist on the counter. "What do you know of responsibilities? You . . . ?" Words failed him as he began to shake with anger and exasperation.

"Otto!" Anna Hutten took his arm. "It will be all right, Otto. Please. It will do no good to argue."

"The old woman is right," said the official. "You want to reenter Germany, you pay. Otherwise, you better have a ticket back."

"It is not all right," said Hutten. "First the fees. Then this tax bond. It would take all the money we have with us. We would be left with nothing. From owning our own little vineyards, we would be . . ." His voice caught in his throat until he coughed. "We would be paupers. A whole life of hard work and we would be left with nothing."

"You should have thought of that before you got on the Zeppelin," said the official, holding out his hand for the money.

Anna hugged Hutten's arm. "But we're home, Otto. *Home*."

"Home? The Germany I left did not steal from citizens."

Slowly, he counted the worn German and Brazilian banknotes from his billfold. When he finished, the official quickly recounted the money, jotting notes on his pad. "It's not enough," he said, looking at the locket on Anna's neck and the gold watch on Hutten's vest. He waited until Hutten's eyes followed his, then said, "Those will do."

Hutten's fists tightened again. "To take jewelry from an old woman! Have you no shame? This is not the Germany I left."

"Shut up, old man," said the official, reaching out for the watch and the locket. "You're lucky we let you in at all."

Whitman twisted free from his own line, backing up until he was at the end of the partition, where he saw de Nascimento watching the transaction with his familiar, unctuous grin. "Problems?" asked Whitman as he caught Anna's eye.

"Oh, Captain." She nudged her husband until he looked up.

"Captain Whitman." Otto Hutten managed a smile of recognition through the rimless glasses. His eyes, like his wife's, were red with anger and frustration.

"It seems that for old people to return to the Fatherland is not so simple as we imagined,'' he said. ''They say that we must have a *Steuerverzichtsleistung*. We knew nothing about it. No one in Rio de Janeiro, at the embassy, ever said anything. And without it . . .''

''Tax quit claim?'' Whitman deciphered the compound noun. ''You were living in Brazil for twenty-five years. What taxes could you possibly owe here?''

Hutten shrugged. ''I've tried to explain this to them, but how can one argue with the regulations? We had to pay over all the money we had. And when that wasn't enough, they even took Anna's little locket and my gold watch.'' He pointed to the watch, still lying on the table in front of the official, who was busily stamping and stapling documents.

''We're proud people, Captain. We saved our money so we wouldn't be a burden on anyone in our old age. We don't wish charity, even from our family. But . . .'' He choked up. ''Well, what can we do? We're just old people. And it seems that the New Germany has no need for old people.''

Whitman turned to the immigration official, a long-faced man with closely shaved sideburns and temples, and a stiff-collared uniform that looked too tight and too warm.

''Are you sure there's no mistake here?'' said Whitman.

''Mistake?'' The official answered without looking up. ''There's no mistake. These old codgers! They come back here to die. Think the Reich is some kind of hospice. Nothing but a drain on the State, these old ones.''

''Wait a minute!'' said Whitman. ''The Huttens are German citizens. They've done nothing wrong. How dare you speak of them like that!''

''Who are you?'' asked the official.

''Paul Whitman. Acting commander of the Graf Zeppelin.''

The official went back to his stamping. ''Well, *Acting Commander*, this matter is no concern of yours. We're just taking precautions to see that these old leeches don't suck the blood of the German State.'' He handed Hutten his passport. ''Now move on, you.''

Hutten looked down at the thin book with the eagle emblem on the cover.

''Do I get no receipt?'' he asked.

The official glanced at Hutten, then at Whitman.

''Receipt?'' He laughed. ''What for?''

''For our money,'' said Hutten, red-faced. ''For the savings from our years of work and for my wife's locket and for the watch that I have worn for almost thirty years.''

"What they've paid is actually a bond, isn't it?" said Whitman. "They'll need a receipt to reclaim the funds.''

The official laughed. "Call it what you will,'' he said. Taking a scrap of paper, he scribbled some indecipherable figures and handed it to Hutten. "Now move on,'' he said.

He turned then to Whitman. "You see. Already they are a drain on the State, taking up time with their nonsense requests.''

Flushed with anger, Whitman started to reach over the counter toward the official.

"Whitman!'' It was a voice from the next aisle, where his own papers were going through their trial by ordeal.

'Alles in ordnung, Whitman,'' the voice said, and Whitman felt arms pushing and pulling him through the aisle to the exit point, where someone handed him his papers.

The Huttens were already there, Anna dragging her worn traveling bag, Otto carrying an old valise, held closed with a leather belt around the middle.

"Well,'' said Otto. "We're in Germany again.''

"I'm sorry,'' said Whitman.

"Sorry? What have you to apologize for? You've done everything you could do. I'm afraid that we're powerless, just two old people against a great bureaucracy.''

"Look,'' said Whitman, "give me your address. If I can find out anything about this tax quit claim business, I will. Maybe it will straighten itself out.''

"Perhaps,'' said Otto Hutten as he wrote out the address on the back of the receipt. "You've been very kind to us,'' he said. "But I fear there is nothing you can do. You should perhaps save your energies for your own struggles with the bureaucrats.''

"Oh, Captain,'' said Anna Hutten. "If only we could somehow repay you for your kindness. Perhaps you would someday have time to visit us in Bremen. It is lovely there now. I would make you a fine dinner, real German home cooking. It's one thing I have not forgotten in Brazil.''

"Anna!'' said Hutten. "The captain is a busy man. He has no time for *real German home cooking*.''

Whitman shook off the hand of an official on his elbow.

"Actually,'' he said, "I'd like that very much. My father was from Wilhelmshaven. In New York we ate the old dishes all the time.''

"Wilhelmshaven?" said Hutten. "We're practically landsmen. It is only one hundred kilometers from us."

"You will come then?" said Anna Hutten. "And perhaps you would bring that lovely Fräulein Bourne."

"I'll certainly try," said Whitman.

"Move on," the immigration official barked at the Huttens. "You're holding up things here." He turned to another official and added in a voice loud enough for all of them to hear, "Old farts! Don't know why we even allow them back."

Anna Hutten gathered her traveling bag in one hand and waved with the other. *"Auf wiedersehn, Kapitän."*

"Auf wiedersehn," said Whitman.

Otto Hutten gazed for a minute at Whitman, then through the glass doors at the end of the terminal at the Zeppelin looming on the airfield. He pulled off his rimless glasses and wiped his eyes, as if he were trying to rub away the regret and incomprehension and sorrow from his gaze. To Whitman, the old man looked like he had just come to the end of a rainbow and found a pot of lead.

"Auf wiedersehn," he said finally and turned to walk away.

Thirty-Four

"There is also a phone call for you," said the clerk in the telegraph office. "Long distance. Cabin two." She pointed to the wall next to the offices where the three telephone booths were lined up.

"Long distance?" said Maggie. "From New York?"

The clerk looked down at her papers. "Barcelona," she said.

"Barcelona? Are you sure? I don't know anyone in Barcelona."

"Of course I'm sure," snapped the clerk. "It's my job to be sure. The call could be from anywhere in Spain. All calls from Spain are routed through Barcelona now."

It took a long time for the call to go through, and all Maggie could hear over the receiver was static interrupted by bursts of chatter in German between the operators. She still had no idea who the call could be from, or how whoever it was had found her in Frankfurt, at the Rhein-Main Airport. It bothered her, not only the guessing game, but the intrusion into what had been an interlude of special privacy, a time when no one knew where she was, whom she was with, or what she was doing. There had been few times in her life when she wasn't accountable or didn't have a responsibility. She had treasured this one.

Through the glass window in the booth, she watched the terminal hall empty. Even the plainclothes policemen who had questioned her about the admiral and about Paul Whitman were gone. *Sicherheitsdienst,* they had called themselves. Security Police. When she asked them where Paul was and when he would be finished, one answered curtly, "Herr Whitman is quite occupied. I think he will be busy for a long while."

For the first time since boarding the Zeppelin, she felt dirty. She was wearing the same clothes she had worn for four days, rinsing them out each night in the tiny sink in the washroom and hanging them to dry in her cabin. Now, the blouse felt limp and gray, the suit was a map of wrinkles and spots. Would they ever be clean enough to send back to that Lopez-Otero woman? she wondered.

Slowly, Maggie realized what was really bothering her. Why hadn't she told Paul about David? It wasn't an effort to deceive. She had never even thought about it until the man from the embassy came over with the temporary passport. She had just forgotten David, forgotten him completely. He was out of her life, gone. She had taken the Africa assignment to get as far away as possible, to forget everything about those years. And it had worked. Too well.

"Mrs. Sinclair, we have your call."

Her insides fell. Even before the "Mrs. Sinclair" registered, Maggie realized who the call was from.

"Margaret?" The connection was poor, but the voice was unmistakable. In just the name, she recognized the hard edge, the tone that he used when he was feeling confident. And, of course, no one else ever called her Margaret.

She wanted to hang up, to cut it off before they had the inevitable blowup. Why? she asked herself. How could he ever have found her? She had been at the terminal for less than two hours, had spoken to no one except the immigration officers, the security police, and the woman at the telegraph office.

"David. How did you find me?"

"Morrison. He said you've had quite an adventure."

"Yes," she said, but she knew it was impossible to tell him

what had happened and why it had all mattered to her. He would dismiss it as a ridiculous search for the exotic. He always had a way of making her feel guilty for enjoying her experiences.

"How's Madrid?" she asked.

"Bizarre. The political naiveté of the Spanish is amazing."

There was an embarrassing silence. His comment was one of those pronouncements that cannot be answered. And she had nothing to say to him. Eight years of marriage and they couldn't carry on a conversation. That, more than the silence itself, was painful.

"Actually," he went on, "I'm not in Madrid." His voice rose in excitement, like when he had a new assignment. "I can't tell you where I am now, not over the phone."

"Oh, David—" She regretted her sarcastic tone as soon as it came out. "Still playing games? Trying to make a holiday or a junket sound dramatic. Covering a scoop?"

"No, Margaret. It's not a holiday and I'm not covering a scoop. I'm not an observer on the sidelines anymore."

His words stung. More than once, she had accused him of being an armchair revolutionary, content to criticize but without the conviction to act. Each time the words had hit him hard, like the probe of a dentist when he finds the exposed nerve. When the words came back, she realized how cruel she had been.

"This could be the turning point," he went on, his voice taking on the stagy tone she remembered from his endless pronouncements about the world. "For Spain, maybe for democracy as we know it. I once told you there was little standing between the survival of democracy and the collapse to totalitarianism. Well, right now we're sitting on the last hope. Either we succeed, or Spain—and that means eventually the rest of Europe—falls to the Fascists and the Communists."

"It sounds exciting, David." She found it impossible now to avoid the patronizing tone that crept into her voice. And when he recognized it, he knew he had to convince her.

"I'm serious, Margaret. This is *the* struggle, the real cause."

"What are you talking about, David?"

"I can't explain now. But I should be in Switzerland in three days, four at the most. I'll look for you at the Züricher Hof. I already have a room booked, so just tell them you're Mrs. Sinclair."

"I can't, David."

There was another moment of silence, and she could feel his anger even before he answered. "What do you mean you *can't*?

Morrison told me you have no plans. He said you're just passing the time until you catch a steamer or the Hindenberg back to New York. This is important, Margaret, the biggest thing either of us, *anyone,* has ever gotten into."

"I have plans, David. I'm going to the Olympic Games in Berlin, maybe Kiel too. I'm hoping to do some shooting there. I'll sell whatever I get on speculation."

"Olympics?" He snarled it with the contempt he reserved for sports, Africa, farm workers, and anything else she had ever been interested in. "Who's taking you, some kraut gigolo?"

"Actually . . ."

"This should be good," he interrupted. "I can't wait to hear who you're climbing into bed with to get the tickets."

"David! Please. I don't have the energy for another of these arguments. We promised that we would give each other some room for a few months."

"*Room?* Is that the new word for it? You're still my wife, Margaret. Remember?"

"Yes, David. I remember. But that piece of paper is all there is between us now."

"Well, who is he?"

"He?"

"The kraut."

"David, if you must know, I'm going to the Olympics with an American named Paul Whitman. He's the acting commander of the Graf Zeppelin. He rescued me from that awful schooner . . ."

Sinclair's laughter crackled through the phone, hollow and acrid. "A flyboy? You actually fell for a uniform? That's something I wouldn't have suspected of you. Does he know you're married?"

She felt herself flush at the question. "Please, David. Can't we just be friends and behave civilly toward one another? In another six months the divorce will become final. Wouldn't it be easier to just try to be friends?"

"Friends?" He snarled the word, and she could picture his expression, the slight curl at the edge of his upper lip, the narrowing eyes, the deep furrows across the forehead. "You're my wife, Margaret. When you realize what I'm . . . what's happening in the world and what I'm doing, you'll give up these infantile fantasies of flyboys."

"David. It's no use. It's over. Done. It's just a matter of time until the divorce is final."

"No! Never!" His voice rose, then fell calm again. "I'm *not* the same man I was, Margaret. I'm not on the sidelines any-more. This is the real struggle. Come to Zurich and see for yourself.''

"I'm sorry, David. I can't.''

"I'll never let you go, Margaret.'' His tone switched from plea to threat. "I mean it.''

"Good-bye, David. And good luck with whatever it is that you're doing. I wish you well. I really do.''

"I mean it, Margaret. I'll . . .''

"Good-bye, David.''

When she hung up the phone, her hand was trembling.

"Damn.'' She said it to herself softly. "Damn, damn, damn.''

Thirty-Five

One glance and Whitman knew that Hempe was not a "typical" Nazi.

Most of the Nazi rank and file Whitman had seen were small-towners, men with meager educations and a lingering bitter hostility toward the cities, foreigners, wealth, and culture. With no provocation at all, they were likely to barge into a cafe where foreigners or German intellectuals were discussing films or books, and drown out all conversation with a rowdy rendition of *Wacht am Rhein* or the *Horst Wessel Lied.* In the homes of the rich, they would use the slightest pretext to destroy furniture or art works, less because of party guidelines or policy than because of their own resentments of what the wealth represented.

But alongside the rank and file, or more commonly in charge of them, were a few men who did not fit the stereotype. University educated, though often not in the great universities like Göttingen, Tübingen and Heidelberg, they were men of the cities, men who presented a facade of suave cosmopolitanism, using language and affectations to differentiate themselves from the coarse rank and file. Josef Goebbels with his Ph.D. and especially Hermann Goering with his greed for art were perhaps the epitome of the cultured Nazis. And although they were sometimes resented by the rank and file, they inspired protégés, like Adalbert Hempe, the Director of Operations of the Zeppelin Company, who did all they could to imitate the styles of their mentors.

Hempe was not quite as fat as Goering, and his lips lacked the thin, curling sneer that was so striking in photographs of the air marshal. But his pudgy skin was pink and soft, his eyes tiny and piglike, and he shaved so closely that there was no trace of a beard or moustache in his puffy, round face. His fingernails were long and carefully manicured, with clear polish that glinted in the light. As he looked up at Whitman, he tapped the nails on the desktop in a nervous, annoying rhythm.

"I trust you enjoyed talking with the *Sicherheitsdienst*," he said. "I understand that you were most uncooperative." There was a trace of a Bavarian accent in his voice, which he worked hard to expunge.

"Where is Eckener?" said Whitman.

"Please, Whitman, sit down. We have much to talk about, and you look very uncomfortable. Your friend Hugo Eckener is in Friedrichshafen now, where he can surround himself with memories. He's no longer in active control of the Zeppelin Company."

"Eckener is still chairman of the company."

"In title, yes. But things are changing in the Zeppelin Company, as they are changing all over Germany. I am now the Director of Operations, and it is I with whom you must deal."

Whitman looked around the office. Things *had* changed. It was hard to believe that it was the same room where only a few weeks before he had spent long hours working with Hugo Eckener. Before, the furniture had been shabby but serviceable, heavy oak tables with wicker chairs like the ones Eckener favored in the control rooms of the Zeppelins. There had been maps and drawings on the walls, and models everywhere, of Zeppelins, of a new cross section for frame rings, of a new nacelle design that would house the big diesel engines that were just becoming available.

It was all gone now, and in place of the maps and drawings, the freshly painted walls mounted only two small photographs, the standard framed portraits of Adolf Hitler and Hermann Goering. In place of the old furniture, there were delicate French antiques, and the wooden floors were covered with expensive Oriental carpets. The new decor looked strange in what had been a working office. Whitman searched in vain for a comfortable-looking chair.

"You're surprised by the office?" Hempe waved his hand around the room when he caught Whitman's eye. "You see," he said, "we're not all barbarians."

"It takes more than furniture and carpets," answered Whitman. "And it's not so impressive to someone who has seen your methods. Out there, I just saw one of your customs officers confiscate a gold watch from an old man whose only crime was coming home to the Germany he loved."

Hempe waved the comment aside.

"You shouldn't let yourself be taken in so easily by the old ones, Whitman. Their reactionary views can be more dangerous to the Reich than the Bolshevists and the Jews. But this is really far from our concern, and I suspect that we can only disagree about this sort of matter." He waited for a response. When Whitman answered only with a glare, Hempe went on.

"You're in serious trouble, *Herr Kapitän*. After this recent incident with von Teppler, I suspect that we shall have a difficult time protecting you from the *Sicherheitsdienst*."

"*We?* I was under the impression that it was you who ordered the hearing."

"Whitman, I'm not a petty man. The hearing has been postponed to give you other options, options that may be wiser both for you and for the Zeppelin Company."

"Such as?"

"I'm certain that if you resign your command, *and* if you're willing to work with us in certain other capacities, the police charges against you can be dropped."

"*Police* charges?"

"Assaulting a navy officer. Interfering in the transport of a prisoner. Not to mention endangering the passengers and crew of a German Zeppelin. The evidence against you is quite solid. There are witnesses ready to testify."

Whitman stared incredulously at Hempe. "Are you serious? Do you actually expect me to cower from men like that wretched little lieutenant? He is a pathetic little coward, a man with no trace of honor or decency."

"*Honor. Decency.* Those are big words, Captain Whitman. Your author Hemingway says in his novel on the Great War that he is embarrassed by such words, that they are somehow wrong for our age. Don't you agree?"

"I'm not sure Hemingway had the Nazis in mind when he wrote that."

Hempe reached for a polished wooden box, caressing the inlaid top before he opened it. "Take one," he said, offering the cigars to Whitman. "Canary Islands. They're superb, better than the Cuban cigars."

Whitman waved the box away, then watched while Hempe went through his elaborate ritual, selecting a cigar, sniffing along its length, snipping the end with a silver cutter, moistening and lighting it with fastidious care.

Hempe let the first clouds of smoke drift in front of his face before he spoke.

"It's foolish for us to argue, Whitman. You're an excellent technician. There's no question of your skills in flying the Zeppelin, or your knowledge of the aircraft. But technical skill is no longer the sole criterion for the airship commands. It's impossible for the Zeppelin Company to continue the dangerous apolitical course started by Herr Eckener. Today, to be apolitical is to join the opposition. And these Zeppelins are tools of immense importance for the New Germany."

"Tools?" said Whitman. "I suspect that your new Luftwaffe, and even the air marshal himself"—he pointed to the photograph of Goering behind Hempe—"would agree that there's little military use for the Zeppelins. A hydrogen-filled airship is too vulnerable. A single explosive shell can turn it into a fireball."

"Warfare with guns and bullets is not our intention. The German Reich has no plans for aggressive wars, anywhere. I think that has been made quite clear by the speeches of the Fuehrer..."

Whitman pictured the squadrons of Junkers 52s with their escort of Messerschmitt 109s of the Condor Legion, winging their way over the Straits from Spain toward Spanish Morocco.

"...but there is another kind of warfare that *is* important. The war of words. And in that war, the prestige of the Graf Zeppelin is important, far too important to squander. To the masses, the effect of seeing the Hindenberg or the Graf Zeppelin fly overhead is electrifying. In the plebiscite on the reoccupation of the Rhineland, at the party rallies in Nuremberg, at the Olympic Games this week—the Zeppelins are an effective means of convincing the populace of the might and technical achievements of Germany. These are missions of great political importance and delicacy."

"They're a waste," said Whitman. "The Graf Zeppelin and

the Hindenberg are the only aircraft in the world that can fly the Atlantic with a useful load. Even when airplanes are flying regularly from New York to London, or even Frankfurt to Rio, there's no airplane that can match the payload of the Zeppelins. An airplane can't begin to touch the economics. With the amount of fuel the Zeppelin uses to fly to Rio, an airplane would be lucky to reach Paris. And reliability—these ships are incomparable. To take them out of regular service for propaganda stunts would be criminal."

Hempe stretched back from his desk, puffing deliberately on his cigar.

"*Criminal*, you say? An interesting choice of word. The same word has been used to describe your recent actions. You know, Whitman, the *Sicherheitsdienst* does not rely on the usual channels of justice. On matters of Reich security, their remedies are without recourse to the courts."

"Is it the Graf Zeppelin you want? Or me? Remember, I'm still an American citizen."

"No," said Hempe, with a self-satisfied grin. "You're a dual national. Your residential status and your employment in a German company of the restricted category has in effect suspended your American citizenship, at least in terms of what the people at your embassy call 'the protection of American citizens.' Read the inside cover of your passport if you don't believe me. You are fully subject to the laws of the German Reich, without recourse to American protection. Under the circumstances, I worry that you may have become accident prone."

"Accident prone? What are you talking about?"

"Accidents are all too common in Germany today. It's the price we must pay for rapid economic and political development. I wish it were otherwise, but too often, it seems, there are mistakes. I'm told that among the Anarchists, Bolshevists, Gypsies, and homosexuals in Dachau, there are people who actually don't belong there. Once there has been a mixup, it appears that the matter is not easily straightened out. Records are misplaced, names confused. It's regrettable, but perhaps... inevitable. Surely you have seen the newspapers and realize how often it becomes necessary for a certain element to be incarcerated in places like Dachau?"

"*Der Angriff* is not exactly my favorite reading matter."

"You should read it all the same. I just spoke with one of their reporters, the man who will be doing the story on the retirement of Admiral von Teppler."

"Retirement? The man came back to Germany to speak out. Is he going to end up another of your Dachau statistics?"

"Speak out?" said Hempe incredulously. "Whatever the admiral has told you does not correspond with the official story. And, of course, only the official story can be printed or broadcast in Germany. No government wants to confuse the people with spurious lies."

"It sounds like there's no room in the New Germany for a man of honor like the admiral. Maybe there's no room for me either. Is that what you're trying to tell me?"

"The big word again, Captain? *Honor.* It may be an anachronistic concept."

"Not for all of us."

"Whitman! Captain Whitman!" Hempe waved the cigar histrionically. "You confuse me with the crude excesses of the rank and file. I'm not a man without scruples. As you suggested before, there is an important future for the Zeppelins. And you could be part of it. You *should* be part of it." He flicked ashes into a marble ashtray.

"The future of the Zeppelins depends on helium, Whitman. As long as there is the possibility of a tragic accident, like the fire which consumed the British R-101, the Zeppelins cannot achieve their full potential. Imagine the world reaction if the Graf Zeppelin or the Hindenberg should catch fire and be destroyed. It would be a most terrible blow."

"Is that your concern? Or are you worried that without helium they're useless for military purposes?"

Hempe laughed. "I told you. The Reich has no military plans. None whatsoever. Like you, we believe in the future of the Zeppelin as an instrument of peace, especially with a switchover to helium as the lifting gas. But the United States has a total monopoly on helium production in their fields in Kansas and Texas. We have had exploratory talks, and it appears that your Secretary of the Interior, Mr. Ickes, is opposed to allowing the export of helium to Germany. Like you, he is under the mistaken impression that helium would have a military use in Germany. Attitudes such as his cause even more resentment in this country at Mr. Roosevelt and his statements about Germany. But we believe the situation is ripe for someone knowledgeable in Zeppelin technology and respected in the United States to persuade your government to allow the export of helium to Germany. We think you're the man to do that job."

"You're asking me to become a German agent?"

"Such a melodramatic term, Whitman. We're asking you to serve the interests of your own country, the future relationship of our two countries, and the future of the Zeppelins. Those are all worthy goals, are they not? Worthy even of the noble words you so enjoy."

"And if I refuse? If I insist on a hearing to clear the so-called charges against me? If I take my case to Eckener and the board of the Zeppelin Company, which I believe is my right as a Zeppelin officer?"

"Your memory is very short, Captain. As I was explaining, accidents happen all the time in Germany today, especially to people who—what's the expression you use in English?—people who *look for trouble*."

Part III

Germany

Thirty-Six

"Angry?" Maggie had to shout to be heard over the rush of wind past the windshield of the Auto Union roadster.

Whitman kept his eyes on the road. "Not really," he lied.

They were both avoiding the same topic, the "Mrs." on Maggie's passport. The longer they postponed talking about it, the more awkward it became, but neither of them knew how to bring it up. Whitman was afraid of what the answer might be, worried that his feelings for Maggie might change. And Maggie, with David Sinclair's voice fresh in her ears, was anxious not to compound her earlier mistake of not explaining her marriage. The phone call at the Frankfurt airport had brought back eight years of mostly bad memories, and she couldn't bear the thought of destroying a lovely evening and maybe more with a rehash of those years.

The speedometer in the Auto Union registered a steady 110 kilometers per hour, and to keep the car on the narrow highway, Whitman drove with a concentration that seemed out of character for the relaxed commander of the Graf Zeppelin.

"Why so fast?" asked Maggie. "It feels like we're outdoing the Graf Zeppelin."

"I want to get to Alsfeld before nine o'clock," he answered. "I called the parents of that boy, Jürgen Steinbrenner, and told them I was coming. Folks in small towns in Germany don't usually stay up late."

There was an awkward silence for several kilometers as each of them expected the other to speak.

"They must have really given it to you back there," she said. "Not all because of me, I hope."

"No. They hardly mentioned you, except to remind me about fifty times that you were American. You were only one item in the dossier they seem to be putting together on me. It seems that they just don't want me flying the Graf Zeppelin anymore, and they'll use any ammunition they can get to shoot me down. They've come up with new plans for me.''

''Secret missions?''

''Sort of.'' He went on to explain the helium issue and Hempe's offer.

''Will you do it?'' she asked.

''I don't want to. I do think the Germans should get the helium. It *is* the future for the Zeppelins, and the U.S. is probably being sticky for silly reasons. But I'm just not a diplomat. If I was, I wouldn't find myself in situations like this.''

She looked at herself, then back at him, and laughed. When he realized what he had said, he joined the laughter.

''That's not exactly what I meant,'' he said.

The laughter was followed by another silence as they drove through the wooded volcanic hills of the Vogelsberg.

''Why do you stick it out?'' Maggie asked finally. ''If the interrogation I got from those baggy gray suits at the terminal is an example of German hospitality, I can't understand why you'd want to put up with it. And they hinted that mine was distinctly second class, that you were getting the *real* grilling.''

''I've been thinking about exactly that question,'' he answered. ''In fact, all the way from Recife, where I got the first hint that there was going to be some trouble in Frankfurt, I've wondered what I would do. I think there are good reasons to stick it out.''

He saw her twist in the seat to face him, pulling her jacket close around her.

''Too cold?''

''No, I like it. The wind blows cares away. Go on.''

''First, I still can't dismiss Germany as a lost cause. There are just too many people here who aren't like those *Sicherheitsdienst* goons and the other Nazi heavies. As long as I keep finding men like the admiral, or Hugo Eckener, the head of the Zeppelin Company, or the Huttens, I keep hoping that Germany's going to pull through this little flirtation with madness.''

''But look what happened to the admiral. It was almost as if he was proving that there was no room for him in Germany anymore.''

''Those were almost his exact words,'' said Whitman. ''Over the Straits of Gibraltar, he and I were talking, and he said it was too late for his generation. I told him I hoped he was wrong. I still hope he was wrong. What Germany really needs now is more men like him.''

''And you,'' she said. ''What's reason number two?''

"The Zeppelins. Von Teppler talked about the feeling he had when he was sailing on a training ship as a naval cadet, that sense of being at balance with the forces of nature, of controlling a technology that worked with nature instead of against it. I understand what he meant completely. It's a feeling that's impossible in an airplane or a submarine. In the cockpit of a plane, you're throttling raw power, fighting against gravity and wind resistance. But the Zeppelin just goes by itself, working with nature. It's a feeling like nothing else in the world, except maybe sailing. I think it's a technology that's right for our age." He realized he was speaking as much to himself as to her.

"For me, there's a romance in the Zeppelins, a magic like the old sailing ships. It's probably the same feeling you had when you first saw that old schooner. The riggers who work on the Zeppelin are like sailmakers. They sew and splice, and in a pinch, they climb out onto the skin of the ship, dangling from harnesses like a seaman climbing the rigging of an old four-master. And up inside the hull it's indescribable, like nothing else ever built by man. It's immense, but there's a loftiness, a sense of space that's almost religious. The girders are fine and light, a tracery of duralumin and wire, and the skin is translucent. They're like cathedrals in the sky, and to me there's nothing else that has quite the feeling of light and of soaring. I guess I'm just in love with them and with what they can do."

"Sounds like I should get up there with my camera. When you describe it, it's breathtaking."

"You'd love it," he said. "But they're not too lenient about visitors. And the way things are going, I'm not sure how many more trips I'll have. It seems like the Zeppelins and everything they mean are just slipping away."

"To what?"

"I wish I knew. War maybe."

"It's that bad?"

"It could be."

Maggie turned away, thinking of the phone call and David's cryptic remarks, how he was going to save Spain and the world. It was so like him to describe whatever he was doing as if it were the most important thing in the world. And here was Paul Whitman, in the real center of things, talking as if he were a minor character.

"What are you going to do?" she asked.

"About what?"

"The Zeppelin, Spain, Germany, helium. You seem to be in the midst of it all."

"Right now—" he turned toward her, grinning. "I'm going to forget all of this. I'm going to talk American, try to find an ice cream soda somewhere, eat wurst like they're hot dogs, see a baseball game with a beautiful woman, watch my kid brother sail, and cheer Jesse Owens and the rest of the American track team until they run circles around the theory of Aryan supremacy. Germany and helium and even the Graf Zeppelin can wait."

"A deal," she said with a huge smile.

"Which reminds me. I have a present for you. For the Olympics."

She blushed.

"Actually," he said, reaching behind her seat into his kit bag, "it's a loan, so you don't have to be embarrassed." He pulled out the Leica in its hard leather case. "If you're planning to take photographs at the Games, you'll need a camera. Why don't you use mine? It's the newest model, with the range finder coupled to the lens."

She opened the case and admired the camera, holding it up, twisting off the lens cap and extending the lens.

"You're a mind reader, Paul. I've been thinking of switching to a Leica. Up until now, it's been big cameras for me, Speed Graphics and a four-by-five Graphlex that I could hardly lift. I started in industrial photography, because as a woman they wouldn't ever give me a journalism assignment. You know, 'the front lines are no place for a lady.' When I finally bluffed my way into photojournalist assignments, I was so eager that I wasn't willing to take the time to learn to use one of these. But believe me, there were times when I would have given anything to be able to hold a camera with one hand and hold on for dear life with the other."

She raised the Leica to her eye, sighting through the viewfinder, then turned and framed his profile.

"Can I really use it?"

He nodded. "If you don't, it'll die of boredom."

"Is there film in it?" She focused the lens, then realized that there wasn't enough light for a close portrait in the fast-moving car.

"Yes." He remembered the shots he had snapped over the Straits. "I almost forgot. I better . . ."

"Let me use the rest of the roll," she said, twisting the focus ring as she watched him through the viewfinder. "It'll be a while before I can buy some film. Anyway, I don't plan to be away from you long enough to lose it.''

She watched his smile, then reached over to squeeze his arm. ''While we're talking about loans . . . I owe you some money. After my trip to the telegraph office, I'm suddenly rich. I'd forgotten what good old American green looks like.''

''Forget it,'' he said, ''I can't spend the money I have.''

''Un-uh. I pay my own way. I don't want to be a kept woman. I tried it and I don't like it.''

He downshifted the car and pulled over to the side of the road, as if he were pulling off for a serious talk on the subject her remarks seemed to invite. Instead he turned onto a feeder road, marked with a small wooden sign: *Alsfeld*.

''You'll like this town,'' he said. ''It's the real Germany. Away from the cities and the Nazis and the parades and flags, Germany is still a country of small towns and good solid people like the Huttens.''

He drove slowly through fields set off with hedgerows, and after a few kilometers they were in the narrow streets of the town, paved with cobblestones that made the car feel unwelcome. There were only a few other cars in the streets.

He followed the wooden signs on the lampposts until they were in the Marktplatz in the center of the town, facing a stone building with a stepped gable line. To the side of the building, on another side of the square, was a beautifully timbered house with two sculptured towers in front.

''The peasants come on market days in their native dress,'' he explained, ''just like the picture books.''

''It's what I pictured Germany would look like,'' said Maggie. ''A postcard town. I see why you don't want to give up on the Germans.''

They walked around the square until they found the Rittergasse, an arcadelike street of finely preserved old wooden houses, with a single stone house that looked like it had been built for a movie set. There was no one else on the street, but the front windows of the houses were all brightly lit, the curtains drawn back so they could see into each parlor.

''In small towns,'' he explained, ''everyone keeps their curtains open in the evening. It's so no one will think they have anything to hide.''

Number fifteen was a narrow wooden house, barely wide enough for a full row of the cross-hatched timbers that were the hallmarks of the old structures. In front, a wood sign hung from an iron bracket: *H. Steinbrenner. Kurzwaren*. Through the window on the ground floor, they could see the shop, a narrow counter with bins and drawers behind, meagerly stacked with gloves, handkerchiefs, and belts. None of the merchandise looked expensive.

"Do you want to come up with me?" asked Paul. "You don't have to. I suspect that it may not be very pleasant."

"I'd like to," she said. "It was all because of me. I'd like to try to say something to them."

Paul pulled on the dangling cord, setting the bells inside tinkling. A light came on in the back of the ground floor, and they heard footsteps on the stairs at the back of the shop.

The man who opened the door was tall and very thin, with the faintest resemblance to Jürgen Steinbrenner. His wrinkles and thinning hair made him seem old enough to be a grandfather to the boy.

"Ja?"

"Herr Steinbrenner? I'm Paul Whitman, from the Graf Zeppelin."

Steinbrenner scrutinized Whitman without a word.

Whitman was suddenly embarrassed, wishing he had worn his uniform instead of the soft leather jacket, open-collared shirt and a scarf tossed loosely around his neck.

"I'm off duty," he explained. "After ten days in uniform, I find that I cannot wait to change into other clothes."

Steinbrenner nodded in obvious disapproval. When Paul introduced Maggie, the frown on Steinbrenner's face deepened as he realized that she spoke no German.

"You will come upstairs," he said.

The parlor on the first floor was so filled with furniture that they had to be careful not to bump into chairs and tables. A tall Biedermeier highboy dominated one wall, its shelves filled with photographs, medals, and plaques. Small, uncomfortable-looking chairs and a stiff settee were arranged around it, with tiny round tables between, covered with lace doilies and bric-a-brac. Lace antimacassars were on the arms and backs of the chairs. On one table, a plate of cakes sat forlorn. The Steinbrenners had been waiting for a while.

"You will have coffee?" said Frau Steinbrenner, a severe woman whose skin and brown-gray hair were drawn by the tautness of her expression.

"Or schnapps?" added Herr Steinbrenner.

"Thank you, but we have a long drive ahead of us. Perhaps

coffee.'' Whitman turned and saw Maggie nod and smile. The Steinbrenners answered her nod with stern looks as they passed the cups of coffee and the cakes.

"We are pleased that you have come," said Frau Steinbrenner.

"I came," said Whitman, still standing, "because I wanted to tell you how deeply sorry I am about the death of Jürgen. He was a brave and fine young man, much liked by all his fellow crew members. And he was a superb airshipman. We will miss him very much. I really wish there were something I could say to comfort you, but there is little I can add to what you already know. He died while volunteering for a dangerous job. It was an unfortunate accident.''

"Accident?" said Steinbrenner. His wife stopped pouring the coffee and looked first at him, then at Whitman.

Whitman didn't know how to respond. He had sent a long wire to the Steinbrenners from Recife, through company channels, explaining the whole accident. He assumed it had been delivered.

Steinbrenner went on. "I do not mean to sound rude, Herr Whitman, but we were under the impression that our son died a hero, that he gave his life in defense of the Reich, to defend the Zeppelin and the honor of the Fatherland against enemies of Germany. We expected that you would describe his acts for us. We thought there might be a certificate or a medal of some kind.''

Frau Steinbrenner walked over to the highboy.

"Our older son, Heinrich, is in the SS," she explained. "He serves in the *Leibstandarte Adolf Hitler,* by the side of the Fuehrer. We hoped that young Jürgen would follow in his brother's footsteps, but he was a stubborn boy. When he was only a youngster, he saw one of the early Zeppelins fly overhead. And from that day, he wanted only to fly on the Zeppelins. With all respect, Captain, this was a great disappointment to us.''

She pointed to a photograph, a man in a black, high-collared uniform, the lightning strokes of the SS on the lapels. His features were vaguely like Jürgen Steinbrenner's, but he posed with a stern, thin-lipped expression instead of Jürgen's perpetual grin. The shelf around his photograph was set up like a shrine, and Whitman saw that the shelf above it had a portrait of the Fuehrer in the center with crossed flags, armbands, and military medals on either side.

"At least, Jürgen died a hero," said Steinbrenner. "In his way he was serving the Fatherland. He did die in defense of the

Reich, didn't he, Captain? The letter we have from the Zeppelin Company is not just a form that is sent for everyone who dies on the Zeppelins?''

Whitman knew nothing of the letter, but he could guess the contents, the florid prose with the archaic convoluted phrases and tortured adjectives that the Nazis so favored.

He walked over to the highboy to look at the photographs and medals.

''Yours?'' he said to Steinbrenner as he pointed to a collection of medals from the World War.

''I was privileged to serve in the east,'' said Steinbrenner. ''I was only an ordinary infantryman. But we must each do our part. The Fuehrer has said that if every German does his part, we can defeat the enemies of the Fatherland. At least we know that Jürgen's life was not given in vain. Even in the Zeppelin service, it is an honor to die for the Fuehrer and the Fatherland.''

Whitman caught Maggie's eyes, saw that she understood nothing of the conversation, then looked back at the Steinbrenners, who awaited his answer.

''Yes,'' he said finally. ''Your son was a true hero for Germany. You can be proud of him.''

He and Maggie left as soon as they could. As they walked back to the car, he explained the conversation to her.

''What do they think he did?'' she asked.

''Something heroic. The German papers are filled with tales of Nazi heroism, glorious feats like beating up old Jews.''

''Why didn't you tell them the truth, Paul?''

''Because—'' He hesitated, then said, ''Because they didn't want to hear it.''

''Nobody wants to hear the truth here,'' said Maggie. ''I guess nobody wants to tell it either.'' There was only the faintest tone of accusation in her voice, but they didn't talk the rest of the way to Berlin.

It was late when they arrived in the city, but the Friedrichstrasse was still ablaze with neon, the cafes crowded with officers in uniform who sipped at frothy Berliner Weisse in big bowl-shaped glasses. Women in inviting dresses and even more inviting poses circulated through the cafes offering their wares. Try as they might, the Nazis had not succeeded in scrubbing the 1920s and the Weimar ''system'' from streets like the Friedrichstrasse. The uniformed officers who lounged with the fancy prostitutes seemed oblivious to the codes of morality that had been issued for the New Germany.

The lobby of the Excelsior Hotel was dominated by three large color photographs, approximately half life-size: Hitler in the center, flanked by Goering and Goebbels. They hung on the wall that faced the entrance, and the gaze of the portraits could not be escaped in the lobby.

"You're right," said Maggie when they came in. "He does look like the Little Tramp. Chaplin ought to play him in a film."

"It wouldn't be shown here," said Paul. He was glad that the coolness of a few hours before had worn off.

He turned to the clerk at the registration desk.

"I have a reservation. Whitman, a single room. We would also like another single room."

The clerk looked through a typewritten list.

"*Ja*, Herr Whitman. We have your reservation. But I'm afraid another room is quite out of the question. There is no hotel space available in Berlin. In fact, you are fortunate that we have kept your room beyond the usual check-in time."

Whitman looked at the man, irritated by the permanent ingratiating smile. "What does it take to get you to find a room for"—he saw that Maggie had caught his hesitation, a pause that probably communicated fully despite her ignorance of German— "for my companion?"

"*Mein Herr!* This is Berlin, not New York. The staff of the Excelsior Hotel does not accept bribes."

Maggie was still looking at the photographs. "Goering should be easy to cast," she said, "but that one, Goebbels, is going to be tough. That drawn face, the sunken cheekbones and that gaunt neck—he's the most frightening, I think." Almost giggly with fatigue, she was in a good mood.

"No rooms," said Whitman. "Except mine. You take it and I'll sleep in the lobby. Maybe by tomorrow we can persuade someone to find another room."

"It is absolutely forbidden," said the desk clerk in English. "We cannot have people sleeping in the lobby of the Excelsior Hotel. Germany is under scrutiny of the world while the Olympic Games are in progress."

"Is there a sofa in the room?" asked Maggie. "Or at least a soft chair?"

The clerk dropped the ingratiating smile for a stern expression. "We are not that kind of hotel, Miss."

"We're not that kind of customer, either," said Whitman

angrily. He slapped his passport down on the counter, prompting the clerk into a mumble and shuffle as he wrote the names into the register and put the passport into the cubbyhole box behind him. He took out the key, rang for the bellhop, then looked down at their luggage—Whitman's kit bag and Maggie's shoulder bag—with a lascivious grin.

"Is that your only luggage?" he asked.

"Do we need more?" Maggie asked with a wicked smile.

Inside the room, Maggie collapsed into a stuffed armchair, slipping off her shoes, curling her legs under her, and unbuttoning the jacket which she filled out so generously

"I'm looking forward to a hot bath almost like I was looking forward to getting pulled off that boat," she said. "And tomorrow, as soon as the stores open, I'm going to buy some clothes. You must be sick of looking at this suit."

"You may be a little disappointed in German fashions," said Paul.

"Not after Africa and four days in this." She tossed the jacket onto a chair and twisted until she was comfortable in the armchair.

"Before anything else, Paul, I think I owe you an explanation."

Whitman waved it away. "I think we're both too tired."

"No. I should have explained a long time ago. There was no mistake on my passport. I've been traveling under my maiden name, which is also my professional name, but the 'Mrs.' that fellow from the consulate used is right."

She twisted in the chair to face Whitman, who sat awkwardly on the edge of the bed. Her hands were in her lap, open, as if to show that she had nothing to hide.

"My husband's in Spain. He's a journalist, covering the war. We haven't lived together for almost a year. As soon as we . . . I can, we'll be divorced. It's nothing but a piece of paper between us now. In fact, that's all there's been for years."

She could see that Whitman was troubled. She reached out, a long, awkward reach, and touched his arm.

"I really like you, Paul. I'm looking forward to the next few days more than anything I can remember in a long time. And it's more than gratitude for your coming along like a knight to rescue me. It's been a long time since I've felt like this. I guess I forgot what it's like to be with a man who's strong and still kind and gentle. And who respects a woman's independence."

"Independence is a tricky word," he said. "You're kind of in no man's land now."

"Not any more. For the first time in eight years, I feel free. I'm making my own choices because I want to make them. It's a new feeling for me. David—my husband—always resented my photography. It was all right when it was a hobby. But when I began to get commissions that would have me traveling, or when my credits began to appear in magazines, he started to get touchy. I guess he wanted someone who was always at home to welcome him back from an assignment, someone who would listen to him and tell him what he had written was *very* important and *very* good. For a while, I thought my career was the problem, until I realized that it was only a cover-up for the real problem with our marriage. There was just nothing between us anymore. It was over. Once I realized it, I left. That was almost a year ago."

"Is it over for him?"

She hesitated, not sure what the question meant or how to answer. "It's over. I'm just sorry I didn't explain everything earlier. It matters to me for you to know that I'm not like the traveling salesman who takes off his wedding ring when he's out on the road."

Paul smiled, but not persuasively. "You take the bed," he said. "I'll take the chair."

She looked at the big comfortable bed, made up with a light goosedown comforter and fluffy pillows, then at the chair. She turned her head away so he couldn't see the expression in her eyes.

"Does this mean you're sorry I'm here?" she asked.

He came around in front of her and took her hands in his, smiling the mischievous grin she had seen so often on the Zeppelin.

"I'm delighted," he said. "But tomorrow is a big day at the Olympics, we have a long drive to Kiel, and if you're going to be awake enough to take pictures you'd better get some sleep." He pointed her toward the bed.

She forced a smile. "Afraid of involvements?" she asked.

"Maybe," he said. "Everyone seems to want to get me involved in something now."

Thirty-Seven

Montserrat was mindlessly wiping off the tables at the cafe, each for the fifth or sixth time, when she saw the fishing boat pull up at the quay. For a long time after Sinclair left, she had waited in the room, feeling lonelier than she had ever felt before in her life. In the bed with him, it had not been what she thought it would be. His touch had not stirred her as she had been stirred alone. She wondered what she had done wrong. Was that why he had left? She had been afraid to ask him if she had done what she was supposed to do. Perhaps when he came back, she told herself.

The heavy steps on the quay told her it was not Sinclair, but Pedrito. He was alone. She brought him a bottle of gin and a glass.

"Señor Sinclair?" she asked. "He is not coming?"

"They've gone," said Pedrito. "We finished with the fuel, and they left. Señor Sinclair persuaded Manolo that it was necessary. He can persuade anyone with his words."

"Will he be back?"

Pedrito downed a glass of gin in a gulp. He could read what the question meant in his sister's eyes. Even as a little girl, Montserrat's dreams were not the dreams of the other women of the island.

Pedrito had thought she would outgrow her fantasies, but as she got older and learned to fulfill the duties of a woman, taking care of the little house and working in the cafe and helping with the cleaning and marketing of the fish, she still kept part of herself in a separate world, practicing her French, reading her guidebooks of Paris, dreaming of another life. For a brief moment, David Sinclair had made that fantasy world seem real, and Pedrito had seen what that meant to Montserrat. But Pedrito also knew that the fantasies could never be her future.

"I think he will not come back," said Pedrito. "I'm sorry for

you, Montserrat, but he is not a man for a place like Minorca.
He's a strange man.''

She said nothing, but Pedrito knew she believed him. He
could see it in the look of grim determination on her face. He
wished he knew a way to comfort her, but nothing he could do or
say would matter. It was best, he thought, if she could be alone
with her dreams, until the fantasies of David Sinclair and Paris
went away and she once again learned the hard reality of her life
on Minorca. There would be other men, and someday, he hoped,
she would find a man who could make her forget those dreams.

Montserrat could read her brother's mind. She loved him for
understanding as much as he did, for allowing her a private
world, for never forcing her into a marriage that she would hate
for the rest of her life. But she knew that he could never truly
understand. The brief glimpse of hope she had felt when she was
with David Sinclair, the feeling that she would truly escape to a
world of lights and beauty and fashion instead of fish and cheese
and gin and stones, had inflamed her with a yearning that she
could no longer quench. It would never go away, she knew, no
matter how long she sat in her private place in the Cala, or
retreated into her private world of daydreams.

She dressed without saying a word, putting on shoes and a
sweater, and taking the pocketbook that she carried when she
was going to the market. Pedrito was already drinking a fourth
glass of gin when she left, and he said nothing.

She walked up through the square. The bus for Mahón didn't
leave until five o'clock, so she wandered around the square,
staring at the buildings she knew so well. Of course, David
Sinclair would never want to come back, she thought. No one
who had seen France and Switzerland would ever want to come
back to Ciudadela.

She hardly looked up as the bus huffed its way over the
highway, stopping at the familiar towns—Alayor, Ferrerias,
Mercadal. There was nothing to see in any of them, nothing that
made them really different except the days of their markets and
their festivals, and what kind of shoes they made.

In Mahón, she went straight from the bus terminal to the big
hotel opposite the cathedral. She wasn't sure how to ask for the
man. All she knew was that he dressed like he was from the city
and that he was a foreigner with a flat face and an accent.

The clerk gave her a lascivious look, running his tongue over
his lips. He knows, she thought. It shows. She pulled her dress

around herself, crossing her arms in front of her as if she could hide the secret.

"What is a girl like you doing here?" he asked.

She explained, describing the man.

"You want a man?" The clerk winked. "I can find you a man. Don't you know that the morning is no time for that kind of business?"

She ran from the hotel, and walked from one small hotel to another, more scared each time to go in and ask for the man. She dreaded the way they would look at her, their eyes raking up and down as if they were examining a load of *merluza* or *gambas* at the market, checking for the quality and size of the catch. Wandering about, asking about a man, she was fair game, and the Spaniard's sense of macho and sport meant that he had to try for fair game.

By late morning, she had tried every hotel, even some of the small boarding houses by the quays where she was sure that a stranger who arrived by airplane would not stay. She wondered if he had left, but remembered him saying he would be on the island for a while, that it was so important that he would stay until he found David Sinclair

"It is very important to me," he had said. "Finding him is very valuable." He had rubbed his fingertips together in a universal sign.

Valuable enough, she hoped, so she could leave Minorca. She could not stay now. She was worthless, a dishonor to her brother and herself. Even if she wanted to stay, she could not.

It was almost in desperation that she went back to the big hotel. She hesitated at the door, wondering if the same, horrible clerk would be at the desk. When she peeked in through the open doorway he caught her in his roving gaze.

"*Allo* again," he said with a smile that disgusted her. "You are still too early, but maybe I can help you out. We will have time to check things, no?"

She turned to run away, and as her eyes scanned the lobby, she saw the man she had come to find. He was sitting in one of the overstuffed chairs, sipping coffee, with newspapers spread out on the low table in front of him.

"Señor!" she said, walking quickly toward him. "You remember me, from Ciudadela. I need to talk to you."

"Is this woman bothering you?" said the clerk.

Orlov looked at Montserrat. She stood awkwardly, clutching herself, the sturdy shoes and the childish pocketbook and the worn black shift incongruous in the overdecorated lobby. But her eyes and her hair were unmistakable, and when she spoke clear Spanish instead of the Minorquin that Orlov could never understand, he remembered her.

"It's all right," he said to the clerk, who answered with a knowing wink as he went back to his desk.

"What brings you here?" Orlov asked, offering her a chair.

"I want to talk about David Sinclair," she said.

Thirty-Eight

They met for a late breakfast, the only two people in the vast, ornate dining room of the Excelsior. Late breakfast was an unheard-of meal to the Germans, a mark of Anglo-Saxon decadence. The waiters showed their disapproval by forgoing their usual overprompt and overbearing service, clustering instead at the doorway of the dining room and allowing Maggie and Paul the extraordinary luxury of privacy during the crowded Olympics.

Maggie came in with an armful of packages and a beaming grin.

"You look terrific," said Paul. "I've never seen a woman in Germany wear a jacket like that."

She touched the lapels of her tweed jacket. "I found a store where they sold riding habits. The man was offended when I refused jodhpurs and boots. It seems that everyone here wears boots."

"I was afraid that you'd come back in one of those matronly suits that are all the fashion here, or one of those pinch-waisted things that make the poor woman look like a wasp."

"I'm not sure if I should be complimented or insulted," said Maggie.

She reached into the stack of boxes and pulled out a small one, wrapped with a bow but no paper, handing it across the table to Paul.

He glanced at the cover and recognized the name of a fancy jeweler on the Kurfurstendamm, then slowly undid the ribbon.

Inside was a sterling silver keychain, with a tiny filigree silver Zeppelin on the chain.

"It's for luck," she said. "That rabbit's foot on your car keys is due for condemnation by the board of health. The way they scrub the streets here, they could lock you up for carrying a keychain like that."

He fondled it. "So I'll always have the Zeppelin? Thanks." Then he pushed a carefully wrapped box over to her.

"For me? You're not fair."

"The camera was only a loan, remember? Like the Zeppelin fare."

She grinned. Then she tore into the wrapping paper and opened the box, a fitted case which held a 90-millimeter telephoto lens and auxiliary finder for the Leica. He watched her admire the lens, feeling the fine engraving of the aperture and focus rings and the flawless machining of the nearly friction-free surfaces. To most women a present so devoid of romantic inspiration might have been a disappointment, or even an insult. But to Maggie, it was a statement of admiration for her independence and career. It showed that he knew how to listen.

She reached out and squeezed his hand. "Would they faint here if I jumped up and kissed you?" she asked.

"Herr Kapitän Whitman?"

A uniformed Luftwaffe officer in his gray-blue uniform snapped his heels together just inside the entrance to the dining room. When Whitman turned in his chair, the officer looked disappointed.

"You are Captain Whitman?" he asked.

"Yes."

Expressionless, the officer handed him an envelope, clicking his heels again formally, before spinning about to march out of the dining room.

Whitman's name was handwritten on the creamy white envelope in formal Fraktur script. He turned the envelope over and read the raised, engraved letters of the back flap. *Reichsluftsministerium.* The air ministry.

He set the envelope down on the table and looked back at Maggie.

"Aren't you going to open it?" she said. "If I ever got an envelope delivered like that I'd tear it open in a second. It looks like you're being invited to a royal ball. Or the biggest debutante party in the history of Berlin."

"It's from the air ministry," he said. He lifted the flap of the envelope with his finger, noticing how it had been carefully sealed in a single spot. Inside was a second envelope, with his name again written out in the precise professional script. Then the stiff card, with a raised border, engraved in gold Fraktur letters. He glanced through it, then translated for Maggie.

"The Air Minister, General Hermann Goering, requests the honor of my presence at a reception tonight in honor of the Olympic Games. At Karinhall. That's his hunting lodge in the woods north of the city."

He tossed it down on the table. "*Generaloberst*. I remember when he was promoted. I was still reading the newspapers then. It was in April, Hitler's birthday. He was being traditional, I guess. The kings and emperors used to announce promotions on their birthdays."

Sure he was making it all up, Maggie picked up the invitation. The strange Fraktur type was a blur, but she could make out one word: Goering.

"My God! You're not kidding. The fat one himself. Are you going?"

"No."

"Why not? It sounds exciting. From the pictures and the newspapers, Fatso is number two around here."

Whitman couldn't help smiling at Maggie's casualness. "Would you go?"

"You really aren't a diplomat, Paul. I'd go in a minute. I can't imagine anything more exciting than meeting one of those bogeymen. How else can you ever really know whether this is all real? Just this morning I saw those scrubbed streets and the rows of flags. This city makes New York or San Francisco look like pigsties. It made me almost believe what they say in the newspapers, that they're saving Germany. At least it sure is a change from those photographs of not so many years ago with people hauling a day's pay home in a wheelbarrow. You have the chance to find out whether they are for real or only the *poseurs* that the admiral called them. Maybe it's even an apology for the grilling you got in Frankfurt. Goering is that other man's boss, isn't he?"

"He sure is," said Paul. "And I would venture that the whole thing is to put a little pressure on me. I guess they think I would be impressed by one of their orgies."

"Sounds even more interesting." She laughed, and he smiled at her laughter before he looked away, the lightness disappearing into pensiveness.

"You're really worried about them, aren't you?"

"I'm not sure," he said. "I was just thinking about something the admiral said, how they can distract you with one set of antics so that you can't see what they're really doing. Sort of a shell game. It's strange how much of what he said seems to haunt me."

They ate and sipped coffee silently, picking at the continental breakfast that was all the waiters were willing to bring at the odd hour.

"I couldn't go anyway," he said. "The baseball game is tonight."

"You got tickets? You still have influence, *eh, Kapitän Whitman*?" Her imitation of the German pronunciation of his name was wickedly precise.

"No influence, but I had dollars. Thanks to you. There are some things in the New Germany that haven't changed."

"Don't worry about the game," she said. "I'll write up a scorecard for you. Even errors. In return, you can give me a scorecard on the evening with Fatso. Blow by blow. Really, Paul, you must go to that reception."

"I've got a better idea," he said.

"I take photos of the game?"

"You come with me."

Her eyes widened. "I'm not invited. And from what you said, I might be exactly what you don't need."

"We'll promise that you won't eat much."

He watched the smile spread across her face, sparkles lighting up the corners of her eyes. "You're sensational, Paul. Thanks." She reached again for his hand.

"I don't think you can get away with bringing the camera," he said.

"A promise. I won't eat and I won't take pictures. And I won't wear my un-German jacket. Maybe I should run back and buy those boots. Then I might fit right in."

The stadium was a stark, mammoth, gray slab, looming over the 325-acre *Reichsportsfeld* like an oversized Wagnerian stage set. It reminded Whitman of the great parade ground at Nuremberg, a brooding gray architecture built on a scale to dwarf an individual. Every seat was filled, over one hundred thousand fans, with another ten thousand standing in the fenced areas at the edges of the field.

From the crowd Whitman overheard descriptions of the mass gymnastics display that had been put on for the opening of the

Games, where batons substituted for the rifles of a close order drill. The display was so large that it had to be staged outside the stadium, like the Nuremberg crowds that were artfully massed for the Nazi party rallies and so perfectly captured by Leni Riefenstahl's cameras in *Triumph of the Will*. He could picture her cameramen covering the Olympics, lying on the ground to shoot up at the athletes with wide angle lenses that would make even ordinary men look like giants. He knew that in Friedrichshafen they would be talking about her filming of the Hindenberg flying over the stadium, wondering if excerpts of her films could be used by the company as advertisements for the Zeppelin.

The morning drizzle had temporarily stopped, but the sky over the stadium was still heavily overcast, a heavy gray that merged with the looming stadium and made the green of the infield and the bright red of the track seem luminescent. At the end of the stadium, two clock towers rose up, and between them the huge Olympic torch, a new innovation for this Olympiad. Two weeks before, a relay of three thousand young runners had carried the flame from Greece across Europe to Berlin, where a German athlete was given the honor of running up the steps of the stadium and kindling the flame in the torch.

The signs and programs were in five languages, but around them in the stands, Maggie and Paul heard only German. Fully half of the spectators, it seemed, were in uniforms, the recently restyled uniforms of the armed forces and the many uniforms of the Nazi party organizations.

He watched Maggie frame the flags and towers and the geometry of the field in the viewfinder of the camera as she familiarized herself with the Leica and the new lens. The crowd suddenly hushed when a trumpet fanfare blared over the loudspeakers. An orchestra began playing *"Deutschland, Deutschland über Alles,"* the beat slow and stately, and the stirring words of the old anthem welled up from one hundred thousand throats. According to the program, the anthem was unscheduled, but the fans loved it. When it was over, they stayed on their feet, heads turned toward the president's box in the center of the stadium.

The orchestra struck up again, this time with the catchy melody of the *"Badenweiler March,"* the Nazi equivalent of "Hail to the Chief" and "Ruffles and Flourishes." Before the music ended, the crowd exploded with a roar:

Sieg Heil! Sieg Heil! Sieg Heil!

Arms shot up in the Nazi salute as the crowd went on and on, six, seven, eight times, each shout more frantic than the one before.

Whitman raised his field glasses to watch the Fuehrer make his entrance. His timing was perfect, delayed long enough to create an aura of suspense, but not so long that he lost a single pair of eyes in the crowd. The Little Tramp, with his plain double-breasted suit and his silly fey salute, was a master of drama.

The crowd roared on, chanting out the *Sieg Heils!* even after Hitler sat down, and he had to stand and return the salute a second time, his right arm flopping backwards at the wrist with an embarrassed version of the straight-armed salute of the exuberant crowds.

"My God!" said Maggie. "Is that really him? That was unbelievable. He seems so . . . so ordinary . . ."

"They don't think so," said Paul, pointing down toward the field. "I watched the athletes. Not just the Germans; the Austrians and the Bulgarians were also returning that salute, and their coaches and trainers were with them. It's not just Party members. It's all of them." He said it as if he could hardly believe his own observation.

"Did you photograph him?" he asked Maggie.

"Through the camera, he's nothing," she said. "The real story is these people, the faces and the reactions. I've only seen that kind of crowd once before. In California, at the migrant camps, when the revivalists would come around and pitch their tents. They'd preach for hours at a time, stopping just long enough to pass the plates before they went back to it. After a while, some of the people would get into the spirit and they would begin a kind of hypnotic dancing and speaking in the 'tongues.' They had that same mesmerized expression. But this"—she gestured at the crowds—"this was without dancing or music or the droning sermons. It was as if he were the Messiah."

"That's one claim he doesn't make," said Paul. "Yet."

The field events began without ceremony, and after a few minutes, the results of the first round of hammer throws went up on the scoreboard. The German fans cheered loudly.

"Where else can you find people cheering hammer throws?" said Paul.

"The national sport?" limned Maggie.

"A German is favored to win. It's one of the few field events they could take. They've never won an Olympic field event."

Another throw and the crowd roared.

"I thought it was supposed to be individuals competing," said Maggie.

"Not this time. The Germans are out to prove a point. When a German wins an event like the hammer throw or the discus or the shotput, it puts the seal of authority on the theory of Aryan supremacy. I'm just hoping that the Americans will trip them up."

"I wouldn't count on the American high jumpers," said Maggie, spotting them through her binoculars.

Paul swung his own glasses over. Two black Americans in red, white, and blue track suits were lounging on the infield near the high jump. He watched for a moment, then realized they were shooting craps.

"Maybe we really are decadent," said Maggie.

Whitman glanced through the program, then back at the two men. "Dan Albritton and Corny Johnson," he said. "Our best men."

"*Our* best men? Who's being nationalistic now, Captain?"

Out on the field, an official walked over to talk with the two high jumpers.

"He's breaking up the game," said Maggie. "I guess the Germans don't allow gambling during the finals. Good for them."

One of the black Americans walked over to the runway for the high jump, limbering for a moment by slowly flexing one knee, then the other, with his arms hanging limply at his sides.

"I can't believe this," said Maggie. "All the other jumpers spent a long time pacing off the distance and making trial runs and doing all kinds of stretching exercises. Our guy doesn't even bother taking off that warm-up suit."

"Psychological warfare," said Paul.

The tall black high jumper suddenly stood up straight, waved to the man he had been shooting craps with, then loped effortlessly down the runway, flung himself over the bar, brushed off the woodchips, and walked back to stretch out for more of the craps.

"Incredible!" said Maggie. "It's like there was no bar at all. Half of the others missed at that height."

They watched while the other black American repeated the performance and returned to the crap game with the same nonchalant insouciance. It wasn't until every other athlete but one was eliminated from the high jump that the two Americans even removed their warm-up suits, and by then the competition was strictly between the two of them.

"I don't think a single person besides us is watching that high jump," said Paul. "They're all interested only in the hammer throw. They only want to see winners."

"Don't we all?"

The loudspeakers announced the winners of the hammer throw in a slow, flawless voice. The stadium suddenly quieted as the three winners, the first medalists of the Olympics, went to the three-tiered stand for their accolades.

". . . *Gold . . . Deutschland . . .*" cried out the announcer as he announced the first place winner. The name of the athlete was lost in the shrieks of the crowd. This time they cheered even through the long, slow playing of *"Deutschland, Deutschland über Alles."* When the laurel wreath and medal were draped on the man's neck, the crowd burst into a chorus of *Sieg Heil!* that drowned out even the loudspeakers.

The athlete returned the salute, then marched to the president's box, where the Fuehrer stood and shook his hand for the photographers with their flashing bulbs.

"I bet a copy of that photograph is going to make some front pages," Maggie shouted into Paul's ear.

"Today's hero," he said. He couldn't help thinking of Admiral Wilhelm von Teppler, yesterday's hero. His return to Germany went unmentioned in the newspapers. Like Hugo Eckener and everyone else who had spoken out against the Third Reich, the admiral had become an unperson.

Directly below them, on the straightaway of the track, the contestants were lining up for the finals in the 100-meter dash. The winner would carry the title of the fastest human on earth.

Each athlete went through his own elaborate ritual of exercise before the start. Some bent over, stretching one leg, then the other as they loosened muscles for the explosive start. Others went through what looked like Yoga exercises or meditation rituals to focus their concentration.

On the inside lane, Jesse Owens stood at his blocks, grinning at the vast crowd like a star-struck schoolboy. When the man next to him had trouble adjusting his own starting blocks, Owens dropped to his knees and pushed on the balky block until it worked free and into the position the other man wanted. Then he went back to his own lane, tested his blocks briefly, and peeled off his warm-up suit to await the signals.

Every other event stopped as athletes crowded the edge of the infield to watch the race and the debut of the much talked-about American.

"Auf die Plätze!"

Across the lanes, legs stretched out, shaking invisible cinder from spikes before the feet settled into the blocks in slow, exaggerated motions.

"Fertig!"

Tension rippled down the line of coiled springs. A few men nervously lunged, then quickly pulled back. Owens, at the end of the line, seemed so calm that he could have been unready.

"Los!"

The gunshot echoed as it was picked up through the loudspeakers. All seven men flew out of the blocks, two of them bolting so quickly that it looked as though they had jumped the gun. But the start was good.

Owens got one of the slowest starts, but he was quickly up to pace, his legs lifting high as he swung into an effortless stride. While the other runners struggled, their faces contorted with pain, Owens loped in a gait that made it seem as if there were wings on his shoes. It was impossible to see his feet come down. There was only the blur of lifting legs as he flew down the track.

"I've never seen a human being move more beautifully," said Maggie, raising the camera to her eye.

Owens broke the ribbon with a safe margin between himself and the next runner. Paul and Maggie stood to cheer but felt like they were the only Americans in the stadium, or at least the only fans of Jesse Owens. Everyone in the seats around them stared at them as if they had applauded between the movements in a symphony concert.

Over the loudspeaker the announcer reported the results of the race in a flat voice, without the fanfare with which he had announced the German victory in the hammer throw.

The victory ceremony was repeated, with the laurel wreath and the medals, the orchestra playing the "Star Spangled Banner" in a quick, jaunty cadence that made it sound ludicrous.

"Now comes my photograph," said Maggie. She trained her telephoto lens across the stadium to capture the handshake between the Fuehrer of the Reich and the black American.

Whitman raised his field glasses to watch, and suddenly the crowd burst into another chorus of *Sieg Heil!*, their arms waving wildly.

"They've had a change of heart," said Maggie, putting down the camera for a moment. "I guess the beauty of that man running is enough to break down any theory, even Aryan supremacy."

But when she looked back through the viewfinder of the

Leica, the President, Chancellor, and Fuehrer of the Third Reich had left the president's box and the Olympic Stadium, just in time to avoid the prospect of congratulating a black American for being the fastest man on earth.

Thirty-Nine

The long drive to Kiel gave them a chance to talk—about Germany, the States, Paul's brother, Henry, and each other. For the first time in months, Paul found himself relaxing, pushing away his worries about the Zeppelins and Germany.

It was late afternoon when they arrived at the Quai Hindenberg. Paul drove straight to the yacht club docks on the northern edge of the vast *Kieler Bucht,* where they boarded a spectator launch for the ride out to the Olympic sailing course, skirting the protected beaches of the wooded shore, and far away from the towering gantries of the naval yards in the distance.

Maggie had sailed before but had never raced, and she listened bemused as Paul tried to explain what was happening on the race course. The German navy patrol boats kept the spectator fleet far enough away so that they could barely follow the races through binoculars, and even with Paul's careful efforts to explain, Maggie found it as confusing as watching a first chess game.

Henry Whitman was racing in the Six Meter Class, the second largest of the Olympic boats and in many ways the boats that came closest to looking like pure racing sailboats. The boats were remarkably similar, slim and powerful, each about thirty-five feet long, with masts that towered fifty feet off their decks. Everything that was not essential to speed had been eliminated, leaving barely enough room for the five-man crews that were needed to adjust the dozens of lines that tuned the boats for maximum speed. And from up close, the look of power in the sails as they were trimmed in by powerful winches and tackles was awesome. The tall masts and sweeping mainsails seemed too enormous for the lean boats, straining the rigging and the boats themselves as the crews struggled to counter the heeling that could roll a rail or even the edge of a cockpit under water. But sailing together, their sails filled with the wind, the Six Meters were as beautiful as a sailboat could be, the very image of grace and speed on the water. Watching them, Maggie could understand everything Paul had said about the Zeppelins and the magic feeling of floating with the winds instead of fighting them.

The American boat got off to a good start, squeezing over the line on port tack, just barely in front of two boats that were crossing on starboard tack.

As the boats worked their way up the course, the majority of the fleet stayed on starboard tack, sailing toward the left side of the course. The Americans alone held on the port tack and the right side of the course. When they were halfway down the leg, it was difficult to follow the boats anymore, even to make out which was which, except that the Norwegian and the Swedish boats were finished in varnished mahogany that made them stand out as showboats next to the white hulls of the others.

"It's exciting," Maggie said. "But I really haven't got the foggiest idea what's happening. How can you even tell who's winning?"

"They're going to cross most of the fleet now," explained Paul as the American boat tacked. "If they cross in front of another boat, they're safely ahead. If they have to dip and take the stern of the other boat, they're behind. Unless there is a windshift—" The rest of his explanation was lost in incomprehensible explanations of *safe leeward* positions, *lifts* and *headers*.

"I'll try to explain it all later," he said. "If you're still interested. Or better yet, we can let Henry explain."

She smiled. It really didn't matter. Paul's enthusiasm was contagious, and what she enjoyed most of all, besides the occasional bright splash of sun that burned through the overcast, was the fact that Paul Whitman seemed totally relaxed and at ease. The water seemed to transform him. It was like on the Zeppelin, when he was totally in command, miles removed from the deadening pressures of Germany and the Nazis. She couldn't remember when she had felt so at ease with a man.

The Americans rounded the buoy first, with the British and the Norwegians close behind them. All three boats popped out big ballooning spinnakers of light cloth as they raced back toward the starting mark with the wind behind them. The British and Norwegian boats began to work up from behind the Americans, and Paul explained that when the boats sail off the wind, the boats behind can sometimes have a slight advantage, especially if the lead boat does not react quickly enough to a challenge.

It took only a few minutes for Maggie to see what he meant. The British boat, with a better angle than the Americans, reached up to windward of the American boat, moving fast enough to threaten the wind of the American boat

"They have to luff them up," said Paul, and at that instant, as if they had heard his suggestion, the American boat turned sharply to windward, forcing the British to do the same if they wanted to avoid a collision.

"Smashing the other guy seems a silly way to keep a lead," said Maggie. "It looks like they're trying to collide."

"It's perfectly legal for the leeward boat," said Paul.

The maneuvers were over in a second, and with disastrous results for the Americans. The British boat had kept its sails filled through the entire maneuver, but the spinnaker on the American boat somehow got out of control, collapsing into a trembling sheet of cloth.

"They blew it," said Paul. "Whoever was on the spinnaker sheet didn't trim fast enough. They'll never catch the English boat now."

He was right. The English boat worked ahead of the Americans, then bore down toward the mark, leaving the Americans wallowing until they got the sails refilled and the boat moving again.

"That was really a sloppy move," said Paul.

The three leading boats paraded by, the English boat, followed by the Americans, then the incredibly beautiful Norwegian boat. Maggie turned her binoculars on the Scandinavians, watching the sunlight gleam off the hull when an occasional ray burst through the clouds.

"Wouldn't you know it?" said Paul. "The clown on the spinnaker sheet was Henry."

The Norwegian boat started to make its move after the Americans. The wind had backed so that the boats were sailing with the wind directly over their sterns. Without warning, the Norwegians jibed, swinging their spinnaker around to the other side of the boat and bringing the mainsail over. The maneuver enabled them to hold a course that the American boat could no longer sail, and to cover and keep the Norwegians from overtaking, the Americans too had to jibe.

When the Norwegians did it, it seemed a simple and elegant maneuver, the sails staying full as they switched over. But on the

American boat, something went wrong. In the middle of the maneuver, the spinnaker collapsed, then filled again, tangling and wrapping around the headstay, with filled sections ballooning out above and below until it looked like a poorly engineered vertical brassiere. The Americans immediately started to fall behind, and the boat turned into pandemonium as a crew member ran forward to untangle the sail.

"Damn!" said Paul. "It was Henry again. He should have kept that sheet trimmed. He's not concentrating."

"They have another whole lap, don't they?" said Maggie.

"They haven't got a chance. Not now. He blew it."

"You're really hard on him," said Maggie.

"It's a team out there. It takes the full concentration of five men to sail the boat, and he's just not pulling his weight. It would be one thing if he were sailing alone on a Monotype. Then if he screwed up it's only his loss. But he's let them all down. *Mystery* is a fast boat, and Bill Bartholomae is a good skipper. But there's nothing they can do to recover from that one."

As he predicted, the mistake was fatal. By the time they got the errant spinnaker down, the Americans were next to last. They limped through the final legs unable to change their position. Paul said little for the rest of the race and seemed more angry than disappointed at the American finish.

"Is the team play that important?" asked Maggie. "Isn't it just as important for each man to do all he can?"

It seemed a profound statement, and Paul let it pass.

They were already ashore when the Six Meter yachts arrived at the docking area behind their tow boats. Catching sight of Paul, Henry bounded up the sloped gangway that led down to the dock. Maggie could see that he was almost a carbon copy of his older brother, with the same towheaded shock of unruly hair, the mischievous eyes and strong jaw, and the lanky frame.

He hugged Paul and turned immediately to Maggie.

"So this is the lucky lady?" he said to Paul, keeping his eyes on Maggie. "You weren't exaggerating at all, were you? You sure you didn't plan the whole operation?"

Maggie grinned back and shook his hand. "Some people seem to think he did," she said.

"I can understand why," Henry answered.

The tables inside the bar-cafe at the yacht docks were already crowded. They took one outside, ignoring the threatening drizzle of the dark gray sky.

"Not a great race," said Paul.

Henry ignored the comment and the talk at the other tables, much of it rehashing the Six Meter race. "How was Berlin?" he asked.

"Incredible!" said Maggie. "The Little Tramp himself graced the stadium with his presence, and then took off so he wouldn't have to congratulate Jesse Owens for winning. And that man is the most amazing sight. He doesn't run, he flies. And the American high jumpers must have had springs in their shoes. I loved every minute of it."

"I'm really sorry to have missed it all," said Henry. "The Olympics are kind of a bust here. I thought that at least there would be some Fräuleins—you know, with the tightlaced dirndls and all that—but they have us buttoned up so tight in those barracks that we're lucky to get a breath of air. And believe me, the Navy barracks aren't like that Olympic Village in Berlin. Before the opening ceremonies they took us on a tour. What a showplace! To rub it in, they brought over a cottage from the 1932 Olympics in Los Angeles, one of those bungalows that were thrown up in Baldwin Hills. The comparison makes us look like real pikers."

"Everybody made us look like pikers out there on the course," said Paul. "You really blew that downwind leg."

"Yeah," said Henry. "That was a tough break."

"No, that was a screw-up. You weren't concentrating during the luff *or* the jibe. I've never seen you sail so badly."

Henry shrugged. "We all have our good days and our bad."

"How did you ever get on the Six Meters in the first place?" asked Paul. "You never really explained. I would have been a little surprised if you'd made it in Stars, but at least you had the experience there. And you really were good when you were sailing full time. But Six Meters? How many times had you even sailed one before?"

Henry shrugged again and looked around before answering. "We got a lot of practice in Newport and on Long Island Sound," he said. "It's an easy boat."

"It didn't look like it today," Paul said. "What happened in the Stars?" he asked. "I heard that the Germans have some kind of breakthrough rig—incredible speed and flexibility."

"Yeah," said Henry with no real interest. "The German is supposed to be very fast." There had been a time, only a year before, when he would have discussed details of a Star class rig for hours on end. Now, he seemed eager to change the subject.

"How about dinner tonight?" he said. "Would I be muscling in? I'm dying to get away from those barracks, and I'd really like to hear about the Graf Zeppelin. *That* is what I call interesting."

Maggie started to say something, then stopped when Paul said, "I thought you had to take your meals in the Olympic barracks. Don't you have tactics sessions or something like that? Postmortems on the race?"

"One more session in there and I'll be ready for the loony bin," said Henry.

"Afraid you'll get called on the carpet for this afternoon?"

"Not really. We all flub every so often. Even you, I suspect."

"Hey!" interjected Maggie. "Do you two always go at it like this?"

"Only when either of us slides a notch or two down from perfection," cracked Henry, and the three of them laughed.

"Really," he said. "I would enjoy dinner."

"So would I," said Paul. "But we have to go to some bigwig party. I didn't really want to go, but Maggie thinks it's a chance to see the inside of the zoo."

"Hermann Goering's hunting lodge," she said with an air of excitement and awe.

"*Really?* I don't blame you. What's the occasion?"

"Just a reception for the Olympics," said Paul.

"And you're that tight with Goering himself?"

Paul smiled. "Anyone they need or want for something is suddenly tight with them, I suspect."

Henry looked interested, leaning over the table, taking his eyes off Maggie for the first time since they had been introduced. "What do they want from you?" he asked.

"I'm not really sure," said Paul.

"How about lunch tomorrow?" said Henry. "I'm dying to hear what happens at the big spread."

"What about your practice sessions?" said Paul. "I thought you spent mornings on the water."

Henry waved the question aside. "A couple of guys are so red-hot they'd practice all night if they could," he said. "But I can easily get out of the morning sail. I might try to take a look around the city. Want to come?"

Maggie looked up and across the docks toward the single tall spire of the City Hall that dominated the modest skyline of the city, then beyond to the rows of immense naval gantries of the shipyards. "It sounds like fun," she said. "But we promised to visit some people who were on the Graf Zeppelin. In Bremen."

"Bremen?" said Henry, the interest obvious in his voice.

"If the thought of Bremen can excite you," said Paul, "you really are itchy here. What about the Olympics? I thought you weren't supposed to leave the team barracks. The Olympic Committee certainly didn't bring you here to be a tourist."

Henry grinned mischievously. "Am I going to get a lecture about the Olympic spirit?"

"No," said Paul. "But you don't have to say it as if it were a dirty word."

"The idea's fine," said Henry. "But it really doesn't fit. Not this time. Some of the sailors are pretty friendly in the cafeteria, but the officials, especially the Germans, treat the whole thing as if it were part of their diplomatic offensive. We won the sailing events in 1932, so we're the enemy. And they're prepared for this like it was the second Battle of Jutland. Their boats have us outclassed, they train like they're preparing for a military siege, and in a couple of classes they behave on the race course like maniacs. It's just not my idea of sailing."

"It's competition," said Paul. "There'll come a time when you'll remember being in the Olympics as a high moment in your life."

"The way the world is going, Paul, I'll be lucky to live long enough to look back."

"You're sounding very fatalistic for a young man."

"And you're sounding very paternalistic for an older brother."

"Hey! Both of you. How about a little less arguing?" said Maggie. "Couldn't we talk about something else?"

They did, for the rest of the afternoon, but the unspoken tension between Paul and Henry remained just below the surface of their small talk. Maggie found it hard to understand. Paul didn't seem like the kind of man who would be so ill at ease with his brother. And despite his boyish charm and looks, Henry didn't seem the devil-may-care blade he pretended to be.

Forty

Each night, the jailer had a new excuse. The wrong guard was on duty. The moon was too bright. Another prisoner might arrive. But even as he rattled off his excuses, he would pause, crouching on his haunches to stare at Conselheiro.

"You're certain?" he would ask. "Two millions *milreis*. You're certain?"

Conselheiro would smile and nod his head, knowing it was only a matter of time before greed overcame the jailer's qualms.

"Tell me again how the money is kept," the jailer said one night. "How is it placed on the airship?"

Conselheiro explained it all again, patiently, watching as the jailer swallowed every word. "It's packed in metal cases, and the cases are then crated in wooden boxes." The description seemed to fascinate the jailer. Just hearing those details was enough to assuage his doubts. He smiled broadly, spreading his legs and standing with his hands on his hips as if he were already a grandee with no worry in the world except how to spend his one million *milreis*.

It was so simple to leave the jail that Conselheiro could hardly believe it had happened. The jailer opened the barred door to the pen, walked with Conselheiro out into the big room where he had first been beaten and interrogated, then down a hall to a heavy planked door with old-fashioned iron straps. Once through that door they were in a road behind the jail. There were no other prisoners in the barracks prison, and the only guards were busy playing cards and drinking beer at a table in the office in front. The jailer had even brought a clean blouse and drawstring pants for Conselheiro. Once he changed, he felt and looked no different from the thousands of displaced backlands peasants who wandered the streets in search of work or food.

They disappeared quickly into the *favelas*, scurrying through the narrow streets like land crabs as the jailer led Conselheiro to a plywood and tin shack deep among the mangroves, one more shack scarcely distinguishable from thousands on every side of it. As they walked, Conselheiro found that he had trouble keeping up with the jailer. His foot, crushed and pounded during the beatings, had again begun to swell and throb with pain.

Before they set off for the last stretch to the house, by boat from an overgrown riverbank, the jailer suddenly stopped. "Now," he said, "you will tell me how it is that we will get the money boxes from the Zeppelin."

"So you can kill me in my sleep and take all of it for yourself?" said Conselheiro. "You'll know what you need to know when the time comes."

"And you promise that my wife and children will be safe?"

"They'll be safe. The Integralistas won't dare to search in the backlands. They know that *we* rule there."

"We? Who is this we?"

"The *Serteños*. You, me, all the people of the backlands. We will rise again, as we did with the first Conselheiro, as we did with Lampiao. When there is a need, a leader comes to give the signal to the people. And then nothing can stop the forces of the masses."

The jailer shook his head in ignorance. "Sometimes I think you're truly mad. Why do you talk of the Great Conselheiro or Lampiao? Why do you not talk instead of what you will do with your one million *milreis*?"

Conselheiro threw his head back, booming out a deep, rolling laugh that shook his beard and rangy hair. "My million! You fool! You're just like those swine of Integralistas. Everything is only for the money. You cannot understand that some things must be done for the people, for justice. It was when the German Zeppelin landed that the people were crushed, on the very field of the Zeppelin. While the Germans watched for their mighty airship, our people were cut down like pigs at the slaughterhouse. It was German guns that shot them down, Germans who trained the Integralistas to fire the guns. Now, the Zeppelin must be destroyed—to avenge the people and to signal the coming of a new age when the people will triumph again."

"But what about the money? The new *milreis* notes in the metal cases inside the wooden crates?"

Conselheiro laughed again. "There is no money."

"No money? You lied to me? You told me this only so I would let you out of jail?"

Conselheiro grinned through the bushy moustache, nodding his head so the thick beard shook.

"Then you are worse than they say," said the jailer. "A liar and a cheat. Do you know what you have done to me? Now I am an outlaw. My wife and children are outlaws. They will chase us anywhere we go, and when they catch me, they will throw me into jail or even kill me. My wife and children will starve and there will be no one to bury them. Their bodies will end up in the river to be eaten by the crabs." He reached up with his fists, trying to pound at the man who stood grinning at him.

Conselheiro caught the fists and held them in his own powerful grip.

"Thousands starve every day," he said. "And those who do not starve die of the fever. So now you're one of the people again. We're all outlaws. It is better to be an outlaw and to die in the struggle than to work for them."

"You talk of the people. Have you ever buried the body of a child? Can you know what it is to carry a tiny form to a grave in a box so small that you can pick it up with one hand? Can you know what that is for a man? You've tricked me, and now I will die, and my wife and children will die. You're worse than they are."

Conselheiro waved his hand, brushing away the torrent of words. "The people will be avenged," he said. "From the backlands a new Conselheiro will lead the people against the foreigners and the Integralistas and the Southerners, until the backlands are truly free for the people."

"You believe all these words of yours, don't you?" said the jailer. "If I die and my children and wife have the fevers or starve, or if others are punished and killed because of what you do, it means nothing to you. You care nothing about the people. They should kill you, or send you back to Fernando de Noronha so you can die like a lizard in the sun."

Conselheiro grabbed the jailer by the upper arms, pressing hard until his fingers dug into the smaller man's skin.

"Remember, jailer, if you say one word to anyone, you will die a death worse than a lizard in the sun. You have no choice now. You help me, or you are caught by the Integralistas. And then, no matter what you say, they will beat you until there is almost no life left in your body. Could you stand such a beating, jailer? Could you stand it when two men hold you down on a table and another uses the rubber hose upon the soles of your feet? Could you stand it when they hold your fingers on the floor and a man places the butt of his rifle on the fingers and slowly puts his weight on the rifle so the metal plate of the butt crushes your fingertips? Could you stand that, jailer?''

Conselheiro watched the jailer's face turn ashen with fear.

"Now," said Conselheiro, "you've been inside the armory. I want you to tell me exactly how it's guarded, and by how many men. And I want to know where inside they keep a weapon that looks like this." In the dust, he drew a crude sketch of a mortar tube, a simple capped cylinder with two legs to elevate the muzzle. "Somewhere near this weapon, they will have the rockets for it. They are shaped like this." He drew another sketch with his finger in the dust, a full-sized outline of the finned mortar shells.

The jailer tried to look away, as if just glancing at the sketches would involve him even more deeply in the project he now so feared. But Conselheiro held him firmly, forcing him to look.

"Think," he said. "Try to remember the inside of the armory. Where do they have a weapon that looks like that? And while you're thinking, think of your wife and children, realize what will happen to them if I am caught. Does that help your memory, jailer?''

Forty-One

The damp air of the North German plain put a film of condensation on every surface, and Maggie leaned close to Paul in the seat so they could hear one another over the roar of the airstream past the open car.

"What's with you and Henry?" she asked. "You were really hard on him. It doesn't seem like you."

"I don't think I've changed," said Paul. "But he has. He used to be a real competitor. To get on the Olympic team, he has to be good. But he really blundered out there on the course. Those weren't little slips or bad luck. They were the kind of moves that shouldn't happen. And he didn't even seem interested in the boats. He's a naval architect, but it's as if his mind is somewhere else."

"Do you think he was *trying* to get the Americans to lose?"

"No, of course not. I suspect he just doesn't care. That's what bothers me."

"It's this country," said Maggie. "It's strange. The uniforms, the music, the rituals—it does something to people. It's too organized. Everything is so precise, a place and a way to do each thing, as if they're afraid of surprises. Like with the admiral, the way they were waiting for him. It's almost choreographed. I'd just love to pop a balloon and see what would happen. Maybe Henry had the same feeling. Don't you?"

"What bothers me . . ." he started to say, then didn't finish his answer as they turned off the highway at a small marker sign pointing the way to Karinhall. The access road was new, cut straight through a dense pine forest, a landscape like the Russian steppes.

The first sentry station was five kilometers from the highway. A pole gate across the road blocked all traffic, and bright floodlights illuminated the area. It had the appearance of a guardpost for a top-secret installation, or a border crossing where every vehicle was to be inspected for smuggling.

"Are you sure this is okay?" said Maggie. "I had no idea it would be so . . ."

"If it's not okay, I'm not going either. And then we will have hustled away from Kiel and Henry and changed clothes for nothing. Except that I get to see you in that dress."

"Basic black," she said.

"On you, it's more than basic."

The guard was a young soldier with a smooth oval face and a forelock of blond hair that leaked out from under the peak of his cap. He checked Whitman's name off a list and telephoned before raising the gate. He worked hard not to smile in response to Maggie's grin.

The next checkpoint was at an iron fence where Luftwaffe guards stood at the gates with machine pistols slung across their chests. These older guards needed no efforts to maintain blank expressions, and after more checking of lists and telephoning, they passed the car on with a wave, pointing them toward a circular driveway that afforded a glimpse of Karinhall.

They stopped for a moment on the road, looking down on the setting of what Goering affectionately called his lodge, nestled in a dense wood but with an architecture that could only be called palatial, a deliberate effort toward magnificence that combined the worst features of one of Mad Ludwig's fanciful castles and a bunker. More than the Olympic Stadium, it was a structure built to awe, an effort to create instant majesty and permanence. Nazis like Goering did not see themselves as passing politicians.

The ballroom was a staggering display of ostentation, uniformed and bemedaled men, and heavy bare-shouldered women, acres of pasty white flesh, the occasional beautiful woman easy to spot amidst the elaborate pastel ballgowns of German women whose figures betrayed a belief that pounds of flesh are a symbol of well-being. An enormous buffet table at one side of the room was piled high with elaborate food, platter upon platter of caviar and pâtés, whole roasted piglets, boned pheasants encased in their own feathers. In the center stood a top-heavy ice sculpture of a futuristic airplane in flight, and around the perimeter of the room were funereal arrangements of flowers in statuary displays. A small orchestra in one corner played chamber music that was far too serious for the loud chatter of the crowd.

Whitman recognized Luftwaffe and army generals in their dress uniforms, and well-known industrialists in formal wear, with decorations arranged on their colored sashes. He secretly enjoyed the out-of-place feeling of his simple double-breasted uniform, and the fact that Maggie in her simple black dress stood out among the flowery pastel gowns of the other women.

"It's a wonder they didn't have a butler in livery announcing us," she said.

"You're attracting enough attention anyway," Paul answered. "At least two hundred pairs of eyes just nominated you the most beautiful woman in the room."

The first sign of Goering's entrance was a murmur rippling through the room. The mass of people began to part, like the Red Sea in the face of Moses, and Whitman and Maggie caught a quick glimpse of Goering standing in the doorway, the baby blue of his uniform vibrant against the gray-blue of the Luftwaffe officers in his entourage.

The official photographs didn't do him justice. He was immensely fat, and the expanse of pale blue uniform with its extra-wide lapels accentuated his shape. His skin was soft and babylike, an almost rosy pink, rolling in undulating waves as he moved his jaw. His lips were a thin scarlet line, and his smiles lifted only the corners of his mouth, as if he were a potentate saying *we are pleased*.

But it was the eyes that drew Whitman's gaze. They seemed all wrong. Instead of Hempe's beady little pig eyes or the expressionless squint of the official photographs, Goering had deep, dark eyes that lent him an aura of cunning. As he walked, his steps set the rows of decorations on his uniform into a ridiculous jiggle, but with those eyes, he was not a comic figure.

He walked slowly through the crowd, pausing after each step or two, saying a few words that invariably brought titters of polite laughter to the lips of the women as he kissed their extended hands. The procession wound its way through the ballroom, an aide whispering into Goering's ear as he faced each group. Generals and captains of industry could be seen edging their way toward Goering, controlling their ardor lest anyone perceive them as *too* anxious to be seen with the *Reichslufts-marshall*.

Whitman gradually realized that Goering was coming toward him. Maggie glanced at him with a look that said *you really are amazing*. Then the crowd in front of them parted and Goering was there in all his majesty. Up close, his bulk looming in the clownish uniform and the soft leather boots, he seemed both more absurd and more threatening.

"So you are the marvelous Captain Whitman about whom we hear so much?" The ingratiating smile barely parted the thin scarlet lips, revealing tiny white teeth. "There has been much talk about your exploits, Captain. Whatever the detractors might say, surely no one can question your judgment of female beauty. The lady is lovely. We understand your motives completely."

Goering extended his hand to Maggie, the diamonds on his rings glittering like the chandeliers dangling from the vaulted ceiling. The jewels were enormous, but scaled perfectly to his pudgy fingers. Although his German was incomprehensible to her, the flattery in Goering's tone was obvious to Maggie, not very different from the equally unctuous words of Senhor de Nascimento on the Graf Zeppelin. She extended her hand, shaking Goering's hand instead of offering her fingers to his lips.

The *Reichsluftsmarshall*'s smile collapsed as quickly as it had formed. "A modern woman?" he said in English. He quickly regained his composure and added, "You have never seen Karinhall. Perhaps you would like a tour."

Before Paul or Maggie could respond, they were swept past the watchful gaze of hundreds of eyes to the arched entry of the ballroom, surrounded on all sides by the uniforms of Goering's entourage.

It was impossible to comprehend the layout of what Goering called his "little retreat." The long halls of the lodge formed a maze of corridors and reception rooms, all with high vaulted ceilings, the walls hung with paintings and tapestries, the sides of the corridors lined with glass cases displaying objects of every description, vases, sculpture, antique firearms, armor, gold jewelry, samples of almost anything that could be collected—no order to the collection beyond whimsy, the overall effect not so much beauty as lushness, the results of a drunken buying spree.

The Nazis had a word for such items, whether the modest antique furniture in Hempe's office or the splendors of Karinhall, *Objekte,* a euphemism for the riches and splendors that were appropriated from Jews and others, all quite legally of course, according to the strange codes of legality that governed the Nazi Reich. Everyone in Germany knew about the *Objekte* and how the picks of the lots found their way to officers and party higher-ups, but until he saw those halls at Karinhall, and the overwhelming scale of the operation, Whitman had no idea of the extent of the appropriations. In just a few halls and rooms he saw enough to stock several fair-sized museums.

Goering pointed out only a few items, his favorites, or perhaps items he felt would impress—a Leonardo drawing on an easel, a flawless set of Aubusson tapestries, a display case filled with matched antique dueling pistols. He walked alongside Maggie, speaking to her in his stilted English, asking questions or making statements that seemed to call for replies, but never pausing long enough for her to respond.

"You are a photographer, *Mrs*. Bourne?" He accentuated the *Mrs*., the scarlet lips again parting into a lewd grin. "I should like to show you some of the collections of photographs we have here, but I fear that Captain Whitman would think me tasteless unless he is a modern *man* as you are a modern *woman*. Perhaps someday I will have the opportunity to see *your* photographs. There is nothing of beauty that we do not try to collect. We have so little time on this earth, and there is so much beauty that deserves our attention."

He paused by one doorway, open to expose a den, a man's lair. It was a winter room, with a bearskin rug in front of a huge stone fireplace, surrounded by oversized leather club chairs. Stag and boar heads hung on the walls, and just inside the door, two Luftwaffe aides stood obsequiously, their sidearms plainly visible.

"As much as we hate to give up your charming company, *Mrs* Bourne, I hope you will excuse me if I have a few private words with Captain Whitman? I can arrange for someone to show you more of Karinhall, although of course we must skip those photographs this time."

With the grin still frozen on his face, he turned and saw

Whitman halfway down the hall, staring at a pair of deep red
Titian portraits that hung high on the wall of the gallery, almost
lost amid hazy German landscapes and a suit of heavy chain mail
armor. Impatiently, Goering kept talking, as if a moment of
silence would be painful.

"You enjoyed the Olympic Games today?" He looked away
absentmindedly, not expecting an answer.

"It was spectacular," said Maggie. "I thought Jesse Owens
running was the most splendid sight I've ever seen. The beauty
of that man competing makes sport into an art."

The corners of the scarlet line dropped as Goering's face
mirrored his distaste. He watched Whitman leave the paintings to
join them, and waited for him to come within earshot before
answering Maggie.

"It's too bad that the Americans are doing so badly in the
Games," he said, "except for the *black auxiliaries*. I do think
there is something very wrong when a great and potentially
progressive nation like the United States uses former slaves in
this way."

Whitman bristled, angered as much by the opulence of Karinhall
as by Goering's words. "Those 'black auxiliaries,' as you call
them, seem to be sweeping the track and field events. It looks
like their performance may necessitate some new footnotes on
the theory of Aryan supremacy."

"Captain Whitman!" Goering's voice lost its unctuous tone
and the face became sharp and argumentative, the cunning eyes
draining the softness from the pudgy skin. "I'm surprised that
you would leap to the defense of the blacks. After all, they're a
bigger problem for America than the Jews, at least in numbers.
And sending them as auxiliaries with the American Olympic
team only compounds matters by focusing world attention on an
unsolved problem."

"What do you think should happen to the Negroes?" asked
Whitman. "Should they become slaves again?"

"*Slaves?* Really, Captain Whitman. Of course they should not
become slaves. If I'm not wrong, that would be illegal, or as you
Americans say, unconstitutional. I do not believe any nation can
survive when it is led by a government that permits illegal
measures. That is why the Third Reich is so scrupulous in its
adherence to the laws. But there are other laws that we in the
progressive nations must also follow—the laws of nature. What
you have so contemptuously labeled the *theory* of Aryan supremacy is in fact a demonstrable law of nature, one of the

bedrocks of modern geopolitics. You need only look at Africa for your proof. A proper adherence to natural law would suggest that if they cannot be returned to their own homeland in Africa, the blacks should at least be kept in their *appropriate* place in society. Surely the latter course would be far kinder and more humane than the murders and lynchings of blacks that take place all the time in America. It's ironic, Captain Whitman, that a society which would pretend to make judgments on the New Germany would itself permit such oppressions of peoples.''

Whitman turned away to control his anger, catching again in his gaze the two Titian portraits, of a duke and duchess. They were magnificent paintings, the deep red color capturing the majesty and authority of the somber figures.

He turned back to face the *Reichsluftsmarshall*, resplendent in his uniform, his hand on his hips and his feet apart as he stared in defiance. Even in the gloomy hall, the man glittered, the four stars of his rank gleaming on his shoulders, the jeweled medals and rings reflecting the faint light of the dangling chandeliers.

"At least in the United States," said Whitman, "we honor our heroes. When Jesse Owens comes home, he'll get a parade. No one will take his gold medals as *Objekte*. You don't seem to treat your heroes with the same respect."

Goering's tight grin relaxed, as if a wave of anger had passed. "Is it Herr Eckener that troubles you, Captain? There's much about the future of Germany that you unfortunately do not know. I hope our little talk can enlighten you."

"Not just Eckener," said Whitman. "What about Admiral von Teppler? His reception was hardly a hero's welcome."

Goering's grin tightened again. "Von Teppler has retired from active service," he said flatly. "Many who cannot meet the pace and the demands of the New Germany have chosen to retire."

"Retire?" Whitman's voice hardened. "Is that what you call it? It's a whole new language, isn't it? *Objekte* for booty, retirement for..."

Goering's face froze, the cunning eyes narrowing, glaring at Whitman. "I don't think our little talk will be necessary after all," he said, spinning on his heels. The thick legs in the flaring trousers rubbed against one another as his boots clacked away down the polished floor. His retinue followed him, leaving Paul and Maggie alone in the gloomy hall.

Maggie looked up at Paul, put her arms around his neck, and kissed him on the lips, first softly, then with an electric excitement. "I don't know what you said, Paul Whitman, but you're a strange, brave, wonderful man."

They arrived at the hotel feeling sleepy and mellow, exhausted from the long day, but not at all tired of one another. After hours together, they were attuned to one another, a feeling neither of them could help noticing. The unanswered questions of the night before were gone, brushed away by the subtle signals that had gone back and forth between them, casual touches, spontaneous smiles, open and unrestrained talk.

When they got back to the room, past the intimidating stares of the desk clerk, Maggie disappeared into the bathroom, reappearing a moment later in a black slip, appliquéd with a border of gay flowers and butterflies, her jacket tossed over her shoulders. She stood at the doorway with her feet apart and her hands on her hips, thrusting her jaw out and puffing her cheeks.

"So you are the marvelous Captain Whitman about whom we hear so much," she said in a flawless imitation of Goering.

Paul looked at her and burst out laughing, then walked over and took her in his arms.

"Really, Paul. You were dynamite. Meeting you is the best thing that's happened to me in a long time."

"You'd say that to anyone who plucked you off that sinking hulk in the middle of the South Atlantic."

"No, Captain Whitman. I have the feeling that I was out there waiting for you to come along."

She let the jacket fall to the floor as she put her arms around him. Her embrace was strong. He kissed the crook of her jaw, where the neck curved up, and realized that he had been staring at that spot, picturing himself kissing it. They kissed sleepily, their lips barely brushing against one another, slowly and gently exploring with no sense of time or goal or conquest. They seemed to need no talk or brandy or cigarettes or music. They were just two people who wanted one another very much. The sleepiness made it seem even more right, slower and gentler and tenderer than any experience either of them could remember.

They ignored the ringing of the phone at first.

But the ringing kept on, five, six, seven rings. With both of them counting, the moment was shattered.

Paul instinctively brushed the unruly shock of hair off his forehead as he reached for the phone. He listened for only a few seconds before he handed the phone to her, the expression on his face suddenly alert and puzzled as he left the bed.

He watched her hand begin to tremble as she listened to the phone, then heard her voice rise in unfamiliar anger.

"David! How'd you find me here?...You're like a child. Can't you understand? Can't you just leave me alone?... Where?...*Why?*...No, I told you, I'm busy. I have my own life, and that's the only one I'm going to live now....Can't you even explain what it's all about? What's the big mystery?... Oh, of course. David Sinclair would never stop short of saving all of Western Civilization. When are you going to grow up, David?...It's none of your business and the answer is still no. If I ever see you again, it'll be for one reason, and that's to sign those papers. Now just get out of my life and leave me alone."

She was trembling when she put the phone down.

"My husband," she said.

"He really gets to you."

"Some people know how to get to a person. It's like a surgeon who knows his anatomy, knows exactly what does what and how to get to the right little vessel or nerve. He *knows* what words do. And he always uses them to make guilt or pain. Never to make a person feel good or loved or just content. He just digs that little verbal scalpel in right up to the handle."

Paul wasn't sure how to answer. "He does really matter though, doesn't he?"

"Matter? All that matters to me is that it's over. He's an impossible man, really. What he wanted was for me to come to Zurich, probably to read something he'd written. But he wouldn't say that. What he said was that he was about to save Spain. He can't get through his head that a thousand beautiful words or a spectacular picture still won't make a revolution. He doesn't even write because he cares about things. He does it for the praise, so someone will say how good he is. And what makes it so sad is that he's good. Behind a typewriter he's the best. If he could only care..."

Whitman was affected by what she said, and not sure why. "I envy him," he said.

Maggie laughed. "You wouldn't say that if you met David. It's all talk. I can't imagine two men more different than you and he."

"He has you and he has a cause. That's enough to envy."

"The only cause he has is David Sinclair."

Whitman smiled, shyly. "He still has you."

"No, he doesn't. But if that's jealousy I'm hearing, I feel very loved. It's a nice way to feel. I'm not used to it."

She came over to him and he took her in his arms, but both of them could feel the hesitation in his embrace. It wasn't the same. A shadow had come between them.

"Still afraid of sticky involvements?" Maggie asked.

"I guess so."

She crawled off the bed and padded into the bathroom, splashing cold water on her face before she came back and curled up in an armchair, hugging her legs under her and rolling herself into a compact ball.

"This is going to sound crazy," she said, "but I think I'm going to go to Zurich. Once he signs the papers, it's all over. There's no other way to end things. I can't win with words. He's just that kind of man, a verbal virtuoso. When we argue he can finally bully me into anything. That's why Africa was so wonderful, or the days on the Graf Zeppelin. He couldn't reach me with those words. And now that you've come along . . ."

"Are you sure it's only his words?"

"As sure as I've ever been of anything."

"When will you go?"

"I guess tomorrow, after we visit the Huttens."

"And when will I see you again?"

"That's not a real question, is it? If we could find one another in the middle of a whole ocean, anything else is easy. Europe is a small place. I can be down to Zurich and back to Friedr— What's the name of the town?"

"Friedrichshafen."

". . . right, before you're through with that inquiry."

"And then?"

She looked away, then back to his eyes. "No plans," she said. "These have been some of the best days of my life, because of you and because there are no plans. Let's keep it that way."

"Okay," he said. "No plans." He reached out toward her, taking her hands in his, feeling the softness of her as she came toward him.

"*Almost* no plans."

Forty-Two

Sinclair was smiling when he came out of the cafe. He could remember every word of the phone conversation, every nuance of tone. He knew Margaret's voice, knew how to interpret the inflections that said more than her words.

The little Citroën van parked by the dock looked woefully inadequate, overloaded, sorely in need of repair, too anonymous for its history-making task. He remembered when they had first glimpsed it, as they came up the narrow channel of the river and he shouted out to Manolo.

"How did you ever pick such a place?" Manolo asked them. "It feels like malaria here."

They were motoring up a dank channel of the Petit Rhône, a backwater of the Rhône delta that runs through the edges of the vast swampland of the Camargue west of Marseilles. They had navigated without a chart, Sinclair tossing out a leadline from the bow of the boat to find the shoals as Manolo maneuvered within meters of the banks. They had seen no other boats on the river, only the encampments of Gypsy caravans around open fires, and wild horses braying defiantly at the boat from the grassy banks.

"It's Gypsy country," Sinclair explained. "Every year, in the spring, they gather at Stes. Maries de la Mer for their festival. The rest of the year, they use the town for their smuggling. Even the gendarmes are afraid of the Gypsies, so for us it means no questions, no customs, no pratique." He remembered picking up the scraps of information long ago, on an unrelated story, filing them away in his mind with no idea how or when he would use them.

Manolo swung the boat parallel to the crumbling dock, using the shift levers of the two engines to bring the boat within a foot of the pilings before he jumped up with the lines.

"You're in the wrong business, Sinclair," he said as he wrapped the lines around the pilings. "With a mind like yours

ou could have been a *contrabandista*. You could have been a
ch man.''

"I'll remember the invitation."

Sinclair found Martine at the cafe, distancing himself from the
ypsies as he tried to keep his suit prim. From the terrace of the
afe they could see Manolo carrying the crates on his shoulders
the waiting van.

"Well?" said Martine, his shrug registering his skepticism.
What happened?"

Sinclair grinned and nodded toward the boat and the cargo.
There it is.''

"You did it? I thought it would be . . . different. Just wooden
oxes? They look like ammunition crates.''

Sinclair told them the story of their raid.

"That easy?"

"That easy," said Sinclair. "Any problems with the van?"

"The van is fine," said Martine. "And the papers are flaw-
ess. With the stamps of the union on them, they will ask you no
uestions at the Swiss border. But you must still be cautious.
Orlov, the NKVD man in Madrid, suspects something. He was
sking questions before I left, lots of questions. No one will tell
im anything, of course, but he's persistent. It's only a matter of
me before he knows something.''

"No one will tell him anything, of course," mocked Sinclair.
You idiots. Somebody already talked. He was in Minorca.''

"Minorca?" Martine's face went blank.

"Not to worry," said Sinclair. "No one in Minorca will talk."

The phone call took longer to place than Sinclair expected.
√hen he finished, Manolo was covering the cargo in the back of
\e van, spreading the load carefully over the rear axle and tying
\e crates in place with a tarpaulin.

"We're ready," Manolo said to Sinclair.

Sinclair lifted a corner of the tarpaulin and counted the crates.
There are only sixteen here," he said. "We took twenty-two
ff the ship.''

"Your plan was for sixteen boxes, Sinclair. The others are for
pain.''

"For Spain?" Sinclair snapped. "That's a grand cause for a
nuggler.''

Manolo climbed into the cab of the van, closing the door and
urning to face the road ahead of them.

"Save your breath, Sinclair. We have no time for argument that do no one any good."

"*We* have no time?"

"It's you who were in the great hurry, Sinclair."

Sinclair climbed into the cab, pushing himself back in the seat and gripping the wheel with both hands.

"Can you speak German, Manolo? Or even French? How will it look if I walk into a bank with a man who speaks only Spanish? What will they say at the Swiss border when we drive up and you have only a Spanish passport? Alone, I'm an American driving a van with spare machine parts. That's what the papers say. They're all in order. But with you along, there are all of a sudden too many questions to answer."

Manolo reached for Sinclair's arm, holding the wrist in his grip. "You think I'm going to let you take this by yourself? Just drive away with it? You think men died and we used the petrol and the weapons that could have saved lives on Majorca so you could take this alone?"

"What choice have you?"

With his right hand Manolo pulled up his pants leg. The long knife blade seemed to spring into his hand. "Choice? One choice is for me to take the gold to Marseilles and buy enough arms to kill every Fascist in the Islands. That's not a bad choice, is it Sinclair?"

Sinclair was ready with his answer. "And while you kill the Fascists on your little island, what happens to Spain? They will cut you off and let you starve like fish in the reeds. Do you still think I want this for myself? To be rich? It is I who am doing something for Spain and for democracy. Or can't you understand that?"

Manolo let Sinclair wriggle free. He lifted his pants leg again and the knife disappeared as mysteriously as it had appeared. For a long moment, he stared at Sinclair without blinking, until Sinclair turned his own head away.

"I know you will not take this for yourself," said Manolo. "You are not such a man. That I can see. But why must it be alone? Why must you be such a hero?"

Manolo opened the door of the van, half climbing out before he finished.

"You say you are doing this for Spain, so the Germans and the Russians will not use Spain. I will tell you what I think, Sinclair. I think that you, too, will use Spain. For what, I don't know. But you will use her."

Forty-Three

"I really like your brother," said Maggie. "He's full of life."

Henry had shown up bright and early in their hotel room, clutching a nosegay of colorful flowers for Maggie. He had decided to stay in Kiel, he said. The weather looked promising, and he wanted to spend the morning on the water. He was all smiles and enthusiasm, eager to hear about their evening with Goering, overjoyed at Maggie's description of Paul standing up to the air marshal.

Maggie had the flowers with her when they drove to Bremen.

"He really is a good kid," said Paul. "But I worry about him."

"Kid?"

"I guess that's the problem. We're far enough apart in years that I've never been sure whether I'm a brother or a surrogate father. I always have a nagging sense that tells me I am supposed to take care of him and keep him out of trouble."

"Right now," said Maggie, "you'd better worry about keeping yourself out of trouble."

"You mean last night? I can't believe that will matter much. Goering must have something on his mind more important than one more airship pilot."

Unlike the Olympic cities of Berlin and Kiel, Bremen had not been cleansed of propaganda for the benefit of the world press. Posters were still on the lampposts and the sides of buildings, bold cartoons of hideous bearded rabbis holding bloody daggers, overprinted with warnings about the dangers of doing business with Jews. There were proclamations of the Nuremberg Laws, which forbid most forms of social, commercial, and sexual intercourse between Germans and Jews. As they drove from the Marktplatz toward the warehouses and shipyards of the River Weser, through streets of bars and whorehouses and bawdy clubs that rivaled the daytime tawdriness of Hamburg's Reeperbahn, they passed occasional boarded shopfronts, with the word *JÜDE* and crude six-pointed stars splashed in yellow on the boards.

Otto Hutten's directions were easy to follow, and they soon found themselves at the edge of the vast harbor, overlooking the forest of cranes and gantries at the quays and facing an imposing warehouse facade with a sign painted on the bricks. *HUTTEN u. SÖHNE*. The strong smell of coffee beans from the warehouse competed with the dead fish smells of the harbor.

"Doesn't smell like wine to me," said Maggie.

"He quit coffee in Brazil," explained Paul. "Didn't like the way the big landowners ran the coffee plantations or the ghetto the Germans built for themselves."

They were directed from the front of the building to an alleyway behind, through a freight entrance that led into a storage area piled with pallets, dollies, and bundles of burlap sacks. The roar of coffee grinding machinery and conveyor belts made it impossible to talk, the heat from the ovens was stifling, and a fog of fine greenish-brown powder filled the air, settling everywhere.

They were ready to turn back when Maggie spotted a freshly painted door in a niche behind a stack of pallets.

When the door opened, they could smell strong disinfectants and fresh whitewash.

"You're surprised?" said Otto Hutten, greeting them formally.

The inside of the flat was scrubbed and freshly painted, thick coats of whitewash covering the irregular surfaces of what had once been a storeroom. The air was so close that it took away their breaths, hotter than the air outside. They could hear the starting and stopping of machinery above the room.

Maggie began to say something about how clean the flat was, but Hutten sensed their reaction and hurriedly explained.

"It's not what we expected either. We must pay rent to our relatives, you see. And now we have no money. So I work in the warehouse, and Anna works cleaning some of the houses of the relatives, and they have let us have this room. It's not so bad at night, when the machines have shut down."

They all sat down around a cramped table, the only place with room for four of them. Their conversation, mostly about the Zeppelin, was strained. Anna, sensing the awkwardness, rushed to set the table and lay out her banquet of Bremen specialties— *Vegesacker* herring, chicken ragout, tiny sausages cooked with broccoli. Explanations of the dishes and the enjoyment of the food soon filled the awkward silences. Otto uncorked a bottle of white wine—"Our last from Brazil," he said—and filled their glasses whenever either of them took a single sip. Maggie proposed a toast: "To homecoming."

When they put their glasses down, Otto looked up with a gaze that Whitman remembered from the Frankfurt airfield, a forced smile that couldn't hide his feelings.

"It's not good, Captain," he said. "This Germany is not the country we left so many years ago. Even our family is not the same now." He looked over at Anna and reached out for her hand. "Our people are part of this madness that is the New Germany. Perhaps they are not truly believers, who is to know? Perhaps it is necessary for them to do their business. But we cannot be part of this Germany. We cannot talk with this hatred for Jews and Poles and French and Gypsies."

"We have no one to blame but ourselves," said Anna. "But that does not change the fact that we're sorry we have come back. We wanted to spend our old age among our family, with our own people. In truth, it's as if we have no family now. They will never see us. They make us live here, in what was once a storeroom. It's so hot that we cough from the heat and the coffee dust. In the winter it will be cold, and we have only the stove. Otto is too old to drag sacks of coal. And because we have no money, we must work to pay the rent. I do not mind the work. I do not have such pride that I will not clean the house of another. But it doesn't seem right. Otto should not have to carry heavy sacks all day. We left a fine house and our vineyards and now we are laborers again."

"Can't you go back?" asked Maggie.

"Ah, Fräulein Bourne," said Otto. "How much we would like that! But we have no money now. Did Captain Whitman explain to you about the tax quit claim? And in another week, it will be too late. After thirty days, our land in Brazil must be sold."

Hutten explained the Brazilian law. To discourage foreign ownership of land, the Vargas regime had promulgated decrees that required all foreigners leaving Brazil to sell their land to a Brazilian within thirty days.

"Can't you have them hold up the sale?" said Paul. "Wire them that you'll be coming back to live on the land again as soon as you can."

Hutten shook his head. "They make no exceptions. Why should they? And we could never get back in time."

"What about the Graf Zeppelin?" asked Maggie. "That would get you back in time."

"Ah—" said Hutten. "What a wonderful journey! We will remember it always. But that was before our money was taken away."

"I can loan you money," said Maggie. "American dollars."

"We could not take your money, Fräulein. It wouldn't be right."

"You offered me money when we were on the Zeppelin. What are friends for?"

"It's very kind of you. But it will do no good. If we were to try to buy tickets, they would confiscate the money because they say we still owe them for the tax quit claim. It seems that we're not really welcome in the New Germany, but that it's also impossible for us to leave."

Maggie looked at Paul, expecting him to say something.

"When the funds from the auction of our land are forwarded to Germany," Hutten went on, "they will also be seized because of the tax quit claim. They say that if there are no taxes owed, I will get the money back. But I don't trust them. Would you?"

Whitman leaned forward. "You mean that you'll get nothing from the sale of your land? You'll have to stay here like this?"

"It's only temporary, we hope," said Hutten. He glanced at Anna, then back at Whitman.

"I tell you this because you're a friend," he said. "I hope you will not judge me harshly for what I do. When we arrived here from Frankfurt, we knew already that we would have more troubles with the authorities, that the business at the airfield was only the first encounter. And we knew that if we couldn't get our money, we would have a terrible time here.

"Well, we were no sooner settled here when we had an unexpected visitor. Senhor de Nascimento, from the Graf Zeppelin. It seems that he does much business in Germany and travels often between Brazil and Germany. He said that he had overheard our difficulties with the customs people at the airfield, and he wanted to help. We were unsure of him at first, because on the Graf Zeppelin he seemed an unsavory man. But when he talked with us he was very sincere and sympathetic. He said that he would be glad to bring us the money from the sale of our land personally so that it would not be seized by the authorities. He says it can be brought as diamonds. I know what we're doing is not proper, but we have no choice. I'm already an old man, and I don't know how long I can work carrying the coffee bags."

"Did you agree?" Paul asked.

"I don't know much about the legal details," said Hutten.

"With Senhor de Nascimento's help we signed a paper, a power of attorney so he may act in our stead at the sale of the land. Since he's a Brazilian, there will be no questions, he assured us. He was very kind to Anna and to me. He's a man we can trust, isn't he, Captain?"

Whitman didn't answer, mumbling something about getting to the airport in Hamburg in time for Maggie's flight. He found it hard to look at the Huttens.

"We should not be so sad," said Anna Hutten. "It's a happy occasion when the Captain and Fräulein Bourne can visit us. We should toast our friendship and the future when we can again have dinner together."

"Yes," said Otto, raising his glass again. "No matter what, they cannot take away our friends and our memories. I will always remember the taste of the new wines. It was as if the sunshine were inside the grapes. And the wonderful views of Brazil from the Graf Zeppelin. The memories are enough for us."

"What will happen to them?" Maggie asked in the car. "Will that de Nascimento really bring their money?"

"What do you think?" said Paul. "Do you know why that parasite comes to Germany? He brings diamonds, cheap Brazilian stones that he sells to Jews who are desperate to get their money out of the country. He gets them when they have nowhere else to turn, and they pay him fabulous sums for junk. And then when they finally get to England or Holland or Switzerland and try to resell the stones, they discover that they've got nothing."

Maggie sat silently for a while, looking at the flat Autobahn ahead of them, before she returned back to Paul. "Why didn't you tell the Huttens?"

"And break their hearts before it happens?"

"You'd rather their hearts be broken when you're not around?"

"No. I'd rather their hearts not be broken at all. I keep hoping that something will change."

"Who will change it?"

"Maggie, I hate this rotten business as much as you. If there were something I could do, I would. But I'm only an airship pilot. I can't change the world by myself, even if you and the admiral seem to think I can."

She turned in the seat, looking at him as if she had never seen him clearly before.

"It's really strange," she said. "Without the Graf Zeppelin

you're a different man. It's like those big albatrosses, the dodo birds. Up in the air they're the most graceful creatures alive, soaring for hours on end, in complete control. On the ground, they can hardly keep from tripping on their own feet. In the Zeppelin you were the commander, totally in charge, equal to any situation. Now you seem like a rider without a horse. Or is it a captain without a ship?"

"Try a man without a country."

"That's a little melodramatic, I think. You can always just leave this whole mess and go home. Which I guess is just what they want you to do. Is that why you won't—the stubborn man?"

"Maybe," he said. Then he turned and tried to smile. "This doesn't seem like the best sort of good-bye, does it?"

"No." said Maggie. "It doesn't."

Forty-Four

For two days Conselheiro hid in the shack in the mangrove swamps. He had been planning to steal the mortar himself because it would be one more insult to the stupidity of the Integralistas, but he could no longer run or even walk on the swollen foot, which had become discolored and odoriferous. The wife of the jailer cooked for him and washed the foot and put poultices on it, but it didn't seem to help, and while Conselheiro never complained about the pain, even he could not help but notice the nauseating smell of the festering flesh.

"You should see a doctor," the woman said. "The foot is very bad."

"I should be a rich man too," he said. "With a house in the city."

"The doctors here will not recognize you," she said. "No one remembers."

She meant well when she said it, but her words made him angry. She didn't mention the foot again.

Conselheiro sent the jailer to get the mortar and the rockets, insisting that it would be easy to steal.

"But they're already looking for me," said the jailer. "If they catch me, they will kill me."

"If you don't go, I will save them the trouble."

"There are guards at the armory."

"There were guards at the jail. They're nothing."

Conselheiro was right. Most of the Integralistas were involved in the search for Conselheiro, an impossible task once he had reached the safety of the *favelas* where the Integralistas would not venture. Only a skeleton crew was on duty at the barracks and the armory. The jailer, knowing they would stay inside the screened guardhouse playing cards and drinking beer, had just walked into the building they called an armory, taken the mortar and four of the rockets and put them into a basket with a headstrap, then walked back out and boldly crossed in front of the guardhouse as if he were one more peasant carrying fruit or crabs to the market. To the guards, one man in peasant garb looked just like any other, and the search for the jailer had been less than half-hearted. They assumed that Conselheiro had killed him and thrown him in the river.

He swung the basket off his head and put it on the floor in front of Conselheiro. "Now," he said, "you must go to the backlands."

Conselheiro tried to get up to unpack the mortar, but he stumbled and fell. The foot was so swollen and tender that he could put no weight on it.

"You must see the doctor," said the woman. "If you won't go to the doctor, you can go into the backlands, to the clinic of the English doctor. He cannot know you. Even now, you cannot walk. In a few more days it will spread up your leg."

Conselheiro knew they only wanted him to leave. He also knew the woman was right. He let them take him by boat up the river, far into the backlands, where the drought-shrunk river threaded through the parched land until they finally stopped alongside a ramshackle building with *Clinica* painted on the tin roof. The woman had already shaved off his beard and moustache and cut his hair and rubbed leaves on the pink skin under the beard. No one recognized him on the boat or at the landing for the clinic.

Alongside the central building with the sign there was a long shed, with a corrugated roof and screened sides and a long row of pallets inside. Nurses in soiled uniforms walked up and down with buckets, offering cups of water to the patients. While Conselheiro waited in the line that curved down from the front of the clinic, he saw men come in with a cart to pick up those who had not survived the previous night.

Most of those who waited in the line with him had distended bellies and flushed skin with sunken gray eyes. Some had come by themselves, supporting their weight on sticks or collapsing after every few steps. Others were carried on shoulders or in arms. From the smell of the bundled rags in one woman's arms, he knew she had come to seek not a cure but a miracle for her child.

It was the fever. It had come before in the backlands, killing hundreds and even thousands before it ran its course and stopped. Nothing anyone did helped. The peasants used their own herb medicines, but they did no good. Many went to church, where the priests recited special prayers or told them to say a hundred *Ave Maria*s or five hundred *Our Father*s. Still others went to Macumba rites, including many who had abandoned the old faiths long before. But the fever went on, taking its toll. Medicines and prayers and rites were useless.

To Conselheiro, the causes of the fever were obvious: poverty, crowding, poor sanitation, oppression. And the cure was even more obvious: revolution. Let the people seize power and throw out the Integralistas and the rich and take the land back to grow food on again, and there would be no more fevers. Nothing else would help. The people needed a sign, a signal, like the destruction of Zeppelin. Then they would make their own destiny.

Conselheiro had heard of the English doctor before, a man of the Anglican Church who had chosen the backlands of Brazil for his mission. He had built the clinic himself, bringing supplies from England, training nurses from the cities and the countryside. He did not recognize Conselheiro—to him, just another of the peasants. Everyone had forgotten him.

"What is it?" said the doctor.

Conselheiro held out the foot. The doctor examined it without flinching from the smell.

"It is festering," he said. "You should not have been walking on this wound. How did the foot get so mangled?"

"I hurt it."

The doctor asked no more questions as he prepared an injection, then busied himself cleansing and cauterizing the wound. He warned Conselheiro that much of what he would do would be painful, but Conselheiro didn't flinch even when the doctor probed and cut the blackened flesh.

"What's the use of this?" asked Conselheiro as the doctor started to bandage the foot. "What good is the clinic? They will die of the fever anyway."

"We must try. We can comfort."

"Comfort? But still they will all die. Without food and medicine and work, they will all die. Maybe it's better that they die quickly from the fever. Maybe it's a sign."

"I do not think that the Lord would send such a sign to his poorest children."

"The Lord?" said Conselheiro. "And would the Lord let the government spend millions on the army and the Zeppelin flights for the rich, with nothing for these people?"

"Perhaps the Lord has secrets that we do not understand yet," said the doctor. "Soon we may have medicine for the fevers."

"Medicine? There is such a medicine?"

"We hope so. It can do nothing for those who have the fevers, but it may stop the spread of the disease and save the others." He finished with the bandage and added, "You must stay off the foot and change the bandages each day. In five days, come back and I will look at it again."

Five days, thought Conselheiro. In five days he would be on the Zeppelin field, waiting with his mortar, ready to give the signal that the end of suffering and oppression was near. For a fleeting moment he wanted to talk with the doctor, to find out more about this medicine that would someday come. The Englishman was a man of the Church, educated, intelligent. You could tell from talking to him. Perhaps he was a man who would understand.

But the doctor had already turned to the next patient in line, a woman carrying a tiny bloated body, its frail limbs trembling with every labored breath it took.

Conselheiro looked at the child and realized that he too had no time to talk.

Forty-Five

Paul made it to the dock minutes before the spectator boat was scheduled to depart. A VIP party—German navy uniforms, civilians in white flannels and blue blazers with crested pockets, ladies carrying parasols—was taking its time in boarding, pre-empting the desirable seats on the fantail and the port rail as they tossed out words like ''regatta,'' oblivious to Whitman and the others who were eager to see the start of the Six Meter race.

Trying to control his temper and at the same time not think about Maggie, Whitman glanced at the bulletin board with the posted results of the previous day's racing. A man had just asked him to explain the complex Olympic scoring rule when Paul spotted a handwritten notice at the bottom of the race schedule, a single line announcing a crew change on the American Six Meter entry: Henry had been scratched. Paul offered his ticket on the spectator boat to the first man he saw.

It took an hour of patient argument, telephone calls, and heel-cooling at the gate before the officious guards at the Olympic barracks would allow him in. They searched him at the entrance, explaining that it was a normal precautionary procedure, then led him into what they called the lounge.

The room was a former officers' wardroom, freshened with a coat of bright paint and with Olympic flags and large line drawings of the Olympic class sailboats in place of the usual naval regalia. But the long tables still bore the scars of years of naval service. Rings had been burned into the wooden tabletops by countless mugs of steaming tea, and even through the fresh paint, the room wreaked of stale pipe smoke.

Henry came down in dungarees instead of the usual white trousered uniform, the irrepressible grin plastered across his face. ''How was Bremen?'' he asked.

''What happened?'' said Paul.

''I got scratched.''

''I know that. How? Why?''

"Take it easy!" said Henry. "It's not the end of the world. The Whitman family will still have its day of glory. You've scored enough honors for both of us anyway."

"Henry, please! Just tell me what happened."

"Okay, big brother, but I warn you, it's not what you think at all. No one was really upset by yesterday's screwups. It's just that they're really stiff around here, and I seem to have broken some of their sacred rules. This morning there was a sensational breeze blowing on the bay, and I just really wanted to sail. So I borrowed a Monotype . . ."

"Borrowed?"

"That's what I would call it. There are twenty-five of them, all identical, just lined up on the docks. I even made sure that I took a practice boat and not one of the competition boats. It seemed a shame to pass up the good breeze, so I walked out on the dock, rigged a boat and took off."

"And?"

"It's a terrific boat. Like having the power of a Star on a hull that you can handle by yourself. I tore straight across the bay on a wild, screaming beam reach, and before I knew it, a German patrol boat was behind me with a big klaxon on top screeching right in my ears. I tried to wave them away, lost control in a disastrous jibe, and they ended up hauling me and the Monotype out of the water and depositing us back on the dock. Then there was a lot of screaming and sharp looks, like I'd broken into the cookie jar and eaten all the treats, and before I knew it I was scratched from the team and confined to these lousy barracks.

"I would've thought that the American coaches or the team manager could have gotten me out of the mess, but it seems they called old Avery Brundage himself, the head of the U.S. Olympic Committee. Mr. Supernazi personally ordered me off the team."

"What happens now?"

"They sail without me. There are alternates on the team, and the guy for the Six Meters is pretty good. Maybe without my screwups they'll do better today."

"Henry! What happens to you?"

"It's all right, Paul. I join some good company. After all, Eleanor Holm got booted for drinking champagne on the ship coming over. And then there were two boxers who were sent home. The official explanation is that they were homesick, but the scuttlebutt has it that they were caught shoplifting cameras.

Compared to the other sinners, I'm not much of a *cause célèbre*."

"It seems a harsh punishment," said Paul.

"*Discipline*. The Germans have it, and the Americans are envious. With better discipline, they think we can equal the German athletic machine. Who knows, maybe we'll do better today. If I were you I'd get out there. There was a terrific breeze blowing earlier. It could be a great race."

Paul started to answer, then caught a very different look in his brother's face, completely devoid of the mischievousness. Suddenly Henry seemed pensive and serious.

"I need to talk to you," said Henry. "I mean really talk, without these heavies breathing down our necks. They all understand English, and they've got ears like microphones. I feel like a prisoner."

Paul glanced over at the uniformed Olympic official sitting in the corner, not close to them, but easily able to follow their conversation in the quiet room. "You should have thought of that before you borrowed the boat," he said.

"Whose side are you on?" said Henry.

Paul hesitated. "Everyone seems to be asking me that question."

"It's the only question now, Paul."

Forty-Six

Maggie carried her shoulder bag and the battered fiberboard case with her as she walked into the airport terminal at Hamburg. Arriving three hours before the scheduled departure of a flight seemed to destroy any advantage of air travel, but as soon as she was inside the terminal she understood the airline warning.

The single cramped window that serviced international flights faced a crowd at least three times as large as any airplane could accommodate. From scattered bits of conversation, Maggie discovered that people were waiting not only for the flight to Zurich, but for flights to London and Stockholm that were not scheduled to depart for at least six hours. Everyone, it seemed, wanted to leave Germany.

She found the end of the disorderly line and passed the time, as she often did, by taking imaginary photographs, framing individuals or groups of people and freezing emotions and expressions by clicking an imaginary shutter.

An hour of waiting passed quickly, and she found herself at the head of the line, facing a cheery official. She presented her ticket and the temporary American passport.

"This document has expired," said the official.

Maggie started to explain her absentmindedness, gearing up to do battle. The official quickly cut her off with a wave of his hand. "When you reach Zurich," he said, "you should go to the consulate there and get a new passport."

She smiled as he looked up her name in a looseleaf notebook, scanning his finger down a page of names and numbers. Then she saw him reach with his other hand to the edge of the counter and push a button. Maggie assumed it was to summon the baggage handler.

"I'll carry them myself," she said. "They're small."

"This way, please," said a customs officer in uniform. She followed him to a small office. He knocked, opened the door for her, then shut it behind her.

The walls of the office were barren, the only furniture a table and two chairs. In the chair behind the table sat a man in a light gray suit. He glanced at her passport and said, "Good afternoon, Mrs. Bourne."

"What is this about?" she asked.

"Would you please put your bags on the table?"

She put the two bags down, and he quickly opened the fiberboard case.

"What are you doing?" she said.

"My job. If you are embarrassed to have a man look through your personal effects, I can have the matron inspect your bags. I suspect that is not the case, Mrs. Bourne."

"I have nothing to hide."

"Of course."

He unpacked the film plates and cans from the case and the shoulder bag and lined them up on the table, making sure they were squared to the edge of the table and in even rows.

"What have you been photographing?"

"The plates are from an assignment in Africa," she explained. "They were with me when I arrived in Germany. I even have the form they gave me in Frankfurt."

"And the miniature films?" He pointed to the row of 35-millimeter film cans.

"Snapshots. I took snapshots at the Olympics."

"*Snapshots?* Mrs. Bourne, a person who takes snapshots does not label the film cans or keep a notebook detailing every photograph." He held up the small notebook from her handbag which had the exposure notes on her photographs. "You are a professional photographer, are you not?"

"Yes. But those are snapshots. I borrowed a camera from a friend and snapped some pictures. Is that a crime?"

"Captain Paul Whitman is the friend you are referring to?"

"Yes." She tried not to react to the name.

He began comparing the film cans with the notes, going through her scrawled handwriting meticulously. Then he picked up several of the cans.

"A matron will wait here with you," he said.

"Where are you going with those films?"

"We are doing you a favor, Mrs. Bourne. We will develop the films. You have no cause for worry. It is an excellent darkroom."

"I have a flight leaving in less than an hour."

"That will give us plenty of time. Surely you prefer the privacy of this waiting room to the crowds in the concourse."

The matron was neither old nor formidable. She searched Maggie's clothes, then sat with her, affecting a stern expression that seemed out of place on her cherubic face and refusing to answer any questions except the time. She fondled, then stared at the hacking jacket that Maggie had bought in Berlin, probably comparing it in her mind with the dull, sturdy green-gray fabric of her uniform.

When the man with the gray suit reappeared, the matron hovered for a moment, touching the jacket that still hung on the back of the door, then left without a word.

The man laid a stack of contact sheets on the table, printed on single-weight paper and badly curled from being dried too quickly.

"You're an excellent photographer," he said.

"If those sheets are an example of your darkroom work, I'm afraid I can't return the compliment."

"We didn't want to delay your departure."

He picked up one sheet. "Would you explain please, Mrs. Bourne, where these photographs were taken?"

She didn't look down. "They're just snapshots, I told you. You have my notes."

He held the sheet in front of her. "There do not appear to be any notes for these photographs. Why is that?"

She glanced at the row of prints on the contact sheet. The images were hard to make out with the naked eye, patches of grainy gray with dark spots, all almost identical except for different exposures. She had not taken them, and she remembered that Paul had told her that there were a few shots on the roll in the camera that he wanted back. She looked more closely and saw that they were airplanes, flying in tight formations. Then she remembered Paul's description of the German planes over the Strait of Gibraltar.

"Where were those photographs taken?" asked the gray suit.

"I don't remember."

"You don't remember? How often do you see a sight like that?"

She shrugged. "I see lots of things. I'm paid to see things."

"Exactly. And surely you know, Mrs. Bourne, that it is strictly forbidden to photograph military aircraft of the German Reich, whether on the ground or in flight. There is no aesthetic value in these photographs. They could not have been taken for any purpose except espionage."

She looked at him with a carefully contrived expression, two parts boredom, one part disbelief.

"Who were you planning to meet in Switzerland?"

"No one."

"You are not a very good liar, Mrs. Bourne."

"I wouldn't know. I don't have much experience."

"Your American humor does not amuse me," said the gray suit. "I'm afraid that you do not understand the gravity of this matter."

"Look," she said, "I'm an American citizen, right? I think I have the right to call the American Embassy if you're going to keep me here for more silly questions."

"Of course. But it will be over an hour before anyone from the embassy can get here, and by then you will have missed your flight to Zurich. The next plane is not until the day after tomorrow."

"Then I can go?"

"You are free to leave Germany. And the films of Africa and the Olympics may go with you. These negatives will stay here, and unless you are willing to tell us to whom these photographs were to be delivered, you will not be welcome to return to Germany. Even the Third Reich does not appreciate abuse of its hospitality.''

''You Germans really know how to make people feel welcome,'' said Maggie as she gathered her films. ''You seem to have a knack for it.''

Forty-Seven

Before he put the key in the lock, Paul sensed that something was awry. Nothing he could put his finger on, just an inchoate premonition that he could neither trust nor ignore. Maybe it was a leftover bitterness from being searched when he left the Olympic barracks, or a reaction to the desk clerk at the hotel who stared at him as if a request for a room key in midafternoon were sign of madness.

He opened the door slowly to find a man in a baggy gray suit sitting at the small round table in the room, his legs crossed and his hands folded on the table, as if he had been expecting someone. There were wrinkles in the light fabric of the suit where it had not been unbuttoned across his chest. He hadn't been sitting long, and he was not as comfortable as he pretended.

The man had the kind of fatuous oval face that's difficult to remember or describe, but the suit, Whitman knew, was a uniform, as unmistakable as the elaborate paraphernalia of the SS or the SA. The Gestapo with their gray suits had long given up the guise of being *Geheime Staatspolitzei,* secret state police. They were an organized and recognized force, and the gray suits were important not for anonymity but precisely because they were supposed to inspire recognition and fear.

''What are you doing here?'' asked Whitman. He tried to keep his voice calm.

''That's not a very intelligent question, Captain,'' said the gray suit, his voice almost an octave higher than Whitman had expected. ''You know exactly what we're doing here. There was a suspicion that you were illegally in possession of paper containing secret information. That suspicion has been amply confirmed.'' He waved a handful of papers that were on the table as if they were self-explanatory.

Whitman thought of questioning the use of the imperial *we*, the same voice that Goering and Hempe affected, a form of speech that made it seem as though the speaker represented a vast organization, perhaps the masses themselves. But his anger would not permit games. "How dare you come into my room?''

"Ah, yes,'' came the calm response. "The American obsession with legality. We have full authorization issued by the *Reichsluftsministerium*. You should realize, Captain, that in matters of security we have the right to conduct searches without special authorization. In this instance, there is no question that we are dealing with a matter of state security.'' He began stuffing the papers into his open briefcase.

Paul tried to make out the documents in the man's hand. From the shape and thickness of the bundle, it looked like the papers in his flight bag—operations manuals for the Graf Zeppelin, blank log sheets, maintenance and flight notes. There were a few sketches that he had made, ideas for future Zeppelins, but it was all so vague and undetailed that they couldn't be of real interest to anyone. Everyone knew that there were no plans for future Zeppelin building beyond the LZ-130, the sister ship to the Hindenberg. It was hard to imagine what secrets the man was talking about.

"The papers are being confiscated, Captain. You will not be detained at this time, but be assured that you are under surveillance. Any contacts that would be deemed suspicious will be noted. Further associations of the sort you have been making or visits to restricted areas would not be to your advantage. And while I must agree that Frau Bourne is as beautiful as the reports say, your living arrangements are not proper for an airship commander.''

"Get out!'' shouted Whitman, though not before the man slithered by him with a gumshoe walk, the briefcase buckled under his arm. He paused at the door, touching the brim of his hat with his fingertips before he said, "You will find that it will not be possible for you to visit your brother again.''

Whitman stared at the closed door for a moment, started to reach for the phone, then changed his mind, leaving with the binoculars he'd carried to the race still in his hand. In the lobby he passed the trio of official portraits: Hitler, Goebbels on his left, and on his right Hermann Goering, looking out of his wide-lapeled uniform with a tight-lipped, enigmatically benign grin.

The post office was across the street, a full block from the hotel. He forced himself not to look around to see if he was being followed as he went up to the counter where arrangements were made for telephone calls. He filled out the slip, paid, then went into the cabin to wait for the call to go through. Through the glass window in the cabin, he could see a gray suit standing in the foyer of the post office, unable to hide himself. Whitman stared at the man until he finally retreated into a line at the stamp window. He wondered if the gray suits had always been there and he was just noticing them, or whether he had been tagged with whatever foul substance made the Gestapo maggots swarm.

"Züricher Hof," said the voice on the phone.

Whitman spelled out the name, described Maggie, tried everything. They had no record of a Frau or Fräulein Bourne. "There are many hotels in Zurich," the hotel operator insisted. "Perhaps at one of the others." But Züricher Hof was all she had said. He glanced at his wrist chronometer. She should have been there already.

He went out onto the street, leading down toward the tall spire of the City Hall, one of those monuments of Imperial architecture, built just before the war when Kiel was the base for the High Seas Fleet, the special pride of the Kaiser, the hope of Germany, the challenge to the British. The Kaiser never failed to find opportunities to come to Kiel, whether to sail on his own yacht, or to review the fleet. But those glories were gone now, destroyed with the fleet.

Kiel was not a city for the New Germany. It was older than the Nazis, with traditions of its own, bound up with the honor and glory of the navy. The Nazis had neither time nor resources for a High Seas Fleet, like the main battle fleet that had sailed from Kiel in 1916 to do battle with the British Grand Fleet at Jutland. And with their paranoid horror of Bolshevism and revolution, the Nazis could never tolerate the kind of navy that had given birth, in Kiel in November 1918, to the German revolution, when seamen mutinied rather than participate in a last-ditch fanatic attack on the British fleet. Red flags went up on the battleships, and Sailors and Workers Soviets were formed, spreading so quickly through Germany that they would have infected the troops on the Western Front if the Armistice had not been signed in time to abort the Revolution.

Nor could the Nazis ever appreciate the suave gaiety of *Kieler Woche*, the spectacular week-long gathering of yachtsmen, diplo-

hats, and royalty each June, a regatta that rivaled Cowes Week in England. For a full week, cultural interchange and diplomatic cabal would be played out against the backdrop of five hundred racing sailboats from all over Europe, watched over by the royal yachts of the Kaiser's many relatives who sat on the thrones of Europe.

Now, instead of the color of Kiel Week, there were the ubiquitous gray suits, anonymous, expressionless, draining the life of the city, making it impossible to think. Had they followed him to Bremen? To the airport? A day before, he had been floating, soaring like the Zeppelin he commanded. Now, everything that really mattered had gone sour—Maggie, Henry, the Huttens, even the admiral. And Whitman was powerless at the center, watching while they confiscated papers, questioned his relationship with Maggie... was there any limit to what they would do?

He needed room to think, space without the gray suits glaring at him, without that cunning, benign smile of Hermann Goering. He walked to the Auto Union and drove out of the city, along the edge of the bay, watching through the rear view mirror to see if they would follow him. The road wound past the pretty little beaches of the northern shore all the way to Laboe, guarding the entrance of the bay, dominated by the *Marine Ehrenmal*, the monument to the sailors lost in the Great War. It was a spectacular monument, enormous in scale, sculpted so that light and space enveloped a visitor in a mood of solemnity and awe and respect for the thirty-five thousand sailors and the many ships that had gone down.

The monument was shaped like the stern of a ship. An underground gallery, luminescent with soft skylight, led up to the base of a 250-foot tower. A hall with plain gray walls displayed the outlines of each ship that had gone down. Simple tablets recorded the count: 210 major ships, 122 minesweepers, 211 U-boats. Above the ships were outlines of the 46 naval Zeppelins that had been destroyed in the war.

Whitman pictured the flaming wreckage of a Zeppelin shot down in flight, the hydrogen burning so rapidly that the ship becomes an instant fireball, the men inside incinerated. Hempe was right, he thought. An accident in a hydrogen-filled airship would end all flying of the Zeppelins. The disasters of the American airships had been awesome, and they were filled with safe helium. What would happen if an airplane or a madman like that lieutenant who had guarded the admiral were to take it into his head to destroy the Zeppelin in flight? A single disaster like that would end the Zeppelins forever, and with them, a whole era of technology.

He was alone in the monument, and it was so close to closing time that he had to plead with the guard to be allowed to ride the elevator up to the observation platform. From the top he looked out on the dense gray sky, broken into patches where low oblique rays of sunlight cut through the overcast to illuminate the vast harbor and the fields that stretched off to the north as far as Denmark. The sun glowed an unearthly orange and gold, and waves rippled the yellow charlock of the fields, scurrying across the grain like whitecaps on black water. A forest of radio masts in the midst of the fields seemed unwelcome intruders, water-spouts in a quiet sea.

Beyond the fields, it seemed that he could see out to the Frisian Islands, speckled across the horizon like shimmering mirages. Was it possible? he asked himself. Or was his imagination playing tricks? He remembered the admiral's description of his house on one of those islands, a house built by shipwrights so he would always have a vessel to command even if they stripped him to an unperson. What a waste! Everything in this country was slowly being reduced to waste.

He turned around, to look at the bay and the entrance to the Nord-Ostsee Canal. The German strategists had to wait for the completion of the canal before they could wage war in 1914. What would be the final preparation this time? Enough practice in Spain? Or the completion of the secret fleet that the admiral had described? He looked down along the shores of the bay where the tall gantries towered over the navy docks. Where there had once been rows of battleships, the awesome dreadnoughts of the High Seas Fleet, there were now only the silent pens of the submarines, floating bulkheads to house the silent weapons that could never defend, but only attack, waging distant war on the lifelines of commerce.

Across the bay, at the yacht docks, the spectator fleet was returning. Launches were towing in the Six Meter boats. It was directly across the harbor, a few miles and a cordon of buoys and patrol boats from those secret submarine pens.

He suddenly realized what Henry had done. It wasn't the stealing of the boat that had enraged the Germans. Henry had sailed blindly toward one of the most secret facilities in the Reich, the staging area for the submarines that only Admiral von Teppler seemed to recognize as a threat to peace. The forced retirement of the admiral now made as much sense as anything these madmen did. With their total control of the news, they had made him into an unperson. And as long as voices like the admiral's were silenced, the Nazis could continue their rough

od ride over Germany, trampling people and institutions and
aditions and finally everything that was the real Germany, until
ven the boundaries of Germany itself were not enough and they
arched off to start the war that would bring those lethal
bmarines out of their pens and into the oceans of the world.

Whitman knew he was making a decision, and he knew too
at it was too late to weigh arguments or list advantages and
sadvantages. "Men make their own circumstances"—the ad-
iral's words haunted Whitman, inviting him to actions he could
ot be sure of, moves that were instinct as much as thought.

"Yes," he said finally, loud enough to startle himself. Then he
n down the steps of the tower to his car. He drove through Kiel
ithout stopping, until he reached the Autobahn that would take
m back to Bremen.

Forty-Eight

or all its staid elegance, the lobby of the Züricher Hof was no
fferent from thousands of hotel lobbies in thousands of hotels
verywhere. A few guests scurried in and out, picking up and
aving messages at the reception desk, the quickness of their
ovements suggesting cabal. A newspaperboy offered the latest
ews in half a dozen languages. A page periodically held up a
ackboard with a name printed on it, ringing a bell to call the
tention of the men camped on the brocaded chairs and sofas,
eir faces hidden behind newspapers. Mostly, people in the
bby waited, for lovers, friends, accomplices, colleagues, con-
cts. It was hard to tell whether some of them had been waiting
r hours or days.

Maggie was the only woman there. Men stared at her, but in
vitzerland men arranged their dalliances in quiet private rooms
te at night, not in the lobby of the Züricher Hof in midafternoon.

Across from her, a heavy-set, flat-faced man toyed with his
wspaper. He seemed neither nervous nor unaccustomed to
aiting, and from the way he held the newspaper, not so much
ading as processing the pages, it was evident that the newspa-

per was only a way to pass the boredom. When Maggie looke
up, he spoke to her in heavily accented English.

"You await someone." There was no interrogative in h
inflection, and something about his voice, a vague Middl
European mystery, was off-putting to Maggie. She answered wit
a curt yes, hoping to discourage more conversation.

"Perhaps you would join me for a glass of wine, or
liqueur," he said. "The hotels are the only place one can have
drink in Switzerland. These Swiss have scoured not only the lan
but their palates with their despicable *Alkohol-frei* restaurants.

"No, thank you."

"It is a man you are waiting for."

Maggie smiled.

"He's a very lucky man, madam. I hope I have the opportu
ty to tell him myself."

Maggie almost didn't recognize Sinclair. His clothes we
filthy, and his jacket hung limp over a dark shirt and a knitte
tie, without the aura of deliberate casualness that was his usu
style. His face was grimy with road dust, his beard overgrow
his hair matted and unruly. Even the detached cynicism was go
from his expression; in its place was a fire and excitement th
made her remember the man she had once fallen in love wit
whose words had been like torches. When he embraced her, s
felt a sinking sensation in her stomach, as eight years of b
memories evaporated in a flash.

"Mr. Sinclair!" said the accented voice of the flat-faced ma
who had offered Maggie a drink. "How very fortunate you ar
Beautiful women wait for you wherever you go. I hope you
not treat this beautiful lady as badly as you have treated yo
woman friend in Spain. You never know what people can s.
about you when they've been mistreated."

Sinclair held onto Maggie, pulling himself back to look at t
other man.

"You need not look puzzled, Mr. Sinclair. We've never me
but I think you know me. I am Gregory Orlov."

"You'll have to excuse us," said Sinclair.

"Of course," said Orlov. "We will have plenty of opportu
ties to talk. You may be here for a long time. Perhaps you d
not know that there have been recent changes in the Sw
banking laws. Large deposits of bullion are no longer acceptab
against currency withdrawals. It is a courtesy the Swiss ha
extended to my own bank. As a major trader in bullion, t

viet Union must use every means possible to control pilferage.
n sure you understand.''

"I have no idea who you are or what you're talking about,"
id Sinclair. He led Maggie toward the desk.

Sinclair was shaking when they got to the room. He began
eling off the filthy clothes, then ordered whiskey sent up by
om service.

"Do you know that man?" asked Maggie. "Whatever is he
lking about? Bullion? The Soviet Union?"

Sinclair walked slowly around the room, lifting pictures from
e walls, looking behind drapes, making sure the windows were
mpletely sealed and trying the locked door that connected the
om to an adjoining suite. He moved deliberately, aware that
aggie was watching him. When he was satisfied, he lay down
a the bed, his hands folded behind his neck. He'd been waiting
r this moment for a long time.

"His name is Orlov. He's NKVD, their top man in Madrid.
fore that he was in Austria, and before that, Germany.
herever there's trouble, they send Orlov."

He watched Maggie's eyes follow his every move.

"I told you that I was in the thick of things, Margaret. You
re right—there's nothing like it. Right this moment, in a
rage near the railroad station, there's a Citroën van parked in
rage. I drove it here, alone, from the French coast. In the back
the van there are some ordinary-looking wooden crates with
ough gold in them to buy a whole squadron of attack bombers,
ough planes to make a difference between survival and col-
pse for the Republic in Spain."

"Gold? Airplanes?" Maggie's tone registered genuine sur-
ise, without a trace of the bored contempt that Sinclair had
own to fear. From the first moment that he had seen her eyes in
e lobby, he had recognized the admiration and even awe in her
ze. It was more than he had expected.

He explained his plan slowly, no longer afraid of her reaction.
: told it as he would have written it, using detail and twists of
rrative to build suspense, emphasizing the spectacular success
a few men against the entire Spanish navy, the Italian air
rce, and the Russian NKVD. "As soon as I can arrange for the
livery of those planes," he concluded with a tone of triumph,
he Republic will have its own air force, with nothing owed to
e Russians or anyone else. This could be the turning point for
ain, and for every other country caught in that vise between

the Fascists and the Communists. If we prove that Spain can s▪
free, then so can the others.''

Maggie was fascinated by the tale, even as she recognized ▪
Sinclair touch in the telling, the way the whole complica▪
venture seemed to depend solely on his judgments and mov▪
She was so absorbed that she didn't notice the knocking at ▪
door until he waved and pointed.

"That's the whiskey," he said. "Get it, will you?"

He sang in the shower, holding the whiskey glass in one ha▪
while he scrubbed, bellowing out songs that Maggie could bar▪
remember from eight or nine years before. She couldn't reme▪
ber ever seeing him so exuberant.

She remembered why she had come to Zurich, but it was ha▪
to put the words together now. He was so different from the m▪
she had left at the Union Station in San Francisco, so differe▪
even from the insistent voice on the long distance telephone. S▪
had expected the tight, controlled David Sinclair, hiding eve▪
thing behind the cynical grin and the pursed lips. She had be▪
prepared to argue, to demand that he sign whatever it was th▪
they needed to end their relationship, finally and completely. S▪
had meant to tell him straightaway that she would get her o▪
room, as a signal that she was there for one reason and ▪
reason only. But she hadn't said a word. And when he went i▪
the shower, grinning as he stood there naked with the whisk▪
glass in his hand, he had said, "There are just three things I ne▪
right now: a hot shower, a glass of whiskey neat, and a g▪
screw." Even the way he talked about making love had chang▪

It was hard to believe that a man could change so much. ▪
then they said that war changed men, and David Sinclair h▪
certainly been in the war.

Forty-Nine

The Huttens were not surprised to see Whitman. It was as ▪
nothing that happened in Germany could surprise them anymo▪

neither good news nor bad. Anna began to apologize for not having a meal ready when Whitman sat them down and quickly explained his plan. They looked at one another, conferring with their eyes before they turned back to him.

"This would be wonderful for us, Captain," said Hutten. "But what will happen to you? Will you not be on the Zeppelin, as the commander?"

Whitman shrugged off the question. They had enough troubles without sharing his. "Don't worry about me. Just remember to arrive at Friedrichshafen late in the afternoon. Wait at the Kurgarten Hotel and buy your tickets within an hour of the departure of the Zeppelin. That will leave them no time for questions. There's space available to Rio, and they'll gladly sell you a cabin if you pay in American dollars. Once the Zeppelin is airborne, you'll be fine. They can't call it back, and from Brazil I'm sure you can straighten out the whole land business."

"But Captain—how can we ever repay you? You know that we will never recover the money we gave them for that tax quit claim."

"We'll worry about that when we meet again."

The Huttens both smiled, Otto with the enigmatic smile Whitman remembered from the airport, a smile that said *we can pretend not to know the truth*. Anna leaned over to give him a motherly kiss on the cheek, and Otto shook Whitman's hand in both of his own.

"Thank you," he said. "You've given us back our happiness."

Whitman kept telling himself that he had a plan. What he really had was memories of a book, *The Riddle of the Sands,* a story of sailboats, tide, wind, and quiet espionage in the Frisian Islands. His father had read the story to him—the diction always precise, the accent heavily German—from the time that Whitman was six years old. He could draw every chart in the book from memory.

He knew it would be impossible to telephone the admiral. Even if he did, there was no way to say what he had to say on the phone, no way to convince a man unless you were there. And the only way to go without the gray suits in pursuit was the way of *The Riddle of the Sands*—by boat.

As he boarded the train for Norddeich, he kept looking behind him. Even on the train, he waited for the familiar, baggy-suited figures to appear, to take the vacant seats across the aisle. He couldn't believe he had lost them so easily.

Outside the windows, the country was low and flat, never far from the sea, one of those places that made him feel he had been there before, even though he knew it was only memories of his father's stories and the book they had shared. More than anything else, that book had been the meeting ground between his father's love of Germany and Whitman's youthful dreams.

Getting hold of a boat was easier than he thought it would be. He wandered along the bulkheads at Norddeich, poking among the fishing boats until he spotted what he knew wasn't a working boat. It was heavily built, but totally neglected, the paint gone, the bulwarks and decks pockmarked with rot, the mast long beyond varnish, the sails cancerous with mildew. But this was the kind of boat he needed, round-bottomed, shoal draft, a boat small enough to be handled alone, maneuverable enough to poke its way unnoticed through the islands. He asked the first man he saw on the docks, who directed him to a seedy tavern. One look inside, at the fishermen who were down on their luck, and he knew they would agree on a price.

He found the owner at the bar and bought him a beer before he asked the price.

"You want to *hire* the boat?" The incredulity was obvious through the strong Frisian accent. The price he asked was a token, but after Whitman readily agreed, the man insisted on a 500-Mark cash deposit.

"Never know what you might do to her out there," he said. "How do I know you can find your way in the sands?" The man was hoping he would not return with the boat. Five hundred Marks in a tavern was worth more than a useless hulk rotting at the bulwark.

The man pocketed the bundle of bills as he came out to the boat with Whitman. He pointed out the lines, the two sturdy leeboards that took a hefty pull to raise, the oversized gaff that had to be sweated up with the main, and the tiny jib, scarcely large enough to balance the barndoor rudder.

"There's an engine," he said, but his voice told Whitman it wouldn't run. He peeled off his jacket and got out the sculling oar before he tossed off the forward line, coming back to the stern where the man held the last line.

"Is it ducks you're after?" the man asked.

Whitman hesitated. The same excuse had been used in *The Riddle of the Sands*. What else could he answer? He nodded.

"What are you going to do for a gun?"

Whitman looked down at his small traveling bag, much too short to hold a shotgun. "I take photographs of them," he said.

The man shook his head and tossed the line to Whitman, heading back to the tavern without watching Whitman scull off through the harbor. He had no way of knowing that his questions had turned Whitman's memories back to a beautiful woman who seemed very far away. And with his mind on Maggie and the crowded channel that led through the harbor, Whitman had no idea that the old fisherman was met on his way back to the tavern by two men in baggy gray suits.

The tide was rising, and a gentle 10-knot breeze was blowing in from the northeast. Whitman couldn't have picked a better time to go out. He hoisted the worn mainsail in the middle of the harbor and threaded his way out to where the line of booms led off into the sands. The boat rolled gently on its slack bilges as he gradually accustomed himself to the oversized rudder.

It was a strange, twilight world, neither land nor sea, just miles of flat wet sands on both sides of the channel, sculpted by the tides into swirls and sand castles. Footprints of birds skittering along the dunes and the rows of booms were the only landmarks on the waterland desert.

In *The Riddle of the Sands*, the tiny charts had been crystal clear, every hazard and channel marked, the rows of booms carefully delineated. But the waters had changed in the years that had passed, and the only chart Whitman could dig out of the cabin of the boat was almost useless, its scale too large to show the pitfalls that awaited the unwary. The sun was already low on the water, and with the tides swirling it was impossible to read the bottom.

He ran aground before he reached the start of the booms. By raising the leeboard and jibing, he sailed off, but a few minutes later he was aground again, and this time he had to use the sculling oar to pole the boat off the sand. He started down the row of booms, trying to judge how far off them to stay. At a sharp turn in the channel he went aground again, this time hard. Raising the leeboards, jibing, poling, even sculling didn't work. He stripped down and jumped into the water, digging the rudder loose with his fingers under the water and trying to push the boat off. Nothing worked, but the tide was still rising, and after another half hour he was floating free.

He started off again, concentrating even harder on the faint booms that he could barely see against the sun. The tide was all the way in now, and if he went aground again, he knew he wouldn't be able to get off. He wondered about the futility of what he was doing, thankful that the concentration on the booms and the twisting channel kept him from thinking very much about just what he would do if he did not find the admiral.

He finally worked his way out of the Buse Tief, along what he remembered as the Nordland Sands until he was close enough to make out the shoreline of the Island of Juist. There was a cluster of houses around a fishing village that he remembered from the book as being Westdorf. He sailed along a barren stretch of sand dunes on the shore, until he reached the beacon at the end of the island, at the extreme mouth of the River Ems. The water around him suddenly deepened, and the lines of booms gave way to the open waters of the North Sea. He jibed and reached around the end of the island to trace the opposite shore.

He sailed almost three miles on the seaward side before he spotted a lone house, isolated on a point that thrust out into the sea. There was no doubt in his mind when he saw it. Even from the distance, it was like no other house he had seen on the shore. Completely alone, built on a knoll of sand, it looked more like the peaked hatch of an old yacht than the weatherly cottages of the fishermen. Its view was out to the North Sea, not turned back into the shelter of the lee like the other houses.

There was no dock or jetty in front, only the endless sands that stretched out to the sea. He raised the leeboards and steered the bow straight into the beach until it nudged up on the sands. Then he jumped off with a line, hoping to find a post or tree or a big enough rock to keep the boat tethered in place if the tide lifted it any further. In an hour or two, he calculated, the falling tide would leave him high and dry. He would be there for a while.

As he looked around, a wizened, lanky old man appeared on the beach, wearing a fisherman's smock and an inscrutable expression. He seemed unperturbed by the unlikely appearance of a stranger and walked over slowly.

"Is this Admiral von Teppler's house?" asked Whitman.

"If a good northerly makes up, your boat could be in trouble," said the man in a strong Frisian accent. "She'll want a stern anchor out."

The old man tied Whitman's line to the remnants of a jetty, and Whitman instinctively checked the hitch. When he looked up, he saw a familiar figure walking across the sand, that same tall arrogant walk he remembered from the airfield. The admiral was wearing a fatigue uniform, open at the neck, and he was hatless. His silvery hair was wispy in the breeze.

Like the Huttens, he did not seem surprised to see Whitman. "I'm delighted to see you, Captain. I have few visitors here. No one else, it seems, is enterprising enough to come."

Whitman kept thinking that it was not at all what he expected— no guards, no walls, nothing more than a lonely retirement cottage on a windswept island. Was this really the man whose knowledge was a threat to the Nazis, whose name had stirred Goering to such ire?

Von Teppler seemed to read Whitman's mind. "You expected a fortress, Captain? The only walls are within. I am not a traitor to my Fatherland."

Whitman didn't know how to answer. They walked on, the silence feeling close, until they covered the hundred yards of beach in front of the house. Von Teppler showed off the cottage with pride. The joints between the oak frames had been fitted as a boatwright would fit ribs, with solid treenails, and the planking was beveled and caulked against the wind and the sea spray. "This is what good German craftsmen can do," said the admiral. Whitman agreed, recognizing the same pride he had felt toward the construction of the Zeppelin.

They sat down to a dinner of wurst and applesauce, simple peasant fare served by the same old man who had helped to tie up the boat. Through dinner, each time Whitman started to raise the questions that troubled him, the admiral subtly turned the conversation to the sea, or ships, or the Zeppelin.

It was not until after they had finished and gone into a tiny paneled study, the walls lined with books and mementos of the admiral's military career, that von Teppler seemed ready to talk. He brought out a captain's decanter of port and poured two glasses.

"Now, Captain. Tell me why you have come."

Whitman hesitated, the words suddenly failing him in the face of the admiral's bluntness. "To take you away," he said. "That's why I brought the boat."

Von Teppler laughed. "Do I seem unhappy?"

"You're under house arrest?" said Whitman.

"I suppose you could call it that. They need no guards. They know I will not leave."

"But for you to stay—that's surrendering to them."

"And if I leave, Captain—is that not a surrender?"

Whitman thought for a moment. "Not to escape," he said.

"To speak out. Only you have the stature to make Germany listen."

"Against the Fatherland? You want me to speak out against the Fatherland, the Germany I have sworn to serve and defend with my life?"

"Against *them*." Whitman described his meeting with Hempe, the talk of hydrogen, and what he had seen in Kiel. "You were right. Those were real sub pens in Kiel, and over the Straits, there were Luftwaffe planes, flying support for the Nationalists. And no one will believe it. The world is asleep. The French shriek about war, and no one believes them because they have their own revanchist plans. The English are pacifists. The U.S. is isolationist. If no one speaks out, there's nothing to stop the Nazis. No voice from outside and no voice from inside. Except you."

"I'm flattered," said von Teppler. He sipped the port with genuine satisfaction. "You ask me to be a leader of men again. From you, that is a compliment."

"Admiral—you're a hero to most Germans, a man decorated with the highest awards for valor. If you speak out, people will listen. And if enough people listen . . . That boat can carry us to Holland, and from there you can go to England. You would be honored and respected in England. And you would be heard."

Von Teppler smiled. "And so you've come to take me away." He looked up at the bookshelves, then got up from his comfortable chair to browse the volumes with his fingertips. Whitman's eyes followed him, thinking they would be books of the sea, Conrad, Melville perhaps, *The Riddle of the Sands* even. He watched the admiral's fingers march over the spines until he pulled out a volume.

As the admiral thumbed through the pages of the book, Whitman thought about their conversation. Almost imperceptibly, the admiral had switched to the familiar voice, *du* and *dich* instead of *sie*. It was not a casual move for a North German to make. Even Whitman's own father had rarely used the familiar voice when he spoke German at home.

What was the bond between them? wondered Whitman. He felt it, it had drawn him to that barren, forsaken island. The admiral obviously felt it too. Why? A shared hatred and fear of the Nazis? A sense of frustrated honor in the face of barbarian morality? Loneliness and shame at being forced to cooperate? All of those, he thought, but there was something else too. The bond seemed less equal and more intimate than shared feelings, and despite the admiral's candor and familiar voice, there remained a strange, strained formality in their relationship, at once intimate and awkward. Like a father and son.

"Do you read Latin, Captain?"

Whitman nodded no.

"A pity." Von Teppler held out the book. "Vergil's *Aeneid*. I have just been rereading the passage where Aeneas tries to rescue his father from the ruins of burning Troy. It is very moving, but . . ." When he looked up at Whitman there was an elusive smile in his gaze.

The admiral put the book down. "You have thought this through," he said. "It is not a whim. But what you ask of me is not something a man can decide lightly. I'm not a young man. To leave the Fatherland and know I can never come back is not an easy choice to make. For you, the choices are perhaps easier. What *about* you, Captain? What will you do?"

"I'm nothing. An American. I have no influence here, and even if I were to speak out in the U.S., it would be to deaf ears."

"Speaking out is not the only response to them. Can you continue to fly for them? The Zeppelin is a symbol of their prestige, a flag for the new Germany. Will you still fly it?"

"I guess I'm trying to decide that right now."

"And I too must decide," said the admiral. "The tide will not be high enough for your boat to leave until morning. Perhaps we both need time alone to think."

Whitman wanted to talk more, but the finality in the admiral's voice invited no answer.

The guest bedroom was a paneled niche that felt like the cabin of a ship. He found a shelf of books, glanced at the titles, and knew he couldn't concentrate enough to read. He stretched out on the berth, but sleep too was impossible. It was as if he were awaiting a verdict—not just the admiral's decision, but his own. He had dreamt for years of flying the Zeppelin, and now, even as the dream had come true, it had gone sour, leaving only bitterness and frustration. There was no future, not even a choice, because he hadn't focused on his own dilemma. Coming to the admiral had been a way of avoiding the question.

Moonlight played through the porthole-window, and Whitman watched the somber moonshadows grow long on the wall. Outside, a breeze was blowing in off the sea. The full moon made a heavy chiaroscuro of the portentous clouds.

He dressed and went outside—for air, he told himself. As he

walked down the beach, the sky shifted its pattern, growing darker, then lighter. He remembered watching clouds as a child, guessing what animals they were, envying the animals because they could float with such ease, the ease he had known only on the Zeppelin.

He was half a mile down the beach when he saw the silhouetted figure facing the sea, recognizable even from behind by the tall, erect stance. The admiral seemed to be studying the sky over the sea, as if he too expected an answer from the wind and the waves and the clouds. Whitman watched in silence for a moment, until he felt that he was violating a privacy. He turned and walked back to the house, leaving the admiral alone with the sea and his own impossible dilemma, whether to betray his Fatherland or his conscience.

Whitman was still dressed and didn't realize he had fallen asleep when he was awakened by a loud report. He jumped up and ran out of the room. The caretaker was waiting for him, barring Whitman from going any further. The old man's face was as expressionless as when Whitman had first seen him on the beach.

"What happened?" said Whitman. "That sounded like a shot. Where's the admiral?"

"There has been an accident," said the caretaker. It came out in careful phrasing, without the heavy Frisian accent. A rehearsed speech.

"The admiral? Where is he?"

"You had better leave," said the caretaker. "The tide will be turning soon."

"But the admiral—he was . . . An accident? What kind of accident?"

"Please. You must leave now."

Whitman tried to look over the caretaker's shoulder, toward the little study where he had talked with von Teppler the night before. The lanky man blocked his view, his slim body taking charge as if he were physically big enough to block the way. When their eyes met, the caretaker lowered his glance, and just from the cast of those old eyes, Whitman knew what had happened.

The admiral's words came flooding back. *A question of honor . . . a man of the eighteenth century . . .* In the Prussia of the eighteenth century, an officer suspected of dishonoring the strict code of an officer was led to a room and left alone with a loaded pistol on the table. A trial, the airing of charges, was unthinkable.

"He . . ." Before the words came out, the emotions caught up with him. His hands went to his face as he flushed with rage and incomprehension and bitterness.

The old man let him have a moment alone before he said, more firmly this time, "The tide is right now. You had better begin sailing back."

Fifty

Sinclair was impatient on the telephone. He spoke louder than he needed to, explaining everything too clearly. He glanced at Maggie while he talked, making sure she was listening.

"We're going to have a visitor," he said when he hung up. "A salesman."

The man from the Northrup Corporation wore a beige gabardine suit, with straight pants legs and scalloped pocket edges that would have looked right over cowboy boots. He spoke with a broad Texas twang, complaining about the Scotch that Sinclair offered him and the absence of ice with a generalized condemnation of the Europeans as "citified snits."

Maggie didn't understand much of the first part of their conversation, the intricacies of banking in Switzerland and the uses of the new numbered accounts that had recently been introduced by the Swiss banks. "It's for Jew money," the Northrup man said. "These greedy little Swiss will do anything to get their hands on somebody's dough."

Sinclair got up and strode across the room, as if he were beginning a lecture. "I didn't ask you here to talk about banking," he said. "I want to talk aircraft."

The Northrup man took a long sip of his whiskey, wrinkling his face at the bite of the neat liquor. "Switzerland's no place to talk," he said. "We're still under the U.S. Neutrality Act, and the Swiss are prime subscribers."

Sinclair swung around angrily. "Then why the hell are you here? And why do you let everyone in Europe know that you've got planes built and ready to go?"

"It's a good spot to watch both sides. When things start up, everybody's gonna know just where to find me."

"What if someone wants to buy planes now?"

"Mr. Sinclair—I don't know who you represent, but we can't sell here. We thought we had a deal with the Spaniards, but Uncle Sam doesn't want Americans involved in that one, and that means us too. Right now we export only to nonbelligerents. Nice peaceful countries that no one pays attention to."

"What if someone were willing to pay cash up front?"

"Cash?"

"Better than cash, *gold.*"

The Northrup man's face brightened at the talk of cash, then clouded again. "Gold's a problem," he said. "It's not readily negotiable now. We'd have to trade it in a banking area that is beyond the reaches of the U.S. In any case, Mr. Sinclair, like I said before, we only export to nonbelligerents. That means a nice quiet place like Honduras or Pernambuco. We've never had a problem there. Or Argentina is all right. You can pay for aircraft in gold there, and the paperwork is simple if the right people get their gratuities."

"What about delivery?" Sinclair asked his questions as if he were a regular buyer of aircraft. The way he tossed his eyes in Maggie's direction as she sat quietly in the corner of the room indicated that it was as much performance as negotiation.

"No problem. If it's the A-17s you're interested in, they're waiting to go. They can be in Honduras in a matter of days. Once they reach Honduras, no more questions. We're not responsible for final destinations or end use certification. And those A-17s are still damn good planes. Except for some of the really hot stuff, they can fly circles around almost any fighter out there. We built them on speculation, and we almost had them on their way when it turned out that the Ethiopians weren't going to be around to pay the bills. We had pilots lined up for the ferry over, landing rights and fuel cleared right down to Pernambuco and over to Sierra Leone. Would have been an easy hop over. They're still ready to go, but if someone wants to pay in gold, it has to be done on the other side. That's the only way we can do it."

"*The other side?* How the hell am I supposed to get a ton of gold across the Atlantic?" Sinclair slammed his empty glass down on a table.

"Never had the problem myself," said the Northrup man.

"Damn you," shouted Sinclair. "We're talking about the future of Spain, of democracy itself."

"You are, Mr. Sinclair. I never talk politics. I'm just a salesman."

"You mean, unless I pay in Honduras or Argentina or wherever, you won't sell?"

"We don't have much choice. The Neutrality Act is pretty specific about not selling to belligerents, and that means Spain. The currency laws are even more strict. American companies can't play around with gold."

"You don't care which side I'm on," said Sinclair.

"No," said the man from the Northrup Corporation. "I don't."

Maggie wasn't sure when she started to be afraid of Sinclair. She had seen him rage before, knew that his feelings of impotence could erupt in volcanic anger. But this time it was different. He talked with the anxiety of a man who has bet everything on one roll of the dice. And he talked not so much to her, but through her, as if there were another audience, a court to whom he was making a plea.

"What does that little cowboy bastard expect me to do?" he shouted. "Put the gold on a steamer and ship it to Honduras? It would take over a month, *if* I could ever get it on a ship. It doesn't matter to that bastard how many men have died for this. They're all like that. No one gives a damn. Even the Spanish. Why should I care? Why should I break my ass for them? Honduras. Argentina. Pernambuco. Shit . . . I've never even heard of Pernambuco."

"It's on the bulge of Brazil," said Maggie. "Most people call Recife."

"How do you know?" he snapped.

"Because the Graf Zeppelin refuels there on its run from Rio to Frankfurt." She realized that in all the talk about what he had been doing, she hadn't even mentioned her own adventure. "We stopped there after they picked me up. Flying on the Zeppelin was incredible. They're marvelous machines, like cathedrals in the sky. The space and that feeling of floating, it's incredible." She realized as she said it that she had picked up the language from Paul Whitman.

"The Graf Zeppelin stops there?" It was all Sinclair had heard. He smiled suddenly, a conspiratorial grin. "Margaret—

your flyboy with his magic balloon may be the answer to all our problems.''

''Our problems?'' Suddenly the old Sinclair had come back, the bullying, cajoling David Sinclair she remembered so well. She remembered too why she had come.

''There is no *our* anymore, David. For a while I actually forgot why I came here. You seemed to have changed. You actually seemed to care about something other than David Sinclair. But now, all I hear is the old David Sinclair.''

''Margaret.'' The fire slipped out of his voice as easily as it had come. ''Your little problems and my little problems don't amount to a hill of beans. We're talking about life and death. Not just for you or for me, but for Spain, for democracy. This is the only struggle.''

''They're great words, David. You were always great at words.''

''And what's your flyboy great at, bedwork?''

When she turned away, he quickly added, ''Never mind. I'm sorry. As long as he can fly that thing to Brazil, I don't care what you and he do. This matters too much...''

''You don't really think that I...?''

''You're damn right I do. If you care at all about what's happening in the world, you don't have any choice.''

''It's impossible, David. The Zeppelin is guarded day and night. They monitor every pound of weight that goes aboard. It's not like a ship where a few hundred or even thousand pounds doesn't matter. The load and the ballast and the lifting gas have to be perfectly balanced. It's complicated and exact.''

''That's why we need flyboy. He seems to have taught you a lot already.''

''David, you're being ridiculous. He would never do it.''

''He will when you ask him.''

''Not everyone is as pliable as you think. Not Paul Whitman and not me. I can't go back to Germany anyway. They took my passport number at the airport and I'm officially *persona non grata*.''

Sinclair looked surprised. ''Why? I would think flyboy' bedmate would be the guest of honor in Germany?''

Maggie walked away, toward the door. ''I don't really think we have much more to say to each other, David.''

''All right.'' He ran after her, reaching for her shoulders, then pulling back when she flinched from his touch. ''I'm sorry for the crack. What happened at the airport?''

David's change of pace was disconcerting, and it took her a ›ment to collect herself. "I had film with me," she said. "The rica plates and some rolls that I had shot at the Olympics. Paul at me his camera, a Leica. It turned out that he had left some gatives at the beginning of a roll, and when the security police the airport developed my films, they latched onto those ›otographs. They were of German planes flying over the Straits Gibraltar, a big formation of heavy transports. Paul said they re probably helping ferry Franco's army from Africa to the anish mainland. He said the Germans have never officially mitted that they are helping Franco. Those photographs would've de a great story."

"Why'd he take them?"

"Because he hates the Nazis," she said. But she wasn't sure.

"Margaret, don't you see?" David reached for her shoulder. 's all the same struggle. Spain is where the Nazis have to be pped. That's why the gold has to get on that Zeppelin."

She hesitated, putting it all together. "I'm not sure Paul will ll be flying the Graf Zeppelin. He's already in trouble for a lot petty nonsense—mostly for just being an American. And yway, I can't get into Germany. I told you."

Sinclair rummaged in the pockets of the tired jacket he had en wearing in the lobby, pulling out a green American passport. "Have the Germans ever seen this?" he asked. He tossed the ssport to her.

She opened the cover and flushed. It was an old joint passport. ey had fought often over it. To David Sinclair, it was a kind of curity that she would never again travel without him, and to aggie it was the most egregious symbol of what had been ong with their marriage.

She fought down her anger. "How can I believe you? How 1 I make myself believe that you would do anything for yone except David Sinclair?"

"No, Margaret, that isn't the question. You'll believe me cause deep down you know what I'm doing matters. You said pretty well in San Francisco. 'There are three sides to the uggle,' you said. 'The right side, the wrong side, and just tching.' I know and you know that I'm on the right side now. e question is which side your flyboy is on."

As much as she wanted to, Maggie wasn't sure she could swer that question.

Fifty-One

Whitman sailed back mechanically, all adventure and hope gon
It was a bright, clear day, but he hardly noticed the sun on t
water or the breeze in the sails. The boat seemed to find its ow
way among the booms, taking away even the dry, mathematic
pleasures of navigation.

He wasn't surprised to find two men with baggy gray su
waiting for him at the fishing harbor in Norddeich when he ti
up the boat at the bulkhead.

The gray suits said almost nothing on the long drive
Friedrichshafen. They were not hostile, but beyond a temper
curiosity about his being American, they were silent escor
never leaving his side, even when he went to the bathroo
during a meal stop. It was impossible to think with the two
them always there.

He was taken straight to the Zeppelin headquarters
Friedrichshafen and met at the door by Hempe with a frien
handshake. "You almost didn't arrive in time," said Hemp
"We were worried about you."

With those two heavies along, I'd have a hard time getti
lost," said Whitman.

Hempe ignored the remark, escorting Whitman into a sm
conference room where four somber faces waited around
circular table. Whitman recognized only Hugo Eckener, b
when the others were introduced, he vaguely recognized t
names as industrialists and air officials. There were no armban
no insignia, no hint of the cool formality that Whitman associat
with Nazi ceremonies. The only uniform was Eckener's; the o
man as a matter of habit wore a captain's uniform of t
Zeppelin Company.

Even Hempe seemed to have changed. His warmth seem
genuine. Without his ornate office, his manner was less impe
ous, his stature and affectations less imitative of Goering.

haps, thought Whitman, after seeing the master himself, the
ciple paled in comparison.

The table was clear except for a single accordion folder in
nt of Hempe. When they sat down, after the introductions,
mpe tapped the folder with his polished fingernails. "I must
l you at the outset, Captain," he said, "I think all of us find
prospect of this inquiry distasteful. It has never before
ppened in the history of the Zeppelin Company. It would seem
t little is to be gained by the airing of dirty linen." He looked
und the table to collect the quiet murmurs of agreement from
others.

Whitman wasn't sure how to react. Hempe's friendly tone
ly confused matters more. What *did* they want?

"I don't understand," he said. "You send the Gestapo to
low me when I'm off duty in Kiel, have them tear up my hotel
m, drag me down here in what I think the new language calls
'escort,' and now you suggest that it's all for nothing."

Hempe's face softened into a tiny cat grin. "The escorts,
ptain Whitman, were for your own protection. You seem to
e a penchant for misadventures. In any case, what I am
gesting is that your—shall we say, indiscretions?—can be
erlooked if we could just focus on the matter we discussed
viously. The directors of the Zeppelin Company are in unani-
us agreement that there are capacities in which you could be
portant to the future of the Zeppelins. And the future of these
ps, after all, is our only real concern."

"You mean the helium? Being a German agent?"

Hempe shrugged with exasperation. "You're a difficult man,
itman. Especially on yourself. Your conduct has been intem-
ate at the very least. You refuse to cooperate with us. When
Reichsluftsmarshall himself approached you to elaborate
on this generous offer, you responded with an inexcusable
burst. Your manner and conduct do not become a man of your
elligence and talents."

Whitman still wasn't sure what to expect. Hempe's language
s more threatening in its omissions than its inclusions. He
ked at Eckener to see if the old man shared his perception of
charade.

"For the last time," said Hempe, "can we not persuade you
cooperate—for your own good and the good of the Zeppelin?"

There was no reaction from Eckener, and Whitman nodded
. Hempe slid the accordion file across the table to one of the
ectors, a round-faced, balding man named Kuntz, who had

been introduced as a representative of Lufthansa, which course meant Goering's office.

Kuntz took the papers without looking at them. "The question before us, Captain," he said, "concerns your conc as the acting commander of the Graf Zeppelin in its rec crossing from Rio de Janeiro to Frankfurt. The record shows unscheduled and unauthorized deviation from course, a serie maneuvers which resulted in the death of Apprentice Rig Jürgen Steinbrenner, a willful defiance of Zeppelin Comp orders in striking an officer from the crew roster at Recife, questionable activities on board the Zeppelin after its landin Frankfurt am Main. I think we can agree that your conduc these instances is the primary issue, can we not?"

Whitman said nothing. Kuntz waited for a response, then up and went to a back door of the room. He returned with H Stifel, wearing a fresh and neatly pressed Zeppelin Comp uniform.

"You look surprised, Captain," he said. "Officer Stife here through the courtesy of the German Condor Airmail Li He has undoubtedly had a most uncomfortable crossing in Dornier Wal flying boats, but I think it is to everyone's adv tage that all parties be present. Don't you agree?"

Stifel's eyes darted around the faces at the table.

"From Officer Stifel's affidavit," said Kuntz, "it appears in spite of his repeated warnings, you made decisions in course of the flight which endangered the passengers and crew the Graf Zeppelin. Maneuvers ordered by you directly resulte the death of Apprentice Rigger Steinbrenner and jeopardized ship. Apparently, it was due only to the quick actions of Off Stifel himself that the ship was brought under control, the res maneuvers successfully concluded, and the airship returned safe course. Is that correct, Officer Stifel?"

Stifel's eyes avoided Whitman as he answered. The quick *sir* seemed to stick in his throat.

"Do you dispute this account, Captain Whitman?" as Kuntz.

Whitman looked around the table, expecting a reaction fr someone, if only Eckener himself. The summary of Stif account so completely contradicted the logs of the Graf Zepp that it was preposterous. And an entire crew of men could tes to the validity of the logs.

But no one reacted. Whitman felt suddenly like a characte a play he was watching from outside, a charade that had to played out. The stony expressions of the other players suggested that any change in the script would be unwelcome.

"May I speak?" he said.

"Of course."

He paused, looking over at Stifel. "Those flying boats must be very uncomfortable," he said, "because it seems that the flight over has addled Herr Stifel's memory. He did disapprove of our efforts to respond to the distress bulletin, but he was not present on the flight deck during the final rescue maneuvers, since I had already relieved him of further duty. I think the logs of the Graf Zeppelin and the testimony of the other officers should corroborate those facts."

Kuntz answered without hesitation. "The logs, Captain, are of course only your own record. And I'm afraid that no other officer is willing to testify before this board."

"Did you ask Zekner?" said Whitman. "He was present the entire time."

"Officer Zekner has declined to testify, perhaps out of respect for a fellow officer."

"Respect?" said Whitman. "Or fear?"

"Fear of what, Captain? I cannot see what an officer of the Zeppelin Company would have to fear from appearing before this board."

"No one from the crew will testify?" said Whitman.

"I'm sorry, Captain."

Whitman looked around the table of stony faces.

"Steinbrenner was a volunteer," he said. "His death was a terrible and sad accident. To the extent that responsibility must be assigned, I accept full responsibility. The ship and the passengers were never endangered, and the successful rescue of Fräulein Bourne was due solely to the competence of the crew and the bravery and skill of Admiral von Teppler. Stifel was not present during those maneuvers."

"Unfortunately," said Kuntz, "the issue is reduced to a question of your version of events against the testimony of Officer Stifel. And this casts your motives in removing him from the crew roster at Recife into a most unfavorable light, doesn't it? It would appear that you removed him from the crew— against specific orders of the Zeppelin Company—in the expectation that he would not be able to give testimony about the matter in question."

Whitman fought back the feelings of exasperation. What was left? he asked himself. If not a single member of the crew would stand up to the Nazis, the hell with them. What was there to fight for anyway?

"I was convinced that Officer Stifel's continued presence on the airship would endanger passengers, crew, and possibly the ship itself," answered Whitman. "Especially after he permitted one of the guards accompanying Admiral von Teppler to recover a firearm from the bosun's safe."

"Really?" Kuntz pulled another sheet of paper out of the accordion folder. "You're referring to Lieutenant Beck, are you not? According to his sworn affidavit, he found the gun in question on the person of the admiral. He states that *by your orders* the admiral was never searched for weapons. Would you like to see the affidavit?"

"The admiral?" Whitman pictured von Teppler, standing in the open doorway of the Zeppelin in full dress uniform, his chin jutting, his hand resting on the hilt of his saber. "The admiral is *dead*. He killed himself because he didn't want to betray his country. Can you understand that?"

A murmur jostled the stony looks for an instant until Kuntz cut it short. "The admiral is not our concern, Whitman. Your actions are. Would you please explain why you removed Stifel from the crew roster if it was not to keep him from testifying as to your conduct?"

Whitman hesitated. They were right. The admiral was something they would never understand. There was nothing left but to play out the drama.

"Stifel had recklessly attempted to abort our response to the distress signals," he said. "Then in Recife I discovered that he had ordered a special review of the flightworthiness of Elevatorman Stein. Stein is the finest elevatorman in the Zeppelin service; he needed only two more flights to qualify for his pension. Stifel's action struck me as an act of vindictiveness that could only undermine the morale of the crew."

Kuntz glanced quickly at Stifel, sitting stone-faced like the others at the table. "Is it not possible that Stein's skills *were* questionable?" said Kuntz. "Stifel had flown with him longer than you. Perhaps he was in a position to know something you did not know."

Whitman answered, "I've flown with many men and in many situations. I have never seen a man handle an airship as Stein does. I don't believe any competent officer would seriously question Stein's flying ability. He did pass the examination,

didn't he?'' He was guessing, but something told him that he
was right.

"Are you suggesting, Whitman, that Officer Stifel had some
kind of vendetta against this airman? Do you actually believe
that an officer of Herr Stifel's experience and station would stoop
to a vendetta against an ordinary airman?''

"Why don't you ask Stein?'' said Whitman.

He saw Stifel lean toward Kuntz and whisper something.

"This is an officer's inquiry,'' said Kuntz. "It would hardly
be appropriate to involve an ordinary airman. I recognize that
you may take the responsibilities of rank rather less seriously, but
there are some distinctions we must preserve.''

Whitman looked around the room. No one seemed to react.
The whole inquiry was a kangaroo court, a rigged drama staged
to satisfy the letter of the law. That the Nazis on the board would
go along he could understand. But at the head of the table was
Hugo Eckener, a man who had never caved in to the Nazis.
Despite a uniform that was too short and served only to accentu-
ate his corpulence, Eckener had the bearing and appearance of a
composite Prussian king. His eyes were bright blue, one slightly
higher than the other in the deeply furrowed face. His hair was
cut short, and the Van Dyke beard, like everything else about the
face, seemed asymmetrical. His clothes, even now, were covered
with cigar ashes, the final irony for the head of a Zeppelin
Company and a man who had spent so many hours in command
of airships

Eckener returned Whitman's gaze without expression. Then,
still without as much as a nod, he turned to Kuntz.

"Stein is more than an ordinary airman,'' said Eckener. "He's
flown Zeppelins as long as any man in the company.''

"An ordinary airman?'' said Kuntz. "There's no precedent for
this.''

"It would be most unusual,'' said Hempe.

"This inquiry is unusual,'' said Eckener.

Whitman eased back into his chair, barely controlling an urge
to smile. Now, at least, the drama would be interesting.

Stein seemed embarrassed by the assemblage of men. He
managed a half-salute at the doorway, an atavistic reaction from
his days in the navy, then mumbled something like "Gentlemen''
before sitting down. He seemed surprised to see Stifel and
Whitman at the same table.

"Airman Stein!" said Kuntz. "Is there any reason why Officer Stifel would bear you ill will?"

"Ill will?" repeated Stein, obviously confused.

Kuntz looked at the others with a patronizing lift of his eyebrows.

"Is there any reason why Officer Stifel would . . . would have a grudge against you?" he asked.

"Grudge, sir?" Stein still seemed confused by the question. "I guess that's for him to decide, sir. He's an officer and I'm just an airman. As long as I've been flying, officers make up their own minds without asking us."

Kuntz turned to the others, shrugging his shoulders and prompting a rapid exchange of glances around the table.

"Stein!" said Eckener. "How long have you known Officer Stifel?"

"Sir, we were both based at Ahlhorn in the war, on the navy ships. He was a gunner then."

"Did you share any experience that might be considered remarkable?"

"Remarkable?" repeated Stein. "Every day that we didn't get killed was remarkable, sir. The British planes flew higher every day, and they carried incendiary bullets that could turn a Zeppelin into the biggest hellfire you ever saw. Every day that we didn't lose a ship was remarkable."

Stifel whispered something to Kuntz, who promptly interrupted with his own question:

"Did you ever fly with Officer Stifel during the war?"

"He wasn't an officer then, sir. He was a gunner."

"Did you ever fly together during the war?"

"No, sir."

"Then there is nothing you can tell us that would not appear in his naval record?"

"I wouldn't know about that, sir. I've never seen his records. I guess officers' records is none of my business."

"Thank you, airman," said Kuntz. "You may leave."

Stein started to get up, fumbling the beginnings of another salute.

"Wait a moment, Stein," said Eckener, catching Stein in the middle of his fumbles. "Was Officer Stifel popular among the men in the navy?"

"Eckener!" said Kuntz. "That hardly seems an appropriate question under the circumstances. It is one thing to permit an ordinary airman in our proceedings. But to ask such a question? Really!''

"Was he liked by the men?" repeated Eckener.

Stein looked around the room at the awesome, expressionless faces, and finally at Eckener, under whose martinet leadership he had flown for over twenty years.

"It's all right," said Eckener. "You may answer."

"Well," said Stein, "there was lots of men who didn't want to fly with Stifel."

"Why?"

Stein squirmed, lowering his eyes to the table. His normally gruff voice was almost inaudible as he began a rambling narration.

"Well, sir, like you knows, airshipmen are pretty superstitious. Sometimes it's little things, like not liking to fly in some kinds of weather or on certain ships. But in the war it was different. We didn't have no choices about when we flew or on which ships. Mostly the men were superstitious about who they flew with. We thought some officers and men were lucky, like *Fregattenkapitan* Strasser and von Buttlar and von Schiller. Others weren't so lucky."

"But Stifel was not a captain," said Eckener. "He was only a gunner. Was he considered unlucky?"

"This testimony is totally inappropriate," said Kuntz. Next to him, Stifel turned pale.

Stein had already gone back to his story.

"Not exactly *unlucky*, sir. When we said unlucky, it meant lots of things. When Stifel came to Ahlhorn, it was late in 1917. We were flying the height-climbers then, and they were hard ships, stripped down to frames and bags, and pumped up with so much gas they'd have liked to burst. It was the only way we could stay clear of the English planes. We were flying at around six thousand meters then, higher than even the best English planes could climb, so it was almost safe. But there was the cold and the oxygen. We wore leather pants and fur coats and sheepskin gloves, but it was still so cold that when a man worked hard, his breath would freeze on his face so that he had trouble opening his mouth to say anything. And of course there wasn't no air to breathe up there. You couldn't go too long without the oxygen equipment. But the ships were so stripped out to keep them light that all we had were a few bottles of oxygen and hoses that the men shared. You had to be real careful to make it last, especially when there was a strong wind and you would have a long flight back after you dropped your bombs.

"You know, sir, it's funny with oxygen and flying high like that. When you need the oxygen you don't really know it. You get a feeling like your head is all empty, and some men start to giggling like little schoolgirls. When that happens, one of your comrades has to make you take the oxygen hose before you lose your head. It's not like when a man's thirsty and he knows he wants water. With the oxygen you just don't know it until it's too late. You depend on your mates."

The long-windedness of Stein's story prompted yawns and impatient looks around the table. Even Whitman had no idea where the story was leading.

Kuntz interrupted. "Since Airman Stein has testified that he never flew with Officer Stifel in the war, I hardly see the relevance of this testimony."

Eckener, listening intently, waved his cigar to dismiss Kuntz's comment. The ashes spilled on his jacket and the table as he motioned with his fingers for Stein to continue.

"Well, we were pretty short of men by 1917. Lots of Zeppelins had been lost, and men had been pulled out of the service to go to the fronts. I was a rigger then, but I doubled as ground crew. Most of the men did the same. There was times when we would take the lines to bring a ship in, load up the bombs and fuel for another run, then climb aboard as the crew.

"I was on ground crew one night when the L-54 came in from a mission. Over Birmingham I think it was. They came in real fine, no damage at all, but the winds had been strong that night and they had a long flight back. And since the English even had planes in Belgium then, they had to stay way up there the whole way back. They were venting a lot of gas as they came down, and that meant that they had almost no fuel left, so we were ready to run over there and get those men out and get mugs of tea or hot chocolate into them real quick to thaw them out. I think it must have been Strasser in command, because that ship eased down real smooth with no hesitations. He landed a ship like Captain Whitman lands 'em.

"Well, as soon as those lines were down, the rear hatch on the bottom of the gondola opens and out jumps Gunner Stifel, real spright. We were sure happy to see that. See, the gunners' compartment is pretty cold. They have open ports for the Parabellum machine guns, and it gets so cold that the men have to keep moving to keep from freezing. The only thing they can even eat up there is chocolate bars, and when an engine stops in that cold, the radiator will freeze before it can be restarted.

That's how cold it is. There's some flights that would come in and no one in that compartment could even open the hatch from the inside. We'd have to climb in and get them. So we were real happy to see Stifel jump down like that. 'It was tough,' he said. 'We were close to seven thousand meters.' Then he pointed to the hatch and said, 'They didn't make it.'

"Well, we were all real sad then. No one likes to lose a comrade. But then there ain't much that can be done about it. Some men can only take the cold for so long. You struggle with them and try to keep them moving and make them slap their hands together and especially you get that oxygen hose into them. But sometimes, no matter how much you struggle with them, you lose 'em.

"It was me that had to climb into the hatch and get the others, and that's a real tricky job, because those hatches on the old eight-climbers were pretty small, and I'm not so small myself. And after a flight like that the men can get real stiff. I climbed up in there and looked around. The three o' them were sitting on the bench-perches with their hands locked around the grips of the handholds. They were young lads, not much more than seventeen. And you know, sir, they were smiling. All three of them. They were cold like fish from the North Sea, but they had the most peaceful looks on their faces you ever saw. It's what happens when a man don't get the oxygen hose. I looked all around, and I couldn't find no oxygen tank. The tanks were all up inside the hull. There's an ammunition compartment up there with room for one man, up out of the cold. Stifel's parka was up there.

"There weren't no inquiry or nothing, but word gets around among the men real fast. And after that, most of the men didn't want to fly with Stifel."

"Thank you, Stein," said Eckener. The look on his face was controlled but smug. "You may go now."

Fifty-Two

Eckener's new office in Friedrichshafen was a cubbyhole on the outside of the smaller of the two building sheds, a cramped, windowless room that had been used by the floor foremen when the old wartime Zeppelins were being constructed on a crash assembly line, rolling out of the shed almost as fast as the English could shoot them down. The drawings and models that had given a pulse of mad activity to his spacious old office stood forlorn in one corner, like the beginnings of an archive collection that wouldn't be looked at for a long time.

"It's all over," said Eckener when he saw Whitman staring at the boxes. "They've relegated me to this dungeon because they don't care about building new Zeppelins anymore. I'm what they call an *unperson* now. I think your admiral received the same honors. I don't mind being left alone by the reporters, but with no hope for new Zeppelins, I'm a man who's not allowed to dream anymore."

"You got me through that inquiry," said Whitman. "Without Stein's testimony I'd have been lost. There was no way to answer that trumped-up nonsense."

"You're not through," said Eckener. "That was nothing. A private show by Kuntz to secure the command for his protegé. Stifel will still get the command. I just wanted them to know what they're getting, a coward through and through."

"But after Stein's testimony discredited Stifel, what's left to throw against me? They're not going to try to make a case out of my little blowup with Goering, are they? Even Hempe wouldn't stoop to that."

"Whitman! They're hardly begun. And you're being a fool. I don't know what they have in store, but you can't win."

The look in Eckener's bright blue eyes, the beaten and resigned look where there had once been fire and enthusiasm, backed up his words. Almost single-handed, this man had developed the Zeppelins, fighting the collected wisdom of scien-

312

sts and engineers and politicians, overcoming the initial fears of
passengers, the opprobrium of the wartime bombing, the wide-
spread fears of lighter-than-air flight bred by the crashes of
British and American airships. Alone, he had built the reputation
of reliability and safety that made the Zeppelins the technological
glory of Germany, a reputation that could boast that not a single
passenger life had ever been lost on a Zeppelin. For him to say
that Zeppelins were without a future was to hear the death knell
rung.

"Why do they care?" asked Whitman. "Why the mockery of
the inquiry? If they want me out, they can just kick me out. I'm
not even a regular employee."

"They don't want you out. They need you. The future is
helium, and they think you're the only one who can get it for
them. Until now, the U.S. has been icy to the requests for
helium."

Whitman shook his head. "I don't get it. You said they have
no building plans for new ships. And with helium instead of
hydrogen, the Graf Zeppelin and even the Hindenberg won't be
commercially viable. They can't carry the payload with helium."

"Commercial airships are dead," said Eckener. "It's a matter
of a few years until airplanes can fly the Atlantic with profitable
passenger loads. The Americans and the British are already
setting up weather stations and building flying boats. They will
take over the North Atlantic traffic."

"Then why does Hempe want the helium?"

"There are other uses for a Zeppelin besides flying passengers."

"Propaganda?"

"That too." Eckener looked away.

"Military?" asked Whitman. "Flying command posts? Electronic reconnaisance. The Zeppelins too?"

"It's inevitable. There's nothing you can do about it. Don't
try to fight them, Whitman. You can't win."

"You fought them. You called Hitler a 'conscienceless rabble-
rouser.' You said that Germany was a nation governed by
criminals. And when you spoke out, you were probably the
best-known German in the world to speak against them. Maybe it
did some good."

"You think so? Look where it got me. Whitman, I'm telling
you for your own good. Resign. Go home. If you don't want to
work for Hempe and the helium, don't. But forget the Zeppelins.
They're a memory for old men like me. Another year or two of

flights over the Atlantic and then they'll use them for their own purposes."

"Did Hempe ask you to talk to me?" said Whitman.

"It's for your own good."

The hearing reconvened in the same room, with everyone in the same seats except for Stifel. But the atmosphere had changed. The directors were all stone-faced men, used to concealing their emotions and reactions. Now their expressionless faces took on a grim cast that made the earlier session seem playful.

"Whitman," said Hempe, "do you insist on continuing this inquiry?"

It was a ritual question. They knew what his answer would be, and before Whitman nodded, someone had already gone to the rear door to bring in a sallow-faced man in one of the familiar baggy gray suits.

"Herr Kutner," said Hempe. The others nodded.

It took only a glance at Kutner to know whom he worked for. If Hempe's genial cosmopolitanism and affectations of fastidious grooming and highbrow culture represented the Nazism of Hermann Goering, Kutner's sloppily fitted clothes, close-cut temples and unstylishly short hair were the no-nonsense, unsmiling mien of the naked power of his mentor Heinrich Himmler. He wasted neither words nor gestures, not even acknowledging his introduction or the presence of the other men in the room.

"Herr Kutner is from the *Reichssicherheitshauptampt*," said Hempe. "As I explained to you before, the *Sicherheitsdienst* has taken an interest in these proceedings."

The cool smiles of the other directors reflected their own embarrassment that they had to rely on the likes of Kutner.

Kutner waited until the doors were secured, then placed his briefcase on the table and withdrew an envelope, sliding it across to Whitman. "Open it," he said.

Whitman took out the six photographs inside, grainy enlargements on glossy, high-contrast paper.

"What are those photographs, Herr Whitman?"

Whitman looked closely. His first thought was that the lens on the Leica had remarkable resolution, another masterpiece of German craftsmanship. Every detail of the Junkers 52s was clear, the nacelles on the landing gear, the thin radial cowlings on the engines, even the intersecting radio direction finder loops behind the cockpits. The Messerschmitts were much smaller images, but he could make out the black wingtip markings and the unmistakable outlines of the swift fighters.

"Where did you get these?" said Whitman. Before the question was out of his mouth, he remembered. The film was in the camera when he gave it to Maggie.

"Where is she?" he said. He remembered the unsuccessful call from Kiel. He meant to call again, but he had been on the move ever since.

Kutner didn't answer, apparently enjoying Whitman's anxiety. When Whitman repeated the question, he ignored it again.

"Where were the photographs taken?" asked Kutner.

There was no reason not to respond. It was a pro forma question, not a search for an answer. "Over the Straits of Gibraltar," said Whitman. "From the flight deck of the Graf Zeppelin."

"The flight deck?" interjected Kuntz. "You allowed a passenger into the flight deck?"

"Passenger?" said Whitman. "*I* took those photographs."

He watched Eckener's face drop. Even Hempe seemed surprised.

"You *took* the photographs?" said Kutner. "And can you explain why they were found concealed in the baggage of Frau Bourne when she was flying to Switzerland?"

Whitman realized the futility of trying to answer, even as he patiently explained how he had loaned her the camera and forgot about the few photographs he had snapped. The explanation rang frail in his own ears.

"Why did you take those photographs, Whitman? Surely you are aware that it is forbidden to photograph German military aircraft. Of what possible use could these photographs be, except for espionage?"

"I had never seen so many planes in formation before," said Whitman. "Thirty transports, with escorts, is not an everyday sight."

"Who was Frau Bourne supposed to give the photographs to? Who was her contact in Switzerland?"

"This is ridiculous," said Whitman. "She went to Switzerland for personal reasons. She didn't even know she had those negatives."

"It is you who are being ridiculous, Whitman," said Kutner. "Do you seriously ask us to believe that Frau Bourne *just happened* to be a professional photographer who could be expected to carry undeveloped film in her baggage? And that she just

happened to be meeting a well-known propagandist who has
written anti-German articles?''

"My God!'' said Whitman. "You talk as though this whole
thing were planned from the moment we picked up her distress
signals in the South Atlantic. If I were really trying to reveal
some well-kept secret, do you think I would go to the trouble of
planting her on a sinking hulk in the middle of the ocean? There
are easier ways to get a few photographs out of Germany.''

"Apparently you have also explored those avenues,'' said
Kutner. "And in the same bumbling fashion.'' He pulled another
envelope out of his briefcase, opening this one himself and
placing sheets from a sketch pad on the table.

From where Whitman sat, the sketches were upside down. The
faint pencil lines were almost illegible.

"Who drew these sketches?'' asked Kutner.

"I have no idea. I've never seen them before.''

"They were found in your hotel room in Kiel, hidden among
your own papers, carefully interleaved into an operating manual
for the Graf Zeppelin.''

"Where your man planted them, no doubt,'' snapped Whitman.
"I told him that I had no idea what he was talking about, and
I'm telling you the same thing.''

"*Look* at them, Whitman!''

He picked up the sheets, twisting them around until the
writing was right side up. They had been hastily drawn, the
printing vaguely familiar, but he still had no idea what they
were.

"Let me refresh your memory, *Kapitän*. Those are drawings
of submarine pens. They were given to you by Admiral von
Teppler, or at least described for you by him before you went to
Kiel. He undoubtedly attempted to supply further information
during your misguided journey to his retirement home. What you
did not realize is that von Teppler had no idea at all about the
actual construction plans of the submarines or their bases.''

At the reference to the admiral, Whitman's expression changed
from incredulity to anger, a transformation that Kutner seemed
not to notice.

"The drawings are worthless,'' Kutner went on. "You are
welcome to take them. In fact, you can even go ahead with your
plan to let your brother smuggle them back to the United
States.''

"Henry? What has Henry got to do with this?''

"Let us not be dissembling, Herr Whitman. We are not fools.

Your brother is not an Olympic caliber yachtsman. He is distinctly second rate. Does it not seem odd that a nation so anxious to succeed in the Olympic Games that it employs black auxiliaries on its track and field team would then place a second-rate yachtsman on the team? Perhaps he was put on the team for reasons other than sailing. His being picked up in the restricted area of the naval anchorage at Kiel, where he claims to have wandered accidently, only confirms our suspicions."

"Where is Henry?"

"Your brother is in custody in Kiel. We have no intention of making an international incident out of this episode and further embarrassing the United States. Your own efforts with your brother and with Frau Bourne are so feeble that they do not constitute a serious threat to the security of the Reich. If anything, they confirm the bumbling of American espionage, and the Fuehrer's assessment of the United States as a decadent nation. But even a bumbling spy is not fit to command the Graf Zeppelin."

"What's going to happen to Margaret . . . Fräulein Bourne and Henry?"

"We have no idea of the whereabouts of Frau Bourne. Your brother will remain in Kiel until the close of the Olympic Games, at which time a decision will be made as to his future. We have no desire to embarrass the American Olympians any further. The black auxiliaries who have been sent back to the United States after being caught shoplifting are already sufficient humiliation to the Americans, don't you think?"

Whitman scanned the faces around the table, wondering if anyone, Eckener, even Hempe, would find the whole inquiry as absurd as it seemed to him. What they had trumped up was insufficient even for a minor scandal. Photographs of minimal propaganda value. Planted sketches that they admitted were worthless. A plot so farfetched it was ludicrous. But the faces around the table were expressionless, the stony gazes reflecting perhaps embarrassment at the ritual of the inquiry as much as the proper attitude of stern disapproval which loyalty to state and party required.

"Am I under arrest?" Whitman asked.

Kutner turned to Hempe, conferring quietly.

"You could be," said Hempe. "This is a serious matter. But the *Sicherheitsdienst* is willing to drop all charges if you will only assist us."

"Become a German agent?"

"If you insist upon the melodramatic language, yes."

"Will all charges against my brother be dropped?"

Hempe leaned over and appeared to consult with Kutner before saying, "Your conduct will certainly be taken into account. After all, Whitman, it would not look good if an official representative of the Zeppelin Company were to be found the brother of a bumbling spy, would it?"

Whitman looked long and hard at Eckener, hoping for the slightest hint of a response, even a flicker in the eyes. But Eckener looked down at the table. Like the others, perhaps, he was too embarrassed by the absurd ritual to speak.

Fifty-Three

"Promise me, David. Just promise that you'll sign those papers."

"Promise you?" said Sinclair. "Why? For flyboy, so you can jump back into his bed? You don't need a divorce from me for that, Margaret. Being married didn't stop you before."

He glanced over and saw her look away angrily.

They had left the hotel an hour before, after Sinclair shook off the watchful tail of the Russian with an aplomb that Maggie had never seen in him before. They went out through a servant's entrance, across Zurich in three taxis, finally walking to the garage where they picked up the old Citroën van. A few minutes out of the city on Route 1, the highway that led to Winterthur and then to Constance, and they were already in the low slopes of the Toggenberg. In any other circumstances, the mountains would have been spectacular, low and green, without the harsh ruggedness of the high Alps. But Maggie found that she couldn't watch the road. David's concentration on the driving, the hunched pose over the wheel and the deadly speed, frightened her.

David Sinclair had changed. The blithe contempt for everyone and everything, the inability to seize a cause and fight for it, or even to admit belief in anything, the mocking tone of cynicism he hid behind—it was all changed. Maggie realized that she never before could have pictured David driving like this, just as she could never have imagined him dirty and unshaven, with the smell and grease of adventure in his skin and hair. It was as if he vere uncovering a part of himself for the first time. She didn't know how to react to him anymore.

"You don't even know what kind of a man he is," said Sinclair. "Which side is he on, Margaret? That used to matter to you, didn't it?"

Margaret ignored the provocation.

"What about that man in the lobby?" she asked. "Won't he find out we've left and follow us?"

Sinclair laughed. "Orlov? He's persistent, but he isn't bold enough to be a threat. He'll plod and track and pull stops and bribe informers. By the time he figures out what has happened, those planes will be on their way to Spain. This is too big for Orlov to stop. It's too big for any of them."

"You really think we'll get into Germany on that old passport? With those?" She gestured over her shoulder to the flat crates in the back of the Citroën van, stacked under loose tarpaulins.

"I got this far. We can't stop now. Men have died for this, men with nothing to gain put themselves on the line. If I give up, they've died for nothing."

He glanced over to make sure she was listening before he went on.

"It's the real war now, Margaret. No one who hasn't been in it can know what it's like. In Madrid there are only the frightened politicians saving their own necks, and the Russian advisors gorging themselves on Spanish food and women. But outside the city you can see what the war is doing to the country and the people. You can see a country being crushed by the madness of a world gone insane.

"The Fascists are taking hostages now—poor peasants. They come in the evenings, pick up the men at the gates of their houses when they're returning from the fields. Then they line them up in rows to make the work of the gravediggers easier, shoot them without so much as saying a word over them. It's not politics anymore. It's the wars of religion all over again. And this is only the beginning..."

In Sinclair's words, Manolo's story took on the quality of an epic, a struggle of good and evil. And as Maggie listened, she remembered the best of his writing, when language seemed to leap off the page, details and insights that could make the most ordinary individual come alive, turning a factory worker into a hero and the most powerful politician into a villain.

"Would you die to get those planes, David?"

"Is that what it would take to convince you?" He laughed. "Then you wouldn't have to worry about a divorce."

"I didn't mean it that way. But if you keep driving like this you'll end up killing both of us. These little mountain roads weren't meant for this kind of speed."

"What would your flyboy be willing to die for?" he asked. "Is there anything that matters to him besides his magic balloon?"

He watched her squirm as she avoided his glance and the question.

"I guess we'll find out," he said.

Fifty-Four

Whitman walked quickly past the huge hangar, trying not to look at the Zeppelin inside or at his watch. The departure of the *Graf Zeppelin* was only a few hours away. He knew ground crews would be swarming over the ship, loading on cart after cart of provisions—vegetables and fruit, racks of fresh meat and fish, wines, fresh linen and towels, flowers for the dining room, late-night chocolates for the passengers. Riggers would be combing the hull, monitoring the cells for leaks that might leave the hydrogen inside *ripe*, contaminated with air that would combine with the pure hydrogen to make explosive oxyhydrogen. Mechanics and electricians would be going through long preflight checklists, looking for tiny structural weaknesses, vibration strains in the engine mounts, fatigue cracks in the girders or the axial wiring of the hull. The doors of the hangar were already closed, which meant that it was close to the time when the hangar would be cleared for the fueling, the final step before departure. As a safety precaution, the hoses were connected and the Blaugas pumped into the ship with no one in the hangar. Only then would the doors be reopened and the ship walked out for its departure.

The air was unusually clear, and a warm, dry breeze was blowing across the lake. It was the beginning of a foehn, the wind that the French call a mistral and the Italians a sirocco—a fierce, hot wind generated by a depression along the northern

lopes of the Alps. After a few days of the foehn, even the most
elaxed of souls would be affected, becoming tense and irritable
s the relentless wind took away every last breath of free air,
eaving only a dryness worse than a desert.

Whitman wasn't sure what he would say to the Huttens. He
ad assumed that even if he were to lose command of the Graf
Zeppelin, he had enough friends in Friedrichshafen to get them
board. He had thought of Friedrichshafen as different from
ities like Frankfurt and Berlin, where the regulation books were
ll powerful. The men in Friedrichshafen were Zeppelin men,
oyal to those great ships more than to any government. Some of
hem had been with the company since the last days of the
Jerman Empire, hanging on through the barren days of the
Veimar Republic when Germany was forbidden by the Versailles
reaty to have any but tiny, impractical airships. They had been
here when the renaissance of airships began with the building of
he Graf Zeppelin in 1928, and most of them loved that ship as
nuch as he did, shared his pride in its accomplishments and
apabilities. Building that Zeppelin had been a defiance of the
aw. Was it expecting too much to hope that the men who had
uilt the ship would substitute a little Swabian *schlamperei* for
he prescribed procedures, at least enough to loosen up the
assport and customs checks for an old couple?

But now there was no one he could turn to. Not one of the
rew had been willing to come to his defense, except Stein. And
f the crew, men he had flown with and depended on as only the
rew of a ship can depend on one another, had been so taken in
y the Nazis, so threatened that they were afraid to come to a
earing and speak the truth, then he knew he could expect
othing from the ground crew.

Eckener was right. It was all over. He would have to tell the
Iuttens to rush back to Bremen, hoping they could get back
efore the criminal police were informed that they had left. With
uck, they might avoid imprisonment and be left alone to live out
heir days in the warehouse in Bremen, carrying bags of coffee
ntil they dropped.

Out on Lake Constance, the foehn was kicking up whitecaps.
Ie saw a sailboat heel precariously, and the ferry charging across
he lake from Romanshorn, kicking up a big bow wave. He
ould picture the scene from the flight deck of the Graf Zeppelin,
he mountains and the lake scaled into a wonderland that could
e seen in its entirety from that incomparable platform in the sky.

"Paul!"

The voice, coming from the shadows of one of the ol
whitewashed rooming houses with views down over the prome
nade and the lake, surprised him. No one in Germany called hir
by his first name, not even in Friedrichshafen, where everyon
was so much more casual with manners and language than in th
rest of Germany.

He turned around, looking into the shadows of the porch o
the house. The tall figure wore an ill-fitting German suit, and i
took him a moment to recognize the face without the Olympi
blazer.

"Henry! What the . . . ?"

Henry answered with a sheepish grin, exactly as Paul remembere
it from the days when he had to bail him out of trouble at school

"You're in trouble," said Paul.

"Uh-huh."

"Henry, this is serious. It may sound preposterous, but the
think you're a spy. They claim they found some drawings an
they caught you sailing near the navy area. In their pett
conspiratorial minds that makes you a spy."

Henry was still grinning. "Where can we talk?" he said. "W
really need to talk."

Paul started to lead him toward the Kurgarten, where th
Huttens were supposed to be waiting, then changed his mind an
went down to the promenade along the lake, deserted now tha
the stiff wind was blowing off the water. As they walked, th
wind billowed their jackets and made their pants legs flap. The
were at the widest part of the lake, the stretch from Romanshor
to Friedrichshafen, and the open water ahead of them looked lik
an inland sea.

"You don't know, do you?" said Henry. "I tried to tell you i
Kiel, but there was no time. And you were so damned *straight* i
was hard to get through."

Paul didn't answer. He suddenly knew what Henry was abou
to tell him. The realization didn't surprise him at all.

"I'm not here for the Olympics," said Henry. "It's a sham,
cover. I came for information."

"Submarines?"

This time Henry looked surprised. The grin disappeared as h
queried with his eyes.

"They found your sketches," said Paul. "That was a stupi
place to leave them."

"They?"

"*Sicherheitsdienst*. Himmler's heavies."

"You got the rap? I'm sorry. I had to hide them because they ere starting to snoop around the Olympic barracks. I was going explain to you, but there was never time. And it doesn't atter if they got those. On the water I saw the real stuff, up ose. What they're building is incredible. Those pens aren't for tle coastal subs. This time they're building the real thing, tack subs, a whole new class. And if the dimensions of the ens are any indication, they have the range to cross the tlantic."

He reached inside his pocket and took out some folded etches, drawn on the same finely gridded paper Whitman had en only hours before. The handwriting was familiar, even the arp lines of the hard draftsman's pencil were the same. They ere not an artist's rendering, but a draftsman's sketches; no fort at accurate perspective, just a wealth of detail and nota- ons of dimensions.

"There's nothing defensive about those subs," said Henry. And all Hitler's talk about rearming to protect themselves is nk. They're building those subs to interrupt shipping from the .S. to Britain. There's no other explanation. It doesn't take uch to know that if we can't ship to England the English won't able to hold out for long."

The admiral's description of the Nazi shell game flitted through aul's mind.

Henry slipped back into his puckish grin. "I hate to destroy usions, Paul. That nice peaceful Olympic village in Berlin, ith the arching birch trees and the quiet ponds . . ."

Paul looked at his brother, wondering what surprise was ming.

". . . it was a training base for the Condor Legion. And have ou noticed that they're using human silhouettes for the targets the pistol shooting events? The war is on, Paul. It's just a atter of time before we're in it. The only question is whether ou want to enlist now or later. Unless you still have doubts out which side you want to be on."

Paul ignored the taunt as he looked through the sketches, visting them so he could read the tiny lettering and dimensions. e knew little about submarines, but even the little he knew told im that the rows of pens in Kiel were the base for a major bmarine fleet, large enough to disrupt all transport across the tlantic.

"We can be ready for them if we start building now," said enry. "But with the doubters in the U.S., drummed up by

Lindbergh and Henry Ford and the rest of the America Firster
we need evidence to get things rolling. This is the evidence w
need. You've got to get them to the States for me, on th
Zeppelin.''

"You're too late."

"What do you mean? It hasn't taken off."

Paul glanced at his wrist chronometer. "Not for almost thre
hours. And when it does, I won't be on board."

Henry looked puzzled. "Goering's own boy not on board
What happened?''

"It's too complicated and stupid to explain. There was a b
sham of an inquiry, mostly nonsense and games on their pa
The bottom line is that they agreed to go light on you if I w
willing to work with them.''

"Work with them? Isn't that what you've been doing?''

"Different work. Helium—they need it, only the U.S. has i
and they think I can help them get it. You're their guarantee th
I'll cooperate.''

Henry shrugged his shoulders, a boyish gesture that made th
awkward-fitting German suit even more absurd. "They just lo
their guarantee."

"Henry!" Paul reached toward his brother, then pulled bac
when he realized how patronizing the gesture might seem. '
don't know how you got down here, but the Gestapo plays f
keeps. Every border in Germany will be closed. And when the
find you . . .''

Henry shrugged again. "A risk of the game. The importa
thing is the information. And getting it back to the States.''

"Game!" Paul's face tightened. "You really enjoy it all, don
you? The chase, the drama. It's all just high jinks, like practic
jokes at school.''

"Beats sitting behind a desk. Or trying to hustle helium f
their Zeppelins.''

Paul flinched, then relaxed. "Does it beat rotting in a Germa
prison?''

"Hey, big brother! I thought we were on the same side.''

"We are. And I'm probably being watched as closely as yo
I can't take those drawings anywhere.''

"What's that leave me, buying a ticket on the Graf Zeppelin?

Paul stared at his brother and grinned. "That," he said, "ma
not be a bad idea.''

Fifty-Five

clair knew exactly what to look for in Romanshorn. He
lked slowly up the row of warehouses that led back from the
ry terminal until he saw what he wanted, a second-floor
ndow over a shabby, single-bay garage. A sign was backpainted
the glass: *C. Nadler, Warensendung*. With big, reputable
ipping houses available to handle every kind of commerce,
re could be only one reason for the survival of a tiny agency
e that one: every port needed specialists, men who were
ling to handle the unusual cargo for a price, and to do it
thout questions for a better price. Of late, the major business
those agents had been from Jews who fled Germany for
itzerland. If they chose not to try to smuggle money out as
monds, the only way they could later recover the property and
ds left behind was to hire one of the shipping agents in
itzerland.

It took Sinclair a moment to find the unmarked Judas window
into the jointed door of the garage. He pushed the buzzer
xt to the door, waited for a response, then pushed again,
lding the buzzer down.

Nadler was a trim man, wearing a lightweight black suit jacket
d a narrow tie, like an undertaker. He looked at Sinclair
ough gray-tinted glasses with heavy frames, and spoke in clear
chdeutsch*. He knew he was not speaking to a fellow Swiss.

"You have the wrong address," he said.

Sinclair had already formulated a sentence in his broken
rman. "I have some special goods to consign."

"*Special* goods?" repeated Nadler. He opened the door a
ck, and Sinclair saw that the garage was filled with furniture
d cartons of books stacked as high as the ceiling.

He led Sinclair upstairs to the office, a tiny room with
thodically neat stacks of forms on the desk and an orderly
okshelf of looseleaf books against one wall.

"Furniture or funds?" said Nadler.

Sinclair looked puzzled.

"Is it Jew furniture or Jew money that you wish to bring in Switzerland? Doesn't really matter, because the procedures a the same. We do not take *consignments*, to use your term. Y sell us the goods in Germany, then purchase them back here. Th difference in the prices is our fee."

"How much is the difference?" The reporter in Sincla surfaced.

"Fifty percent," said Nadler. He seemed impressed whe Sinclair did not bat an eyelash.

"What I have is for shipment the other way," said Sinclair

"*Into* Germany? What do you need me for?"

"I told you, it's special goods."

"What kind of special goods?"

"Let's just say that it's compact and heavy." Sinclair watche Nadler's eyes behind the tinted glasses and added, "Machi parts."

Nadler reached behind him and consulted a looseleafed vc ume, thumbing through the pages, then reaching for anoth before he started mumbling, "Tryptique, bill of lading, declar tions, bonded certification... Who is the consignee?"

"I am. And I go with the shipment."

Nadler pushed the books away. "Let me see your passport.

He thumbed through the worn green passport, glancing bac and forth at the photograph and at Sinclair.

"The woman?"

"She goes too."

"She is very beautiful."

"How much?" asked Sinclair.

Nadler looked back at the photograph, then at Sinclair. "Th depends on the special goods," he said. "You pay in advance.

"And how do I know that the goods will be cleared throug German customs?"

"You trust me."

Maggie took an instant disliking to Nadler.

"Just like that?" she said to Sinclair as they drove to the fer terminal. "You walk down the street, pick a window, wa inside, and he's your man."

"After a while, you get to know who you can trust."

"*After a while?* You talk as though smuggling were a lifetin specialty."

"I can trust him, Margaret. He knows what will happen him if anything goes wrong. It's that simple."

"Is it?" Maggie wondered if she really liked the new Sinclair any more than the old. "You really like that language, don't you? '...what will happen to him.'"

"Men have already died for this," Sinclair said flatly.

"But those were accidents, in the heat of battle."

"Are you still testing me? First I have to be willing to die. Now I have to be willing to kill."

"I'm not testing, David. I'm trying to understand. I don't know what to believe anymore."

Maggie felt that she recognized Friedrichshafen, even though she had never been there before. Paul had described every detail of the town, the huge hangars that dominated the flat city, the promenade with its view over the lake, even the inescapable feeling that the town saw itself as one of the capitals of the world. The Zeppelins might be of passing interest elsewhere, but in Friedrichshafen, they were everything, on every postcard in the racks, on every shelf in the souvenir shops, on every signpost.

She looked in vain for her old friend the Graf Zeppelin, but the doors to the hangars were closed. Outside one, there was a caravan of wheeled trollies, piled with baggage and cargo.

"What is this?" said Sinclair impatiently after they had made a slow circuit through the city. "A sightseeing tour? Where's our flyboy?"

They pulled over in a parking area close to the hangars, where a sign described the guided tours offered each afternoon at two o'clock.

"He's here," she said. "The Graf Zeppelin departs tonight, and his hearing was over this morning. He's here."

"What the hell are you waiting for? Afraid he'll turn you down?"

"Remember your promise," she said. "You'll sign the divorce agreement." But Maggie knew he was right. She was afraid. She had misjudged one man—one she had lived with for eight years. How could she be sure of Whitman?

Sinclair laughed. "Are you really that sure?"

"Promise me," she said. "I mean it, David. I want to hear it from you."

"If flyboy comes through, I'll sign anything."

She was reluctant to walk into the office. There had been no questions at the passport control, not even a hesitation, but she still had the feeling that her picture and her name were in files or on posters, and that she would be spotted. She waited outside the commissary building until she spotted a man in a steward's uniform.

"Where is Commander Whitman?" she asked. "Does he have an office somewhere?"

The steward shook his head, answering in uncertain English. "He's not *Commander* Whitman anymore."

"They booted him?"

"Booted?"

"Did they take away his command?"

"Whitman resigned. They say he is going to work for the Zeppelin Company in the United States. It was just announced."

"You're sure?"

"If you heard the grumbles of the men, you'd believe me. They liked Whitman, and they don't like the new man." He pointed to the huge hangar behind them, where a single guard stood next to one of the side doors, a bay large enough to drive the biggest truck through, but only a tiny aperture in the immense windowless facade of the hangar.

"They're fueling now," said the steward. "And for all I know, Captain Whitman is already on his way to Frankfurt. They'll be briefing him there. That's what they say."

Sinclair lost control when she told him. "Coward! You knew he wouldn't. You knew what kind of man he was. What's he going to do for them in the States, sell Zeppelins?"

"It's something to do with helium, I think. The U.S. has a monopoly, and he's supposed to try to buy helium for the Zeppelins."

"To keep up German prestige, no doubt. You still want that divorce?"

Maggie spun around in the seat, fury in her eyes. "You're actually glad, aren't you? You don't really give a damn about the gold, planes, Spain, democracy . . . any of it. It was all just words to you, a chance to be somebody. David Sinclair, the man with a gun, the adventurer who knows about smuggling and ships. What are you going to do now, make the story into a novel? You always wanted to do a novel, didn't you? This time you even came up with a plot."

"Hold it," said Sinclair. "I'm not the one who blew it. Your flyboy did. He chickened out of flying the Zeppelin for a nice easy job. He's still on the wrong side, but now you can see it

at's what you're so pissed about, Margaret, so don't blame
e."

"Maybe he had a reason."

"I'm sure he did."

She turned away, staring at the hangar where the bored guard
ced aimlessly. He sensed her vulnerability.

"It's not the end of the world, Margaret. In a few weeks the
viss will relax this stupid regulation at the banks and we can
posit the gold against a check. The Swiss will always take the
oney in the end. Why do you think they introduced those
mbered accounts? It's so they can get all the money the Jews
e sending out of Germany."

She turned back, angry again. "You bastard! Yesterday you
id a delay of a month was impossible. Spain would fall apart.
ow it's no problem. And after a month you'll probably decide
it the money is really a nice little nest egg for David Sinclair.
 more deadlines, right? No more crummy little articles for
etin editors who don't know what they're talking about. I can
ar it now, the way you'll spin the words around and convince
urself and maybe even me that the Spanish aren't worth it, that
mehow what you've already done for Spain deserves that
yment. Golden words, spinning off the golden tongue of David
nclair."

"What do you want me to do, sprout wings and fly it
yself?"

"Just *care*. Care about anything in the world except David
nclair."

"Care?" He turned around and lifted the corner of the
paulin in the back. "What does that look like? Do you know
at it took to get that?"

"And what are you going to do now? What you started to do is
right, but you have to care enough . . ."

"I do care," he said. "I care about you, Margaret. I love
u."

"Go to hell!" She stormed out of the van, walking toward the
ngar in the distance, the dry wind brisk at her back, spreading
r jacket like a spinnaker. She was planning to walk to the
ppelin offices, determined to find Paul, but when she turned,
e wind caught her in the face, leaving her breathless, her eyes
ared.

She pictured the Graf Zeppelin behind the hangar walls, and
ed to imagine the takeoff from the lakeside town, the ship
ing, looming over the picturebook mountains and lake before

it turned off toward the west. She had no wristwatch, but sh
remembered the steward saying it was only a matter of hours
Paul's description of the Zeppelin came flooding back. They too
off from Friedrichafen in the evenings because the high altitud
reduced the amount of hydrogen that could be pumped into th
ship. An evening departure, in the cooler air, meant that mor
gas could be pumped aboard, an extra reserve for emergencies
She could almost hear his words. He really believed in th
Zeppelin. When he talked about it, it was more than a machine
it was a work of technology that had become art. *A cathedral i.
the sky.*

She watched the guard in front of the hangar. He was obvious
ly bored, moving aimlessly, sitting for a while, then wanderin
off to find better shelter from the hot wind. She didn't envy him
Paul had said that the fueling could take hours.

There were big *No Smoking* signs posted on both sides of th
door, written in German over a large graphic symbol of
cigarette with a red *X* drawn through it. She remembered Paul'
description of the cautions the Germans always took, clearing th
entire hangar area while the Zeppelin was being fueled, doin
everything by remote control from a distance to avoid even th
slightest chance of an accident.

He had seemed so proud of his command. She couldn't hel
wondering why he would quit. Maybe she didn't know him ɛ
all.

Then suddenly she ran back to the van, fighting against th
wind at every step. She was breathless when she opened th
door, and she could hardly hold it open.

"David! How heavy is it?"

"What?"

"*It.*" She pointed to the flat crates in the back of the van.

"Almost a thousand kilos. Why?"

"What do you need to lift it?"

"I can carry the individual crates myself. Why? What ha
gotten into you?"

She looked back at the hangar, where the forlorn guar
huddled in the shelter of one of the corner posts, then climbe
into the van and shut the door. She started explaining rapidl
telling Sinclair everything she could remember about the Zepp
lin. A little she had seen, in Recife and in Frankfurt. Mostly sh
repeated what Paul had told her in the long hours of their drives
She knew a lot.

Sinclair listened with a smug, condescending smirk on hi

ace. "Forget it," he said when she finally stopped explaining.
"It's too risky."

"Damn it, David. Anything worth doing is risky."

Fifty-Six

he two brothers stood close to one another, facing the lake.
Mist, blown up by the steady wind, turned the normally placid
ake into a mysterious sea.

Henry shook his head. "It's ridiculous, Paul. I appreciate
vhat you're trying to do, but it sounds stupid. Like a circus
tunt."

"You've got no choice. If it's any consolation, it's been done
efore. A kid stowed away the first time the Graf Zeppelin flew
he Atlantic. They've kept it a secret because they were afraid
ublicity would attract imitators. That was almost eight years
go, and I'd guess everyone has forgotten by now—except me.
'm probably the last fanatic who keeps track of Zeppelin
ninutiae."

As Henry turned to face his brother, the wind whipped his hair
to his face, which made him seem even more boyish. "And
vhat happens to you?" he asked.

"Me?" said Paul. "They want that helium too much to do
nything to me. I can stall until I know you're clear. Then—who
nows? 'No plans,' was Maggie's line. I guess in this crazy
vorld she's right."

"What *about* Maggie? Where is she?"

Paul shrugged, looking away across the lake into the wind. "I
aven't heard from her. I've tried to call Zurich, but there's no
ace of her. I guess she decided to go her own way. It was really
oo good to—"

"Try harder," said Henry. "She's the best thing that ever
appened to you." He turned and started for the hangar in the
istance, then turned back and hugged his brother.

"Good luck," said Paul.

Henry grinned. "Welcome back," he said.

The direct route to the Kurgarten Hotel and the Huttens was through the Zeppelin facility, but Paul hesitated, anxious to avoid the Zeppelin crews. They were men he had worked with, trusted, depended on; he wanted to remember them that way. They would do their jobs, fly on schedule, get the vaccine to Brazil in time, keep up the reputation of the Zeppelin. That they had chosen to go with the Nazis was something he just didn't want to think about. After all, he admitted to himself, he really hadn't chosen any differently himself. And he supposed that they had been subjected to the same pressures. Naked force could be resisted, but to fight the Nazis was to abandon the sure future they promised for a vague uncertainty.

There was a time when he had defied tradition and protocol by spending his free time in the crew commissary, grabbing lunch or a cup of tea with the airmen and letting them regale him with stories of the Zeppelin service. No other officer would go near the crew quarters, and several times the regular officers had spoken to him about his frequenting the commissary. In the end they excused it because he was only an American visitor.

An American visitor. He thought of Maggie. Why hadn't she called? Why was there no trace of her? He could remember their conversations, the times when they had hinted toward the big questions but never really talked them through. There was never enough time, it seemed. Yet it always seemed so right, relaxed and easy. She *was* the best thing that had happened to him in a very long time. But now . . . ?

A man in uniform came out of the commissary, running across the grounds of the field toward Whitman. Whitman walked faster.

"Captain Whitman!" It was Zekner. He would probably be senior watch officer now, thought Whitman. A reward for keeping his mouth shut at the right time.

"The men want to talk to you," said Zekner.

"I don't think we have much to talk about," said Whitman, regretting the hostile edge in his voice as soon as he said it. "And you have a lot of work to do." He glanced at his chronometer. "You're departing in less than two hours."

Zekner shook his head. "I'm not sure we're departing."

"Why not?"

"The men. They don't want to fly with Stifel. They say he's *unlucky,* whatever that's supposed to mean. They want to talk to you."

"Me? I'm scratched. You know that. And I don't really think the usual good-byes are in order."

"Look, Whitman," said Zekner. "The men need to talk to you. We *all* need to talk to you."

"Nobody wanted to talk when I had that hearing," answered Whitman angrily.

Zekner responded with a quizzical look. "*Your* hearing?"

"This morning. The only one who would testify was Stein. Everyone else wanted to save their own necks and let Stifel's testimony stand."

"Oh," said Zekner. "You mean Stifel's certification hearing. They never asked us to testify. I think they were afraid of what we might say. I was really surprised that they let Stein testify, but it didn't seem to matter. Once you resigned, Stifel was in."

Whitman looked at Zekner for a long moment as the truth of the situation sunk in. "Where are the men?" he asked.

The commissary was crowded. The room would normally hold fifty men at a sitting, and with both the flight crew and the ground crew there were over one hundred men there, most of them clustered in a tight knot. They buzzed when Whitman came in, gathering around him.

"Where's Stein?" someone shouted. "Let Stein tell him."

Stein pushed his way forward, and Whitman expected some kind of ceremony, maybe a present, like a model of the Graf Zeppelin. He pictured it sitting on a shelf, next to the keychain Maggie had given him. Souvenirs of an era.

"Sir," said Stein, "the men don't want to fly with the new commander. It's like I said in there, some officers are unlucky, and well, no one wants to fly with Stifel."

Shouts came up around the room: "We won't fly! Stifel won't command!"

Whitman shook his head. "I know how some of you feel, but the Zeppelin has to go on schedule. People expect it. That vaccine has to be delivered to Brazil, thousands of people are waiting for it. You're the only ones who can get it to them in time."

Another grumble rolled through the room. "Not with Stifel!" someone shouted. Others echoed his cry.

"You shouldn't have resigned, sir," said Stein. "I know you might of had your reasons, but we need commanders like you."

"I had no choice," Whitman explained. Without going into details, he told everyone what the hearing had really been about.

"But you men have to keep flying," he went on. "You're

what holds the Zeppelin Company together. If you stop, the Zeppelin will die, and a part of what's great in Germany will die with it."

Zekner stepped forward and stood next to Stein. "The men want to fly, sir," he said. "To the man."

Whitman looked out over the room, recognizing faces from the flight crews and ground staff, old-timers who had been with the company as long as Stein, and new men, mechanics who had arrived with Luftwaffe training and were subject to temporary ostracism by the old-timers. There were apprentices as young as Jürgen Steinbrenner, faces that made even Henry look like an old-timer. When the Nazis completed the *Gleichhaltung* of the company, Whitman knew, the old-timers would be retired off, and the youngsters would become the core of military crews, lured with offers and promises that they couldn't refuse.

There was a hubbub at the door. Whitman recognized Anton Lehrmann, the chief radio operator, working his way across the room.

"Captain!" he said. "Sure glad you're back."

Whitman shook his hand, then looked at the bulletin Lehrmann was about to post. It was a short typed order, imposing an indefinite delay in the departure of the Graf Zeppelin due to weather.

"Why?" said Whitman.

"The foehn. Stifel doesn't want to fly in the foehn."

"But it's just begun to blow. If he takes off now, it'll help his crossing. If he waits, it could be two or three days before it's calm enough for a departure. And then it's too late for the vaccine." As he said it he thought of Henry, perched on the hull of the Zeppelin just below the great axial catwalk of the hangar.

"He's the commander," said Lehrmann.

"No!" shouted someone, beginning another round of the chorus: "Stifel won't command!"

Zekner glanced at the weather report, then looked hard at Whitman. "The men are ready to fly when you give the word, sir."

"I'm out," said Whitman. "Dumped, through, scratched, relieved. How many words do you need for it?"

"Not to these men," said Zekner. "You give the word and the ship will be walked out. Once he's out, they can't stop the lift-off. Trying to put him back against this breeze would destroy him."

A quiet settled over the room as one hundred men looked at
Whitman.

"Well, sir?" said Lehrmann.

Fifty-Seven

Crouched on top of the huge airship, the thin rigging wire cutting
into his palms, Henry Whitman found even the voluminous
space of the hangar claustrophobic. The skin of the ship, inches
from his face, smelled of dope, and the smell made him
lightheaded and dizzy. When he turned away for a breath of pure
air, he could smell the cloying sweetness of escaping Blaugas,
rising from the clamshell ventilators on the back of the ship
toward the humming exhaust vents in the ceiling of the hangar.

Everything had gone as Paul said it would—sneaking past the
guard who was hiding from the wind in the shelter of a corner
post of the hangar, climbing shoeless up the tall wooden-treaded
ladder, walking across the narrow catwalk until he was directly
over the access hatch on the back of the ship. He hadn't looked
down, for fear of losing his balance on the railless catwalk, but
now he was beginning to feel the effects of the height. His
fingers ached from the thin wire and his body protested at the
forced crouch. He knew it could be hours more.

He kept wondering what would happen when they found him.
It was no use trying a wild story. One look and they would know
he was the brother of Paul Whitman, and one radio call and they
would know why he was there. But Paul's plan sounded good. If
the wind held, and if he could stay in hiding until they reached
the Mediterranean—no more than twelve hours—the Zeppelin
would no longer be able to turn back. And in Recife, he would
be met by Americans.

He was getting ready to shift his position, to work a cramp out
of one leg, when he heard one of the side doors of the hangar
roll open. Last minute preparations, he guessed. It wouldn't be
so long now before they rolled the ship out.

He heard a cart roll through the doorway, the rubber-tired

wheels rumbling on the floor of the hangar. Then indistinc
voices and the purr of an electric motor, one of the cable hoist
suspended on tracks, under the ceiling of the hangar. H
remembered Paul saying that the electric hoists were never use
during the fueling because of the danger of sparks.

He craned his neck trying to look down, but from his perch h
could see nothing but the vast expanse of fabric leading down o
both sides of the ship, long inviting slopes that concealed a
activity on the floor of the hangar.

"The ballast is nothing but water?" The man's voice echoe
through the hangar like a whisper in the vaults of St. Paul's
"We need a drain."

"Over here, in the floor," came the answer, a woman's voice

With a bolt, Henry realized that they were both speakin
English.

"Is the hose connected?"

"Ready."

"Here it comes."

He heard the sound of water pouring into a drain.

Henry stood up, reaching for the catwalk overhead to stead
himself. The voice of the woman was hauntingly familiar, bu
impossible to place. He hadn't heard much English spoken sinc
he arrived in Germany, except with the team and Paul. And ther
were no women on the sailing team.

He got up, ready to walk aft on the backbone of the ship, the
changed his mind and used his arms to pull himself back up ont
the overhead catwalk so that he could look down at the ship. Th
size of the hull was overwhelming, like the view up at
battleship in drydock. He couldn't see the floor of the hanga
and he realized how far away the voices and the running wate
were. His stocking feet made almost no sound on the meta
catwalk, but he wondered if even the soft footfalls wouldn
somehow echo in the vast space.

The rushing water stopped, and the man's voice asked, "Hav
you got the first load ready on the hook?"

"Ready." Again, the woman's voice. Achingly familiar now
like a voice he had known all his life.

He was finally far enough down the catwalk to see down th
tapered tail of the ship. Just below the tail was a small rubbe
wheeled cart, one of the trolleys he had seen scurrying around th
outside of the hangar with baggage and cargo when he first g
there. Flat wooden crates were piled on the trolley, wrapped wit
cord and hooked to the cable that descended from the ceilin

he woman was bent over the trolley, her back to Henry. Then
he raised her hand, signaling with her thumb up before she
urned to watch the crates ascend.

Henry ducked, but not before her eyes caught his.

Maggie!

She took two steps to the side, pinning him in her gaze. The
ook on her face was not so much surprise as confession, a mask
aat dropped in place when she had been caught *in flagrante
elicto*. He started to shout to her, then caught himself when he
eard the winch start again and the man spoke to her.

As the hook came down, she busied herself with the crates.
hen she looked up again, this time with her finger held up to
er lips and a grin in her eyes. She winked, as if to acknowledge
secret that they shared.

Then he saw an unfamiliar man, working with what looked
ke a heavy crate. He suddenly wondered about his taciturn and
ysterious brother. Maybe Paul was not so straight. Maybe he
as doing more with the Graf Zeppelin than he let on.

Nothing was what it seemed anymore . . .

Part IV

Recife

Fifty-Eight

Stifel shrugged his shoulders, letting the jacket settle onto his frame. It was snug, but a glance down at the shoulders with their old stripes and he didn't mind the fit. He reached up to the hat, handling the scrambled eggs of braid on the visor. At least he knew how to wear a hat, he told himself. He knew how to conduct himself as a commander.

The foehn-blown sky was a lucid deep blue, and the light from the stars and moon was the only illumination on the tarmac. With the departure postponed, the runway lights were out, the hangar doors shut, the ground crews nowhere to be seen. The field was eerily quiet. He knew he had plenty of time to move his gear into the captain's cabin, and he looked forward to the quiet time alone on the Zeppelin. The delay of a day or two wasn't enough time for what he really wanted, which was to get the Zeppelin Company joiners to repanel the captain's cabin with lighter woods. It was details like that, the details that could make the Graf Zeppelin into a first-class command.

Stifel was in the middle of the tarmac when the doors of the hangar began to swing open, like the cover of a giant cocoon. Why? he wondered. He hadn't looked at the maintenance procedure charts, but he couldn't remember anything that would require opening the doors.

Inside, the Zeppelin was poised in stillness, a giant chrysalis. Then, with moonlight shimmering off the silvery skin, the Zeppelin turned into an enormous metallic caterpillar, its legs the dozens of men holding the restraining ropes along both sides of the hull. Two towing tractors came out like friendly beetles to lead their gigantic friend, and almost imperceptibly, the great caterpillar began to move, poking its nose gently into the world outside, gradually straining at its slender legs as the ground handlers walked the ship out into the clear evening air.

When the end of the gondola cleared the hangar doors, the

propeller of the wind-driven main generator began to spin, an
the ship seemed to come alive, lights in the windows glowin
like phosphorescent spots. For an instant, Stifel thought the gia
caterpillar would turn into a butterfly before it flew away.

Then he panicked, running toward the ship until he found th
chief of the ground crew giving arm signals from under the nose

"What's going on?" shouted Stifel. "Why is the Zeppeli
being walked out?"

No one answered him as the ship continued its steady march

"Who ordered this?" he shouted. "Who gave the order?"

"The commander, sir," said the ground chief.

"I am the commander."

The ground chief grinned, then nodded toward the windows
the control room. Stifel looked up and saw the face of Pa
Whitman, hatless, looking down at him from the ship.

Whitman turned from Stifel to look around the control roon
Stein was at the elevator wheel, his legs braced, scanning th
dials in front of him. He looked old and tired. Sweat alread
stained his shirt, and his hands trembled. When he notice
Whitman watching him, he quickly put both hands on the whee
clamping down to stop the palsy.

Across from him, the engineer surveyed his control panel
pretending it was just one more routine flight. But the exciteme
in the control room was impossible to ignore. The men responde
to one another with a crackling quickness, without a trace of th
bored familiarity that a summer of routine flights had bred.

Everything had happened quickly. Paul Whitman had go
from the commissary to the telephones in the deserted passeng
lounge. The call to neighboring Zurich was easy to place. Ther
was still no trace of a Frau or Fräulein Bourne at the Zürich
Hof. This time he pressed the clerk with a description: "A
attractive woman, brownish auburn hair, a warm smile." Th
rest of the image was vivid to Paul—the laughing eyes, th
toothy smiles that grew out of grins—but it meant nothing to th
clerk. Then Paul mentioned that she might be wearing a twee
jacket. The clerk paused, the silence of recognition.

"She left no messages and no forwarding address," he said
his haughtiest *Hochdeutsch*. "*Mrs*. Sinclair left early this morn
ing with her husband. They were in a hurry."

Whitman forced himself not to think. He went straight back
the commissary, losing himself in the flurry of orders, drawin

ose to the crew as they began to function as a team, methodi-
l, thorough, flawless.

The stewards brought the passengers back from the Kurgarten
otel, where they had been taken after the indefinite delay was
nounced. They were hustled through the empty customs and
migration shed and boarded inside the hangar.

The bosun recovered the vaccine, which had already been
crated for shipment back to the Höchst Laboratories. It was
aded directly into the Zeppelin's refrigerators, while the me-
anics and riggers went about their final tasks, working through
e checklists that had to be completed before the ship could
part. And all the while, the wind blew, not strong yet, but
lentless, hot enough to turn mouths dry, eyes wet, tempers to
der.

Whitman remembered a takeoff from Los Angeles, years
fore, when the Macon had the advantages of semiautomated
ound handling equipment and a massive mooring pylon with a
rcular track for the tail that let the ship swing to face the wind.
a breeze of little more than fifteen knots, the American ground
ews had botched it, leaving the ship with a smashed-up tail.
e vulnerability of the American airship in that wind had
elled part of the beginning of the end for American airships.
nd the wind outside at Friedrichshafen was blowing almost
ice as hard. But, Paul told himself, Zeppelin men were
fferent. They knew that machine so well they could all but
al it from under the eyes of the Zeppelin Company.

"Sir?"

The steward waited for Whitman to turn from the window.

"The passengers boarded without a hitch, sir. That German
rty of six left the Kurgarten when the delay was first an-
unced, so there's plenty of room. The Brazilian ambassador
as a little upset about having to walk through the hangar floor
here it was wet—I guess they must have overfilled some of the
llast tanks—but everyone has settled into the cabins now."

"The last-minute passengers . . . ?" asked Whitman.

"They're just fine, sir. Lovely people, the Huttens. And I had
idea that . . ."

Suddenly the floodlights on the tarmac flashed on, surrounding
e ship.

"RETURN THE SHIP TO HANGAR. THE DEPARTURE
AS BEEN POSTPONED. THE SHIP MUST GO BACK INTO
IE HANGAR."

Whitman heard the blare of the electronic megaphone before

he saw Hempe and Stifel together, waving frantically to attrac
his attention.

The chief of the ground crew answered Hempe after th
towing tractors had been disconnected from the Zeppelin. "Si
we can't walk him back, not in this wind. If we tried to take hir
in against the wind, it'd destroy him. The wind would swing th
tail around and smash it against the hangar doors."

"There was no order for this departure," shouted Stifel. "
specifically . . ."

"The commander, sir," said the chief, grinning again as h
pointed up to the windows of the control room above them.

"*I* am the Commander," said Stifel.

The chief looked up at Whitman, then crisscrossed his arm
over his head, signaling that the ship was clear of the hangar.

Whitman stared at Stifel and Hempe as he began the fina
check sequence.

"Control check, up elevator!"

"Up," repeated Stein, swinging the wheel aft.

"Elevator up," came the distant voice on the intercom, from
man stationed in the auxiliary steering station at the tail of th
ship.

"Down elevator!"

"Down." The wheel swung back.

"Elevator down."

As he went through the rest of the checks, Whitman kept hi
eyes on the men and the gauges, avoiding the windows and th
floodlit tarmac.

"Altimeter?"

"Calibrated," said the navigator. "Pressure nine-eight-eigl
millibars."

"Nine-eight-eight?" said Whitman. "How much gas are w
carrying?"

"Overpressure," said the engineer. "And we've got fiftee
hundred kilos of extra ballast to hold it down. That's why you
passengers got wet feet."

"Fuel?"

"Full load. All cells topped. Normal leakage from cells thre
and thirteen. Never get those down to zero anymore. The othe
are tight."

"Batteries?"

"Full charge. In this wind we're generating full power ju.
sitting here."

"Gyro?"

"Power on. She'll settle in a minute or two."

"Anemometer?"

"Steady sixteen knots, sir. Gusting to twenty-four. Could be thirty-five or more aloft."

"Standby the mooring lines!"

Outside on the tarmac Hempe and Stifel were running up and down the rows of ground handlers, shouting. They avoided looking up at Whitman, as if by not acknowledging him they would somehow make him disappear.

"ANY MAN WHO RELEASES THIS SHIP WILL BE SEVERELY PUNISHED!" shouted Hempe. His voice was high and shaky. The manicured and polished man seemed unable to direct his anger, and his ample flesh shook ludicrously as he ran up and down the rows of men.

"DEFLATE THE SHIP!" he shouted, this time at the ground chief. "RELEASE ENOUGH HYDROGEN TO LESSEN THE BUOYANCY SO THE SHIP CAN BE WALKED BACK INTO THE HANGAR."

From behind him, a gravelly voice boomed out: "You can't deflate the ship. Without buoyancy it would collapse into a heap on the ground."

It was Hugo Eckener, holding an unlit cigar, his jacket covered with cigar ashes as he stood staring up at the ship he had made into the most famous aircraft in the world.

Hempe glanced at Eckener, then back at the Graf Zeppelin. He knew next to nothing about airships. He could give orders, but he couldn't challenge the knowledge of Eckener.

Raising the megaphone again, he shouted: "ANY MAN WHO RELEASES HIS LINE WILL BE SEVERELY PUNISHED! THE SHIP IS NOT TO BE RELEASED! THAT IS A DIRECT ORDER!"

The chief, directly below Whitman's starboard window in the control room, looked up at the commander in the window, waiting for the two most exciting words of the Zeppelin lexicon, the words that would signal freedom for the ship.

"...DIRECT ORDER...SEVERELY PUNISHED..." repeated Hempe's chirping voice. "THE SHIP IS NOT TO BE RELEASED."

Whitman waited for a pause in the shouts before he leaned out the open, downward-sloping window. Hempe looked up, eye meeting eye.

"Schiff auf!" commanded Whitman. Ship up. It was a ringing

command to Zeppelin men, like the umpire's "Play Ball!" or the report of the starter's gun.

The chief raised his arm. He glanced at Hempe, who held the megaphone away from his face, frozen in the realization that there was nothing he could do. Then he turned to face Eckener.

Ashes swirled off the old man's coat, and his hair stood on end as the wind blew under his clothes, making his already corpulent figure a mimic of the Zeppelin. He caught the young American commander's eyes with his own. Then, without a smile or a nod, he raised his right hand, extending the thumb upward.

The chief's arm fell, and men up and down the sides of the Zeppelin released the restraining ropes.

The Zeppelin lifted slowly from the ground, moving up so gently it was as if an autumn leaf could magically float up instead of down.

A single quiet cheer went up in the control room, like a collective sigh.

Ballast was released a moment later, delayed just long enough to miss the men on the ground, and the ship began to rise more quickly. It was still floating, its engines not running yet, the only sign of life the whirling blades of the wind-driven generator at the aft end of the gondola.

Below the ship, the lights of Friedrichshafen were a random grill of dim flickers. Out on the lake, where the moonlight turned the wind-shipped water into shimmering silver, the running lights of the Romanshorn ferry stood out like rubies and emeralds among the diamond whitecaps.

Whitman stood behind Stein for the weigh-off, glancing over his shoulder at the inclinometer.

"Stern down," said Stein. "Four degrees. Could be under pressure in one of the aft cells."

"What was the final gas loading?" Whitman asked the engineer behind him.

"All cells fully pressurized. With that low from the foehn, we were able to pump them tight."

"What about the stern breeches—could they be overloaded?"

"The ballast loading was checked before fueling, sir."

"Right," said Whitman. "Release ballast, station nine, four hundred kilos."

Stein reached up, pulled a toggle above him, then watched the inclinometer level off, slip slightly forward, and finally correct itself.

"Weigh-off complete," said Whitman. "Start all engines."

The telegraph flashed, answering lights came on above them,
d outside the ship the great propellers slowly began to whirl.
side the control room there was no roar, not even a murmur.
til the speed indicator dials began to record the forward
ogress of the ship, the only sign that the great engines were
nning were the lights on the control panel.

"Rudderman, steer two-four-seven," said Whitman.

"Two-four-seven, sir."

"Stein, take him up to five hundred meters."

"Five hundred meters, sir."

The bow of the ship rose gently as Stein swung the wheel aft.
 last the Graf Zeppelin was flying on its own, taking command
 the air instead of drifting. The bow swung around to face the
ad of Lake Constance.

There was only the slightest hint of acceleration, more like a
ip gradually picking up power as it comes away from the dock
an an aircraft taking off. When the turn was complete, Whitman
id, "All engines ahead standard." He waited for the soft clank
 the telegraphs, then turned back to Lehrmann.

"As soon as we reach antenna height, file our flight plan with
iedrichshafen. Standard course—Rhine Valley, over France to
 e Mediterranean, then across the Straits. You can radio Lyon
 rectly to confirm overflight permission. And if you can get
 rough, send the same flight plan to the Hamburg Network
 erator and the Condor Syndicate Network in Buenos Aires.
 nd try to pick up the British and American weather reports."

Lehrmann asked, "Do we really need to notify Friedrichshafen?"

"This is a scheduled flight," said Whitman. "We follow all
utine procedures."

Lehrmann barely concealed his grin as he walked back to the
dio room.

Fifty-Nine

 n the map, it was only a lake, twelve miles wide at its broadest
 int. On the ferry, with the wind smashing waves over the blunt

bow and whipping cold spray across the decks, it felt like t
North Atlantic on the off-season.

Somehow, Orlov controlled his stomach, no easy task whe
the rails were lined with the queasy and the lounge crowded wi
the tail end of the queues from the WC. He had fought off t
nausea because he was preoccupied with his quest.

Sinclair had almost gotten away. Orlov's smugness had let t
American slip away in Zurich. And after a day of searching t
banks, and finding that Sinclair had not gone to the railro
station or the airport, Orlov had been desperate. It wasn't un
late afternoon, when he received a call from the Swiss bord
police—another of those courtesies the Swiss were so gracio
about extending—that Orlov discovered that Sinclair had tak
the unlikely route of driving north into Germany. It was pu
luck. A customs man who had not received an expected bri
from a smuggling agent had reported the crossing.

Orlov followed in a hired car. Germany? he wondered.
Sinclair's place he would have gone to Italy, to Lugano, whe
there were still bankers who would perform transactions
different from what the Swiss had always done, transactions wi
no questions asked. Mussolini needed the Lugano bankers for h
own dealings, and he left them unrestricted, available for anyo
else to use.

But Germany? It would be hard to pick a more inhospitab
place, crawling with suspicious Gestapo and criminal polic
Hitler needed hard currency, and the Germans would never allo
an exchange of bullion at a useful rate. There was no blac
market worth trying, unless Sinclair had a way to get fro
Germany to Beirut or maybe Istanbul. With Sinclair anythi
was possible. But why would he come to this wretched flat litt
town, nothing but a few low factories, the hangars, and t
dreary lakeside rooming houses for absurd Germans who came
wade in the water with their trousers rolled up?

As the ferry eased into the slip, the engines reversed with
roar, tossing up a powerful turbulence in the water that slowe
the heavy boat with a shudder.

Before the boat was tied up, heads all over the deck we
canted up, watching the spectacle overhead. The Zeppelin wa
low enough for individual lights to show in the windows of t
gondola, and for the huge red, white, and black swastika on t
tail to be plainly visible. It floated serenely against the deep bl
of the sky, accentuating the vulnerability of the ferry that ha
labored against the wind and waves on the lake.

"Always on time," said one passenger, glancing at his watch.
"Never a problem. No matter what, the Graf Zeppelin is always
time. The one thing you can depend on in this crazy world."

The dry foehn tore into Orlov's eyes and throat as he followed
craning heads on the bow of the ferry. It was hard not to envy
comfort of the passengers in the Zeppelin, and harder still to
ignore the awe everyone on the ferry seemed to feel toward that
masterpiece of German engineering. A people who could produce such a machine, it seemed, would be excused their excesses.
The Russians might give money and men to aid the Spanish
Republic, but that brought no awe or respect for the Soviet
Union. It was the building of machines that inspired awe.

"Where is it going?" Orlov asked, to no one in particular.

Heads swung to stare at the man who had asked such a naive
question. How could anyone not know where the Graf Zeppelin
is going?

Someone pointed out a poster on the wall inside the ferry
cabin, a rich azure sky shading down to green water surrounding
a rocky tropical island, studded with palm trees, the Zeppelin
floating magnificently overhead. *In 3 Tagen Nach Sud Amerika!*
read the caption at the bottom of the poster. In three days to
South America!

Orlov's jaw dropped. His stomach rushed up into his mouth.
South America. Three days!

He pushed and jostled his way to the head of the line of
passengers waiting to disembark, provoking complaints and
rude comments from the patient Swiss and German passengers.
As soon as he cleared customs on his diplomatic passport, he
hailed a taxi.

"Take me to the Zeppelin field."

"You're too late, sir." The driver pointed up to the receding
shape in the western sky.

"Hurry!" said Orlov.

He spotted the Marseilles license code on Sinclair's van as
soon as they pulled into the visitor's parking lot. He turned from
the van to look up at the sky. Dim blinking lights were all he
could see of the Zeppelin as it flew off toward the west.

Orlov knew he was finished. There was nothing he could do,
no way to catch up with Sinclair without admitting what had
happened. In seven days, the freighters would dock in Odessa.
The crates would be unloaded and stacked on the docks, surrounded
by armed soldiers while a count was made. The tally would go to
Moscow, ahead of the crates, and it would be compared with the

official count that he had signed in Spain. As soon as
discrepancy was noted, Orlov would receive official notificat
asking him to return to Moscow by the fastest available transp
tation, probably by air. He would never leave the Soviet Uni
again.

If he was lucky, he would be sent to an obscure labor facil
a lumber camp maybe, or a coal mine. His fate would
production schedules, quotas, vodka and loneliness—*if* he w
lucky and the discrepancy was considered minor. But 1.
kilograms of gold was not minor.

How did Sinclair do it? he wondered. How could he ge
German Zeppelin company to transport it? If one was to belie
what he wrote, the man hated the Germans more than he ha
the Russians. No, thought Orlov, Sinclair didn't deal with
Germans. He was too clever for that. He was clever eno
to . . .

What did it matter? No explanation would help. In the pu
trials, they expected only confessions, not explanations. Th
were no pleas of innocence, no extenuating circumstanc
Treason was treason, whether by Zinoviev and Kamenev, or
Orlov. And the punishment was always the same: *oblivion*.

Unless . . .

He looked around the promenade that bordered the win
whipped lake, lined by tiny, quaint rooming houses. It was
so very different from the Black Sea, not such a terrible pla
after all. With the right arrangements, a man could live well
Germany. After all, he was not a Gypsy or a Jew. He was a m
with information. Even the Germans respected information.

Sixty

Whitman couldn't remember seeing the chief rigger smile
fore. He was a gruff man who usually seemed oblivious to jo
and kidding.

He intercepted Whitman in the corridor aft of the chart hou

This is an unusual flight, sir," he said. "But we never pected . . ."

Whitman knew immediately. "You found him," he said. How?"

"Humming, sir."

"Humming?"

"That's right. One of the riggers was monitoring the fuel leak the number thirteen cell. We never trust those electronic onitors. The safest bet is to get back there and sniff. When he ent down the axial catwalk—this was just before lift-off—he ard a humming noise from somewhere up the main vent shaft. thought it was maybe loose fabric, or the hatch not secured operly, so he started up the shaft. That's when he heard the pping and he came to get me.

"I know it sounds crazy, sir, but the men are superstitious. ey talk about poltergeists in the ship. Once they start that kind talk, I know I have to investigate myself. So I scrambled up at vent shaft, and what do I find but the spitting image of urself, in civvy clothes, sitting there plain as day on the hatch atform, humming away and tapping his foot to the music like doesn't have a care in the world.

"He came right down with me, and I took him into the crew arters. When I told him you were in command, he got real gry, said that you tricked him and that he could have bought a ket just like anyone else. Guess he's a real prankster, that one. ght now he's telling stories about the Olympic Games to the -duty crew. Says he actually ate dinner with Jesse Owens on ship coming over to Germany. Can you beat that, sir? Ate nner with Jesse Owens himself."

Men had begun to gather around the two of them. Whitman sn't sure how to react until he saw the smiles on all sides.

"We were talking, sir," said the steward. "And the men seem feel that it might not be a good idea if . . . well, since he does k so much like yourself, we were thinking that it might not be good idea if he was to move into the passenger cabins. Could use some misunderstandings, you know. We were thinking that could just stay in the crew quarters and share a hammock with rest of us. If that's all right with you, sir. Except that if he eps telling stories of the Olympic Games, the men may not get ch sleep."

Whitman grinned. "I'll be up to see him later," he said. Ve'll see how much truth there is in those stories of his."

Whitman felt so light-headed he had to compose hims
before he went into the passenger lounge. Just flying t
machine did it to him, and now he was soaring higher than
Zeppelin. He had made his own circumstances.

He paused at the binocular rack, restraining his grin as
picked up the commander's cap. After the drama of the lift-o
the passengers on the Graf Zeppelin would expect a sober a
thoughtful commander.

He stuck his head into the radio cabin on his way aft. "A
reply to our flight plan?"

"They acknowledged with *Flight Plan Received*," said Le
mann. "Nothing else. I guess we're just one more routine flig
following our course and schedule."

"They may have another response in due course."

"Like what, sir?"

"Maybe orders to land at Frankfurt."

"But a detour to Frankfurt would throw us off schedule. T
vaccine shipment will be worthless after ninety-six hours. The
are warning labels all over it."

"Then we may have to reject the suggestion of a detour."
Lehrmann smiled.

"It may not be that funny," said Whitman.

"Actually, sir, I was just thinking how much I would ha
liked to see the expression on Stifel's face when . . . if he h
been in command when your brother showed up."

Whitman could not abort his own smile. It was hard
imagine a finer group of men than the crew of the Zeppelin.

Paul saw her from the doorway, as soon as he opened the do
to the passenger lounge. His gut twisted into a knot.

She was sitting at the aft table on the starboard side of
lounge—the admiral's old table—looking out the window at
panorama of lights along the river valley below. She looked
when the other passengers stirred at Whitman's entrance, and
eyes caught his. There was no smile, only a dry, expressionle
gaze that he couldn't read. He started to walk over to her, th
hesitated, unsure of his feelings, afraid to surprise himself.

A man was at her table, his back to Whitman. He turned wh
she looked up, twisting around in his chair so that Whitman co
see his blond beard and narrow, deep-set eyes. She had ne
described him, but Whitman knew this man was her husband

Why? he asked himself. If she wanted to disappear from
life without explanation, that was her choice. She was marri

had admitted it. And she had a right to be angry after the
pections and interrogations or whatever the *Sicherheitsdienst*
put her through to get those photographs. But Maggie wasn't
to be scared by them. And why did she have to come on the
af Zeppelin? Three days to Recife, four to Rio. He would be
the passenger lounge at least once each day. It would be
possible to avoid her. Why?

Every eye in the room, it seemed, was on him, but he was
rcely focusing. He heard his name, looked down, and recog-
ed Otto Hutten, smiling broadly. Anna was sitting next to him,
arm on his, with her own warm smile. Whitman sensed a
mmer of a question in their eyes. A few days before, Maggie
been Fräulein Bourne to the Huttens, Whitman's friend. Now,
was Mrs. Someone or Other, another American woman
veling with her husband. Who would explain it to them?

With all eyes on him, Whitman began an explanation of their
ty departure from Friedrichshafen, losing himself in the dry
k of the weather and their planned course down to the
diterranean, through the Straits of Gibraltar and out across the
antic. He explained that the Graf Zeppelin was carrying the
cial vaccine for the epidemic in northeast Brazil, and how
ud he and the rest of the crew were that they were flying this
pment that only the Graf Zeppelin could deliver in time. He
ieved what he said, but the words seemed stale. When he
ished he quickly excused himself, saying that it was late and
t the passengers were surely interested in dinner. His abrupt
parture from the lounge cut off both questions and complaints.

When he got back to the control room, he relieved Zekner,
ing the watch himself. If tradition hadn't ruled it out, he
uld have taken the helm as well, just to lose himself in the
ing of the Zeppelin.

Sixty-One

Vhy don't you *do* something? Are you just going to treat it as a
rmal flight?'' Stifel leaned over the desk in Hempe's office,

pointing down at the flight plan that had been filed by the G
Zeppelin. He was a big man, heavily built, and with expansi
jowls that shook like baby fat when he whined.

Hempe tapped his polished fingernails on the desktop. "A
just what do you propose I do?" he asked

"Order them to Frankfurt. Order them to land at Frankfurt.

"Do you really think Whitman would heed such an order? N
everyone is as eager to please as you, Stifel."

Hempe took out a cigar and fondled it, almost mocking
gruff manner of Hugo Eckener, who all but devoured his che
cheroots.

"In fact," he said, holding a light to the tip of the cigar, "i
hard not to admire Whitman. There is more to the man than t
test pilot front he puts on. I think he really does believe all th
big words, like *honor* and *duty*."

"Send airplanes to escort them back," said Stifel. "*For*
them to land."

Hempe waved the cigar, as if he were brushing away a fly.

"Don't be asinine, Stifel. We can't send airplanes to interce
them in France. And Whitman knows that. No..." He let
chair swing around until it faced the large map of the world
the wall behind his desk.

"With the whole world looking, I think we may have to ju
announce the departure of our mission of mercy to Brazil. It m
be a real credit to the Zeppelin Company that one of c
commanders was willing to lift-off in a foehn to deliver th
vaccine to the needy poor of South America. Ironic, isn't
Stifel? Commander Whitman may end up a hero after all."

"But the command was to be mine," whined Stifel.

"*Yours*, Gunner Stifel?"

The phone buzzed once, quietly. Hempe picked it up befc
the end of the buzz. He stood behind his desk to speak, snappi
off an alert "*Jawohl!*" at intervals. He was no longer smili
when he replaced the receiver.

With a scowl, he dismissed Stifel, then sat down at the de
nervously passing a few minutes until the door of his offi
opened and Kutner appeared with another *Sicherheitsdienst* ag
in a baggy gray suit. A heavy-set, flat-faced man stood betwe
the two agents.

"This is Herr Gregory Orlov," said Kutner, "formerly of
NKVD. He has some interesting information for us."

Sixty-Two

Whitman let Zekner relieve him at midnight. There had still been no message from Zeppelin headquarters except the terse acknowledgements of their position reports, and he left word with the radioman that he was to be awakened immediately if there were any messages regarding their course to Brazil.

At the top of the ladderway leading from the control room, he walked past his own cabin and the officers' cabins to the crew quarters. It was unprecedented for a commander to enter the crew quarters except in unusual circumstances—another of those barriers of rank that were so important to the Germans—but there was no other way he could see Henry. He rapped lightly on the frame members that outlined the doorway to the hammock-strewn space.

"Captain!" acknowledged a crewman, surprised but not unfriendly.

"Paul!" Henry was astraddle a lower hammock, looking very relaxed. "We've decided that Jesse Owens will take a fourth gold medal in the relay. None of them will believe me when I say that he's actually a very reserved and modest fellow, even if he is the fastest man on earth."

Paul gestured for permission to enter the crew quarters, then sat down on another of the hammocks. "Go on," he said. "Don't let me stop you."

A few men tried to keep the conversation going, but years of tradition could not be erased in an instant. Even Henry sensed the barriers, and when other men drifted off, leaving the two of them alone, he pointed to the corridor outside where they could talk in privacy.

"Welcome aboard," said Paul.

"What the hell is going on?" asked Henry. "Whenever I ask anyone how you ended up back in command, they answer with silly grins. Someone would think you had stolen this monster."

"That's pretty close," said Paul. "Let's just say that you had

355

better appreciate that you're flying with the finest group of me ever assembled on a ship.''

Henry laughed. "I know it's natural to you," he said, "but can't help laughing when I think about ships flying." He turne and looked straight at his brother. "What about Maggie?" h asked.

"What about her?"

"Come on, Paul. What's going on? I saw her when I wa waiting in the hangar. She was back at the stern of the ship. I ge the feeling that you're some kind of Pied Piper, and we're a stringing along."

Paul shrugged, looking away for an instant. His voice brok when he answered. "Maggie's her own woman. She was proba bly sneaking a photograph. I told her it wasn't easy to ge permission to photograph the ship. She and her husband are bot journalists. I guess this is their new story."

"I don't think so. What happened to you and her?"

"Why don't you ask her yourself when we land at Recife Who knows, once she finds out what you're doing here, yo could end up the hero of the story. Photos and all."

"Whew! Never heard you so bitter before. You two are reall through, huh? I'm sorry."

"Nothing to be sorry about. I guess it serves me right fc messing around with a married woman." Paul tapped his knuck les against the filigree framework of the ship.

"I guess if I stay loyal to this old ship," he said, "I can really blame her for staying loyal." He tried to smile, the hugged his brother and turned for his own cabin.

When he got there, Lehrmann was standing outside the door, message blank in his hand.

"Still on duty?" asked Whitman. "I think we both need son sleep."

"I was just listening for the late British weather bulletins, si when this came in." He handed the blank, with its neatly printe block letter message, to Whitman.

DEUTSCHE ZEPPELIN REEDEREI F'HAFEN. DENNE, LZ-127 GRA ZEPPELIN, EN ROUTE RECIFE DE PERNAMBUCO. URGENT. HÖCHS VACCINE SHIPMENT DEFECTIVE. NEW VACCINE TO BE FLOW VIA LUFTHANSA COURIER PLANE TO SEVILLE SPAIN FOR PICI UP BY LZ-127. FLYOVER PRIVILEGES CLEARED WITH SPANIS GOVERNMENT. REPEAT. URGENT. ACKNOWLEDGE COURS CHANGE IMMEDIATELY.

"Do you believe it?" asked Lehrmann when Whitman looked
up.

Without answering, Whitman led the way down the steep
adderway to the chart house. He leaned over the chart table and
used the parallel rules and divider to plot off the course for
Seville. To avoid crossing the Sierra Nevada, they would have to
follow the coast as far as Málaga, then swing through the
mountains and up the valley of the Guadalcivir into Seville. It
would mean a delay of over half a day, even if they could do a
pickup by lowered hoist instead of touching down to transfer
packages.

"What do you think?" Whitman asked Zekner.

The junior watch officer read through the message and handed
back.

"I think it's a trick. Stifel would come up with a stunt like
that. And Hempe would have to back him. I'll bet the only thing
waiting there is Stifel himself."

"Can you reach Höchst Laboratories directly?" Whitman
asked Lehrmann.

"It may take a while. I have to go through the Hamburg Net."

"I still think it's a trick," said Zekner. "They had a week to
repare the vaccine. Why would they discover a mistake only
after we left?"

Whitman glanced out the window of the chart house. They
were approaching the Mediterranean, close enough to the coast
of France for him to recognize the loom of the lights of the shore
towns.

"If that vaccine is no good, we have no choice," he said.

He stared out the window for a minute longer, then leaned into
the radio cabin. "Can you get a message off to Friedrichshafen
telling them their message was garbled and made no sense?"

Lehrmann looked up, smiling. "Yes, sir."

From the corner of his eye, Whitman saw Zekner's smile.
"You're doing the right thing, Captain."

It was almost half an hour later when Lehrmann came forward
with two message blanks.

"Friedrichshafen sent a repeat of the first message. The only
change was to put another *urgent* in it."

"Did anything come through from the Höchst Labs?"

Lehrmann handed over the blank. "It's gobbledy-gook to
me."

Whitman read through the medical terms. It sounded authentic, but all jargon sounded authentic to the uninitiated. "Is ther anyone on board who would know what this means?"

Zekner volunteered. "There's a physician traveling with th Brazilian ambassador, a member of his staff."

"Is he Brazilian?"

Whitman smiled at Zekner's nod.

Whitman found Doctor Altschul in the lounge. He was a elegant man, with a vested suit, a goatee, gold-rimmed hal glasses, and a large gold caduceus—the serpent and staff of th physician—in his lapel. When Whitman addressed him in haltin Portuguese, the doctor answered in fluent German. "I wa educated in Germany," he explained. "At Göttingen."

Whitman showed him the message from the Höchst Labs.

Altschul read the blank with half-glasses perched well dow on his nose.

"What does it mean?" asked Whitman when the docto looked up.

"It couldn't be clearer, commander. There has been an erro in the match-typing of the vaccine."

"Could it be true?"

"Commander! This message is from the Höchst Laboratories Surely you are not questioning the expertise of one of the fines medical laboratories in Germany."

"Does what they say about the vaccine make sense?"

"Of course. In making a vaccine the exact strains of bacillu must be matched or the vaccine will be invalid. The Germans ar world leaders in the technology, especially Höchst." He looke up, weary of the simplified explanations for a layman. "Is ther anything else you wish to know?"

"No, and thank you." As Whitman walked back to th control room, a sentence of the doctor's played over and over i his mind. "The Germans are world leaders in the technology." I was true of the Zeppelin too, and the Zeppelins were alread under the thumb of the Nazis.

But he knew he had no choice.

Sixty-Three

nclair woke Maggie early. The Zeppelin was flying a few miles
rth of Minorca, close enough for him to be able to point out
e huge harbor at Mahón and the serpentine inlet at Ciudadela.
e described the cove at Cala Morell and the grotto where they
d hidden the boat, and pointed out the approximate locations
the barren rocky island. Before they went ou* *o the lounge
r breakfast, he had recounted the whole bone-shaking two days
had spent in the open boat on the sea below.

He told the tale well, but his story did not have the effect he
ticipated. He hoped that hearing the saga and seeing where it
d happened would reawaken in Margaret the feelings he had
en in her eyes and heard in her voice that first day in Zurich.
e waited for her to smile and open up to him. Yet no matter
w often he hinted at the grandness and boldness of what he
d done, or the dangers and excitement of his scheme, Margaret's
sponse remained cool and formal. She seemed barely to toler-
e Sinclair, putting up with his presence as if they were reluctant
rtners in a business enterprise. She seemed further from him
an she had been in San Francisco, and at night it was worse.
e dressed and undressed with a modesty he had never seen
fore, flinching every time he so much as brushed against her.
e effect was more chilling than if she had just walked away.

He said little in the lounge after breakfast, consciously avoiding
y mention of Whitman. Time would change it all, he thought.
time Maggie would realize that her dashing captain was only
ing the Germans' bidding. She would realize what really
attered, who was really doing something.

Just after lunch they could see Cartagena through the starboard
ndows. Sinclair pointed it out, eager to resume his tale.
aggie glanced down for a moment and then asked, "Could we
back to the cabin?"

Inside the doorway, Sinclair pulled her close to him, kissing
r hard on the lips.

She didn't resist, but she didn't respond either.

"What is it with you?" he said, pushing her away. "You sa
you want to come back here, then you act as if I were a strange
You're still my wife, Margaret, remember? It's because of y
that I—"

"When do we tell him?" Maggie asked.

"When the time comes. From what you said, nothing is goi
to happen to that emergency ballast in flight. And the less
knows, the better."

"I want to talk to him," she said.

"Him?"

"Paul. I want to talk to Paul."

Sinclair laughed. "You can talk to him whenever you want.
he gets up the courage to come back into the lounge again, yo
can talk until you're blue in the face. If last night was a
indication, I don't think you'll find the conversation ve
scintillating."

"Alone, David. I want to talk to him alone."

"I don't think that's a good idea," he said.

"What makes you so sure he'll help us?"

"Oh, he'll do it, Margaret. The wrong reasons, but he'll do
Didn't you see that look on his face? The cool voice? And th
nonsense about the photographs you told me before—it's all
setup for you. He knows that little Margaret likes her heroe
And you're too blind to see him for what he really is."

"I don't believe that," she said. "I don't know what
happening or why he's flying the Graf Zeppelin, but I know he
not that kind of man. I want to know from him what he's doi
and why."

Sinclair laughed. "Ask him anything you want, Margaret. Ju
remember that I'll be there. Until we land, you aren't leaving n
sight."

He watched as she turned to face him, her face void
emotion.

"I love you, Margaret. What will it take to convince you
that? What do I have to do?"

He waited for her to answer, but she said nothing, and
followed her eyes to the window. The Zeppelin had crossed t
coast of Spain and begun to fly over land. He watched for a fe
minutes, expecting the ship to turn back to the Mediterranean,
perhaps for Gibraltar to appear, but below them was only the f
fields of Andalusia, stretched out in vast *latifundia*.

He pointed it out for her.

"Another scene of your glories?" She refused to look.

"No. But I think flyboy has some surprise in store for us. This n't the way to Gibraltar." He rummaged in his flight bag. "If e tries anything . . . I'll . . ."

"You'll what?" said Maggie. "Paul's not the enemy. He's our nly hope. If you really care about Spain and getting those irplanes, you need him. We need him. When are you going to ealize that?"

Sinclair stared at her, listening to the words. Then he turned ack to the window and the flat fields below.

Sixty-Four

Whitman took command again when they crossed the coast, elow Málaga. They flew a dead reckoning course from the oastline to the valley of the Guadalcivir, which they would ollow up to Seville.

They had just reached the river when the rudderman spotted two irplanes coming toward the Zeppelin. In a moment, they were so lose that everyone in the control room could make out the nmistakable outline of the new Messerschmitt 109 fighters with eir black wingtip markings. The two planes split when they were vithin a few hundred yards of the Graf Zeppelin, one diving below nd the other peeling off in a sharp Immelmann over the bow.

"What the hell?" said Whitman. He was into the radio cabin a two steps.

Lehrmann looked up, the headset cocked over one ear. "They're n escort," he said. "One pilot says we're the prettiest sight he's ver seen. He keeps trying to tell the other one about the eppelin. Must be an old-timer, he remembers seeing the ship ears ago, when he was still buff colored."

Lehrmann grimaced, shaking his head with incomprehension. My God! The men they have flying those planes. The other ilot is a kid. Never seen a Zeppelin before. The only thing he ays is that it's vulnerable, that a single burst from his cannon ould bring it down." He peeled off the earphones, offering them to Whitman. "What kind of men do they recruit for thos planes? Talking of destroying the Zeppelin . . . ?"

Whitman waved away the headset. "Tell them to keep clear They're endangering the Zeppelin by flying so close. And the get the airdrome in Seville and see if there's an old-timer there who still remembers when the Zeppelin landed there in 1929. I would be a good idea to have at least one person on the groun who knows what he's doing."

He stepped outside to the chart house, looking down at the plot of their course.

"May I?" he said to the navigator as he took the dividers an measured off the distance to the landing field. It was slightly mor than thirty kilometers, less than one-half hour of flying time.

Lehrmann came forward and pointed out the window to th two Messerschmitts, coming back for another pass by the Zeppelin

"Did you tell them to keep clear?" asked Whitman.

"We don't have a crystal to transmit on their frequency," sai Lehrmann. "It's a military channel. We can only listen."

"Then get the ground and tell them to call off their dogs. Unti those planes land we're not going to approach the field." He wen forward to the control room, picking up his field glasses on the way

"Elevatorman, ease him down to two hundred meters," sai Whitman.

As he spoke, the two planes made another pass, diving sharply in front of the Zeppelin before they peeled off toward the city i the distance. Whitman watched them through the field glasses flying toward the distant spire of Seville Cathedral. They covere the distance in moments, then swooped down for quick landing at the airfield.

When the field came into view, Whitman saw the two plane taxi up in front of rows of parked aircraft. He pulled the glasse away and rubbed his eyes, then raised the glasses again to coun the planes. There were over one hundred of them, and in a fev minutes they were close enough to identify. Four squadrons o Junkers 52s, twelve planes in each squadron. Across from then were fighters—some old Heinkel 51 biplanes and more of th Messerschmitt 109s, believed to be the fastest and most moder fighters in the world. The four squadrons of fighters were parke in front of service hangars, and just under the covering of th hangar Whitman could see a squadron of Fieseler Fi-156s, *Stork* the pilots called them, light, high-winged airplanes that coul take off anywhere and fly so slow they seemed to be standin still. There were also planes he didn't recognize—reconnaissanc

ines from the looks of their bulbous canopies. In front of the
port terminal building he spotted a new Heinkel 111, a fast
o-engined attack bomber he had heard about but never seen,
e of the newest planes in the Luftwaffe arsenal.
He let the field glasses rove slowly over the field, taking in the
ectacle of concentrated military aviation, a spectacle that dwarfed
e displays of military airplanes at the Rhein-Main field in Frankfurt.
day before, the Junkers 52 transports that he had spotted over the
aits of Gibraltar had been the great secret— and they were nothing
t transports. Here was the Luftwaffe in all its might and glory, the
west and best planes Germany had, untried and untested airplanes
th the potential of changing the nature of warfare.
Whitman said calmly to Lehrmann, "I want to speak to the
ector of the airdrome, in Spanish."
Lehrmann excitedly pulled the headphones off. "Sir, the
rman commander at the field wants to speak with you person-
y. It is General Hugo Sperrle himself."
Whitman waved the microphone and headset away. "I want
e manager of the airdrome," he said. "I want to know from
m whether the vaccine is at the field."
"But General Sperrle is the commander in chief of the Condor
gion," said Lehrmann, unable to conceal his awe.
"I don't care if it's the Fuehrer," said Whitman. "If that
ccine isn't there, we're not getting any closer to that field."
Below them he could see the preparations that had been made
r the Zeppelin—not just a pallet and lines for a cable lift, but
ooring ropes and almost two hundred men standing in rows on
e empty tarmac. They were planning on a full-scale landing of
e Graf Zeppelin.

Sixty-Five

e two Messerschmitts swept down onto the field, landing
ter than Juan Sebastien Birlan had ever seen a plane land, so
t that it looked like they wouldn't stop before reaching the end
the runway. Birlan watched the pilots climb out of their

cockpits as the chocks were put under the wheels and t
mechanics went to their tasks on the engines. Like everything t
Germans did, even the quick search for the Zeppelin w
conducted with a military precision.

Birlan had been the managing director of the airdrome
Seville for five years, long enough to see the Spanish repub
come and go in Seville. Now, as the German "volunteer.
poured in, he was beginning to feel like a bystander in his o
country. First, it had been airplanes, then communications equi
ment, field kitchens, a portable hospital, repair shops, fueli
equipment. Nothing Spanish was good enough for the German
The Spanish mechanics at the airdrome had become janitors, t
Spanish radio operators were now stewards in the German mes

Well, thought Birlan, perhaps this was the price one must p
to learn superior technology from the Germans. No one el
would bring modern airplanes to Spain—certainly not the Repu
licans or the Nationalists, who cared only about politics and
civil war that was destroying Spain.

He saw the Zeppelin when it was still far in the distance, a
he remembered how it had been in 1929, when the Zeppelin fi
came to Seville. He had been a mechanic then, and he was aw
when the great ship came, so grand and peaceful, hovering wi
such grace over the field where there had been only ti
awkward biplanes. As the ship came closer, he realized that t
color was different from what he remembered, silver now inste
of the tawny buff color. The ship had looked better without t
enormous swastika on the tail, he thought.

But even with the Nazi insignia, the Zeppelin was a gre
ship, like the sailing ships that had once left Seville to discov
the New World. Maybe, he thought, this landing could be t
beginning of a new era for Spain.

Out on the field, two hundred men were lined up with t
heavy cables and mooring lines. But they were not Birlan's me
At the last minute, the general had decided that the enti
mooring crew should be Germans, technicians and mechani
from the shops. The Spanish crew that Birlan had assembled w
dismissed, and the entire field was closed to all Spaniards. Ev
he, Juan Sebastien Birlan, the managing director of the a
drome, could not go onto the field.

The Zeppelin was almost overhead when men came to ta
him to the communications office. The commander of the G
Zeppelin wanted to speak with him, they said, in Spanish.

It is impossible to understand these Germans, thought Birla

they wanted him to organize the landing of the Zeppelin,
use he could remember the landings in 1929; then they
ded that they would do it without him and his Spanish crew.

now, after weeks when the Spaniards at the base had been
ted for not knowing German, a German Zeppelin command-
anted to practice his Spanish with Juan Sebastien Birlan.

e was led into the communications office, a small building
ded with the special equipment that the Germans had
ght, and made even more cramped by the presence of
ral Sperrle himself. The general was an enormous man,
a deeply furled brow, hooded eyes, and lips that curled
n at the corners in a permanent scowl. He was talking with
her man, in German, and didn't look up when Birlan was
ght into the room.

om the conversation, Birlan heard the other man's name—
er—and realized that he was a security man who had arrived
he He-111 that had flown in early that morning. Their
ersation seemed to suggest that they were interested not in
ering something *to* the Zeppelin, but in getting a special
from the Zeppelin.

ow like the Germans! thought Birlan. Special couriers arrive
e middle of the night on new attack planes; special equip-
t arrives on the Graf Zeppelin. The Spanish could learn
h from these people. You didn't see the Germans frittering
their resources and their energies in a civil war.

oth of the men seemed to notice Birlan, but they kept talking
e another, and from the little German he could understand,
n gathered that whatever was to be unloaded from the
elin would not stay in Spain but would be loaded on the
ng plane for immediate departure back to Germany.

It certainly cannot be left in Spain," said General Sperrle,
only the faintest effort to raise the downward curl of his

e other man laughed.

rlan felt like a bystander in his own country.

You are the director of the airdrome?" asked Kutner. He had
g, drawn face, close-cropped hair, and wore a baggy gray

Juan Sebastien Birlan, at your service," he answered.

You are to speak with the commander of the Zeppelin," said
er. "You are to say exactly what I tell you and nothing else.
ember—I speak Spanish and I will understand what you

rlan nodded.

"If he asks, tell him the vaccine is ready for the Zeppeli
he wants to know why the airship must land, it is becaus
containers of vaccine are too delicate for the hoist."

"But where is the vaccine?" asked Birlan. He wanted t
about the mysterious equipment that was to be unloaded
returned to Germany but didn't dare admit that he had u
stood a conversation that was clearly not intended for his

"Just say what I told you to say," said Kutner.

Birlan raised himself up to his full height, which made
difference alongside the bulk of General Sperrle. "I am
managing director of this airdrome," he said. "I have resp
bilities. I cannot..."

Kutner pulled a Mauser service pistol from a shoulder h
under his arm. "There is no time to argue," he said. "Rem
ber, I understand Spanish. One slip and you will be mana
director of nothing."

They handed him a set of earphones and a microphone,
Kutner put on another set of earphones. Through the windo
the communications room, Birlan could see the Zeppelin hov
over the field. It had dropped to a height of about two hun
meters, directly over the landing area.

"Señor Birlan?" came the voice over the headset,
Spanish with the twanging accent of an American. "You ar
director of the airdrome? This is Paul Whitman, the a
commander of the Graf Zeppelin."

"Yes, Señor Commandante. This is Juan Sebastien Bi
managing director of the Seville Airdrome."

"Why has the field been prepared for a landing of
Zeppelin?" asked Whitman.

Kutner grabbed the microphone from Birlan's hand, gua
the button with his thumb. "Remember," he said, "the va
is too fragile for the hoist."

Birlan repeated the words, wondering why even the
mander of the Zeppelin seemed not to know about the myste
cargo that was to be unloaded—a cargo that could not st
Spain but had to be rushed back to Germany.

"Then the vaccine is already there?" said Whitman. '
have the new vaccine on hand and ready for us?"

Birlan hesitated, just long enough for Kutner to grab
microphone from him.

"I warn you, Spanish dog—one slip of the tongue and
die. Remember the words of your general? *¡Viva la Muert*

The words stung. Everyone in Spain was repeating

rds of General Millan Astray, the founder of the Tercio, the
anish Foreign Legion. He was a terrible cripple of a man,
unded so often that his body was twisted and scarred, missing
arm and an eye. To many, he was the epitome of the Fascist
vement, single-minded in his dedication to the Spain of king
church and order. All his fervor had come out in a single
gan, his battlecry—¡Viva la Muerte! Long Live Death. The
ech had been printed everywhere, in newspapers and on
ters, and broadcast every day on the radio, proclaiming the
barity of Spain for all to hear.

he radio crackled again in his earphones, the twang of the
erican commander of the Graf Zeppelin.

"Señor Birlan, are you still there? Is the vaccine at the field?
t your request that we land to pick up the vaccine?"

he ship was slowly descending, the propellers feathered and
. Out on the field he could see German technicians running
k and forth, shouting orders to get the crews into position.

"Why do you say nothing about what you are unloading from
Zeppelin?" Birlan asked Kutner. "Even the commander of
Zeppelin seems to know nothing about this secret cargo for
ch you bring the special courier plane."

utner waved the pistol, as if he were going to pistol-whip
an across the face. "There is no time for your foolish
stions. Just say what I tell you to say. Tell him that the
cine is ready and waiting here for him to land."

irlan twisted away from the muzzle of the Mauser. He held
microphone in front of him, the way a priest would hold the
ss. Both of his thumbs held down the button.

"But there is no vaccine," he said, loudly and clearly. "Why
you ask me . . . ?"

utner glanced at the microphone and saw the thumbs on the
on.

he two shots from his pistol hit Birlan squarely in the chest,
ting his body against the edge of the table before it crumbled
he floor.

Sixty-Six

Whitman dropped the headset and ran from the radio room to control room, the piercing overmodulated crack of the p shots still ringing in his ears.

"All engines ahead flank speed," he said.

"All ahead flank," repeated the chief engineer.

"Rudderman, come to one-nine-zero." Whitman's voice firm but unhurried. "Elevatorman, release three thousand k of ballast, stations five, seven, nine, and eleven."

"Three *thousand* kilos, sir?"

"Right. Maximum bow up attitude."

The engine telegraphs clanked, lights flashed on the co panels, the rudder and elevator wheel spun. As the ba dropped, the ship seemed to leap, pitching its bow up so ste that charts and instruments tumbled off the chart table onto sloping floor of the chart house.

The navigator nudged Whitman and pointed out the window of the chart house to the field below. Two pilots sprinting across the tarmac and climbing into the two Mes schmitts that had landed. Ground personnel pulled away wheel chocks and started the engines, and minutes later planes took off at high speed, climbing steeply until they level with the Zeppelin.

Zekner came forward from the radio room.

"They have ordered us to land," he said. "General Sp made it a direct, priority order. The planes are to escort us to the field. Sperrle is a very tough man, Whitman. I don't t you can get away with defying him."

Whitman glared at Zekner.

"It's the same pilots as before," said Stein, leaning his aft to look out the window beyond his station at the elev wheel. "They're so close you can see their faces."

The two Messerschmitts paced alongside the Zepp

368

agging their wings up and down in the airman's sign for *follow
e*.

"Get those pilots on the radio," said Whitman. "Tell them to
ay clear." He turned to the window and watched as the two
anes peeled off in tight turns and flew back toward the stern of
e airship so they could make another pass.

"No," he said. "Let me talk to them." He walked back and
ok the set of earphones from Lehrmann, pulling the long cord
ith him so he could stand in the corridor and see the men in the
ntrol room and the view through the panoramic windows in the
ont of the airship.

This time the planes came closer, passing within meters of the
indows, so close that they could see the lips of the pilots
oving as they talked to one another on their radios.

"Get on their frequency," said Whitman.

"General Sperrle and a man named Kutner demand that you
me to the radio," said Lehrmann.

"Try to get on the frequency of those fighter planes," repeat-
 Whitman.

Forward, in the control room, Stein pointed up through the
per window. "That's the way the English used to attack during
e war," he said. "Always from above, out of the sun. They
ew our parabellum machine guns couldn't swivel up, so they
uld come down on us and let loose with the phosphorus
llets. That's why we had to outclimb them."

"Whitman!" said Zekner. "We have to land. It's too late
w."

"What's the armament of one of those Messerschmitts?"
ked Whitman.

"You aren't thinking . . . ?" said Zekner. "No one would fire
 a Zeppelin."

"I don't have time for thinking now," said Whitman. "Does
yone know the armament of an Me-109?"

"Two machine guns and a cannon," said Lehrmann.
The machine guns are on the engine cowling and the
nnon fires through the propeller hub. I've got them on the
dio now. We can listen, but I don't have a crystal to
ansmit to them."

Whitman took the earphones, holding one to his ear and
tting the other dangle free so that everyone near him could
erhear the pilots.

The two planes swooped down across the bow of the

Zeppelin, wagging their wings in another signal before peelin off.

"I'm going to fire a warning shot," said the younger pilo "That will make them turn."

"Fire?" said the older pilot. "You're crazy! You can't fire liv ammunition at a Zeppelin. The tracer shells would blow it u What's the matter with you? That's a *German* Zeppelin, th pride of Germany."

"Pride? It's a ponderous old hulk. Let them see what Messerschmitt can do."

"We have no orders to fire. If you slip, you could destro it."

"I don't slip," said the younger pilot. "You watch. They' land when they see what a 109 can do."

"Storch! Don't fire!"

Every man in the control room was hypnotized by the tinn chatter of the pilots in the earphones.

"This is madness," said Zekner. "You've got to land."

"I hope that kid knows what he's doing," said Stein. "I sa the L-48 blown up by English planes. They were a few hundre meters below us when a tracer bullet got them. It was all over i less time than it takes to tell. The hydrogen went all at once then the fuel. And when the fireball collapsed, there was nothin left but the frame and a few chunks of engine. We could feel th heat of that blast in our faces, thought it would get us too."

Whitman watched the planes peel off, one close behind th other as they drove up toward the sun. To attack out of the su was a standard maneuver for a fighter pilot, but only in a re dogfight, where it was important to reduce the visibility of a opponent. This was only a game: the Zeppelin was defenseles

"Tell them that we'll land," said Zekner. "This is madnes Whitman."

Whitman moved forward until he was standing directly behi Stein, watching through the upper window as the first plan appeared in the glare of the light. The young pilot grinne fiercely in his leather flying helmet as he lined up the sight rin on his windshield, dipping one wing, then the other to level th plane off for his final approach.

"I'm warning you," said the voice of the older pilot on th headphones. "Don't fire."

His answer from the younger pilot was laughter.

"He better guess our speed right," said Stein calmly. "Eve with this climb, we're making close to seventy knots now. If

esn't lead enough, those tracers are going straight for the
umber one hydrogen cell.''

The Messerschmitt dropped his nose, refining his aim. Along-
de the Zeppelin, the airplane looked like an angry bee trying to
ing an elephant.

"He still says he's going to fire," said Lehrmann from the
ack of the control room. "The other pilot is arguing with him,
it he says he's going to show the Zeppelin . . .''

"Whitman!" shouted Zekner, his voice taut. "Tell them
ju'll iand. You can't play games with a maniac.''

Whitman lined up the sights of the Messerschmitt, extrapolat-
g from the nose of the closing fighter to the bow of the
eppelin, projecting in his mind how far the Zeppelin would
jove in the next instants. He could see the hands of the
idderman tighten on the wheel in front of him, the white-
nuckled tightness that said the man might not be able to react at
1. Behind him, Stein's grip on the elevator wheel was still
ose, but he was staring at the attacking plane rather than at his
istruments. He had suspended the continuous, almost subcon-
:ious movements of the elevator wheel that kept the ship steady
s it climbed.

"He's not leading enough," said Stein. His voice was no
tore excited than if he had been describing the style of a boxer.

Whitman waited another instant, then reached over Stein's
toulders and pulled five gas toggles at once, holding them long
tough to release thousands of cubic feet of hydrogen.

The ship dropped straight down, over fifty meters, just as they
:ard the rat-tat-tat-tat of the machine gun on the airplane. An
istant later the plane disappeared above them.

"Cannon fire!" someone shrieked. *"Mein Gott!"*

The Zeppelin shuddered. The snare drumming of the machine
un was so close that it was impossible to tell whether they had
:ard only the firing of the guns or the impact of bullets against
e frame and skin of the Zeppelin.

In the back of the control room, a white-faced Lehrmann held
it the headset.

"Storch!" shouted the older pilot. "You're insane. If they
idn't dropped, you would have hit them. Turn back now. We're
iing in. That's an order!"

There wasn't a sound in the control room, not even the quiet
:hale of a relieved sigh, until the planes turned in sharp
nmelmanns and banked back toward the airdrome.

Whitman watched them until they disappeared behind the

Zeppelin. Then he looked at his own hands, white from the grip on the girders of the control room framework.

Sixty-Seven

The thick foliage of the swamp muffled the noise, but Conselheiro could still hear the wheezing steam engine on the patrol boat. He had been moving all day, from one abandoned shack to another, concealing the waterlogged pirogue among the stilts of the shacks while he hid from the patrol boat. With his mind on the patrol boat, he couldn't plan exactly what he would do when the Zeppelin came, and he knew he was running out of time.

After the visit to the clinic, his foot had healed quickly. He had been able to walk on it for much of a day, enough to get him back to the safety of the swamps. But then, when he finally sat down to rest, he felt hot and flushed, his whole body on fire. His mouth turned to sand, and when he tried to get up again, his legs collapsed under him. He began to shiver.

He didn't remember drifting off. When he woke, he was back in the house of the jailer, deep in the mangroves. The wife of the jailer was bathing him, sponging the sweat and filth from his skin, touching him with a softness he had not felt in a long time.

"Must you go soon?" she said. "You are a strong man, but perhaps it is too soon."

Her hands moved over his skin with a gentleness that stirred his flesh. There was none of the antiseptic distance that let a doctor or nurse touch even a man's sex organ without arousing him.

Conselheiro raised himself on his elbows. There was no one else there in the tiny one-room house. "Where is he?" he asked.

She kept sponging him. "He has gone. You needn't worry."

Conselheiro relaxed again as her hands caressed his chest.

"What will happen to you?" she asked. "Where will you go after . . . ?"

Conselheiro didn't answer. He was thinking not about her question but only of the feel of her fingers on his skin, a feeling he had missed for so long he had almost forgotten what it could be like.

She unbuttoned her blouse and let her heavy breasts tumble
ut into her hands, holding them up and bringing them to his
ingers. "You have not been with a woman in a long time," she
aid, watching his eyes on her breasts. "I can tell." She
ndressed slowly and lay beside him, reaching up to stroke the
ough stubble on his face.

He took the breasts in his hands, touching her tentatively
efore he suddenly stopped.

"What is it?" she said. "You are a man with feelings like any
ther man. You cannot only do great things." As she spoke, she
ressed her body against his, and he responded, drawing her to
im, feeling his own body come alive, the strength flowing into his
nuscles as the last of the sickness and fever was driven out by the
tirring of his flesh. She was right, it had been a very long time . . .

He twisted on the narrow pallet, bringing himself over her,
eeling her legs part underneath him as he pulled his body down
o her, her lips hot on his skin, her body warm and damp. His
lan, the thoughts of revenge for the hundreds who had been
laughtered on the Zeppelin field, even the memory of the great
Zeppelin as it taunted him by flying over Fernando de Noronha,
aded far away . . .

Then he saw it, on the table. A basket holding a tiny sack of
our and another of beans.

Market day!

He tried to count the days in his mind. How long had it been? If
his was market day, how long would it be until the Zeppelin landed?

And how far did he have to go to get across the vast delta to
he landing field at Giquia? How long would it take him with the
ntegralistas patrolling with their boats in the swamp?

Sixty-Eight

he passenger lounge was a shambles. Unoccupied chairs were
verturned, books had toppled from the shelves, platters had
umbled off the galley trolley. A cabin boy was on his knees,

mopping spilled cakes and tea off the carpets. The steward was
doing his best to placate the angry passengers.

Whitman heard the squabbles as soon as he opened the door.

"He's a dangerous man," said de Nascimento. "An incompe-
tent maniac. We should demand that he be removed from the
command of the Zeppelin."

Otto Hutten was standing at his own table, red-faced, the
rimless glasses sliding down his nose as he shook with anger.
"He must have his reasons," he said. "Captain Whitman must
have his reasons."

"Reasons!" answered de Nascimento. "What do you know of
reasons, you old fool? That American is a maniac, I tell you.
First it was for her." He pointed to Maggie, sitting quietly with
Sinclair in the back of the lounge. "Now, who knows why the
man endangers the ship and the passengers. Only one thing is
certain: he is not fit to command this airship. And the sooner the
Zeppelin Company does something about it, the better. If necessary, I will personally demand that the man be removed."

He was the last one in the room to notice Whitman come in.

"You were saying, Senhor de Nascimento?" said Whitman.

De Nascimento glared at the bareheaded commander, his own
brow tightening into a pattern of fine lines that glistened with
sweat like his moustache.

The ambassador stood up. "I believe Senhor de Nascimento
was asking the questions that trouble all of us, commander,
questions which the steward seems unwilling or unable to answer
adequately."

"Yes?" said Whitman.

"I think you know what we mean, commander. What is the
meaning of these violent maneuvers? Instead of flying through
the Straits of Gibraltar, we go overland to an airdrome, obviously Seville, then just as suddenly we leave the field without a
landing. These wild maneuvers are surely dangerous to the ship.
And airplanes shooting outside the ship! We did not book
passage on the Graf Zeppelin to be witnesses to the Spanish
difficulties."

Whitman scanned the lounge. Every eye was on him. Even the
cabin boy and the steward seemed to melt back into the bulkheads, motionless as they awaited his explanation.

He debated in his own mind. How much should he tell? What
could he say? That they were a renegade flight? They weren't.
The Zeppelin Company had become the renegade. They were
doing what the Graf Zeppelin was supposed to do, flying on

edule, carrying the cargoes that had to be delivered to Brazil,
nging people across the ocean faster than any other carrier.
t could he say that?

He spoke in a calm, unruffled voice. "I'm sorry for any
onvenience or discomfort. There has been a communications
oblem. It appeared that we would have to land at Seville, and
airplanes you saw were sent up as an escort. It now turns out
t the landing will not be necessary. We are proceeding on our
antic crossing, and we should have a smooth flight from here
Brazil."

"Communications problem," spat out de Nascimento. He
dressed himself less to Whitman than to his audience. "Were
u planning to land in Seville to find a new lady friend?"

Whitman spun angrily toward de Nascimento, then caught
nself, forcing calm into his words. Somehow, the Brazilian
d put too many of Whitman's preoccupations into the single
nt.

"In fact, Senhor de Nascimento, the reason we approached
ville was because there was some concern about the vaccine
're carrying in the Zeppelin's refrigerators. The only reason
the detour was to make sure we were bringing the correct
ccine to Brazil."

The ambassador turned to the doctor at his table, saw him
d, then turned back to Whitman, apparently placated. But de
scimento wasn't ready to quit. He switched his attack.

"Can you also explain why the Graf Zeppelin is carrying
gal passengers?"

Whitman looked at the Brazilian as if he had no idea what the
er man was talking about.

"Them—" said de Nascimento, pointing at the Huttens.
hey're not supposed to leave Germany. I *know*. You have
uggled them on the Zeppelin. It is true, isn't it? As soon as
land, I intend to inform the German Consulate."

Hutten turned crimson. He jumped up from his table until
na caught him by the arm and held him.

From the corner of his eye, Whitman saw Maggie lean
ward, as if she too were awaiting his response.

He turned to de Nascimento, lowering his voice, though not so
v that everyone in the still lounge could not hear what he said.
Vhile you are at the German Consulate, Senhor de Nascimento,
haps you could report on the nature of your business activities
Germany. Germany today is a nation of many laws, and quite

proud of its observance of those laws. I wonder how the con
would react to your business activities?"

"How dare you speak to me that way?" said de Nascimen
Sweat beads stood out on his forehead, and he reached up
wipe his moustache with a handkerchief. "You are not one
lecture me on the law. It is not I who have smuggled illeg
passengers onto the Graf Zeppelin and endangered the passe
gers with bravado flying maneuvers."

Without answering de Nascimento, Whitman walked to
Huttens' table, turning his back on the Brazilian.

"He said the most terrible things, Captain," said Otto Hutte
"We tried to silence him, to say that what he was saying w
wrong, but he just kept repeating these terrible things. He is
despicable man."

"Did you get your business with him straightened out?" ask
Whitman, this time in a voice low enough to keep their conver
tion private.

"No. He refuses to discuss matters in a calm and prop
manner. He will not surrender the document we signed, and
says that it cannot be rescinded, that since we have left Germa
illegally we will have no power to oppose him in Brazil. He
truly a despicable man. I don't know how we let ourselves
fooled."

Whitman glanced over at de Nascimento, who glared ba
with a self-satisfied grin.

"Believe me, Captain," said Hutten. "We are still happy tł
we have come. It will be better for us in Brazil, and the la
does not matter so very much. We came once before as imn
grants with nothing, and we can do it again. It is a rich lan
And this time, we come not on a leaky old steamer, but on
Graf Zeppelin." He forced a smile, but Whitman could read
real feelings in his eyes.

Anna placed both of her hands on top of her husband's ha
and smiled with him, the warm grin of the never daun
woman. "We will be all right, Captain," she said. "A
whatever happens, we will always remember what you ha
done for us. He cannot take that from us even if he does get t
land. Friends matter more."

Whitman took their hands, one in each of his. "You'll g
your land," he said. "I'm not sure how, but you'll get it."

Whitman continued his slow circuit of the lounge, making t
required small talk at each table. He had postponed his duties

mmander for too long, and the excitement of the day made it
en more necessary.

The ambassador was cordial, his teen-age daughter charming
d flirtatious. "We were told that the Zeppelin is a calm and
mfortable journey," he said.

"It's usually quite peaceful," said Whitman. "This is in some
ays a special flight."

"Special? How is that, Captain? Because you are an American?"
Whitman smiled.

"I have said something amusing, Captain?"

"Not really. It just seems that everyone wonders about my
ing an American." As he started to explain, he thought of his
nversations with the admiral.

"The world is a small place today," he went on. "National-
m no longer makes it impossible for an American to serve on a
erman airship."

"Really?" said the daughter. "There was plenty of national-
m at the Olympic Games."

"You were at the Games?" asked Whitman.

"Only the opening ceremonies," said the ambassador. "We
ft when the Brazilian team was not recognized by the Olympic
ommittee. That is the reason for my journey home now."

Whitman raised his eyebrows, inviting an explanation.

"Some misguided political groups in my country organized
hat they called an 'alternate' team," explained the ambassador.
And the Olympic Committee refused to certify either the
ficial team or the alternate. Brazil is the fifth largest nation in
e world, and we are not allowed to compete in the Olympic
ames. A great nation must not allow itself to be snubbed so
sily. It would be a sign of weakness."

"No," said Whitman wistfully.

"No?"

"I mean yes, of course."

"Exactly, Captain. Politics has no place in the Olympic
ames," said the ambassador with a tone of finality.

Whitman couldn't help noticing Maggie the whole time he
oke with the ambassador. She was watching him, not staring
t observing, with what appeared to him the detached clinical
e of the photographer. He felt like a potential subject for her
mera, as though he hardly knew her.

"I'm surprised to see you in command," she said when he
oved on to her table. "But delighted, of course."

Both Whitman and Sinclair reacted to the word "delighted," Whitman with a faint smile, Sinclair with a nervous glance.

"What was that whole business really about?" said Sinclair. "The dogfight, the hovering over the field—it seems rather dramatic for what you so cavalierly describe as a 'communications problem.' Unless you were trying to show us something."

In those few sentences, Whitman understood what Maggie had said about her husband, his facility with words, the way he could use language to control and dominate.

"It was just a misunderstanding," said Whitman. "As I'm sure your wife has told you, misunderstandings are not unusual on the Graf Zeppelin." He regretted the sarcasm as he said it and purposely avoided Maggie's eyes.

"And what about those airplanes?" asked Sinclair. "If I'm not wrong, those fighters that performed for us were the new Messerschmitt 109s, supposedly the finest Luftwaffe fighter. I saw the rest of a squadron of them on the field at Seville, parked next to those workhorse Junkers and some old Heinkel biplanes. What do you suppose all those German airplanes are doing in Spain now? Do you suppose it's a good will mission?"

"I just fly, Mr. Sinclair. I don't make German policy. You don't need a comment from me to write a story about those planes."

"Indeed! It's an excellent story—how the Germans, despite Hitler's straight-faced proclamations of neutrality, are aiding the Nationalists in Spain. What effect do you think that aid will have on the war, *Kapitän*?" His German pronunciation of the rank was excessive, but effective.

"I guess that depends on what planes the other side has," said Whitman.

"Precisely. And what do you think would be a good match for those Messerschmitts?"

Maggie looked back and forth until the stalemate of sarcasm was unbearable. "I lost your negatives," she said finally, interrupting their duel.

Whitman seemed startled.

"The negatives that were on the roll of film in your camera. I was searched at the airport in Hamburg, and they took them. I had the feeling you would get in trouble. That's why I was surprised to find you in command."

"It's a long story," said Whitman.

"I'd really like to hear it." Maggie ignored the tightening of Sinclair's expression. "I think we have a lot to talk about."

"Maybe," said Whitman. "But if I don't get back to the trol room, I have the feeling that some of our passengers may ry about an American conspiracy."

Whitman was acutely aware of the glances shooting back and h between Maggie and Sinclair. He wondered what he had gered.

"I'm sorry if those photographs caused you any inconve-nce," he said.

Maggie shrugged it off.

"You seem a very apologetic man," said Sinclair. "I thought pelin commanders were men of action, heroes."

here was no way to answer Sinclair. Whitman didn't try.

Sixty-Nine

itman spent most of the day in the chart house. Zephyrs of sip were in the air, but no one spoke directly to him about the nts at Seville. The conspiracy of silence also avoided mention Henry, the Huttens, Maggie. Although he said nothing, he nted the kid glove treatment. He would have preferred if the w had questioned him, probably because he would have liked ear his own explanations.

here was little operational responsibility for a commander ing a smooth watch. His responsibilities were the executive ority of a ship's master, not the minute-by-minute operation-ommand of an airplane pilot. He was there in case of trouble, it looked like they had already had their share of trouble for flight.

Whitman busied himself with the kinds of tasks he had ertaken as a test pilot, plotting alternate courses, calculating consumption curves and ballast versus cell pressure graphs— resting busywork, but not at all necessary for a scheduled ht, especially a route that had been flown hundreds of times.

Ie spent the late afternoon plotting a synoptic weather chart of South Atlantic. In the operational areas of the U.S. Navy, t radio stations broadcast weather bulletins in encoded letter

groups, and a skilled operator with the correct handbook an
blank chart could produce a synoptic weather map in half
hour. But the U.S. Navy broadcasts didn't cover the So
Atlantic, and that meant that the Zeppelin had to depend on
German weather bulletins, made up of spot readings from
Dornier Wal flying boats on the airmail service, the catap
boats that refueled the planes, and their ground crews in So
America, Africa, and the Mediterranean.

The German weather reports showed a small, localized
pression northwest of Cape Verde. The navigator had alrea
noted the low and had plotted a course for the Zeppelin to sh
south. The figures were sketchy, and Whitman decided to try
interpolate the British weather reports with the German ones
task that was complicated by the rivalry of Germany and Engla
in the South Atlantic, a rivalry that manifested itself in a to
lack of cooperation on technical matters.

When he finished plotting the German figures, Whitm
glanced at the latest British bulletin, written in the usual te
BBC style. He looked back at the chart where he had sketched
the small depression. It was hard to believe they were talki
about the same ocean.

The British shipping bulletin was couched in the famil
English calm: wind Force six to eight, wave conditions moder
to rough. The summary didn't trouble Whitman. High se
bulletins were often based on the report of a single ship, a
seamen had a nasty habit of overestimating the weather con
tions they encountered, so that a severe but local line squ
could be reported as part of a major front. What did trou
Whitman were the pressure readings in the detailed section of
British bulletin, readings that were far too low and far too spre
out to be anything other than a major depression. And once
began superimposing the English figures onto the charted G
man figures, the two sets of figures meshed into a single lav
depression, still diffuse, but with the potential of making up in
a tropical cyclonic disturbance—possibly a hurricane.

Lehrmann, Zekner, and the navigator were all looking o
Whitman's shoulder when he finished plotting the figures a
sketching in the isobar curves that connected the isolated re
ings into a synoptic weather map. They had all seen weath
maps before but never had seen one made up from those pal
figures.

"What do you think?" he asked the three of them.

Lehrmann answered. "I wired the Condor Syndicate ag

fter I saw the British figures. They say the path is clear in the
outh. If we hug the African coast until we're well below the
quator, we can cross over in headwinds of no more than twenty
nots.''

Whitman laid out the course with the parallel rules, then
easured it with the dividers against the latitude scale on the
de of the pilot chart. He calculated for a moment before he
aid, "We would lose at least fourteen hours. The refrigeration
on't hold that long. The vaccine would be worthless."

"What choice have we?" said Zekner.

The navigator leaned over the chart, picking up the parallel
ales and sketching a modified thumb-line course, closer to the
epression, without the detour.

Zekner gulped when he saw the navigator's course.

"That's the alternative," said the navigator. "If your figures
re right, we would encounter winds of forty knots during the
rossing."

"Close to no progress," said Whitman. "The depression will
robably intensify, which could mean winds of fifty knots or
ore. With reduced power we would be lucky even to hold
osition. It's too risky, and just as slow. Even with full power, it
ould cost us most of a day against those winds."

"Unless the front moves north," said Lehrman. "If it goes
orth, we could scoot right under and miss most of the wind."

Whitman pointed to the clouds in the sky to the southwest—
ale mare's tails, like brushstrokes. The sea below them was
reaked with long, slow swells, piling up at half the usual
idocean rate.

"They always go north," he said, "but this one isn't moving
st enough to help us down there. They rarely move fast when
ey're as disorganized and spread out as this mess."

"Then there's no choice," said Zekner. "We take the route
own the coast of Africa. Who knows, maybe the vaccine will
rvive anyway. We've done our best, haven't we?"

As Zekner spoke, Whitman began plotting with the dividers
nd parallel rules, swinging off a series of points that made up a
rge loop from Madeira across the mid-Atlantic.

The other men gaped as he marked off the course, a bold hop
way from all the familiar navigational checkpoints of the Zeppe-
n route to South America, across a portion of the ocean that
as devoid of islands, out of range of the usual radio direction-
nding stations—nowhere.

"Sir!" said Zekner stiffly. "What if the storm does move

north? We could be caught in the heart of it. You said yourse
that it could pack fifty-knot winds."

"It could," said Whitman. "But that wind is with us, on o
tail, and when we cross—" He swung the point of the divide
across the middle of the empty ocean, "—we can follow th
edge of the storm right down the coast of South America. If w
watch our pressure readings we can pick up a steady thirty- c
forty-knot tailwind all the way. We'll be making one hundre
knots over the surface, and we can keep our schedule int
Recife."

The engineer, standing behind them at the engine telegraph
leaned his head in.

"I don't think he can take that kind of flying, sir. Not now,
he said.

"Why not?" said Whitman. "The Graf Zeppelin has bee
through storms that make that kind of tailwind nothing."

"But that was before, sir. When maintenance was up to th
limit. It's not the same anymore. Since the Hindenberg wa
built, we're second class. The ship is an old man now, with to
many miles and too many hours in the air. There are girders wit
hairline cracks, rings that should have been rebuilt, rivets th
are starting to fatigue. There's no telling how he'll work in
storm. A girder deflection that he could have handled easi
years ago could mean popped rivets now. The fabric is tire
worn and patched too often. Ask the riggers—it's not just tea
and patches now, but weak cloth, fine for normal flying, but n
a ship to fight a storm. They can only patch and dope him s
much, and he can only take those stresses for so long."

Zekner looked up admiringly at the gruff engineer. "And we'
low on gas and ballast," he added. It was the first reference t
Seville and the drastic maneuvers that had cost them dearly
the reserves of gas and ballast that they could usually count o
for the long flight.

Whitman looked back at the chart, then measured off th
coordinates of the points that marked his great circle route an
the bearings of the legs.

"How can we follow a route like that?" said the navigato
"No interim checkpoints, no radio signals of any use. If th
storm is heavy, we won't be able to drop flares or fly fla
patterns. We could end up anywhere on that ocean and not eve
know where we are. And then whatever time we save will be lo

ing in circles to figure out where we are. I say the only choice
the safe route south.''

Whitman pointed to the shelf over the chart table, where his
rcraft sextant was braced in its polished mahogany case. There
d been only the most polite comments when he first brought it
d the nautical almanacs aboard, no real interest in an instru-
ent that was not part of the canon of Zeppelin flight.

Outside, the sky was exceptionally clear, almost sparkling.
e high before the storm, thought Whitman. A good time to
oot a fix on planets or an early star. The practice would be
art. But he saw the eyes staring at him.

"We'll find our way," he said, tapping the wooden case with
s fingertips. "As long as we can shoot the sun or a few stars,
'll find our way." He looked long and hard at each of them,
ting his eyes say, *it's my responsibility, I must decide.*

No one answered. When their eyes went back to the chart, he
nt forward to the control room.

"Rudderman, come to two-seven-nine."

"*Two*-seven-nine, sir?"

"Correct."

The rudderman shrugged, then disengaged the autopilot and
ung the wheel over.

"All engines ahead standard," said Whitman. He listened for
e clank of the telegraphs, glanced up at the ship's chronometer,
en settled back into the wicker chair in the corner of the control
om.

His watch was beginning.

Seventy

aggie was only half asleep. The voices in the corridor kept her
ake, and she finally gave in and listened. De Nascimento's
ice she recognized immediately; his ingratiating tone came
rough in any language. David answered him in a familiar
rogant tone that would never admit to being surprised by any
formation.

The door clicked open and shut. Sinclair made no effort to ┃ quiet.

"You're awake?" he said.

She answered groggily. "Almost. What's the commotion?"┃

"It seems that Whitman is playing the hero again. I guess ┃ just doesn't know when to give up."

She shook the sleep away and stared at Sinclair, flipping ┃ tangle of hair away from her face.

Outside, the sky was murky, deep gray and black. The air w┃ muggy, and a light rain pattered on the skin of the ship, runni┃ down the pane of the sloped window.

"He's flying into a storm," said Sinclair. "And some of t┃ crew don't think it's necessary or wise. I guess he's trying ┃ prove a point or something. That nonsense over Seville apparent┃ cost the ship a lot of lifting gas and ballast, and now we'┃ headed for some rough flying. Are you sure they never use t┃ emergency ballast in flight?"

She shook her head again before propping herself up in t┃ upper berth.

"I wouldn't believe everything you hear," she said, "esp┃ cially from that slime, de Nascimento. I was told that he ma┃ the same kinds of comments when they came to fetch me off th┃ sinking schooner. He's apparently the type who would watch h┃ own mother drown. And don't worry about your precious car┃ either. Whatever you want to say about him, Paul Whitm┃ knows how to fly this machine. Without him, we're nowhere ┃ remember?"

Sinclair's upper lip puffed into a scowl.

"You really don't see through him yet, do you? This is ┃ empty heroics. Did you see his face in the lounge when I ask ┃ him about his being so apologetic? It's a show for you, Margar┃ Just what you want."

"Not everyone thinks the way you do," she said. "Wh┃ bothers you is that he seems to care about something."

"*Care!* Did you hear his answer when I asked about tho┃ planes in Seville, the German fighters? 'I just fly. I'm n┃ responsible for German policy.' You call *that* care? He's in fo┃ real lesson about caring. I guess you are too."

"David, you're really beginning to sound like the villain in┃ B-grade movie. You seem to forget that we need Paul."

"We'll see who is the villain," he said, turning for the doc┃

Maggie listened to Sinclair's footsteps in the corridor outsi┃ the cabin. Probably in the lounge for more camarilla with ┃

cimento, she thought. Or snooping for more anti-Whitman
ip.

he rain outside was getting louder and steadier. She was
re, too, of a loud whirring hum that she had never heard
re, and every so often the ship would shudder, a motion
ceable only because she was so accustomed to the implacable
nity of Zeppelin travel.

he was still listening to the hum and the rain and the rumbles
n she realized how long Sinclair had been gone. She had no
ch, but she knew it was well after midnight.

nally, she reached over to the buzzer, summoning the stew-
to her door.

Is Mr. Sinclair in the lounge?'' she asked.

No, madam. Perhaps in the lavatory.''

When did he leave the lounge?''

He hasn't been there, madam. Not since you both left after
er. There's no one in the lounge.''

You're sure he hasn't been there?''

Quite. I was working on menus at one of the tables. There
no one there at all. The noise of the generator seems to drive
passengers off when it's blowing outside. He's probably just
ne lavatory.''

laggie hardly heard a word he said.

I want to speak with Captain Whitman,'' she said.

He's on watch, Miss Bourne . . . eh, Mrs. Sinclair. In the
rol room.''

It's very important,'' she said. ''Would you just tell him that
nt to talk with him?''

he steward looked down at her black slip.

I'll be dressed in a minute,'' she said. ''I'll wait for him in
lounge.''

laggie had never unpacked her clothes, and as she dug
ugh the shoulder bag for a blouse, she had to push aside the
photo lens in its case and the black dress she had bought in
in. Moments from the whirlwind days with Whitman came
. to her. She remembered how relaxed she had felt with Paul
tman, how he had made her feel like a woman and a person
ead of an appendage. But how much did she really know
? she asked herself. The doubts that Sinclair had planted, or
be only underlined, nagged at her. Whitman was gentle and
ident and sure, but there was a core of the man she hardly

knew. And there had been moments when he seemed to lack
conviction.

She wasn't even sure what she would say to him, how n
she would tell him. Where to begin? Would he even listen

There was no one in the lounge, only the menus spread ou
the table where the steward had been working.

Where was David? she wondered. What was he up to no
She sat at the Huttens' table to wait.

The door to the control room opened and the steward cam
alone.

"I'm sorry, ma'am. Captain Whitman says he cannot leave
control room now. The weather outside is a bit rough, and h
standing his watch."

"Did you tell him it was important?"

"Perhaps tomorrow," said the steward. "You'd best be g
back to your cabin for a bit more sleep."

As she turned, she felt another rumble. This time she d
know whether it was the Zeppelin or her own insides.

Seventy-One

The rumbles of the airship—caused by the deflections of
longitudinal girders and the frame rings—were of little con
in the control room. The sounds of the frame were like
groans of a laborer exerting himself. A little rough weather
no novelty on the Graf Zeppelin.

The rain too was nothing that the crew had not seen n
times. Before the Graf Zeppelin opened up service to the trop
there had been worries that the heavy tropical squalls w
prove perilous to the Zeppelins. The ship was so large that
heavy rainstorm the skin, despite being heavily doped, c
absorb as much as eight tons of water, enough to make the
sluggish at the controls. But the Graf Zeppelin had reserve
buoyancy and power, and usually a small trim of the balla
slight upward attitude trim, and increased power on the eng
would keep up the lift of the ship until the skin dried out.

ill effects would be the water that leaked into the control
n, drenching the floor.

his time the rain was no passing shower. The ship had been
nd out of rain for over five hours, first isolated squalls, then
eady downpour, driven by strong winds so that not only the
of the ship but even the skin underneath was soaked through.

barometer had been dropping steadily, and even with the
eased lift of the gas in a low pressure area, it was a challenge
aintain the altitude of the ship. The engineer was reluctant to
e the engines any harder, so to reduce the load on the ship
released ballast in increments, a few hundred kilos at a
. They were trying to conserve the ballast, but after five
s of steady drops, the ballast reserves were close to the
er point.

he dead reckoning plot of the navigator was useless now. It
been over six hours since the last flare drop, and it was futile
rop another with the visibility so limited and the surface
ds so strong. If they went low enough to see the flare, they
ld risk crashing the ship in the sudden downdrafts that could
etimes drop the whole airship as much as five hundred
rs.

he airspeed indicator hovered around sixty-five knots, even
the engines at cruising speed, but they were flying in strong
wing winds that fluctuated from twenty-five knots to gusts
probably exceeded fifty knots. It was impossible to make
an approximation of their speed over the water without a
drop. It was equally impossible to form any notion of which
the weather system itself was moving, carrying them with it
crept or raced over the surface of the South Atlantic.

heir biggest danger was the inability to keep track of their
ude. The barograph had been jumping and falling throughout
storm, which made it impossible to calibrate the altimeter for
than an indication of their relative height.

very try on the *Echolot*, a device that timed the echo from a
t of compressed air to measure their distance from the ocean
ace, came up with no response. With visibility near zero, a
le drop was impossible. Finally, they tried to time the echo of
le shot, a procedure that had been abandoned years before
use the noise of the gunshot was frightening to passengers.
n with the navigator and an electrician leaning out over the
hatch, the rifle pointed straight down as though they were
lling boarders or hunting whales, it took three tries before

they had a measurable echo. And with the barograph jump
the calibration was useful for only a short time.

The radio had been dead for hours, picking up nothing ex
electric static from the storm. The last bulletin they had rece
was from the Condor Syndicate in Buenos Aires, a confirma
of the size and position of the storm that from their readings
already several hundred miles off. They tried to report their
position, the local weather conditions, and their planned cou
but they were unable to receive any acknowledgement of
last transmission. And when someone spotted blue flicker
static electricity from the storm along the hull—the fabled
Elmo's fire—the antenna was reeled in as a precaution. Sev
hundred feet of copper wire dangling below the ship wa
invitation to lightning.

The men in the control room worked at their posts withou
extra word. Even the change of shifts—they were rotating e
two hours on the helm and the elevator wheel—was don
silence, as if everyone were afraid to miss a single rumble of
ship or a single word between the officers.

"We've still got those two small fuel leaks," said the engi
at one point. "Number three and number thirteen. They d
show up on the electronic monitors, but the men can smell th
It's no problem now, because we're venting the hull pretty v
But if that gas pockets and we get a fatigue break in a bra
wire, the hot metal could cause us some problems." *S
problems* was the deliberately understated euphemism fo
disastrous explosion.

The men in the control room listened, digested the
information, and went back to their work, concentrating, a
deep down to try to put it all together and evaluate the situa
of the Zeppelin.

Four hours into the storm, they hit the first pressure poc
They were flying at an estimated altitude of one thousand me
and the ship plunged a full four hundred meters before it lev
off, but with the bow still down. Whitman watched the eleva
man fight the wheel, swinging it all the way back agains
stops, trying to get the inclinometer to lift back to level and
to the five degrees up attitude that they needed to hold
altitude without dropping more ballast.

The ship responded slowly, swinging up until it was al
level. But then it lost its grip on the air, almost as if it
stalled. The bow dropped again to a four degree down pitc

"Can't hold him, sir," said the elevatorman. He had

el back against the stops and his hands were white with the
n of fighting the pressure on the elevators.

All engines ahead full,'' said Whitman. He hoped that speed
ld bring the ship back into a climb.

he telegraphs clanked, and the navigator began calling out
altitude every five meters. It was only a relative altitude,
ibly in error as much as five hundred meters, but the steadily
pping needle was mesmerizing.

Three hundred eighty . . . seventy-five . . . sixty-five . . . still
pping . . . fifty . . . if we hit another pocket, sir . . . thirty-
. . . thirty . . .''

The ballast, sir?'' asked the elevatorman. His voice was
ous for the order.

Hold course and altitude,'' said Whitman. "Give him a
ce to drive up and out.'' He stood behind the elevatorman,
ching the strain and fear in the man's jerky movements and
white grip of his knuckles on the wheel. He wished it was
n on duty. It was Stein's kind of flying. The more the
ation demanded, the less those palsied old hands shook and
more those tired rheumy eyes seemed to see.

he inclinometer in front of the elevatorman still registered a
dy four degree down pitch as the ship drove toward the sea.
man's left hand was poised at the ballast toggle, ready to
ase hundreds of kilos of water from the number two ballast
on just aft of the emergency ballast tank in the bow.

Vhitman was standing with his legs braced fore and aft so he
ld feel the slightest movements of the ship, including those
small to register on the inclinometer and the other instru-
ts. He sensed a slight upward tilt of the floorboards, a
sure rather than a real shift of attitude. For fear of frightening
elevatorman, he didn't say a word while he waited for the
inometer to register. The elevatorman must feel it too,
ght Whitman. He's more used to sensing those shifts than I
In a minute, he knew, the ship would begin to pull up.

Echolot registers!'' shouted the navigator. "Ninety meters
still dropping.'' There was panic in his voice, and the panic
through the room. Heads turned, jaws locked in fear, eyes
ow and fixed. Before Whitman could give a command, the
atorman reached for the ballast toggle and pulled, an instinc-
move, anticipating an order.

e dropped hundreds of kilos of water ballast, and the bow of
ship leapt up, the inclinometer suddenly swinging from four

degrees down to six degrees up, moving so fast that it signa
that the lounge would be a shambles again.

Whitman started to shout, then realized he was too late.
elevatorman had already let go of the toggle, the ballast w
was already in the sea, and there was nothing they could de
recover it. He watched silently while the elevatorman had
force the wheel forward to get the ship back to a stea
manageable climb.

"I didn't think he'd make it, sir," said the elevatorman.
wasn't really apologizing, only explaining why he had ta
action before he got the order. There was almost a tone
accusation, suggesting that the order had been expected earl

Whitman watched the gauges. They were now close to the
of the ballast, and hence of their maneuverability in the chang
pressure. When they got out of the storm and the sun bega
warm the hydrogen in the cells, they would have to vent off g
and then the next night they would have no reserves of ballas
call on when the hydrogen cooled again and the ship was
heavy. It was like a little girl cutting the hair of her doll,
short on one side, the other side trimmed to match but com
out still shorter, then back and forth until the poor doll is tot
bald. Without ballast the ship had to release lifting gas, and w
the gas gone, they needed to release even more ballast.

But it was too late to castigate the man. No words would bi
the ballast back.

"It's a long shift," said Whitman. "Two hours on that wh
is rough in this weather."

"Yes, sir," said the elevatorman. "Is it to be the emerge
ballast next time?"

"No. Let's stay off the emergency ballast until we've got
water around our ankles. We're going to need something
tomorrow."

"What if we hit another pressure pocket?"

Whitman studied the dials and gauges in front of the ele
torman, jotted some notes on a pad of paper, then went up
ladder to crew quarters, conferred with several men there,
listened while they went through the hammocks, waking
off-watch and putting them all on alert in the crew lounge. E
Henry got up with a grumble, saw his brother, then shuffled
the crew lounge and started on more stories of the Olym
Games to the sleepy crewmen.

Whitman greeted the men, apologizing for the "all hands
deck" call that interrupted sleep, then went back to the con

and told the elevatorman to warn him as soon as possible
ext time they hit a pressure pocket.

e engineer had been reporting every hour since they had
n into the storm, and after the first drop in a pressure pocket
ame back with an off-hour report.

We're getting big deflections on the longitudinals,'' he said,
ng his thumb and little finger apart about five inches to
what he meant by ''big.'' ''Some rivets have started
ing, and we're getting signs of fatigue in the axial bracing
s and some of the joints between frame rings and the girders.
got riggers putting on straps and extra bolts where they look
but we can't refasten the whole frame of the ship.''

How's the skin holding?'' asked Whitman.

ust,'' said the engineer. ''Feels like a sponge in places, and
veight loading isn't good. But it's holding except behind the
er three engine. We're patching there, and as soon as we
ut of this mess I want to send men out for an exterior

.''

How much more can he take?''

How much more do you need?'' asked the engineer.

hitman forced a smile, then started for the chart table to try
timate their position. He was almost there when the ship hit
er pocket. The dividers and parallel rules lifted straight up
e chart table, floating in midair as the ship plunged down.

took two more steps to the companionway ladder that led
the crew quarters, leaped up the steps until his head was in
orridor above and shouted, ''All hands aft! To the end of the
corridor.''

zzled heads looked at him, then everyone scrambled off the
nocks where they were sitting and ran, many of them in
ing feet, to the end of the long walkway that ran the length
e ship.

soon as their weight had shifted aft, the ship began to level
his time without any drop of ballast. Whitman watched the
s form in the control room.

e engineer said, ''Like a bloody U-boat.''

Exactly,'' said Whitman, picturing for an instant what the
ral's response would have been.

om then on, the pressure pockets were almost welcomed by
off-duty men. Those who were involved, whether in the
ol room or inside the hull, had the marvelous feeling of
concentration, of being part of a flying team, alert to the
test signs of a drop, their attention honed by the excitement.

Henry Whitman even organized what he called the spr
offering gold, silver, and bronze medals in a mock presenta
ceremony for the first men aft each time. The men comp
themselves with the crews of wartime U-boats, reveling in
camaraderie that had them depending on one another.

It was hours later when the lights suddenly flashed on all
the control panel. The whining that had been bothering som
the passengers stopped, and men in the control room awaited
news from the engineer.

There was no immediate panic, because the signal lights in
control panel had been intermittent throughout the storm. W
leaked through the skin in places, dripped down the fr
girders and shorted wires.

But minutes later, when the engineer appeared, his face
drawn and haggard, his expression more worried than gruff

"We've got a problem," he said. "The prop flew off the s
on the main generator. A chunk of it ripped through the skin
of the gondola and lodged in the hull. Must have been a w
gust, or maybe the freewheeling mechanism jammed."

"How bad is it?" asked Whitman.

The engineer shook his head. "The skin is no problem. I
small rip, and the riggers have already got a temporary patc
place. The electrician says we can make up the power loss or
auxiliary generators. It'll mean no cooking and holding dow
the radio, but we'll be all right if the passengers don't comp
The real problem is that the chunk of propeller tore open
fuel cells. The Blaugas is venting all right, but we've lost
cells."

He went over to his control panel, jotted some figures
pad, then consulted a table in one of the operating manual

"If we cut down to half-speed, we've got maybe thirty h
of fuel."

"Half-speed?" said Whitman.

The navigator was already plotting a course on the c
extending the DR plot—only a rough guess of their position
the only approximation they had—with a walking motion o
dividers.

He smiled when he finished the last swing of the divi
"We'll make Recife, sir. It doesn't leave much margin, but w
make it. And only about ten hours behind schedule."

Whitman looked down at the chart, then borrowed the div
and swung it off himself, coming up with the same re

Eight hours behind schedule at best,'' he said. "And that means the vaccine will be worthless when we get there.''

"We tried, sir,'' said the engineer.

"Yes,'' echoed the navigator. "At least they can't say the Graf Zeppelin didn't try.''

Seventy-Two

Conselheiro left the swamp at night, when he was sure the patrol boat had gone back down the river. He had hoped the boat would try to patrol at night. He pictured finding it in the morning, the propeller tangled in the mangrove roots, the bodies of the integralistas floating in the water, nibbled by the crabs like the corpse of a poor *Serteño* who could not afford a funeral. It was what they deserved, he told himself.

When he reached the parched plain of Giquia, the horizon was edged with thin lines of gray and yellow. The top of the red and white mooring mast glinted in the sun that had not yet reached down to the field.

He needed rest. His whole body ached from being cramped in the trees, and he longed for shade and sleep. The foot had started to throb again, and he had deliberately not looked at it, ignoring the pain as he ignored the bites of the crabs and the sharp stings of the worms that dug their pincers into the soles of his feet. He knew he was slowing down, from lack of food and rest, but there was much to do, so he kept walking, crouching low, keeping his back down so that the basket with the mortar and rockets would not stick up above the brush as he scurried from one patch of concealing scrub to another.

Soon he was close enough to see the base of the mooring mast and the arid land around it, scraped clean even of grass. The field was empty—no mooring lines, no hoses for the fuel and gas and water, no preparations at all. He knew he was at least a full day early. He had seen it all before, the last time. The Zeppelin had come late, but all the preparations had been made the day before it was due. Now he had to hide another day from the

Integralistas, in the sparse scrub brush and palm groves, when
there wasn't enough shelter to hide a rat.

He let the heavy basket slide off its headband and ont
the ground, and he rubbed his forehead and shoulders when
the ropes had chafed against his skin. Finally, he slumped to th
ground, lying back with his head against the basket, ignorin
the chiggers that were already under the loose shirt, attackin
the sweaty skin where the drawstrings of his trousers had been tie
around his waist. Sharp-jawed ants climbed on his feet and leg
and he ignored them too, trying to think, to plan how he coul
hide for a day on the field.

But with the load off his back, he thought not of the plan, b
of the woman, the wife of the jailer, with the cool sponge in he
fingers. He thought of the soft pallet, the touch of her finger
the feel of her heavy breasts, soft to his own hands, the nipple
hardening to his touch. His body began to stiffen as he thougl
of what he had left, until the image of the jailer cut off h
thoughts with a pang of shame.

He knew he would die. They would put enough men arour
the field to make escape impossible. And when they caught hi
this time, they would kill him. His only hope was that he cou
somehow survive a whole day, long enough to destroy th
Zeppelin, long enough to give the signal that Conselheiro ha
returned to avenge the massacre of the people.

He heard a rustle in the grass and froze, lifting his head ju
enough to see over the dry brush. His eyes roved back and forth
scanning the low scrub out to the distance, toward the field an
then back to the palm groves and the shacks where they ha
caught him before. He saw nothing, and he finally let his visic
soften and broaden so he could take in even the slightest motio

When he heard the rustle again, he spun quickly, directed b
his ears. He was quick enough to catch the scorpion moving, i
tail arched back almost to its head, walking fearlessly towar
Conselheiro now, as if he were an intruder in its territory.

Seventy-Three

we only had a reliable position . . .''

Every head in the chart house nodded at the navigator's words
 their hidden meaning: *If we had flown the safe route,
ping from landmark to landmark on short legs, we wouldn't
in this jam.*

The usual course over the South Atlantic was safe and sure,
er more than half a day's flying time from one island or
ther, so that dead reckoning offered safe position fixing and
quate checkpoints. If for some reason they did not spot the
e Verde Islands on the way to Europe, they only had to keep
ng and they would intercept the African coast. Or if they
sed Fernando de Noronha on the way to Recife, they had
y to fly on and they would intercept the coast somewhere
ween Fortaleza in the north and Salvador in the south. It
ght take more time, but they would always get there.

But now, no matter which way a course was plotted, they were
vhere. In the winds that had been blowing all night, they
ld be as much as one thousand miles off the dead reckoning
rse, without a hint of which direction to look for their error.

night the navigators had kept up a crude dead-reckoning plot,
rking off estimated positions on the basis of the course and
ed notations in the ship's log. The pilot chart was a maze of
ppily penciled lines. Circles of position marched to and fro
 the meanderings of a drunken bug, guess piled on top of
ss until the final estimated position was nothing but a dan-
ng fiction. Relying on a DR plot after seven and one-half
rs in that wind, with no confirmation of surface winds and no
itive fixes, was like setting off blindfolded in a rowboat, into
fused currents, and trying to keep track of your position by
number of times you pulled on each oar.

he DR plot was overlaid with long arcs that the radio
rators had swung off, showing the range of various stations.
 semicircular arcs reached out on all sides of the ocean, from

the African coast, the edges of the Caribbean, and the coast
South America. In the middle of the arcs was a vast area of op
sea, encircled by plotting lines and islands and coastlines,
still empty for an expanse of six hundred miles in every dir
tion, without a single clue, not an island, not even an uninhabi
chunk of rock or reef to tell them where they were.

The navigator spread his fingers on the chart, leaving
thumb on the end of the DR plot and letting his little finger m
off a course.

"If that storm tracked north," he said, "we could be up he
Even if we turn due south now, we're still ten or twelve hours
schedule into Recife. It's the only safe course now." He put
emphasis on the last word, as if it were obvious to everyone
the room that they had made a terrible mistake by flying throu
the storm.

The radio operator nodded. "There's nothing on the set nov
he said. "Not even static. We must be well beyond the electri
storm, but too far from any of the stations. And that would
us right here." He jabbed his hand down in the area of the l
position. "I don't like to navigate by what we can't hear,
that's all we have now. And that puts us in the emptiest area
that ocean."

The navigator nodded and swung it off with the divide
measuring the distances carefully as if the DR position wer
precise fix.

Whitman leaned over the chart, glancing at the figures in
open log, then spanning off distances with his fingers a
shaping his hands into a rough circle to represent the sto
system. He tried moving the circle in different directions,
panding and contracting it, all the while studying the press
readings that had been recorded in the log every half hour.

"There's only one way to be sure," he said, reaching for
sextant on the shelf behind him. "Let's go up and have a look

"Sir," said the navigator, "we've still got near zero visibil
I don't think you'll find clear sky until we go up to twenty-f
hundred or even three thousand meters. You can't see a horiz
and we don't have an accurate altimeter reading." He spo
slowly, as if he were explaining to someone who had difficu
understanding.

"A power climb?" said Zekner. "The procedure manuals
very clear about holding the loading down in heavy weather

"Damn it," said Whitman, taking the sextant down from
shelf. He sensed the sharpness of his tone, a resolution geared

much for himself as for them. "Don't underestimate this ship. The Graf Zeppelin is still the finest airship in the world, and this is the best flying crew ever put together. We can do it."

His words left a stunned silence as he walked forward.

"Stein," he said, "take him up. Twelve-degree climb."

"Yes, *sir*," said the elevatorman. He held up both palms, spit into them, then grabbed the wheel and spun it back, bringing the ship into a steep climb. The control room gradually began to slope, five, nine, then twelve degrees, the maximum safe climb, pitched upward so much that it was uncomfortable to stand. Loose equipment slid off tables and shelves, and men grabbed for the girders to brace themselves.

It was a matter of minutes before the engineer appeared, as Whitman knew he would.

"Up?" he asked, his face twisted into a scowl.

"For a sextant sight," said Whitman.

The engineer grimaced. "How high?"

Whitman pointed out the windows, to a swirling gray and black sky, with scarcely a hint of clearing.

"Until I can see stars," he said.

The engineer looked out the window at the gray. "That could be three thousand meters," he said. "Pressure altitude. We'll have cells expanding to the vent point. And if you keep those engines at that speed, we'll have heavy vibrations in the frame in a climb like this."

"There's no other way to get a look at those stars without dropping emergency ballast."

"Stars, Captain?"

"Stars. Three sights and I can work up a position."

"Let's hope so," said the engineer. "If this old man doesn't make it, we'll all be seeing stars."

At three thousand meters, the overcast outside the windows was still impenetrable. They had reached pressure altitude, and the smallest gas cells, numbers one and seventeen, had begun automatically venting the overexpanded hydrogen. If they went too much higher, the engineer warned, all the cells would begin venting. He reminded Whitman that they were already short of hydrogen, with no reserves of ballast to drop if they later found themselves short of lift. But still they climbed.

At thirty-five hundred meters the air was thin enough for the altitude to be noticeable, but the overcast seemed to climb with them. Whitman could feel the war of nerves in the control room.

They were already far higher than the accustomed altitude fc
operations of the Graf Zeppelin, driving the engines hard enoug
to risk overheating, straining the frame and girders in the powc
climb, testing the tired fabric that had to hold against th
buffeting of the wind. It was not so much the spinning dial of th
altimeter that made the climb seem perilous, nor the radical slo̧
of the control room floor, but the perceptible thinness of the a̧
making breaths light and quick after so many hours close to sȩ
level. Whitman thought of Stifel and his precious oxygen tubȩ

"Sir." It was the rudderman, a passive passenger as th
autopilot steered them through the buffeting of the wind. '
think I can just make out stars above us."

Whitman went forward and glanced through the windows.
took his eyes a moment to adjust from the cabin lights to th
twilit sky, and then to gradually resensitize enough for him ȶ
make out the few stars that were peeking through the patchy hig
clouds.

"Level off at four thousand meters," he said to Stein. It wa
not an easy command to execute. At that altitude, the expandȩ
hydrogen wanted only to lift the airship still higher, until th
pressure valves opened and released the gas. To maintain th
altitude meant holding the elevators down and driving the shȋ
against the lift.

Whitman took the sextant in its case and motioned to th
navigator to follow him with the stopwatch as he climbed up th
companionway, then went into the hull to the vertical accȩ
shaft that rose to the very top of the ship.

There was no proper perch at the top, and the hatch had to ḇ
lashed down to keep it from swinging up in the slipstream
Whitman tried to balance himself on the top step of the laddȩ
and to hold the sextant case between his knees while he took oȶ
the delicate instrument, but he seemed to need an extra hanȡ
Twice the navigator had to reach up to keep the case froȶ
toppling eighty feet straight down to the keel of the airship.

With the leather strap of the sextant buckled tightly across th
back of his hand, Whitman steadied himself to study the sk
Polaris was impossible, far too low and already gone in th
morning glow on the horizon. He let his eyes adjust to the ligḫ
and finally picked up Rigel, brilliant, blue, unmistakable in tḫ
southern part of Orion. A good first star.

The proper procedure with an aircraft sextant was to take
least three fixes on each star and average the sights, because
was impossible to be sure of a single sight with an artifici

bble horizon. He held up the sextant, bracing his knees against
e edges of the hatch opening. The image jiggled with the
brations of the frame of the ship. He couldn't hold himself
eady enough to level the bubble in the cross hairs.

The wind was fierce, chilling his hands, freezing the water-
gged skin of the ship so that it crackled. The sounds of the
gines droned in his ears. Even at half-speed, they were
boring heavily, suffering at that altitude without the air their
rburetors promised them. Whitman's eyes smarted from the
ind, tears ran from the corners, catching in the rubber eyepiece
the sextant so that he had to stop and wipe it off with a corner
his sleeve.

He finally got the bubble centered, then slowly turned the
rnier drum, bringing the dancing star down. The vernier was
iff, sticking in flat spots. The sextant had been neglected, left
oiled. It was the first lesson every navigator learned: a man
ho neglected his sextant deserved the results.

"Sir?" It was the navigator, getting ready to relay a message
om below. And it was enough to throw Whitman off his
ncentration. He closed his eyes tightly, opened slowly, and
ed again to settle the bubble and the star in the jiggling cross
irs.

"The engineer said we can't hold long. They're holding the
essure valves on some of the cells now to keep from valving
f hydrogen. He wants to know if you can hurry."

Whitman didn't answer. He focused everything on the task of
inging the image of the star down to the bubble on the cross
ir, bracing himself, alternately holding his breath and exhaling
wly, like a target shooter at the moment when he is ready to
ueeze the trigger. It took forever, it seemed, for his hands to
ady, but he gradually felt himself adjust to the cold and the
mbling of the ship and the buffeting of the wind.

We're going to be all right, he thought, as he finally steadied
e sextant and lined the image up. *We're going to be all right*.

He let out the rest of the breath and closed his eyes, and only
en realized that he had been so absorbed in the mechanics of
e sight that he had forgotten to say "mark!" to the navigator.
ithout the exact time, the sight was useless.

"Sir!" said the navigator when he saw the sextant come away
m Whitman's eye. "They're reporting a major deflection in
e of the longitudinals, near station eleven. It's close to the

leaking fuel cell. They're trying to strap it, but if a rivet po
there . . ."

"Can they vent the gas?"

"They're afraid of a tear in the skin at this altitude."

Whitman raised the sextant again. The overcast was starting
close on the sky above them, and as the morning glow can
further up, he would have fewer stars to choose. He tried
steady on Rigel again, but his hands were cold, and the finge
of his left hand were getting too numb to turn the vernier dru
with the kind of delicacy he needed. He took the hand down a
stuffed it into his pocket to warm up. He rubbed the finge
together, then fingered the keychain with the filigree silv
Zeppelin. He had to fight the rushing thoughts of Maggie.

With the hand warm, he worked quickly, forcing himself n
to think, making his eyes and his hands function mechanica
with one another, steadying, bringing the star down slowly un
it just touched the cross hair.

"Mark!" he shouted.

"Got it," said the navigator.

Whitman read the figures off the scale and drum. It had f
like a good sight, but there was no sense of triumph. Only wor
that it had been too close, so close he almost missed it. And
had two stars to go.

Seventy-Four

"You'd sleep through anything," said Sinclair. He was sitting
the folding stool in the cabin, his back to the door, a reporte
notepad open on his lap.

Maggie yawned herself awake, rubbing the sleep out of h
eyes. "Sleeping on the Zeppelin is marvelous," she said. "Y
ought to try it." She remembered that he could never sleep on
airplane, or even a ship. He was a terrible traveler, nervous, slc
to adjust to unfamiliar surroundings.

"Sleep?" he growled. "It felt like a roller coaster last nig

:hing up and down, that whining sound, those rumbles. Your
»oy really put on a performance, didn't he?"

The mention of rumbles and the whining noise made her think
her own trip to the lounge. She wondered where he had been.

"Where did you go last night?" he asked.

"I was going to ask you the same question."

"Margaret, the steward said you were in the lounge. Who did
i talk to?"

"Myself, mostly. There was no one else there."

"What did you tell him?"

"Him?"

"Whitman."

she sat up straight on the berth. "David, I didn't see him. He
s flying the ship, so the rest of us could sleep. For God's sake,
i're being a first class fool. How do you think you'll ever get
)ff the ship without telling Paul? Do you really think they'll
k this monster in a quiet, deserted hangar in Recife and
vide you with a chain lift and a trolley? Maybe a truck to haul
iway? Paul is the only hope, whether you like it or not."

"And how do I know you and he wouldn't just take it?"

"Take it? What would we . . . what would anyone do with a
of gold?"

"I don't know what you've planned," he said. "But it ought
pay for a nice comfortable bed, anyway. Lots of comfortable
ls, all over Germany. With big black and red swastikas on the
:n."

Ier face tightened in anger, then relaxed as the wave of
speration passed.

"It's still safe," he said, "as if you really cared. I checked it
ing the storm."

"For how long do you think it's safe? They must have
pped a lot of ballast during that storm, and they probably
i't have much left in reserve. The last time they landed at
:ife they had to drop the emergency ballast at the last minute.
it would be a rather dramatic delivery, wouldn't it?" She
ghed.

"You said they never use it."

"Except in emergencies. The only way you can be sure is to
Paul. He's on our side, I know he is. What was your plan,
"way? Or do you have one?"

she regretted the barb as soon as she launched it. No words
ild make him angrier.

Ie reached for his pistol, a mannered gesture. If only they

hadn't boarded at the last moment, she thought, there wo
have been a luggage inspection and someone would have ta
the pistol away from him.

She looked at the fear in his face, the mask that covered
insecurity. It was the one thing that could drive him to acti
The predictable David who watched and snickered and let
world roll by with nothing but cynical barbs as his salute
gone. He was a determined man now, seized by a cause, dri
by conviction and fear, willing to do anything. She knew he
to be distracted.

"David?" Her voice softened as she turned toward the w
dow. "Isn't it romantic? The Zeppelin—it's like a magic car
You float and the world passes underneath. It's like a dre
Don't you feel it?"

He caught her shift of mood. At the word "romantic"
expression changed, his eyes drooping downward, his mo
twisting into a smile of power and confidence that she coul
remember ever seeing before.

She looked down at herself, wearing only the slip that she
bought in Berlin. She realized that she had made a mistake
single word could be a mistake with David. When he was t
he read what he wanted into words.

She watched his eyes undress her as he took the *Do*
Disturb sign and hung it on the outside of the cabin door.

Seventy-Five

The ship dropped smoothly. They were powering down,
engines at cruising speed, a bow down attitude of seven degr
the slope gentle enough to relax the pressure on the structure
the skin, and to keep Whitman's worksheets on the navigat
bench where he was working up his lines of position.

The calculations went quickly, even though he didn't have
special reduction forms that they had used in the navy.
remembered how easy it had been when they had the
Almanac in 1933. You could do a star fix in ten or fif

utes. But even with the standard *Nautical Almanac*, it was a
ght to work up a fix, the respite of quiet calculations, the
asure of solving a puzzle, seeing the numbers fall into place
a tiny triangle that, if you were lucky, you could cover with a
mb.

As he dipped into the book, he marveled at the delightful
rrie Olde Englishe of the table headings, like *Declination
he Name as Latitude*. Normally, he would plot the azimuth
intercept of each star as he worked the sights, but this time
reduced all three at once, and he could see from the numbers
the intercepts were going to be close. *A piece of cake*, he
ught, glancing over at Lehrmann and the navigator as they
ted at the chart chest, keeping a respectful and skeptical
ance. He smiled a private grin as he jotted the figures down
his pad.

"Coming up on three hundred meters," shouted Stein from
elevator wheel.

Whitman leaned over the chart chest, putting down the pad
picking up the protractor to plot the LOPs. The radio
rator and navigator stood back a step, and the rest of the crew
ed their necks, hoping to watch the culmination of the
sterious process without seeming too obvious.

Whitman took one look at the chart and slumped. His calcu-
d triangle was tiny, but it was approximately two thousand
es off, somewhere over the Sahara Desert in French Africa.
he navigator stretched his fingers beyond the chart table,
cating where the plotted position would fall—an obviously
ossible point. Whitman watched a mistimed grin spread on
man's face.

Shall we turn south at half-speed?" he said.

Whitman looked again at the chart and his figures, then said,
aintain altitude and speed." He went back to the navigator's
ch.

hecking a bum fix was a thousand times more work than
ulating it. When the numbers came easily, he could work up
ar fix in fifteen minutes. A check, going over every calcula-
and every entry, trying to catch an error, could take hours.
wished he had the computation forms that they had used on
y test flights.

he one consolation was that it was a big error. It was the tiny
rs that sometimes didn't get caught at all, leaving a calculat-
osition fifty miles or more off, far enough to lead to untold

disasters. An error of two thousand miles had to be a slip th could find.

He pushed aside the papers and took out a clean sheet, lis all the corrections for the sight. Right away he saw a mist Sextant index error. He had left it out. Every sextant is permanc misaligned by a small but measurable amount. His was minutes of arc, and he wrote it in, wishing he had recheckec index error more recently. It was a quick and easy ch something he did whenever he cleaned and oiled the sextar

He started to smile, then caught himself. An index erro four minutes of arc would put the lines of position off by a dozen miles, not two *thousand* miles.

He went through the rest of the calculations, bringing numbers over from his notes and rechecking each figure in almanac. He got a new set of figures for the first LOP, but it only a few miles from the old one.

He thought of the possibilities. Either the sight was off o time was off. He knew it wasn't the sight. Those stars unmistakable, and a sight was automatic. At least it used to

"Two hundred meters," said Stein. "Can't hold altitud half-speed on this course."

Zekner came over to Whitman, the navigator at his side. ' have to decide, sir," said Zekner. "We can't hover in wind." The decisiveness in his voice surprised Whitman.

"Are you sure you read the time right on those sigh Whitman asked the navigator. "One minute off is fifteen mil the LOP."

"Yes," snapped the navigator in a tone that made it clear he knew he was being blamed for what was not his mistake couldn't have been off enough for an error of two thou miles."

Whitman ignored the tone. "And you rated the chronon against the radio time ticks?"

"I checked it yesterday, sir. The ship's chronometer has a steady error and I check it daily."

Whitman looked up at the man, ready to apologize unti caught himself. There was nothing to apologize for excep own failure to get the fix. He had picked the chancy co against all recommendations, assuring them that he could g navigational fix. Now he had to do it.

He pushed all the worksheets aside, printed up a rough of the navy computation forms, and began all over ag working only from the observation data. He forced himself n

e any shortcuts, purposely didn't look at any of his previous
lculations, dug each entry out of the almanac again. When he
oked up the hour angles, he again noticed the Merrie Olde
glishe headings—*Declination Same Name as . . .*

August, he reminded himself, Northern Hemisphere. He stopped.
uthern Hemisphere. He had gotten it wrong, the simplest
stake, a reversal of signs.

The rest went quickly. He finished the calculations and brought
m over to the chart. They were still off the chart, too far south
s time. He unfolded the chart and fingered the approximate
sition, then excitedly drew in the three lines, grinning when
y intersected in a cocked hat he could cover with the eraser of
pencil.

Everyone in the control room was standing around now,
rdless, holding their breaths in expectation. The navigator
re a smug, knowing grin as he watched Whitman plot the
ee fixes that pegged their position just south of the equator,
ne four hundred nautical miles northwest of Recife. If Whitman
s right, they had flown over thirteen hundred miles in eleven
urs. Instead of being six to ten hours behind schedule, they
re ahead of schedule, well within the margin of safety for the
ccine.

Excitement coursed through the room as incredulity gave way
amazement. Whitman shrugged it off and kept working with
dividers, plotting the pressure readings that had been recorded
the log, trying to estimate the movements of the storm. Finally
took a sheet of vellum drafting paper and laid it across the
art, sketching the rows of points onto the paper and moving
d swirling it until he had what he thought was the behavior of
storm.

"It hardly moved," he said. "Just tightened up and whirled
around, like a skater cracking the whip. If we stay in the tail
l of it we'll be in Recife before nightfall."

Seventy-Six

It took Conselheiro hours to find the right spot, a knoll behind the fuel tanks at the far edge of the landing field, raised just enough above the flat field to give him a clear view of the mooring mast in the distance, and surrounded with a dense low scrub that obscured his hiding place from anyone in the field.

When the sun came up, he had expected troops to be all over the field, combing the shacks around the mooring mast. Instead there was only the quiet of morning, the sun hot and still. He tried to stay awake, but the heat made him even sleepier, and gradually ignored the chiggers and the ants and the sounds of the scorpions in the brush, letting his eyes close in intermittent sleep.

When he awoke, it was to the roar of airplanes.

He watched them land one after another, within a few hundred meters of his hiding place. He had never seen airplanes like these before, with single low wings and huge round engines in front. The only airplanes he had seen before were mazes of wire and fragile braces, awkward, ungainly craft that struggled mightily to lift their impossible structures off the ground. Those other airplanes were like albatrosses compared to these sleek, stream-lined hawks.

He watched the airplanes taxi back along the field to park in two rows, four airplanes in each row. There were no markings on the silver fuselages or the wings, but he knew what the airplanes were. They were there to search for him. The police and the Integralistas were so afraid of him that they had brought airplanes to shoot him down from the air.

He took a deep breath of the dry morning air, expanding his chest. It all made sense to him. The Zeppelin was coming, and the airplanes were sent to protect it from him. They were afraid of him.

He smiled and began his preparations, laying out the morning

406

ets and wiping muck and grease off the rockets and the
ching tube. If he could take on the mighty Zeppelin, he told
self, what were a few airplanes? The Great Conselheiro
ld show them.

Seventy-Seven

fire in Sinclair's eyes was something Maggie had never seen
re. There was no trace of the restraint, the intellectualizing
nce that had clouded sex for them before. As a lover,
lair had always been passive and removed, as if lovemaking
a burden, or at least an act he watched himself perform.
was one of the reasons their marriage had never worked. Or
aps, as Maggie had often thought, the sex had been terrible
use the marriage was deeply troubled. It was something he
ld never talk about.

ut that was long ago. Now, he was bold and passionate,
ping at her, crushing her against him, pressing his lips on
. "You didn't believe I changed, did you?" he asked. When
didn't answer, he pulled her to him again, tearing the thin
lder straps as he stripped the silk slip off her.

e tried to push him back, putting her hands flat on his chest,
e seized her wrists, twisting her hands behind her back and
ng her even tighter to him.

You've become a tigress," he said. "I like it. Maybe this is
we needed all along."

e tried to turn her head, but he pulled up on her arms,
sing until they hurt, forcing her to him. His knee forced its
between her legs as he pushed her down onto the berth.
y move she made, it seemed, fired him even more, arousing
filling him with a strength that she had never seen before.
lips dropped to her breasts, nibbling, licking, engulfing her.
voice was incomprehensible as he spoke into her flesh.

nce again now she was truly afraid of him, not of the pain
vords could inflict, but physically afraid. There had been a
, years before, when she had yearned for some sign of

passion from him, a relief from the deadly dullness of t
ritualized, unsatisfying sex life. Now, she was only disgusted
repulsed. It wasn't lovemaking. It was rape, a gesture of po
and brutality.

The remnants of the slip were off her now, and Sinc
awkwardly groped at his own trousers, grinning an aln
lascivious smirk as he held her with one hand. She twisted a
from him, freeing herself for a moment. He grasped her ag
kissing her hard on the lips, pressing her body against his.

She closed her eyes, trying to pretend it wasn't real, tha
was happening to someone else, when she heard a brisk knoc
the door. Sinclair looked up, putting his hand over her
before she could say a word.

"What the . . . ?" he said.

"Sorry to disturb you," said the steward in the hall
outside, "but breakfast will be served in a few minutes.
captain has an important announcement to make."

Sinclair lifted his head to listen, and she squirmed out f
underneath him, covering herself with the remnants of the sli
if even her nakedness in front of him was a violation.

His expression took a moment to form. Whatever spell he
under snapped, and the reddened flush drained from his fac
his eyes turned narrow and angry. He lifted one arm to slap
She didn't move to block it, holding tightly onto the torn slip
barely covered her. He held his palm a foot from her face,
fingers half curled into a fist, then dropped the hand as
reached for his own shirt and trousers.

He spat out a single word as he bolted from the ca
"Captain!"

Seventy-Eight

The first voice Whitman heard in the lounge was the m
exasperated, slightly pedantic imprecations of Otto Hutten in
of his loving squabbles with his wife.

"You could not have seen that island, Anna. We will no

e for another twelve hours or so. We are still out in the
dle of the ocean.''

Vhen he saw Whitman, he pushed his glasses up his nose and
led. "Captain, I am trying to explain to Anna that we are still
from the coast of Brazil, but she insists that she has seen the
nd with the prison colony. I think perhaps she spends too
:h time at the window. She has been there since before
rise this morning.''

Vhitman grinned, delighting in the closeness of the Huttens.
have a surprise for all of you,'' he said.

. muffled cheer went up when he announced that they were
in a few hours of landing at Recife. Tenseness and hostility
ned to evaporate as the lounge buzzed with excitement. Even
dour Senhor de Nascimento could not find the energy to
plain about the cold breakfast.

Vhitman looked up and caught Maggie's eyes, fixed on him,
ying his every gesture. He realized that it was the first time
ng the flight that he had seen her without her husband. As he
t on to explain the storm and their course during the night,
the steps they were taking to assure the safety of the vaccine,
ouldn't avoid her eyes. When she looked at him earlier in the
it, he had felt self-conscious, as if she were judging him.
v he wanted nothing more than to straighten out some of the
id words between them.

Iaggie never took her eyes off him, and her expression
ually changed into a warm, beckoning smile, the infectious
he remembered so well. He finished his explanation and
ed back to her table, not sure what he would say, but sure
something had to be said. That smile reminded him of too
h to let it all end with silence and bitterness.

Vhitman had just made it to Maggie's table when Lehrmann
:ared in the lounge with a handful of radiograms. "Sir?
se have just come in from the Brazilian stations. And we've
ted the coast now. They're ready to begin the weigh-off.''

Vhitman started to wave him away, then realized that what he
ted to say to Maggie would take more than a fleeting word.
now, it was better to let it ride on the smiles. His own
vant mood and her smile suggested that they had a lot to say.

There are some radio messages I'd like to send," Whitman
to Lehrmann as they huddled in the passageway. "For the
ens, and for my brother. As long as we're close enough now
:ach the Brazilians directly.''

Lehrmann smiled, holding out a telegraph blank. "I took
liberty of sending a wire for the Huttens already, sir. Perhaps
would like to give them the reply."

Whitman looked down at the blank. It took him a minute
decipher the bureaucratic Portuguese, but the message was cl
If the Huttens returned to Brazil before the auction, the l
would still be theirs.

"I also wired the German Consul in Rio about Senhor
Nascimento," said Lehrmann. "It seems that once he has
Germany there is nothing the consul can do about his activitie
Germany. But the consul said that there are laws in Br
respecting the export of gems, and that it would be his duty
report any improper dealings to the Brazilian authorities." Lehrm
smiled even broader. "I suspect that Senhor de Nascimento
not be flying any more on the Graf Zeppelin."

Whitman forced a bittersweet smile, his joy for the Hutt
tempered by the realization that he too wouldn't be fly
anymore on the Graf Zeppelin. But it was impossible to th
glum thoughts in the ebullient mood of the control room. He
never seen the crews in such good humor. The squabbles
barbs that usually marked the exchanges between the watc
had given way to a shared pride in the ship. Everywhere,
were rehearsing the versions of the storm tale that they w
later recount to willing listeners, and even the navigator had
Nautical Almanac open next to his chart.

"Try the sextant," said Whitman. "You could take a
shot with no one to mark the time for you."

Glancing down the pages of the log, Whitman saw nota
after notation of repairs that had been done that morning—s
panels, inspected rivets, lubricated control systems. It was a
the crew were preparing the ship for a special demonstra
flight.

Stein, on the elevators again, was comparing the storm
other, half-forgotten flying feats of the Zeppelin. Even
usually taciturn rudderman piped in at one point, "Can
imagine Stifel in command during that storm?"

Everyone laughed, officers and ordinary airmen together, e
Zekner, on watch in the traditional commander's seat, his
propped on a girder and his hat low on his forehead. He jum
to his feet when he saw Whitman. "Sorry, sir, I was just
.

The engineer and the rudderman snickered, and Whitman
sorry for Zekner. The watch officer was a little too young t
able to take ribbing from the crew.

tay where you are," said Whitman. "Take charge of the
h-off." He stood back, trying to remain inconspicuous so
watch officer wouldn't have the additional burden of a
nander looking over his shoulder.

kner slowly scanned the gauges above Stein's station—
ure, ballast reserves, gas reserves, then the engine gauges
e the telegraphs.

ally, after rechecking every gauge, he said, "All engines
Prepare for weigh-off." He said it too loudly and too
y, forcing a voice of command from his diaphragm. Whitman
d. It would take a while, but with the trust of his crew,
er would be a commander.

the ship gradually slowed, Whitman backed into the chart
, leaving the control room to Zekner.

aptain!"

had never seen the steward so agitated. Even when the
laints of passengers escalated to hysteria, the steward was
y unruffled.

's Miss Bourne, sir... I mean Mrs. Sinclair. She says she
o see you, that it's very important."

nitman shrugged, looking back over his shoulder at the
ol room.

ir, she's quite insistent."

ell her she picked the wrong moment. We can talk after our
l."

e steward seemed embarrassed by the exchange, as if he felt
re in the midst of something that was not for his ears. "Sir,
k this is serious. There's a look in her face that seems very
st to me."

nitman spun again and looked at the steward, whose own
seemed to duplicate the look he described.

1 the lounge?" said Whitman.

he wants to see you privately. Perhaps in a cabin?"

nitman frowned. "Bring her up here, into the corridor."

ggie's eyes were as big as saucers. Her mouth was slack,
ut a hint of the beguiling smile he had last seen.

aul!"

resisted the impulse to take her into his arms.

avid is missing," she said.

lissing?"

le must have gone up into the hull. I think he's afraid you'll
the emergency-ballast."

"Emergency ballast? Maggie—what the hell are you ta▮ about? This is a lousy time for games."

She stared at him, biting her lip as her hands rose involunt▮ in front of her. Then she burst out, "Paul, I know it all so▮ crazy, but David has a plan, and if it works it will ch▮ everything . . . the whole war in Spain . . ." As she describe▮ scheme, she realized once again how bold and daring Sincl▮ idea was, cutting through the paralyzed inaction of men▮ governments. ". . . don't you see, Paul? That's why I'm▮ David. I agreed to help him, to try to get you to help. I be▮ in what he's doing. But now . . ."

The pieces started to fall into place for Whitman. He▮ mention of the two of them near the ship in the hangar befor▮ departure from Friedrichshafen, the detour to Seville, and▮ preparations for a full-scale landing—not for the Hutten▮ Henry or even to wrest the command away from him, but fo▮ gold. The Nazis must have found out about it, somehow. Bu▮ was a prize they would never give up.

But even as it made sense, he was amazed. "How the hel▮ he get his hands on a ton of Spanish gold?"

"Not now, Paul. There's no time for explanations. Just▮ him from doing something drastic."

Whitman pictured Sinclair, the look of defiance and h▮ that the man made no effort to conceal.

"What could he do?"

"I don't know. He's got a gun and he's desperate. He'▮ anything to protect that gold—cut cables, pull pins. I told▮ everything I knew about the Zeppelin, everything you told▮ And that's a lot, I guess."

Paul remembered the long hours they had spent together i▮ car, riding with the top down and talking about the ship.

"Paul—" she caught his eyes again and reached out for▮ "Please be careful."

Seventy-Nine

lair hid for ten minutes in a corner of the keel walkway,
ing for a rigger to finish inspecting the fuel cells. Daylight
red through the translucent skin of the ship, and for the first
Sinclair realized the immensity of the inside of the hull. He
d see the whole way down the length of the axial corridor, to
re the two sides seemed to converge in the distance, like
oad tracks that appear to meet at infinity.

s he began to work his way aft, an acrid smell accosted his
rils, like garlic, but sweeter and heavier. He had to fight
waves of nausea as he breathed it in. He had always read
hydrogen was odorless, and from what Margaret had ex-
ned, it was almost impossible for hydrogen to be trapped
le the ship. He wondered whether she really did know
igh about the ship.

he smell was weaker when he reached his goal, the emergen-
allast sack just forward of the enormous cruciform girders
supported the tail fins. In the warm light that glowed
ugh the skin of the ship, he could see the rubberized sacking
ad over the crates, stretched so smooth that no one would
guess that it wasn't water inside. He remembered how hard
ind Margaret had pulled to get the wrinkles out.

lost of the other ballast sacks were hanging empty now,
pping down to the small valves in the bottoms. They weren't
t like the emergency sacks, with the massive gate valves
e enough to dump the whole load of ballast at once, big
ugh to support the stack of wooden crates inside the rubber-
i sacking.

ie stuffed the revolver into his belt and buttoned his jacket
it, then climbed up the outer netting that supported the sack.
n with the jacket buttoned, the butt of the gun caught on the
ing, and he finally had to climb with one hand, holding the
in the other like a pirate in an Errol Flynn movie.

/hen he got to the top, he pulled the rubberized material

413

down to look at the crates inside. Dripping water had stained
wood of the top crates, but it was still possible to read
numbers that had been stenciled onto the wood. He pict
Gregory Orlov trying to explain those missing crates to
NKVD in Moscow.

It was too big for Orlov, too big for any of them. What
wondered, would the fabled Whitman do when he found or

He fought the threatening image, but couldn't keep it o
Margaret staring at Whitman, the gaze unmistakable. She c
control the telltale corners of her lips, but she could never
the smile in her eyes. And she hadn't taken her eyes of
Whitman. She was like a schoolgirl with a crush, in love w
silly uniform, blind to the truth about the man. He pictured t
together, cheering at the Olympics, easy and relaxed in the c
and in an open car, dancing at a ball, Margaret gay and eas
the black dress, charming everyone; Whitman dashing in
dark blue uniform. And afterwards, her gaze still on him .

He shook off the thought, looking around him at the
interior of the airship. Suddenly he realized that it was compl
quiet. There was no rain on the skin, no wind, not even
steady low rumble of the engines that he had heard when he
climbed up into the hull.

No engines? He felt the girder next to him. During the stor
had vibrated with the rhythm of the engines. Now it was
The engines had been shut down.

Whitman went up the main access ladder to the axial catw
a narrow walkway, without handrails, that extended full le
down the center of the ship, surrounded by fuel lines and wi
All around him was the skeleton of the ship, the imm
structure of girders and frame rings and longitudinals and a
bracing wires, and the miles of ramie cord that held the tau
cells above and the floppy, mostly empty fuel cells below.
fuel cells gyrated against their restraining nets, flapping from
ventilation currents that flowed through the still-moving ship
it was all eerily silent inside, as if even the buffeting of the v
were insulated. The only sound was a soft swishing, like
against skin.

Whitman thought of Maggie, especially that ineluctable sr
From the first moment that he saw her in the lounge, it
always been her smile that drew him—open, warm, beguilin
was hard to believe Sinclair's scheme, harder still to g
Maggie with Sinclair. Whenever Whitman had seen the tw

together, there had been a palpable tension in the air
een them, as if they could barely stand one another. It was
st impossible to believe they were—had been?—married. It
t seem like Maggie.

d yet, he asked himself, how well did he know her? They
spent a few wonderful days together, all easy smiles and
ater and warm feelings. But he hardly knew her. Time was
they needed, and time was something they never had. Even
eppelin was moving too fast for them. Now there wasn't
even to wonder.

ergency ballast? he thought. He traced the control cables as
alked aft, following the maze of wire ropes as they ran over
ys and fairleads to the various ballast and gas valves. Every
of those control systems would have been checked by the
anics in Friedrichshafen, each cable inspected for abrasion,
clevis pins, corroded cotters, anything that could lead to
e. To check the miles of cable now, looking for sabotage,
an impossible task.

pictured the control room, hundreds of feet behind him.
's voice calling off the readings on the inclinometer, the
ator interpolating altimeter readings, ticking off the slow
nt of the ship as it gradually lost the dynamic lift of its
ard motion. And Zekner, nervously glancing back and forth
e gauges, waiting cautiously until the ship came to a
lete halt before he gave the orders to release gas and
st. It would be mostly ballast for this weigh-off, Whitman
. They had already vented off so much gas that ballast was
ey had. And the only ballast was the emergency ballast—
air's gold.

m the walkway inside the hull, it all seemed far away.
e was no hint of nervous voices, no gauges, no view of the
at horizon. The only light was the pale glow of afternoon
hrough the translucent skin, a soft, filtered light that peeked
the vent shafts and around the edges of the bulging gas
modeling the architecture of the frame members, turning
uralumin girders into a vast sculpture.

close, Whitman could see signs of neglect. The green
ctive lacquer was peeling on some of the girders, leaving
aw metal underneath exposed and oxidizing. There were
that needed attention, joints that showed signs of metal
e, gas cells that were worn and frayed from the constant
ng against the ramie cords. There was no immediate danger,
ng that constant maintenance wouldn't keep in check, but it

was obvious that priorities had shifted. The Graf Zeppelin
no longer a flagship, but an old man, relentlessly aging,
with only dignity and reputation hiding his creaky joints
wheezing systems.

As he neared station eleven, almost at the stern of the shi
caught an acrid whiff of the chemical odorant that was add
the Blaugas fuel. It was an unmistakable tocsin of dang
warning that leaking gas was trapped in the ship because
were moving too slowly to ventilate the hull.

He hurried aft, following the cables. The ballast release
led intact up into the tail, where they looped over heavy b
hung from the axial braces and down to the release mecha
for the emergency ballast. The crewmen called the emerg
ballast sacks "breeches," because they were divided into
legs to permit the water ballast to run out quickly. Whi
started to trace the cable down to the Y-junction, where a
clevis pin connected the separate cables that ran to the valv
each leg. As his eyes went down the wires, a voice caugh
short.

"So the bitch told you? I knew she would."

Whitman's eyes swung to the voice. Sinclair was strad
the ballast sacks, standing on top of a stack of wooden crate
rested on the valves. His hands were above his head, reachi
to where the wires were joined at the Y-connector. He had
the antichafe tape off the coupling.

As Whitman looked closer, he could see the gun in Sinc
hand. He was using the lanyard lug at the base of the han
try to knock the clevis loose. The look in his eyes was desp
but his manner, the way he gestured with the gun as he s
was deliberate and controlled.

"Margaret likes her causes, you know," he said.
beleaguered farm workers, the poor starving Ethiopians, the
animals being slaughtered by the poachers in Africa. To he
is all just one more cause, another lark. But she's wrong

He paused, waving the gun.

"Stay where you are, Whitman. And cut the play-
routine. I know why you're here."

"The only reason I'm here is your safety, Mr. Sinclair.
the safety of the ship. They're both my responsibility."

Sinclair boomed out a laugh. "That's good, Whitman.
almost as good as your answer when we saw those planes o
ground in Seville. 'I just fly,' you said. Just a dumb flyboy

scheming for Margaret or the gold—is that what I'm
posed to believe?''

Vhitman didn't answer, and in the silence, Sinclair again
ced the total quiet of the ship.

'Why are the engines stopped?'' he asked.

'Weigh-off,'' said Whitman. ''Before we can land, the ship
to be trimmed into perfect balance. It will mean dropping
ast.''

'Ballast? *This?*''

'There's no other ballast now, not after that storm.''

inclair waved the gun toward the stacked crates under him.
o you realize what this is, Whitman? Do you have any idea
it this could mean?''

Vhitman edged slowly toward Sinclair, keeping his move-
its and his voice gentle so the other man wouldn't panic. ''I
w,'' he said. ''How did you get it?''

'She didn't tell you?''

'All Maggie told me is that you were up here to protect it.''

inclair suddenly waved the gun at Whitman. ''You don't
erstand what it's all about, do you?'' he shouted. ''What did
think it was—contraband, smuggling? Did you think I was
ig this for myself?''

le let the gun fall to his side as he looked down at Whitman.
emember those German planes on the ground in Seville? You
w as well as I do what those planes were there for—the rape
Spain. And what were the Spanish supposed to use to fight
k? Wine bottles? Not this time, Whitman. Spain is not going
e one more Fascist pawn of Germany, because I'm going to
what no one else in Spain was willing to do. The Spanish
ticians are like you: they stashed gold in the Paris banks to
ge their bets. You've got an American passport to cover
rs. You can go either way, stay on with the Germans while
 chew up Europe, or if things suddenly turn around, go back
ie States. But the Republic didn't have a choice—until this.''

he impact and grandiosity of Sinclair's plan had not yet fully
stered for Whitman. It was hard to believe that anyone would
e the imagination and audacity to pull it off. And yet, beneath
ridiculous posturing and bravado there *was* something com-
ed about Sinclair, a vision that seemed to lift him above the
apous rhetoric. Whitman could understand Maggie's partner-
 with the man, and strangely, he found himself feeling like a
ner too, bound not only by the woman they both cared for,
by a bizarre plan that was bigger than all of them.

'How were you planning to get the planes?'' asked Whitman.

"From the States. Northrup built them for export and has b waiting for a customer. They even have the end use certifica worked out." Sinclair enjoyed his command of detail.

"And how were you going to get the gold off the ship?"

Suddenly without an answer, Sinclair glared. "I'll fin way," he shouted. "I'll do it because I have to do it. I took the Spanish navy and the Italian air force and the Rus NKVD. If I have to, I'll take on the whole bloody Luftwaffe Even you."

Sinclair stopped when he felt a tremor in the ship.

"What's that?" he asked.

"The ship is dropping," said Whitman. "We've probably an offshore downdraft."

The ship suddenly plummeted, enough so Sinclair would the downward motion. His face dissolved from bravado to f "What the . . . ?"

"Sinclair!" shouted Whitman. "Get out of there. Grab frame and pull yourself up. That ballast will go any second. the only way they can control the ship." As he spoke, Whit dove for the control cable, trying to hold it with his fingers. cable went taut, inching slowly as the weight of the ba release valve came onto the pulleys. Sinclair froze, the c draining from his face as he watched the cable move

Whitman tightened his grip on the cable, forcing it again riveted gusset brace on the catwalk. The wire cut into his pa slipping as a thin line of blood oozed into the creases of hands. He gripped again, pulling with the full strength of back, twisting the cable around the duralumin brace until could see the plough steel cut into the gusset. The screec metal against metal sent shivers up his spine.

He held until he felt the pressure on the cable relax. The kept dropping, stern down now, and for a moment he fo Sinclair as he pictured the control room—Zekner shouting, S fighting the useless wheel, the navigator hysterically ratt off the altitude readings they could do nothing about wit starting the engines.

"Now what?" said Sinclair. The gun was trembling in hand.

"All I want is to get you out of there before we lose the shi said Whitman. Even as he said it, he could see Sinclair's change. The other man was shaking with rage. He had cro the imaginary line where reason stops.

"So you can go back and tell her I owe you my life?"

lair. "And take the gold for yourself? The gold *and* Margaret,
at it? That was probably your plan all along. You think you
w her. You think she would leave me for you. But you're
ng about that too, Whitman. Because Margaret is never
g to leave me, never . . ."

For God's sake, Sinclair! All I want is to get this ship safely
.ecife." Whitman started toward Sinclair, down the narrow
er that led off the walkway.

I'm not afraid to die for this, Whitman," said Sinclair, the
shaking in his hand. "Some things are worth dying for. You
even tell Margaret I passed the test."

.irectly above them, the number seventeen gas cell was
ched taut against its restraining nets of ramie cord. Below
itman was a half-collapsed fuel cell, number thirteen, the one
leaked. It wasn't slapping, just lying limp. The ship wasn't
ing forward at all. Zekner was taking his time, hoping the
wouldn't drop too far before he started the engines.

Vhitman drew in a breath of foul garlic.

That smell," he said, "it's leaking Blaugas. A muzzle flash
a that gun of yours would turn this ship into an inferno."

inclair laughed again. "Come on, Whitman. I read the
hure. 'The safest ship in the world.' I don't believe you."

Vhitman tried to plan. It was no time for heroics. He had to
, at least until the ship was moving enough to drive out the
:entration of gas. Then Sinclair's gun would be no danger to
whole ship.

e reached up, gripping the towering cruciform girders of the
pulling himself up behind the gas cell, far enough aft so
:lair could no longer see him. The covering of the tail, unlike
rest of the ship, was heavy linen, doped until it was almost
que. He knew he wouldn't be silhouetted by the daylight
e.

e heard Sinclair's shoes as the man climbed from his perch
he ballast sack up to the walkway, swinging on the netting
l he got his own footing on the narrow catwalk.

Think I'm afraid to kill you?" Sinclair's voice echoed in the
space. "Other men have died for this. I'm willing to die for
Vhat about you?"

took a long minute before Whitman could see Sinclair below
, walking slowly, unsure of his balance as he watched his feet
he narrow perforated walk, nothing below him but empty
e as the girders led down into the tail of the ship.

ılling with his arms, Whitman found a foothold on the thin

axial bracing wires, his shoes wedged at angles. He could
blood streaks from his hands on the doped skin of the gas
and the girders, but he felt no pain from the cuts in his pa
All he could think of was time—Zeppelin time, pondero
slow, almost imperceptible in its passage. How long wou
take to get the ship moving and clear the explosive gas out?
long would Zekner wait to start the engines?

Above him, there were light spots where sunlight glo
through thin areas of the tail covering. He wondered if Sin
would see him. But when he leaned out enough to see the c
man, Sinclair was still watching his own feet on the na
walkway, holding the gun out with one hand and with his c
hand cocked back for balance, like a fencer.

Whitman felt a vibration in the girders. One of the eng
turning over. The big Maybachs were cranky about star
They were built to run smoothly and economically for days
time, not to start instantly. The spark was so retarded that
took a long time to catch. From the vibrations, Whitman cou
tell whether it was one engine or all five turning over.

Below him, Sinclair reached a vertical support, grabbed
and looked up. There was no more waiting. It was a dro
twenty feet, and Whitman came down in a crouch, concentr
only on Sinclair's gun, going for that wrist with both of
hands. They tumbled down onto the catwalk together,
Sinclair lashed out wildly, swinging arms and feet all at o
His free hand came around in a barrelhouse punch, his fore
crashing into Whitman's back.

Whitman fought for balance, trying to keep both of them
rolling off the narrow metal catwalk. Sinclair sensed Whitm
momentary distraction and smashed out with his right wrist
hand that held the gun, bashing both of Whitman's hands ag
the metal grid of the walkway.

The gun went off, a *crack,* then a sharper *zing* as the b
ricocheted off a girder.

Both men were so startled by the echoing report that
relaxed for an instant, catching each other's eyes.

Sinclair was the first to realize what had happened. He sv
the gun around, his wrist still in Whitman's grip, but with
muzzle pointed at Whitman's head.

"Well, Captain?" he said. "What happened to the infer
Whitman squeezed down on the wrist, pressing his fin
together until he could feel Sinclair's tendons giving unde
grip. The color drained from Sinclair's hand as the trigger f

ught, but the muscles were in a vise, unable to move. Finally,
e gun slipped from his fingers, bounced on the catwalk, and
l down to the skin of the ship below them, bouncing once
ain before it came to rest on the taut fabric.

Sinclair stared at the gun, then stopped struggling as Whitman
axed his grip.

"Let's go," said Whitman, letting go of Sinclair's wrist,
nsciously giving the other man room.

"You've won?" asked Sinclair. It came out in a peculiar
flection, not quite a question.

"Let's get out of here," said Whitman, trying to call the other
an back to reality.

Sinclair got up, rubbing his wrist. His gaze didn't change until
 suddenly jumped off the catwalk, grabbing at the lower axial
aces with his hands and wrapping his legs around the wires to
de down toward the massive frame ring below them. When he
d a foot on the ring, he leaned out toward the gun, letting one
ot tentatively rest on the unsupported skin between the
agitudinals.

It was too far to reach. He stretched, suspending himself from
e thin axial brace. Sunlight bouncing off the water below them
uminated the worn skin, a diffuse glow that silhouetted Sinclair.

Whitman watched him lean out. His fingers almost reached
e gun, but whenever his foot began to put pressure on the
bric, he had to shift position, dropping his other hand lower on
e wire brace to extend his reach another inch. He almost
ached the barrel of the revolver when the bow of the ship
rted to rise. The gun slid back along the skin, just six inches,
t well out of his reach again.

Sinclair lunged, letting his weight down onto the skin as he
ve for the gun. The taut doped cloth stretched like a rubber
eet, until the worn fibers began to give way, tearing one at a
me with agonized ripping sounds.

Sinclair looked up at Whitman, trying to make contact but
able to focus as fear closed in on him.

Whitman climbed down, sliding on the bracing wires, then
ning out, reaching toward Sinclair's nearest hand.

"Don't move," he said. "That skin is like quicksand."

Sinclair watched Whitman's hand, then shifted his eyes to the
n, still inches from his fingers, and back again to Whitman.
 reached up toward Whitman's hand, then changed his mind
l went for the gun.

The skin tore all at once, a diagonal rip between frame ring
Sinclair's hand came up, grasping. Then he was gone.

The gun hovered for an instant on the torn fabric befo
sliding after him into the sea.

Eighty

Conselheiro's perch on the knoll was the perfect hiding plac
within range of the mooring mast, and with a cover of low scru
brush that concealed him as he squatted over the mortar tube.
was only the airplanes that he feared now.

Why didn't they use them? he wondered. There were m
around the planes, lounging under the wings, with leather flyin
helmets and boots. What were they waiting for?

He had the mortar assembled now, the legs screwed into tl
swiveling mechanism that adjusted the elevation. It was hard
read the inscribed range table, and even harder to guess how
away the mooring mast was. But how hard could it be to hit
Zeppelin? You couldn't ask for a bigger target, and when it can
in for its landing, he knew, it would hover over the field, floatir
like a leaf.

But why didn't they use the airplanes?

Maybe they were saving the planes to use against the peopl
He had heard that the Germans had developed such warplane
planes that would swoop out of the sky with a rain of death ar
destruction. Maybe they were going to try them out in Brazil.
would be like the Germans, using Brazilian peasants as fodd
for their cannons. There were no insignia on the airplanes, r
red and black and white swastikas, but that would be like tl
Germans too.

He picked up the mortar tube and spun it around, planting tl
legs again so that it faced in the direction of the airplanes, the
adjusting the points of the legs in the dust so he could line up tl
airplanes over the top of the tube. The range was about eig
hundred meters, almost the same as the mooring mast.

He wriggled until he was comfortable behind the tube, his le

ddling the elevation supports, his head tilted back to sight in
the two planes in the middle of the parked squadron. Even if
ook two rockets for the airplanes, he thought, he would still
ve two left for the Zeppelin.

Then he saw one of the men lounging near the planes look up
vard the sky. The others also looked up, and Conselheiro
lowed their eyes, squinting against the sun as he scanned the
y, cloudless sky to the east. Dust particles had blown up from
land, and it took him a long while before he could make out
flash of silver against the hazy blue.

The Zeppelin!

He concentrated his vision until he was sure of it, until he
ld see it coming toward the field. There was no time to
ste. The airplanes were not important enough.

Quickly he turned the mortar around again, replanting the
ked legs in the holes where they had been, sighting over the
of the tube, this time at the red and white mooring mast
oss the field. From the corners of his eyes, he could see the
at silver Zeppelin slowly descending toward the field, exactly
it had descended after the people were massacred on that
d.

Eighty-One

l found Maggie waiting in the corridor of the passenger
ins, below the access hatch that led up into the hull. Every-
ig made sense now, but he couldn't get the look in Sinclair's
s out of his mind. There was a conviction in that gaze that
nt deeper than a madman with a gun. He was a man who
uld have led, or at least inspired, instead of being betrayed by
own insecurity, by jealousy.

Maggie looked up as Whitman came down the ladder. There
s no way anyone could have seen or heard what had happened
he hull, but from his face, she knew.

"David?"

"I'm sorry," said Paul, "I tried to reason with him. He

seemed to want to die. He said to tell you that he passed the te
whatever that means.''

She stepped back a foot, looking into his eyes. Then s
melted against him. He held her tightly until he felt the tensen
begin to ebb.

When she looked up, he asked, ''The planes and the gold
it's all real? He actually arranged for delivery of Americ
planes?''

''Yes. I heard him make the calls. I even met the man fr
the aircraft company. The planes were in Texas, waiting 1
export. They had pilots lined up to deliver them to Ethio
before that all collapsed. Now they're supposed to deliver th
to Recife. The Brazilians are getting bribes to ask no questio
David said that aircraft sales like that happen all the time. I
really cared, Paul. Deep down I think he really believed in wl
he was doing.''

''Yes,'' said Paul.

''The gold—did it . . . ?''

''No, it's safe. How did he think he would unload it
Brazil?''

Maggie shook her head. ''He didn't plan that far. Somewhe
he lost track and it turned into this insane effort to prove himse
mostly, I think, to himself.''

''And to you.''

Tears welled in her eyes. ''Yes. He knew we needed you, a
he couldn't admit it to himself. Now, I guess it's really up
you.'' She pulled back, looking hard at Whitman.

''I chose sides a long time ago,'' said Paul. ''Whatever el
he and I were on the same side.''

By the time Whitman reached the control room, the Zeppe
was over the coast, beginning a slow descent toward the fie
Lehrmann was waiting for him outside the radio cabin, a sin
earpiece of his headphones clamped to his ear.

''Why are we delaying?'' said Whitman.

''It's Schaub, sir.'' Lehrmann held out the earphones. ''At
field. Something about a lunatic who wants to shoot down
Zeppelin.''

Whitman grimaced, only half credulous. He had trouble fo
ing his mind off Maggie and Sinclair.

''They think we should delay our landing, sir,'' said Zekr
coming aft.

''We're negative buoyancy now, aren't we?'' said Whitma

ekner seemed stunned by Whitman's words, as if it were a
cism of his weigh-off.

It's his fault, sir," he said, pointing at Stein. The elevatorman
been relieved, and he stood behind the companionway
er, his bulky frame conspicuous even as he tried to melt
self into the bulkhead. Zekner pointed an accusatory finger.
e imbecile! I gave an order for a release from both emergen-
ballast sacks and he released only the forward sack. We could
e lost the ship."

tein was a wretched sight, his hands trembling at his
s, the rheumy eyes red and narrow, the spirit gone from
face.

He's too old, sir. He was a good man, but he's too old
."

It wasn't his fault," said Whitman. His answer was lost
Zekner, who went on, speaking quickly to justify his
ons. "I did some calculations, sir, and the engineer has
cked my figures. If we drop the rest of the emergency
ast, we can stay aloft for as long as six hours. That
ild give us plenty of time to land without worrying about
lunatic down there."

Six hours?" said Whitman. His mind was on the emergency
ast—Sinclair's gold. "And what if that's not enough time?
y might want us to delay all night. It's happened before. And
t about the vaccine? Another hour or two and the refrigera-
will be gone. The vaccine will be useless."

e turned to Lehrmann. "What's Schaub talking about any-
? Some crackpot is always taking a potshot at the Zeppelin.
n if he is down there, the bullets would make little puncture
s in the skin and the cells. He would need a cannon to be a
danger."

Sir," said Lehrmann, "it's the same man they caught at the
l the last time we landed. Only they think he has a mortar
. If he's at the field . . ."

A mortar! Why the hell did they let him out?"

Brazilians," was all Lehrmann answered.

Eighty-Two

They flew directly over the mouth of the rivers, the delta thousand canals. Whitman glanced down at the approach ch then swung off a course that would take the Zeppelin b toward the landing field.

"Come to three-oh-eight," he said. "All engines ahead thirds."

The orders were relayed forward, and the Zeppelin slo swung its bow in the direction of the field. "All right," Whitman. "Get Schaub on the radio for me."

Before they reached the field, the rudderman pointed to airplanes parked at the edge of the tarmac, two rows of planes each, parked close to one another, their wings aln overlapped.

Whitman focused the big 10x70 Zeiss glasses and identi the planes out loud. "A-17s. American attack bombers." tried to conceal the amazement in his voice.

"What are they doing there?" someone asked.

Someone else answered. "Look like old tubs. No match f Messerschmitt 109."

No, thought Whitman, they're not a match. And whe comes down to a real fight we're going to need better plan The A-17s were already obsolete, even in the ill-equip American Army Air Corps. With their air-cooled radial engi and chunky fuselages, they looked like clunkers compared to sleek Messerschmitts. But the A-17s were rugged planes, eas fly, simple to service, and with five machine guns and hundred pounds of bombs, they were an effective attack plane good choice for Spain.

"Sir!" Lehrmann held out the microphone and headset. " the English doctor who's waiting for the vaccine. He wants talk to you."

Whitman came aft to take the headset, holding one earph up and the microphone in his other hand.

426

Captain Whitman?'' The voice was cheery, friendly clipped . ''This is Geoffrey Wade, from the Anglican Missionary c. We appreciate what you're doing, but I must warn you. man is very dangerous. You mustn't underestimate him. He himself *Conselheiro*, the Counselor. He thinks it is his duty stroy the Zeppelin, as a signal to the people. If you've read the first Conselheiro...''

Does he know what we're carrying?'' said Whitman. ''We've much lost our refrigeration, and the bosun says we can't the vaccine below forty degrees much longer.''

He knows about the vaccine,'' said the doctor, ''but I don't he realizes it's on the Zeppelin. He's a deadly serious and mitted man. He believes that the destruction of the Zeppelin d be a revenge for the people killed during the riots last ''

s he on the field?''

We don't know. He has eluded the police for days.''

Damn,'' said Whitman, thinking out loud. How long could it to find a lunatic? Where could a man even hide down there? nothing but flat scrub.

e arching trajectory of a mortar shell seemed timed to er his question. There was an orange flash on the field, and the opposite windows of the control room, they could see ray-brown explosion, the cloud of dust obscuring the moor- mast until the breeze blew it clear.

mortar!'' said Zekner. ''In a few minutes we'll be in his . We must drop ballast and lift out of here.''

llast? thought Whitman. The only ballast left was the aft gency ballast, the gold.

ir!'' Zekner's voice became more insistent. ''We can't risk hip and the passengers. The man will have us in range. We lift out of here.''

We haven't flown that vaccine this far to be stopped by a '' said Whitman. ''If we drop that ballast, we'll be down to ng, no maneuverability at all. And it could take them hours tch the man. What happens to the vaccine?'' He stared at pot where the mortar had been fired through the binoculars, started snapping off orders.

Get the chief rigger to prepare emergency mooring lines, and starboard. Station riggers at each line and put men at the es with megaphones. If those fool Brazilians down on the can't catch that lunatic, at least they ought to be able to take a mooring line. And tell them to have a refrigerated t standing by for the vaccine.''

He pointed down to the field. "The man must be there, on that knoll behind the fuel tanks. He can't fi mortar straight up. If we come down on top of him, the nothing he can do.''

He turned to see the men behind him in the control rc listening to reassure themselves before they scurried to orders.

"And get Stein back on the elevators. We've got some fl to do.''

Whitman stood in the center of the control room, chur out a continuous stream of commands to the rudder engineer and elevatorman, shifting their course to skirt edge of the field, easing them down to 150 meters altit then slowing the ship for its final approach to the spot he picked.

"Zekner! What do you make the wind?" It was obvious the cloud of dust blowing across the field, but Whitman wa everyone involved, especially Zekner.

"Oh-one-oh,'' said Zekner.

"Rudderman, come to oh-one-oh,'' said Whitman. "A s turn.''

"Oh-one-oh, sir.''

The ground crews on the field were in total disa running away from the clouds of dust that swirled around mooring mast from the explosion of the mortar shell. dark green trucks sped out onto the tarmac. When stopped, troops jumped out, holding their rifles at port as they formed into a parade drill before fanning out to se the field.

"Lines ready?" said Whitman. It took two men to pre each of the heavy hausers that would be dropped. Norm the lines would be tied to still heavier lines on the gr with Zeppelin hitches. This time they would have to su alone.

"Lines ready!'' came the call relayed up from the rigge

The fenced-in tanks were directly ahead of them, beyond the enclosure was the knoll where Conselheiro hiding with his mortar. The line of troops began tro across the field, their rifles in front of them. The trucks d behind, officers shouting orders and waving their pistols the windows.

the Zeppelin cleared the top of the tanks, Whitman or-
, "Engines one, three and five, stop. Engines two and four
one-fourth."

asing down," said Stein. "One hundred thirty-five meters.
ping at one meter per second."

ell the men with megaphones to get those troops on the
lined up," said Whitman. "Two even lines. We'll fly the
s right into their hands."

e steward translated Whitman's orders into Portuguese phrases
the riggers shouted through the megaphones at the troops
.

aptain!" said the rudderman. "There!" His arm trembled
pointed to the knoll beyond the tanks.

was a thick patch of scrub, raised some three or four feet
the rest of the field with a perfect view. The obvious spot
you saw it.

nselheiro was barefoot, wearing torn and muddied peasant
es, a ragged growth of beard on his face. Through the
ulars his body was foreshortened, and he seemed squat as
t straddling the mortar tube, two unfired rockets at his feet,
er in his hand.

struggled to raise the tube of the mortar, trying to get it
enough to bring the looming Zeppelin into his line of fire.
the legs wouldn't elevate the mortar tube high enough, he
d it up in his hands, cradling the tube against his body as he
the muzzle and tracked it around to follow the looming
elin.

e troops had pushed through the brush but still couldn't see
elheiro. Most of them had dropped their rifles as they
d to form into lines.

ir!" Zekner stood directly behind Stein, ready to reach
he emergency ballast toggle. "If he's there, sir, with a
r . . ."

hitman didn't look up. He was close enough to see
elheiro's eyes, the unwavering gaze of conviction and
d. What did it take to be so sure? Whitman asked himself.
man knew he would die, yet he was willing to attack the
elin to realize his goal. How could he be so sure? How
any of them—Sinclair, the admiral, this lonely peasant—
sure?

ive me a megaphone," he said. He opened the access
ow and stood squarely in the opening.

"The Zeppelin is carrying vaccine," he shouted. "Vaccin
the fevers, to help the people."

Counselheiro looked up, his eyes blazing defiance. The m
tube was couched under his arm, and the rocket was in his
hand. One motion would do it: all he had to do was drop
rocket into the tube. The recoil would flatten him, but with
Zeppelin overhead he didn't even need to aim.

He hesitated, looking up at the window of the cor
room.

Whitman took away the megaphone, letting the other mar
him through the opening, staring eye to eye at Conselheiro

"Do you understand?" shouted Whitman. "The vaccin
the Zeppelin is for the people."

Conselheiro's expression froze. He remembered the En
doctor telling him about the vaccine. Could he believe it? C
he believe this man in uniform, telling him that the vaccine
on the Zeppelin, that instead of being the symbol of oppres
and death, the Zeppelin could mean hope and salvation fo
people?

There wasn't time to wonder. Conselheiro had hesitated
enough for one of the dark green army trucks to rush up t
the Zeppelin, less than fifty yards from him. He saw it
turned the mortar from the Zeppelin to his real enemy, but b
he could fire, a machine gun in the back of the truck coughe
its deadly burst, the bullets spitting out of the roostertail of
behind the truck. Conselheiro's arm flew back, holding
mortar tube and rocket aloft. Blood red circles spread acros
tunic.

Whitman cringed with the shots, watching Conselheiro's
fall in a heap, crumbling on top of the mortar and rocket.
machine gun kept firing even after he had fallen, the b
making the lifeless body leap and jump in the dust. It was
the troops thought the man could not be killed with a s
bullet like an ordinary mortal.

"Sir?" Zekner gestured at the ground ahead of them, v
the troops were slowly reassembling into lines.

Whitman didn't look up. His eyes were fixed on
lifeless form below, the gaze in the man's eyes burned
his brain.

"Sir?" It was Stein this time, gesturing toward the ra
dropping altimeter.

Whitman looked up, his expression suddenly peaceful

osed. He stepped back from the control room and turned
d Zekner.

e's your ship," he said. "Take him down."

Eighty-Three

eppelin tradition, the commander was the last one to leave
hip. Whitman waited alone in the control room, watching
assengers and crew hurriedly disembark at the temporary
ing.

e bosun had jumped down first, coming through an open
  before the mooring lines were secure. He was on the
d, hugging the tin box with the vaccine vials inside when
umbersome ice van arrived in a spray of dust. Whitman
ted the truck to race away as soon as the vaccine was
d aboard, but instead it motored slowly up to the nose of
eppelin so the doctor could wave to Whitman and shout
nk you!" Then the truck sped off.
  open airfield bus followed the truck, and the bus in turn
ollowed by a parade of other vehicles—a limousine with
plomatic reception party for the ambassador and his daugh-
nother car with airfield officials, and a van from the
lian Customs and Immigration Service. Three burly men
it of the van, two in uniforms with sidearms on their belts.
nan feared the worst for Henry and the Huttens. The wire
  have been phony, and he still had gotten no reply to his
  regarding Henry. The uniformed officials plucked de
mento out of the line of disembarking passengers, leading
ff to the van before he could reach up to stroke his shiny
ache.
nutes later, a U.S. Consulate sedan appeared on the tarmac,
flying jauntily on the fenders. A jacketless official in an
necked shirt bounded out of the back seat, calling out for
  Whitman in a loud voice and eagerly shaking his hand
he found him. The official was all business, and Whitman
it would only be a matter of minutes before Henry's

sketches were in a diplomatic pouch and on their w
Washington.

The rest of the passengers and crew disembarked
avalanche of relief and laughter. The Huttens danced a jig
tarmac, holding the telegram Whitman had given them ir
hands, tears of joy rolling down their cheeks. Even the Bra
ambassador and the dour Doctor Altschul were smiling, t
to anyone who would listen about the remarkable flight.
change, Whitman knew, there would be no complaints a
the passengers about the dullness of travel by airship.

Finally alone on the ship, Whitman stood with his feet
apart, as if he were sensing changes in attitude of the shi₁
hand rested on one of the filigree girders as he let his eye
for a last time from the panoramic windows to the gauge
controls, the ballast and gas toggles, the gyroscope and cor
the engineer's panel, the big elevator wheel and the s.
rudder wheel, the wicker chair in the corner. He walked
through the chart house, past the chest with the spre
coastal chart, past the radio cabin and the galley, past th
with the binoculars and hats, and out to the open hatchw

On the tarmac below, the crew of the ship stood in a c
officers and crewmen talking together, a single team. As Wl
stepped out of the ship, they turned toward him, suddenly
Stein, closest to the ship, snapped to attention and rais
hand to his forehead—the first salute Whitman had eve
given in the Zeppelin service. Lehrmann followed with a
of his own, then Zekner. Then they were all saluting, the
dividing into two lines as Whitman walked toward them.

Embarrassed and proud, he raised his own hand to retu
salute. He realized he wasn't wearing his hat and turned
red. Someone laughed, and in a minute they were all lauₕ

Maggie hugged Paul's arm as they watched the airship
slowly walked over to the mooring mast, Brazilian so
supplying the muscle power while riggers from the Graf Z
lin shouted the orders.

"Do you really think you can get that gold off the ship
asked.

"With that crew? They stole the Graf Zeppelin
Friedrichshafen. It shouldn't be any problem to unloa
captain's private cargo quietly."

"What about the German heavies? They must have so
their agents here."

aul nodded toward the Zeppelin office, where a crowd had hered. "Right now, they're so busy claiming credit for bring- that vaccine to Brazil that they don't have time for anything e."

Maggie grinned, squeezing his arm. "Then I guess it's back to World Series and Amos 'n' Andy and everything else we've h almost forgotten."

aul didn't answer. She looked over to see him staring at the planes parked in two neat rows at the far edge of the field.

'Are those the planes?'' she asked.

He nodded.

'David really did it.'' Her voice choked, a tremor running ough her lips. "Are they good planes? I mean, for Spain?"

'They're perfect. But getting them across the Atlantic is ng to take some fancy flying and navigation. I'm just not sure pickup air jockeys they used to ferry them down here have experience."

Maggie backed up, her hands on her hips. "And you do, I pose."

'Somebody's got to,'' he said.

ABOUT THE AUTHOR

RONALD FLORENCE is a specialist in European History, which he has taught at Harvard and Sarah Lawrence colleges. With his wife and son, he lives on the Connecticut shore, where he sails a 36-foot racing sloop when he is not writing novels.

The electrifying new thriller by the author of
The Formula

THE CIRCLE
by
Steve Shagan

il Ricker, Deputy United States Attorney General, is convinced
has uncovered a conspiracy that places the security of the
tion in deadly peril, a case that dwarfs Koreagate, Watergate,
d all the others: he has evidence that the Reverend Soong
ee, the evangelical guru who built an empire by capturing the
arts and minds of thousands of American youths, is in reality
agent of the Korean Central Intelligence Agency.

it Ricker's certainty turns to confusion when his evidence is
omptly dismissed by the American intelligence community.
d when the breathtaking but deadly KCIA operative Soon Yi
Sonji suddenly volunteers to help in the pursuit of Reverend
ee, Ricker begins to comprehend the horrifying scope of the
se he has stumbled into.

eve Shagan, who thrilled millions with THE FORMULA, now
s the mask off the unholy alliance between the overworld of
litical treachery and the underworld of power-hungry godfathers
this terrifying novel of international intrigue.

sure to read THE CIRCLE, coming from Bantam on April 20,
83 at your local bookstore, or use this handy coupon for ordering:

DON'T MISS
THESE CURRENT
Bantam Bestsellers